G. E. (George Egerton) Strobridge

Biography of the Rev. Daniel Parish Kidder

G. E. (George Egerton) Strobridge

Biography of the Rev. Daniel Parish Kidder

ISBN/EAN: 9783337031015

Printed in Europe, USA, Canada, Australia, Japan

Cover: Foto ©Raphael Reischuk / pixelio.de

More available books at **www.hansebooks.com**

OF THE

REV. DANIEL PARISH KIDDER, D.D., LL.D.

BY HIS SON-IN-LAW

REV. G E. STROBRIDGE. D.D.

"Gentle to others, to himself severe"

NEW YORK
PRINTED BY HUNT & EATON
1894

TO

KATE KIDDER,

UNFAILING IN AFFECTION, IN HELPFULNESS SELF-FORGETFUL,

PRACTICAL IN AFFAIRS, UNFLAGGING IN PATIENCE,

IN COUNSEL READY AND SAFE, OF A TIMELY

CHEERFULNESS, AND, BEST OF ALL

(I AM CONCEITED ENOUGH

TO SAY),

MY WIFE,

THIS BOOK IS

DEDICATED.

PREFACE.

A DISTINGUISHED man, a bishop in our Church, said not long since to the writer: "I am sorry that you have undertaken to prepare a biography of your father-in-law. If I could have seen you in time I would have advised you against it. Methodism in this country, during the last fifty years, has not produced any man great enough to have his life written."

One difficulty in the way of accepting this deliverance is that the speaker himself is an emphatic passage of evidence in rebuttal.

But even were the statement true, the right of this book to be rests on another foundation. The question is not whether Methodism is a failure in the production of great men, but has she lost the art of producing good men? Mr. Wesley published biographies because the subjects were good, and it was his thought that the record of their lives would abound as a blessing to those who should follow them.

This work is a modest venture with the same intent. It is offered to the public with a conviction (which it is believed the readers will share) that it will prove helpful to all those who are striving to build for themselves such a character as means consecration here and coronation hereafter.

CONTENTS.

CHAPTER I.

PAGE

Ancestry, Birth, Childhood, Youth, - - - - 9

CHAPTER II.

Early Traits and Habits, - - - - - - 18

CHAPTER III.

Conversion, - - - - - - - 27

CHAPTER IV.

Joining the Church—Call to the Ministry, - - - 39

CHAPTER V.

Wesleyan University — Professorship in Amenia Seminary — Licensed to Preach, - - - - - - 54

CHAPTER VI.

Preaching as a Supply—Joining Conference, - - - 67

CHAPTER VII.

First Pastorate, - - - - - - - 77

CHAPTERS VIII-X.

Missionary Life, - - - - - - 87–109

CHAPTER XI.

The Sad Return Home, - - - - - - 122

CHAPTER XII.

Pastorate at Paterson, - - - - - - 136

CONTENTS.

PAGE

CHAPTER XIII.

Pastorate at Paterson—Pastorate at Trenton, - - - 149

CHAPTERS XIV-XVIII.

Secretary of the Sunday School Union, - - - 161-204

CHAPTERS XIX, XX.

Professorship in the Garrett Biblical Institute. - - 217-230

CHAPTER XXI.

Leaving Evanston—Professorship in the Drew Theological
Seminary, - - - - - - - - 244

CHAPTER XXII.

Secretary of the Board of Education, - - - - 254

CHAPTER XXIII.

Literary Work, - - - - - - - 269

CHAPTER XXIV.

Interest in Missions, - - - - - - 284

CHAPTERS XXV-XXVII.

Characteristics, - - - - - - 299-323

CHAPTERS XXVIII, XXIX.

Words from the Students, - - - - - 333-340

CHAPTER XXX.

At the Last, - - - - - - - 349

BIOGRAPHY

OF

DANIEL PARISH KIDDER.

CHAPTER I.

Ancestry, Birth, Childhood, Youth.

AT East Grinstead, Sussex, England, was born in 1663 Richard Kidder, who became Bishop of Bath and Wells. He is described by Macaulay as "a man of considerable attainments and blameless character." He belonged to an ancient family with records dating back to the thirteenth century.

A kinsman of his named James, also a native of East Grinstead, and born in 1626, was the first of the family who settled in this country. He married Anna Moore, in Cambridge, Mass. Among his children was a son named Enoch. To him belonged a cane, ornamented with a silver band, on which was engraved " Enoch Kidder, 1664." The tradition is, that this cane was to be handed down through the youngest son. Accordingly it became the property of Francis Kidder, born in 1703; John Kidder, born in 1749; Selvey Kidder, born in Braintree, Vt., March 21, 1792; and he passed it on to his only child, the subject of this biography, Daniel Parish Kidder, born October 18, 1815, at South Pembroke (now Darien), Genesee County, N. Y.

Selvey Kidder, with two or three brothers, emigrated

in 1812 or 1813, to what was then known as the "Holland Purchase," in the western part of New York. Returning to Vermont in 1814, he married on the last day of October, and took to his home in the then far West, Mehetabel Parish. She was the daughter of Jacob and Mehetabel Parish, and was born in Windham, Conn., December 16, 1786. She was a refined Christian woman, belonging to one of the best families in New England. When her son was but ten months old she died.

In accordance with her last request the son was taken to Randolph, Vt., to live with his uncle, Daniel Parish, whose wife was sister to the boy's father. His maternal grandparents also lived in the family. This uncle and aunt having no children, Daniel, as though their son, became the light and joy of their home. The father married again in the latter part of 1818, but as he had no other children, it may be said that the hopes and sympathies of four doting parents were centered upon this favored boy.

Amid a large circle of uncles and aunts and cousins, his childhood days were spent in this Vermont town, pursuing his studies and enjoying the healthful recreations of a farm life. From the district school he passed into the Orange County Academy, now the State Normal School. Here he began his classical studies, and here he remained until he was fourteen years of age.

A relative, giving his recollections of those early years, says that "even in his childhood he was apt and forward, learning to talk with readiness. He acquired easily, and before he was ten years of age was quite a scholar. He was popular with his teachers and a favorite with his associates." Among his schoolmates were

B. Griswold, missionary to Africa, and W. H. Bissell, one of the bishops of the Protestant Episcopal Church. He was of a very agreeable disposition, and the pet of the whole family. He had an exuberance of boyish spirits and jollity, but with no bluster and roughness. He delighted in out-of-door sports, was particularly fond of gunning, had his own rifle, became a good marksman, and often brought in rabbit, partridge, or squirrel.

His young life in Randolph left behind a long and pleasant memory, and the *Vermont Gazetteer*, in an edition of recent date, has this notice: "Rev. D. P. Kidder, D.D., so long connected with the Methodist Book Concern, at New York, and one of the authors of *Brazil and the Brazilians*, was once a boy at home on these hills. It is with honest pride that all the churches unite to do him honor whenever he visits this scene of his boyhood."

In being taken to be reared by his uncle and aunt, it was with the understanding that his father should convey him again to his own home whenever he thought best. The day of separation came, and the uncle writes: "September 17, 1829. Brother Selvey Kidder and wife set off from our home early this morning with our nephew, Daniel P. He has lived with us over twelve years. This parting is very trying, but we hope it is for the best." His stepmother was fond of him and faithful to him. Her counsel at critical periods in his life was helpful, and he records gratefully his recollections of the wholesomeness of her influence in the formation of his character.

Arrived at Darien he was requested by the trustees to assume charge of the district school at that place. Thus as early as his fourteenth year he took hold of the responsibilities of life in the same manner as many other men who have risen to prominence. This school was continued for three months. The following February he taught a school at Darien Center. The highest attendance at these schools was between thirty and forty, yet they were large enough to tax the resources of one so young, and all the more for the reason that, being without an assistant, the entire charge, including organization, management, discipline, clerical work, and instruction fell on him alone. That he was at all equal to it and conducted his school with success, as the trustees were glad to testify, argues an endowment and manliness far beyond his years.

About noon, of one sharp winter's day, the snow being more than a foot deep, the schoolhouse caught fire; and, as he expresses it, "for a few seconds we thought her gone." But the neighbors rallied in true rural fashion and saved the premises without much damage, and with the simple interruption of half a day's session.

While he was a teacher he was also a scholar in the most valuable of schools—human nature—as furnished him in the old-time practice of "boarding around."

Here, then, was a youth fourteen years of age, who must display the ready adaptability of a congenial guest in a variety of homes, who must maintain in undisturbed equilibrium the dignity of one of the most important personages in the community—the village schoolmaster—and who must not be lacking in that fertility of invention and strategy, or that impressiveness of authority which will enable him to control two score of boys and girls, many of them his equal, and even more, in size and age. To endure as he did the strain of these severe tests, requires that there be united in one an elasticity of intellect, a certain fine fiber of character, a generous mental outfit, and a quiet and unpretentious, but none the less genuine masterfulness of will. All hail the " Little Red Schoolhouse," maker of men in the teacher if not always in the scholar, and conspicuously fortunate in this instance in working upon material not only responsive, but rich in results!

During this period he began keeping a journal, a record of his daily life. Although, like all healthy and hearty boys, he enjoyed the sports of his age, yet his daily work each day was the task of a full-grown man, and the sage comments and reflections scattered at this time over the pages of his diary show the sobriety and balance of the adult. He records almost in the dialect of a physician his impressions of the case of a young lady whose abnormal mental condition was then attracting much attention in the neighborhood. He speaks of the "satisfaction" he derived in talking by means of a slate with a deaf-mute. " I was greatly amused," he remarks, in an entry under another date, "with hearing Cole, a sailor, recount many of his adventures in foreign lands—a most depraved character, who cares for naught but grog, and will tease for it as food. He is naturally a sensible man, and when sober will reason like a philosopher on the depravity of drunkards." The pages of this journal also give traces of an early development of the observing faculties, and entered with his boyish hand are records of the changes of the weather, fit almost, in accuracy and fullness, to be preserved among valuable meteorological archives.

The kind of reading with which he employed his leisure shows the maturity of his tastes. Among the books mentioned by him we find the two volumes of Rollins's *Ancient History*.

With the close of his school he started for Wyoming Seminary, now known as Middlebury Academy, N. Y., walking part of the way. His studies were English, Natural Philosophy, Algebra, and Latin. He finished the *Æneid* and began Cicero. He was not so absorbed in his class work but that he could take in a good share of sport. Ball playing, hunting, blackberrying, and swimming were among his amusements. He was nearly a man in stature, for at sixteen he records that his weight was one hundred and forty pounds.

During the August vacation of the year 1831, he made the experiment of mercantile pursuits, and took a clerkship in the store of Collins & Sadler, at Brockport, N. Y. A little more than two weeks of this was, however, enough to satisfy him that this sort of occupation was not to be his calling in life, and he returned to Wyoming to engage in the more congenial work of the student. At this time he began the study of Greek.

The following winter found him at Byron, in charge of his third public school, at $15 per month. This school he closed March 7, 1832, with the expressed approval of the officers of the district, and, as he remarks, "a glowing speech" by himself.

His spare time and evenings were employed during this period in reading such books as Pollock's *Course of Time*, Goldsmith's *History of England*, *The History of South America*, *George Barnwell*, *Mungo Park's Travels*, *The Vicar of Wakefield*, and the *Lady of the Lake*.

His scholarly ambitions were now thoroughly aroused, and in casting about for an institution of curriculum more enlarged than any he had as yet attended, his attention was turned to the Genesee Wesleyan Seminary, at Lima, N. Y., " upon whose records," it has been said, " first and last have been enrolled more celebrated names than any other institution our Church can show." Even before this, when the seminary had been only projected, but not yet opened, he had written for information to the Rev. J. Laning, the agent. During the winter of 1831–32 the matter was frequently canvassed in the family. His father, having no sympathy with the religious or denominational character of the school, was at first disposed to object. But he finally consented because it was supposed that the new and generously advertised institution would afford the best educational advantages available in that region.

This favorable decision having been reached, he spent the two months of his vacation at home in preparatory study, especially of Greek, going regularly, sometimes on foot, to the town of Attica to recite to a Mr. Goodell, taking time also to read Shakespeare's more important plays.

May 7, 1832, he reached Lima. Here he remained until September 27, 1833, when he was graduated. His vacations he spent at his home in Darien. During this time he began the study of Hebrew. Shortly after leaving Lima he made up his mind to attend Hamilton College, Clinton, N. Y.

He says: "My decision to enter Hamilton College was reached in a spirit of compromise. My preference would have been to go to the Wesleyan University. But for this my parents were not prepared. They had a fear of the sectarian influence suggested by the name Wesleyan. Hamilton was nearer and under another class of influences. My fellow-student at Wyoming, J.

S. Fancher, had entered there, and was urgent to have me join him. Besides, although the college year had considerably advanced, he assured me of my being able to enter Sophomore." Accordingly, in November, 1833, he presented himself at Hamilton College, passed his examinations without trouble, and was admitted to the Sophomore class. In December he began the study of French. He remained at the college during the Christmas vacation for special study.

Toward the close of this school year he again became anxious to go to Wesleyan, and so communicated with his father. But in answer his father still objected and said: "It looks shiftless to see persons moving about too much, besides subjects to heavy expenses in many particulars. It has been with you thus far in the process of your education as with me in the ordinary pursuits of life, situations entirely free from embarrassments are only found, if found at all, in the imagination." He then, to turn his son, if possible, away from what seemed to be his set purpose, proposed a compromise and said: "If you should determine on leaving Clinton, I hope that you will go to Schenectady [Union College]. It will be very convenient for us on many accounts. I do not wish to be dogmatical, but I am far from following visionary schemes." It was a depressing message for the ardent, and as we now know, divinely directed youth, to describe as "imagination" what was really inspiration, and to call that a "visionary scheme" which was, in solemn fact, the plan of Providence. But like that other Daniel, to whom the lions were child's play after the battle with the pulse, the victory in favor of Lima became a vantage ground for Middletown, and during the summer vacation at home, with a determination that had nothing unfilial

in it, and with a persistence that was all the more persuasive because it was always gentle, he prevailed ; and
on September 10, 1834, he set off on his long journey,
as it was in those days, for Wesleyan University, to
enter upon a new, and as it proved, critical epoch in his
life.

2

CHAPTER II.

Early Traits and Habits.

IT must be clear to the reader that we have been traveling in company with one who, although by his youth
entitled to that franchise which the average young man
seems to claim, namely, the luxury of throwing away his
days and nights in pleasure and frivolity, was yet the
rather consumed with a regard for the value of time and
was conscientiously industrious. In an oration, one of
his first efforts at Lima, he severely condemns " mental
indolence." " It has long been proclaimed," he said,
" that ' there is no royal road to learning,' and yet how
many of the present day think to make a life of study
that of ease and indulgence! How many, instead of
confining their minds to close culture and profound
science, suffer them to remain untutored and satisfied
with superficial and limited views! How many, instead
of imitating examples of true worth and merit, allow
themselves to be puffed up with pompous and extravagant notions of greatness and glory! How many can
pronounce eulogies upon the eloquence of Demosthenes
and Cicero, the style of Addison, the patriotism of
Jefferson, but how few are willing to make the sacrifices
to become orators, authors, or statesmen! How many
can scribble and declaim, but how few can think!"
After dwelling upon the possible achievements of intellectual activity, he asks, " Who with such prospects opening
before him can be satisfied with shallow and imperfect

investigations, and cast himself upon the shoals of error and prejudice? Who can be content to stifle these immortal energies and close in with the low and sensual promptings of indolence and ease?" These sentiments were spoken not for effect, but were the deliverance of his cherished and controlling convictions. He was in the world, not for gratification, but for labor; the accomplished fact, not the aimless pursuit, was his purpose; and life, he was brave enough to think, was the raw material to be wrought into achievement.

He was always an early riser, and was often up and at his tasks by half past four o'clock. He divided his time by a carefully adjusted plan, but found as has been a common experience with those who have sought to stand guard over their working hours, that an unbroken regularity in these matters is all but impossible; and there is perceptible just the least trace of murmuring in his confession that he is unable fully to accomplish his ambitions because of his many interruptions—the day's tale of bricks must often be catalogued as unattainable, so many hindrances filch away the straw. He did his best, however, to preserve sacred the time allotted to his study, and he had no hospitality, even for friendship, when it intruded upon the hours thus devoted. Sickness was not allowed always to break the current of his application, and Sunday was also with him a day of labor. Not only was he constant in his attendance upon religious services, but formed the habit of taking notes of the sermons which he heard, and then wrote them out in full.

He found exhilaration in music, was very fond of singing, and on the notes of his flute often blew dull care away. He was social in his temperament. To make friends he thought one of his most valued acquisitions.

On leaving Lima he says: "A year and a half ago I
entered this institution an entire stranger; since that
time I have formed an acquaintance more or less intimate
with probably three or four hundred persons of various
situations and residence." He frequently availed himself
of the rigidly regulated privilege of making calls in the
ladies' department of the seminary. But to all others he
preferred the company of men older, wiser, and more experienced than himself. By their conversation he felt
that he could be instructed and stimulated. The reflections he has left show how appreciative he was of these
interviews, and how keen and correct was his estimate of
men. He valued particularly the opportunity of visiting
with Dr. Luckey, the principal of the seminary. No turn
in his affairs which he thought acute enough to be a crisis
was he willing to pass without seeking the doctor's advice.
Their talks together were frequent and lengthened, and
the after years continued and richly ripened the intimacy
which then sprang up.

A man even then of one work, it was his purpose that
his social enjoyments, like everything else, should assist
him to yet better results in his studies. After an early
evening spent in a refreshing visit with some of his friends
he retired to the quiet of his room in trim for a night of
hard work with his books. He writes: "I desire to feel
an anxious, persevering determination to be instant in
season, to perform every work which is before me. Action is oratory, said Demosthenes, and it may be added
with as much propriety and correctness, it is religion, it
is everything." Even thus early had he learned

> "To scorn delights and live laborious days."

Along with the regular and never-neglected demands

of his classes he found time also to study stenography. He attended writing school, and began the formation of that clear, correct, compact handwriting which long after was properly compared to " copper-plate printing."

He still set a high estimate upon the value of wholesome reading, and during this period he fed his growing intellect upon such substantial fare as Locke's *Essay on the Understanding*, Bacon's *Essays*, Chalmers's *Discourses*, *Roman Antiquities*, Chalmers's *Evidences*, Scott's *Life of Napoleon*, *Life of Franklin*, Good's *Book of Nature*, Stewart's *Philosophy*, *Aids to Reflection*, Zimmerman on *Solitude*, Mason on *Self-knowledge*, Maury on *Eloquence*, Byron's *Works*, Abercrombie's *Intellectual Philosophy*, Campbell's *Poems*, Robertson's *History*, *Paradise Lost*, Hale's *Lectures*, Volney's *Ruins*, and Foster's *Essays*. In his journal abound notes and comments on these works, showing that he read not for speed or pastime, but thoughtfully and for assimilation and strength.

Some of this reading was carried on during his vacations. With him to be at home for vacation was apparently to be still at school, and an entry in his diary may be noted here as characteristic. On the very day in which he reached home he records : " Unpacked trunk, took out books, wrote in journal, and by noon was prepared for study."

The program of his vacation also covered work about the place, doing the chores and helping his father in the store. His business qualities were not cheap. He was successful as a salesman and accountant, and at an age when boys are an increasing burden to their parents he was a positive help, took a man's place, a partner's interest, and, with a confidence it is impressive to note, his father relied upon his judgment and sought his counsel in important transactions. His abilities in this line were also seen and appreciated at Lima, and during a good part of his stay there he was employed as the bookkeeper for Rev. Loring Grant, the financial agent of the seminary. In this manner he was able to defray in part his expenses, a result highly gratifying to his natural independence of spirit.

As a teacher, too, his worth was soon recognized, and in his second month at Lima he was employed to conduct some of the classes of the president during his absence. Later on, the professor of ancient languages failing in health, he was elected to fill the vacancy, and at his graduation he was at once a student and a member of the faculty.

His fondness for writing showed itself in almost constant literary exercises. Besides the essays regularly called for in his course, he was generous in his contributions to the periodicals issued by the students, and was among the original projectors of some of these magazines.

The *Young Lady's Album*, with its decorated margins and duly distributed prints, mostly of flowers, too intensely bright to bloom anywhere else, was in those days a modest but important estuary from the sea of literature. For additions to its volume he was constantly in demand. As elsewhere, so here, he was ready and accommodating, dispensing sentiments wise and refined, and in the flush of his surplus afflatus he attempted even the difficulties and delights of verse!

But he preferred public speaking. He met readily the customary demands for original orations, and soon came to the front as a popular declaimer. As often as twice in a week he would appear on the platform. Because of his elocutionary abilities he was frequently selected to read on public occasions the compositions of the young ladies, the relentless modesty of that age protesting against the appearance of the fair authors before an audience. At one exhibition, besides making an original address, he read eight of these productions, having in advance but two hours to look them over. At Wyoming he was active in establishing a Lyceum among the students. At Lima he assisted in the literary celebration of the Fourth of July. And he carried off one of the prizes for declamation at Hamilton College. His maiden attempts at extemporaneous address were made at this time, and he was much sought after as a temperance speaker. His earliest recorded effort for this cause was at West Mendon in February, 1833, and his speech was of so much merit that he was requested to furnish a copy for publication in *The Christian Advocate and Journal*, of New York.

Debates, as they were conducted in the societies of the students, were his delight. At Wyoming and Lima he was one of the founders of such a society. That at Lima was called the Amphyctionic, and having carried on its rolls many names widely and worthily known, it flourishes still, an opportunity for mental athletics eagerly seized by the young. These debates were so much enjoyed by him that he often arranged for extra trials in his room. In his journal he would argue and amplify on some subject that had just been handled.

One of the questions with which these ambitious gymnasts had wrestled was as follows: "Is reading a greater source of improvement than observation?" This question, he notes, was "barbarously decided in the affirmative!" In this criticism he spoke from conviction. High as was his estimate of reading, he also reckoned at generous rates the importance of observation. He practiced it constantly. He loved nature as much as did Wordsworth, and with something like his religious sensitiveness. All his byplay was out of doors, reveling among fields, flowers and trees, hills and vales, of whose variety and beauty he constantly speaks with delight and discernment. In every place through which he passed in his journeys to and from school, he makes the most of the opportunities furnished by the deliberate mode of travel then prevailing, and gives himself up to the detailed description of a gazetteer. Nothing striking escapes the notice of his eye or the record of his pen. On his last trip from the seminary he takes a roundabout route, enjoys a long ride on a canal packet, examines with in-terest the system of locks at Lockport, has his first sight of Lake Ontario, takes in the view from Brock's monu-ment, and is ravished with the glories of Niagara. All these places he describes with fullness and charm, but his setting forth of the wonders of the great cataract is so apt and complete that this page from his journal may well be copied entire:

" October 2, 1833. I am now in the dominion of his majesty, William IV, sitting upon the Table Rock which overhangs the mighty cataract of Niagara, within six feet of the current which sweeps past me with an incalculable rapidity. I am on the edge of this rock, which projects some twenty feet over the stream beneath, and from this point I have the finest view possible of a scene which has astonished the world, and will remain till the consumma-tion of time a magnificent display of eternal power. Before me the whole channel of the river, half a mile wide and to an unfathomable depth, seems to be excavated from the solid rock, which on all sides from the water slopes frightfully inward. This excavation is believed to be the work of the stream itself, which in the progress of ages has worn its way backward from Lewiston, the distance of seven miles, where originally it rumbled its rugged way down the sides of the mountain. But here the yawning chasm finds a boundary, and over its brink pours the torrent of Lake Erie.

" For a mile above, the current begins to foam and whiten on the rapids, from which its slope downward is very apparent. Just on the edge of the precipice it sobers down to a transparent green and in an instant plunges into the abyss below. At the foot of the fall an unwasting column of spray arises, so thick as to obscure a distant view of half the falling water. Ascending to the horizon, this mist moves backward, and at the distance of a quarter of a mile appears like a light, fresh cloud, which is observable to the traveler in any direction long before he reaches the place of its formation.

"At the bottom, all is foam of the most exquisite whiteness, the waters pitching and convolving together. A few rods at my left is the most magnificent rainbow ever beheld. It completes a semicircle very nearly. Far beyond are the lower falls dashing out in startling grandeur from the forest and shrubbery which cover the bank. Here and there along the steeps of the precipice are dropped down spiral staircases which, being tightly inclosed, prevent the passenger from the fright to which a knowledge of his actual situation would expose him. But the attention is drawn from those distant objects by the rising wind which gives additional roughness to the current and elasticity to the spray. An occasional gust dashes the latter over me, while at the distance of a few rods toward my left there falls a constant shower.

" The eye rests for a few moments upon the picturesque scenery of the island before me, the tottering bridge which the boldness of some adventurer has caused to extend quite over the edge of the falling water, again upon the spectators wandering here and there, like myself, all wrapped in silent wonder. The scene outranks every idea of the sublime that ever entered my conception from any source, and the situation inspires enough of awe to make one *feel* what he sees. All things seem trite compared with the plunging and the roaring of the mighty waters. They are beautifully terrible! In their presence language is insignificant, conception is frozen, thought is dumb!"

CHAPTER III.

Conversion.

IT was during his second year at Lima that the great change took place which colored and shaped his whole future. He was converted, and, too, after the time approved Methodist fashion, and with the genuine Methodist results. His parents and friends did not contemplate any such issue from his attendance at the seminary. There was in it no satisfaction for them. They viewed it with regret, if not with disapproval.

"They regarded it as a deathblow to all their ambitious hopes for him. And when subsequently he decided to enter the ministry, it seemed more than his father could endure, ' to have his son a beggar,' as he expressed it. It was no light trial for the son thus to encounter the prejudices of all his relatives, and thwart the wishes of those who had hitherto lavished on him not only their fondest affections, but the means that had contributed to his success and enjoyment. He was enabled, however, to be true to his convictions and, at the same time, conciliate his friends."

His father had no sympathy with the Methodists. The son had had no association with them, nor had he any respect for what he supposed were their religious teachings. His more recent opinions were formed among Unitarians and Universalists, with whose views his father, not a member of any church, openly agreed.

The son had been taught to read his Bible, and, in accordance with a promise made to his mother when he left home for school, this had become with him a daily habit. The occasional repetition of the Lord's Prayer was his only additional religious exercise. He had also been trained to attend church on Sunday. But the Sabbath was not as sacredly hedged about as in his practice it afterward became. Scripture and other reading especially appropriate to this day were readily and without any twinges of conscience displaced by *Shakespeare*, the newspapers, and even Tom Paine's *Age of Reason*. The quiet of the day, and its intermission of other duties, rendered it with him a fortunate opportunity for writing compositions and addresses. On this day he drew up the Constitution and By-laws of a fire engine company, and, during one of his vacations, he did not scruple to spend all its hours in marking goods in his father's store.

Such religious training as he had received rendered allowable to him many pleasures which his moral sense afterward rigidly quarantined. Card playing, the theater, and horse racing had for him successful allurements. But his especial passion was the dance. To its indulgence he would give the entire night, and, a leader among his young associates, he would organize dancing parties, being frequently the master of ceremonies.

And yet during all this time there was an undercurrent of virtuous thought—a serious resolve—which saved him from the vapid career of "an earnest trifler." Both by descent and training he was correct in his morals and reverent in his spirit. Loving hands had already laid polished stones in the foundation of his future Christian character. In the home of his uncle in Vermont there was thrown around him the atmosphere of a pronounced, if not demonstrative, piety. The grandfather, Jacob Parish, of beaming, good-natured face, beloved by all, was a patriarch and priest in this household. Among the old-time customs he maintained was the practice of saying grace at the meals with all the family standing around the table.

Inherited tendencies were also in his favor. On his father's side he was born to high ideals of truth and honor, while from his mother he came into the possession of a refined religious temper. The father was a man as correct in his dealings as he was erect in his person, of imperious integrity, impatient even to irritation with all shams and hypocrisy. His mother died with a quiet faith in the Redeemer she had long trusted. A letter written by her a year before her marriage shows the exuberance as well as the maturity of her piety, and uncovers a heart entirely given up to God. When the prospect of maternity was before her she expressed the desire that her child, if a son, might be a minister. As far, therefore, as nature should be credited, with a work which only grace can accomplish, the statement of another is correct: "His sweet, gentle, and noble life may be attributed in great part to his descent."

In one thus sprung we might look for a sober balance, and need not be surprised to read in his journal the record of his religious musings even in the artless terms of a child. On the New Year's following his fifteenth birthday he writes: "Rapidly and imperceptibly time rolls on, and we heed it not. Sometimes the beginning of a year causes us to reflect on the past more than usual, and well it should. Still we ought to observe every day with the same reflections—every day, be it attended with unusual events or not, assists us to complete our probation, and hereafter let us hope to profit by daily reflections." His New Year's entry two years later was as follows: "I wish to realize my dependence upon the Author of my being for every mercy, and pray to him in fervency of soul to endow me with judgment and strength to do his righteous will and walk in wisdom's paths, which are those of pleasantness."

This latter extract, written amid the hallowed influences of Genesee Wesleyan Seminary, would hint that he was at this time in the enjoyment of a religious experience. But such was not the fact, and he would have been surprised, if not offended, at the suggestion. He had no sympathy with a Christian profession. He considered himself an unbeliever, and in a proud, cold manner criticized those of his associates who claimed that they enjoyed religion. " I attended a prayer meeting of the students in the chapel," he writes ; "some of them strove quite hard in the Spirit, but I imagined that it was as much for the sake of making long, sonorous prayers as anything else."

Miss Frances E. Willard * writes: "During a large portion of his sojourn at Lima the religious sentiments and practices of the Methodists were an unfailing source of amusement to our young friend. He delighted to put their advocates on the defensive, and to puzzle them with the standard questions of Universalism and infidelity. Nevertheless, the generally consistent conduct of those professing to be Christians did not fail to impress his mind favorably respecting a form of religion with which he had not previously come in contact, and of which he had learned through its enemies alone."

---

* Sketch of Dr. Kidder in *The Ladies' Repository*, October, 1871. Acknowledgments are also hereby gratefully made for other extracts from this beautifully written article.

In the fall of 1832 he was called to wait upon a student who was sick. He took all care of him, and when he died attended to his burial, arranging the plans for the public service, collecting funds for the funeral expenses, and communicating with the father. He was also appointed a committee to draft resolutions. These were published in the *Advocate*. This communion with sickness, this waiting upon death, affected him. The night watches by the bed of one of his own age were seasons for the growth of heavenly thoughts, and in the presence of the coldness and the stillness of death purposes that were divine came to the flower. He was also deeply moved by the funeral sermon preached by Dr. Luckey.

Thus was Providence working in him a preparation for the crisis. This came the following spring during a great revival in the seminary. There had been a profound spiritual movement in the neighboring town of Pittsford. Many of the students attended, but he did not go. On March 11 he says: "The people returned from Pittsford, and a protracted meeting commenced at Lima in the Methodist chapel." Under this date he enters in his journal this remark: "Had some reflections upon religion." Still he kept away from the meetings at the beginning, conceiving the idea that there was a purpose among the leaders to make a Methodist of him. In this course he felt justified, because, a public examination being near, his studies were unusually urgent.

"At length," quoting again from the writer just referred to, "one afternoon a student, whose Christian character had compelled his respect, invited him to go to the meeting appointed for that evening in such a manner that neither politeness nor a sense of courage to investigate truth allowed him to decline. He pledged himself to go. That promise was the turning point of his destiny. Once made, it suggested a train of reasoning which convinced him that if he was ever to investigate, practically, the truth of the Christian religion, the time had come. This point gained, good thoughts and influences, which had before floated about him without positive results, seemed to focalize in favor of a prompt and right decision of the mysterious questions involving the welfare and destiny of the human soul.

"When the resolution was taken to attend the meeting it was, before evening, followed by one far higher and more decisive—to make one sincere effort to know and do the will of God. Before entering the church his mind was made up to put himself in the way of any good influences which might then and there be manifest. The sermon was not specially adapted to his mental condition, and while listening to it he was tempted not to act as he had proposed, lest he should appear to be influenced by what had, in fact, made less impression on him than the kind word of his friend. But a better thought prevailed, and, to the surprise of all who knew him, he was one of the first to go forward and kneel at the altar of prayer as a suppliant for wisdom from on high. From this beginning of a sincere religious life the most decisive results ensued. Plans of worldly ambition gave way to an ardent desire to live for the glory of God and the welfare of men. Study, instead of being pursued wholly for the pleasure and profit it might bring, was thenceforth most highly valued as an agency of preparation for a life of Christian activity, and the Church, before despised, was regarded with a warm and pure affection."

The story, as told in his own modest way, is as follows: "I felt disposed to attend meeting, went in the evening, and was found among those who desired to know the truths of religion, and willing to show their interest by doing the will of God. This step was one which perhaps would seem incongruous with the opinions I have heretofore held. But by some agency those strongholds which I have striven to fortify are removed, their strength appears to be weakness, and I am convinced that there needs to be a subjection of the human understanding to the will of God and his revelation. That I may make this lawful submission, be enabled to see clearly by the light which cannot be hid, and to cast my influence upon the side of piety and virtue, has been my sincere prayer. May God hear and grant!" The next day, after remarking that he recited all his lessons well, he observes: "I felt my mind occupied with the thoughts of religion and a desire to know the truth as it is in Jesus." On this day he is, however, tempted to draw back and yields in a measure. He writes: "Although earnestly solicited, I concluded not to attend meeting. I conversed with a friend upon the subject who did not profess to follow Christ. I was strengthened in my determinations, read the Bible." But the next day this interruption—this fatal compromise, this attempt at half way measures—is checked, the evil reaction is broken, the fate of Lot's wife is escaped. He goes to the church and hears a timely sermon from the Rev. Mr. Ferguson upon the text, "My Spirit shall not always strive with man." At the close of the prayer meeting which followed the sermon, he says, "I spoke a few words signifying that I felt differently disposed toward the subject of piety, and was determined to ob-

3

tain it." He heard the next day a sermon by the Rev. Wilbur Hoag, which he describes as "most interesting indeed." "The speaker's flow," he adds, "was easy, simple, and elegant; his argument close, critical, and perfectly satisfactory." The text was, "Strive to enter in at the strait gate." The next day, Sunday, was religiously full and delightful for him, beginning with a prayer meeting in Elder Grant's sitting room. Three sermons and prayer meetings with crowded altars followed this. The next day he says: " My mind is constantly occupied with religious thoughts; everything that I ever held as an evidence that religious professions and delights were merely the offspring of delusion seemed to crowd upon me to persuade me that I was making myself a dupe to the same whims that I had so long ridiculed and despised. But something tells me that I am just beginning to be wise or rational when I forsake these hiding places (which have been hunted out by pride and vanity, but, most of all, for boasting competition), and determine to take refuge in the Rock of our salvation, to subject my weak judgment to the standard of all truth. Elder Grant and Rev. Mr. Hoag solicited me to write a communication to *The Christian Advocate and Journal* of the progress of the work in this place, saying it would be read with more interest from a subject. But what! my name to be found in a Methodist newspaper confessing to the whole world that I am a proselyte! What indeed will my acquaintances say? I can anticipate each individual remark, wherever I have been, wherever I am known. One will say, ' Silly fellow!' Another will be glad he is converted, but will feel worse through fear that he will become a Methodist. But I might make hundreds rejoice who should become acquainted with the circumstances. That, however, comes in for a show of vanity, and I think that I shall not attempt it."

These were delicate balancings. Properly was he governed by a regard for the approval of his friends and relatives. Their good opinion had in his estimate the weight of a moral obligation. And what is more, he would have dealings with himself only on terms of the strictest honesty. He would rather a slighted good should stand against him, than that his personal vanity, like a bird of prey, should frighten away the dove of peace.

Fortunately also for him, at this time he was taught by a simple incident the supreme importance of planting an Ithuriel guard against religious self-conceit, pious self-complacency, that foe of many disguises and shrewd insinuations. He was in attendance upon one of the prayer and testimony meetings of the revival, and observes that "in attempting to say a word, I found myself under the influence of my old desires to do something nice and pleasing. It being a very beautiful morning, the snow melting and the sun beaming in splendor, the thought struck me that I might bring in an apt illustration and expatiate upon the cold, dark burdens which the Sun of righteousness was melting from our souls. I was endeavoring to arrange this figure properly in my mind, so that it half occupied my thoughts during prayers. But my turn to speak came second, and I was as yet unprepared. I faltered and blundered along, till I was perfectly ashamed and sat down. Moral: henceforth, Let your answer be, Yea, yea! Nay, nay!" On the witness stand for Christ, and, by a legitimate application, in the pulpit, not the "desire to say or do something nice and pleasing " (rags, these are, from the old Adam's wardrobe) is essential and imperative, but the truth ; not rhetoric, but experience ; facts, not figures of speech! In these matters whatsoever spreads itself outside of the scant covering of the " Yea, yea! Nay, nay!" is sin.

On this same day he received a letter from a very dear friend with whom he had been long intimate, but who was an unbeliever, and he remarks: " What shall I do? endeavor to persuade him from his infidelity, or keep silence and peace?" Two days after he adds : " I wrote a letter to H., told him frankly of the change I had met, and invited him to an unprejudiced examination of the subject." About this time he persuaded two of his friends to attend the meeting, and remarks: " O that the Lord would strengthen them and bring them wholly from the weak defense of reason to put their entire trust in the divine Spirit!" Coming away from another meeting, he writes: " I felt a pleasure in associating with the meek and humble followers of Christ. I determined then to call off my thought and affections from the things around me, and to pray humbly for this meek and lowly spirit of Jesus. O that God would be with me and make fast my determinations ever after to do his will and be willing to bear his cross; that he would guide and enlighten my understanding, and give that peace which passeth all understanding! I desire that resolution which shall enable me in every circumstance of life to confess with my mouth and show with my actions that I wish to be a Christian, and am willing to sacrifice all else to live and die in the enjoyment of his mercy and blessing."

Now for the first time he attended a Methodist class meeting. " Most of the converts," he adds, "joined on probation. I refused for the present. It would be too much for our people to learn that I have not only become a convert, but a Methodist. This, however, is a poor excuse, and I must examine the subject and its claims."

There was at this point no long halting between two opinions, and the next day he writes: " I joined the class." This was Monday, March 25, 1833. It may be that he was influenced to this prompt decision by a letter which he received at this time from one of his school-mates at Wyoming, informing him that he, too, had been converted.

The following September he records: " Six months have now elapsed since I gave my name as a probationer in the Methodist Episcopal Church, and I am called upon for a determination whether to accept membership or not. I ought, perhaps, to charge myself with neglecting to investigate the subject in all its bearings as fully as I might have done. Yet it has often occupied my mind and occasioned prayerful solicitude. Should it appear obviously my duty to make any such association, I have determined that I should have no excuse to decline from any circumstances of a trifling nature that might seem to forbid. I have thought it would be better for me to see more of the world and of Christians before making a decision of that importance. I concluded, however, to receive the holy ordinance of baptism. The reasons for this scarcely need repetition here. Suffice it to say that the New Testament contains numerous and plain examples and injunctions upon this subject. Repentance and baptism are frequently connected, so it seems a necessary duty in consecration of one's life and hopes to the Lord." That evening, in company with three young ladies, he was baptized.   He says: " It was the most interesting scene of the kind I ever witnessed.   My own feelings were wrought up to a high sense of the sanctity of the privilege, and all present seemed to join most heartily in offering petitions to God that the form of godliness might be attended by the power.   I believe that those fervent prayers ascended to a throne of mercy.   May I never forget this evening!" This was September 22, 1833, his last Sunday in Lima.

CHAPTER IV.

Joining the Church—Call to the Ministry.

THE humility and carefulness with which he proceeded in these early steps appear when it is known that it was fully eight months after the events recorded in the close of the last chapter, or considerably more than a year after his conversion, that he ventured to partake of the Lord's Supper. He says: " The season was impressive. I spoke a few words signifying the great satisfaction I felt in thus renewedly and publicly dedicating myself to the love and service of God. This day abounded in testimony to my own soul of the truth of practical religion, and calls for the warmest aspirations of gratitude to God for the consolations of the Gospel of Christ."

At length, on Sunday, March 23, 1834, while a student at Hamilton College, his former scruples against Methodism having been removed, he was taken into full connection in the Methodist Episcopal church at Lairdsville, a small appointment near the seat of the college, there being no Methodist church at Clinton. Instead of writing and informing his father of this step, which he knew would encounter his most obstinate objections, he waited until his return in the following vacation. Then he took the first opportunity in a long conversation to explain the whole matter and announce his membership in the Church. There were present also, on a visit from Vermont, the uncle and aunt who brought him up, so that to the two fathers and mothers he narrated the story of the great change. Referring to the interview, he says: " Many interrogatories were put." And then he adds: " O, may I show by my actions that I am a member of thine eternal Church, and at all times appear and be one of the ransomed of God ! " His account closes with this short but touching sentence: " This was a deep trial of feeling." A trial, it may be added, that meant disappointment to the father and taxed the heroism of the son.

During this time he never relaxed in the severe fidelity with which he scanned his inner thoughts. " I somehow find myself dull and stupid upon matters of the greatest interest. I cannot enlist my feelings and energies to grasp and desire for divine truths as I wish. O that God would illumine this dark soul and stamp his image on this heart!" More commonly, however, his testimony is that of a joyful and placid spirit. " This has been a day," he writes of one of his Sabbaths, " of much inward satisfaction to me. I trust that God has shed abroad his Spirit more abundantly than I have ever felt it before. O, heavenly radiance, beam still brighter on my soul and wrap me up in visions of eternity! I now begin to know that the King of kings will condescend to commune with the Spirit of the Church, and that this communion infinitely transcends all earthly pleasure. Whatever friends or foes may think, I believe it my dearest, my highest felicity, to serve my heavenly Master, to strive to perform his will upon earth. I see my being, my hopes, my all, proceeding from his eternal goodness, and shall I refuse my heartfelt gratitude to the hand that sustains me? No !

> "'I'll praise my Maker while I've breath,
> And when my voice is lost in death,
> Praise shall employ my nobler powers.'

"With a religion thus unfettered and sincere I go into the world in full confidence and an undisturbed reliance upon the source of infinite mercy to guide me aright and to guard from all delusion, and finally to bring home my ransomed spirit. O, I long for thy wisdom to lead me into all truth, for thy strength to enable me to preserve a Christian character spotless and pure, for thy power that I may perfect holiness in the fear of the Lord!

"I feel a constant inquiry going on in my bosom, 'Am I right?' Reason tells me, 'Yes,' in every form in which I put the question, and the word of God follows with a broad affirmation: 'Remember thy Creator in the days of thy youth.' 'They that seek me early shall find me.' And have I found my Creator? I have prostrated my soul. I have called on him—on the name of Jesus, whose blood cleanseth from all unrighteousness, and the verity of heaven is pledged that I have been heard. Yea, in my own breast I feel a serenity of soul, a devotion and purity of heart which testifieth, 'My Redeemer lives.' May this continue! It is thy will, O Lord! I have prayed more earnestly for pure and undefiled religion than any other thing, and, through the grace of God, I believe I know more about it now than I ever before did."

The benefits he received from attendance at prayer and class meeting are frequently referred to by him, and the band meeting, which had not yet become in Methodism a departed glory, he found particularly helpful. To this service he often opened his own room. Of one such meeting he says: "It was much needed and no less beneficial. The feelings will sometimes, though imperceptibly, become alienated from Christ, and then they need an honest scrutiny and exposition."

Private prayer was his greatest enjoyment. These are some of the expressions in which he refers to it : " I was much blessed in prayer." " I had great enjoyment in calling upon God." " I find relief for a troubled spirit in prayer." " In my evening prayer I had a manifestation of the Spirit of God such as I never before felt." " Praises eternal be to his glorious name ! I cannot sing as I would his praise ! I long for an angel lyre !"

His devoutness, his fidelity to the social meetings, and his attention to his private duties kept him secure amid all surroundings and solicitations. While at Hamilton College he writes : " Christian friends complain that the atmosphere of college is pernicious to piety. I believe as yet I have not been infected, although exposed to the influence of sin and folly in many ways. There is but one antidote, and I pray God that his Spirit may ever be effectual !" The dedication and prayer with which at this time he began a new volume of his journal is the open speech of his heart : "As the journal of my future life, a record of actions and the motives which may prompt them, I would humbly dedicate this yet unsullied volume to my heavenly Master, the only true and wise God, the searcher of all hearts ; praying that through the death and suffering of Jesus Christ, the character of its unworthy author may be wholly transformed to his righteous will ; that my every thought, word, and deed may be wisely influenced by the fear and love of God ; that he may give me grace and wisdom sufficient for every allotment of providence, and finally bring me to the enjoyment of that eternal rest prepared for those that love him.''

The forming and fixing of his religious principles were accomplished to a great degree by the authors with whom he kept company during this interval. Buck's *Theological Dictionary*, Dick's *Future State*, and Paley's *Natural Theology* had been carefully read by him a year before his conversion. But the book that was particularly blessed to him was the *Life of Dr. Adam Clarke*. He found it very stimulating to intellectual effort, but especially did it impress him religiously. "I was much delighted with it, and hope to improve greatly from it." "Noble-hearted, liberal, and pious in every action, I would emulate his virtues." He read also Baxter's *Saint's Rest*, and the *Memoir of John Urquhart*. On this latter his comment is: "By the blessing of God it has in some degree put to flight my languor in his cause. I long for the missionary spirit of Paul, the spirit of my Saviour." The *Life of James Brainerd Taylor* was another book that worked powerfully on his soul. He regrets that he did not note down at length some of the peculiar exercises of mind which he experienced while reading it. "Suffice it now to say," he adds, "that my faith was greatly strengthened, vows renewed, and firm determinations made to strive toward perfecting holiness." But for profit and enjoyment nothing took the place of the Bible. He read it regularly in course, and carried along with it a daily reading of the Greek Testament. "The Scriptures seem to me more fruitful than they ever did before. Every sentence appears to contain some great and striking truth."

How shall they be converted except they hear, and how shall they hear without a preacher?" Our subject was converted largely through the instrumentality of the preaching of the Gospel. Always a good listener to sermons, this time he was also a doer of the word. It was his fortune to sit under the preaching of Dr. Luckey.

Of his sermons he always took and wrote out copious notes, and repeatedly he refers to them as "able," "animating," "instructive." In the historical register of the New Jersey Conference, in answer to the question, "Under whose ministry were you converted?" he has written, "Rev. Samuel Luckey, D.D., Loring Grant, and others." The sermons of Rev. Schuyler Seager, D.D., whom he first met at Lima, who was his roommate at Wesleyan University, and his lifelong friend, he often refers to as very helpful to him. It was also his providential blessing to hear, while he was a student at Hamilton College, a sermon against Universalism by that giant of the heroic period of Methodism, Isaac Puffer. The sermon was preached on a week evening in the Presbyterian church at Clinton. He records: "It was powerful and convincing. I had previously heard so much and so plausibly of that doctrine that my mind was greatly embarrassed by its fallacies. But those fallacies were swept away as by the breath of a whirlwind by his overwhelming Scripture argument. The completeness and efficiency of his work in that sermon were rendered more apparent to me when the Universalist preacher of the place tried to answer him and miserably failed." In a note added many years later, he observes: "Although I did not speak with Mr. Puffer at the time, I always cherished a deep sense of gratitude to that good and in several senses wonderful man, for the service he rendered me in that sermon. Subsequently, when residing as Sunday School Editor in New York, I had an opportunity of expressing that thankfulness by inviting him to the city, entertaining him at my house, and introducing him to the pulpits of the metropolis."

The diligence already observed in Mr. Kidder as a

student appears now as a trait strongly emphasized in his religious conduct. Duty rather than ambition presided over his labor, and work was a large share of the grateful tribute which he was happy to lay at the feet of his Master. An entry characteristic of his feelings at this time was the following: "So the day passed agreeably, especially as I had the satisfaction of doing my duty."

Every opportunity was to him now an occupied and cultivated field. Religion was his favorite theme of conversation. He talked with his parents about the importance of family prayer, and, what was yet more difficult, having gained their consent, he conducted these services in their presence. Many years after, his mother wrote him: "Although you have left us, we forget not to kneel at the family altar, and have found happiness in not neglecting the duty." Visiting the sick was made to him a particular blessing always. He was also full of public spirit, and threw himself heartily into the temperance cause. While yet an undergraduate, he was sent as a delegate from Livingston County to the State Convention at Utica. But it was the Sunday school which earliest enlisted his interest, and in this field, where he afterward accomplished such significant and permanent results, he was unsparingly active. At Lairdsville he assisted in the organization of a Sabbath school, laboring in various departments and working hard to secure it a library. At this date he announced that he intended to make this interest of the Church a large share of his life work.

Seek first the kingdom of God, and all other things shall be added unto you. Before the ship of conduct puts out to sea, adjust the compass of character. Get into right relations with God, before the tasks among men are undertaken. This is the program of wisdom, and this is that dictum of prudence which experience underwrites. Unless Christ's "Seek first" enters into the solution of the question of our calling in life, it will remain an impossible problem; and a dismal eternity will be occupied in traversing, but not correcting, the mistakes we have made.

In studying the features of the critical religious change through which we have followed Mr. Kidder, we have been made familiar with a spirit careful and conscientious, a judgment patiently convinced, a heart thoroughly converted, and a life entirely consecrated. The effect of this remodeling of his character appears now in his choice of a field for his future activities. He had long been perplexed with the question, "What shall be my life work?" In plan and experiment he had canvassed several schemes, with the single result of deciding that he was more than ever undecided.

Although he had shown marked ability in mercantile pursuits, they were with a brief but sufficient trial dismissed as uncongenial. A military career had been at one time seriously considered, and some preliminary steps taken toward an appointment as a cadet at West Point. But in consequence of investigations which he made, this project was marched in double-quick time and out of sight across the field of his outlooks. He was also seriously affected with the fever of emigration then rife, and studied maps and guidebooks, and then again he was found balancing toward the bar. He had in him a propelling power; he meant to do something and something worthy, but what? This was the tangled puzzle that clung about his thoughts and clogged the wings of his endeavor. He writes: " The old subject is hanging around with tenfold earnestness. My mind for several days has been seriously occupied in relation to a course of future life."

And again : " The week past I have been constantly meditating about what course I should next take, or occupation determine upon for life."

But happily now, coincident with his conversion, an end to these buffetings is revealed. The misty envelope which had so long obscured this question was blown into shreds, and out of chaos rolled his duty, a well-defined and sunlit thing! His soul had felt the touch of Deity! Never again could it come down to the pursuit of mere secular ends, nor stoop to a motive so low as either fame or wealth. " Fame," he insists, " is but a bauble, and those who gain it often realize that it is a worthless one." And concerning money-making it was his expressed opinion, that " when a young man engages in the accumulation of property the perplexities and cares of business soon absorb his attention, thought, and time, and by degrees he is led on to a still closer connection with what is deemed his interest, so that the opportunity of cultivating his mind and those powers which would elevate him as an intellectual being is lost, and his life must ever after be confined to the same toils and perplexities of which there can be little melioration. It is admitted on all hands that the more one becomes involved in the possession or pursuit of wealth, the more avaricious and discontented he becomes, and it is rare that anyone rests satisfied with a competency." All other considerations being thus ruled out, there was left to him the one sublime purpose of living for the benefit of others, of imitating Him who went about doing good.

" Should a man's object," he asks, " be in choice to promote his own happiness or the good of others?   Would it not be a happy coincidence if both were connected?" Of course, to a nature thus ardent and wholly given up to God and the welfare of his fellow-creatures, it was natural that the ministry, and even the missionary work with its larger sacrifice, would open up as particularly attractive.   " My mind," he writes, " has been constantly occupied with the subject of the Gospel ministry."   Frequent conversations with Dr. Luckey also pressed his convictions in the same direction.

His delicate sense of filial obligation however forbade that he proceed a step farther in this momentous decision until his father is informed and his consent is secured.   " I am resolved to communicate with my father on the subject."   A few days after this entry he wrote the following letter:

" My dear Father :—I now address you upon a subject which has for some time burdened my mind ; it relates to that of which we have often conversed together, namely, choosing a profession for life.

" You will recollect that when we have heretofore discussed the various conditions and situations of life, there has been one which invariably, and perhaps I may say wisely, has been left out of consideration. It is the Gospel ministry.

" What your thoughts in relation to this may have been I know not ; mine have very seldom reverted to it, and when they have I have always dismissed the subject as one with which deliberate choice had little or nothing to do.   During some portion of the summer of 1833 this rather indirectly occupied considerable of my mind, but was afterward dropped, and I believe I am

safe in saying that until within a few weeks past I have
never contemplated that task as one which would devolve upon me.

"Perhaps any person in determining upon an occupation would avow that to be the object of his choice in
which he could be most useful to his fellow-beings and
himself, could that be ascertained ; and especially every
sincere Christian would feel bound to devote himself to
that calling in which he would best subserve the interests of the Redeemer's kingdom.

"It seems that the declaration of our Saviour was
never more emphatically true than at present, 'Verily,
the harvest is great, but the laborers are few.' From
the islands of the great Pacific, and the Rocky Mountains
of our own continent, even to China and the farther
India, there is one unceasing cry for that word of life
which was sent for the healing of the nations. We are
commanded to 'Pray the Lord of the harvest to send
laborers into his vineyard,' but with what faith or what
sincerity can we pray when we ourselves sit idle ? We
hope, too, for the dawn of millennial glory, but how
heartless must be those hopes when we ourselves are
willing to suffer no inconvenience for the sake of hastening its approach. The parting command of Jesus rests
upon Christians with all the force of a summary, a dying
injunction, 'Go ye into all the world, and preach the
Gospel to every creature.' And it surely proves that
we are none of his if we do not his commandments,
but wish to throw them all upon the shoulders of other
men.

"You are aware that no motives of human expediency
would lead me for a moment to think upon pursuing
such a course of life. And it is well for the cause of

4

Christ that he has made no promises which can tempt
worldly ambition ; he has rather taught his disciples to
expect persecution and hatred from the world.   The
servant of Christ must take his life in his hand and go to
do his Master's will (I speak not of such as call themselves his servants and go to court the favor of men) ; he
must go relinquishing ' all that can flatter, all that can
please ' the earthly mind ; to sustain responsibilities at
which humanity would shudder were it not for the heart-
cheering promise, ' Lo, I am with you alway, even unto
the end of the world.'

"If, perchance, at this unlooked-for intelligence from
me, you should feel a harassing and almost insufferable
disappointment to your expectations (for I know not
what other terms to employ), you may form some idea
of the emotions which filled my mind on first considering
this as above described.   What, to leave all to follow
Him !   To relinquish prospects, which dawn with all the
charms of promise upon the youthful mind ; and that,
too, for the humble office of winning souls to Christ !
And yet in him I hope for eternal life.   He it was that
suffered and died, that whosoever believeth on him might
not perish, but have everlasting life.   But I have since
considered all these things cautiously, and weighed the
sneers of ' worldly wisemen,' which I know will fall upon
me and perhaps upon my friends.   I trust, too, that I
have prayerfully considered the injunction and promises
of the word of God ; the result is that as far as human
reason can perform its office this appears the path of
duty ; and as far as love to God and hope in his glorious
promises can impel me to action, it is to spend and be
spent in his cause.

"We are both aware, my dear father, of the impro-

priety of any person enlisting in any pursuit for life where
he cannot engage with animation and zeal, although
many powerful considerations may incline him toward it.
This has been the chief reason why the kind proposals
which you have so often made me, and which I am convinced were offered with a sole reference to my good,
have never been accepted. I could not accept them, because my taste, my feelings, I cannot say what else, have
forewarned me that I could never be happy in calling
forth all my exertions, in spending my life in the course
they would direct. But here is a cause in which I can
lay out every energy, and when all is gone, weep, not
like Alexander 'that there was not another world to
conquer,' but that I have nothing more to sacrifice for
my Redeemer. I do not know that you will appreciate
these motives, I do not know but you will attribute these
workings of my mind to a false enthusiasm, but I will not
deny myself the illusions of hope if such they must prove;
I can but think that your judgment will approve my
resolutions and your prayers sustain them; I can but
believe that you will be willing and more than willing to
relinquish even an only son to the service of Him who
hath ' died for all, that they which live should not henceforth live unto themselves, but unto him who died for
them, and rose again.' If you are not so, let me entreat
you to ask counsel and wisdom of Him who giveth liberally and upbraideth not. Do search the Scriptures and
see if these things be so; see if the awful warnings and
blessed promises are not directed to us, even us, if we
will but receive them.

" I am very thankful for the full assurance which I feel,
that although such a providence may seem afflicting for
the present, yet we shall all one day have reason to re-

joice on its account; and if the time come no sooner, it
will at least be

> When the dreams of life have fled,
> When its wasted lamps are dead,
> When in cold oblivion's shade,
> Beauty, wealth, and fame are laid.

" I shall wait with the greatest anxiety to receive
counsel and advice from you. I remain, as ever, your
affectionate son.

"HAMILTON COLLEGE, *April* 18, 1834."

In sending this beautiful, impressive, and, as we would
think, sufficient letter, he prays, " May the Holy Ghost
attend that silent and speaking messenger!"

Two weeks after, the following answer came:

"My dear and affectionate Son:—Your letter was received, and its subject fully considered. In answer to the
important question which you refer to my judgment, I am
ready to acknowledge my insufficiency for these things.
I will not deny that I have been much perplexed on account of the profession that you might select; but as far
as I am able to speak I have ever been willing that your
inclinations and desires should govern without being
influenced by my opinions.

" I have long been satisfied that for a person to be useful in any calling his taste ought to be gratified, otherwise a want of zeal and animation in the prosecution of
his tasks would render the incumbent a drone rather
than a profitable member in society.

" Choosing a profession for life, no doubt, is a critical
act for you, and I must say is an anxious one for me. I
had flattered myself that you would not have deemed it
important to select a vocation until you had graduated at

college. Though I had reason to believe that you had many trials on your mind in relation to preparing for the ministry, yet knowing that our minds are susceptible of change, and considering the length of time that would intervene, I always dismissed the subject without much reflection. You now inform me that after deliberating on the matter and weighing all the consequences, the result of your thought is that you *must* preach the Gospel, and you desire my advice. I have endeavored to exercise all my rational faculties in this delicate situation, and I would so communicate my sentiments as not to wound the cause you espouse. I consider the preaching of the Gospel an appointment from heaven learned in the school of Christ, and not a profession to be acquired of man. If I know my own heart I desire your happiness and would not influence you to relinquish a calling that, as you see it, would add to your usefulness and enjoyment. I therefore leave the matter with you and the God of us both. In him and in his government let us put our trust. That good health and the consolations of the Gospel of Christ may attend you is the ardent wish of your father.

"DARIEN CENTER, N. Y., *April* 26, 1834."

Upon the receipt of this loving and considerate message he remarked, " I believe my prayer has been heard."

The following August, while home on a vacation, he records: " I had a long and most interesting conversation with my mother on the subject of my calling. She expressed her perfect willingness that I should go forth, and her belief that it would be for the best. The Lord is merciful ! This is the Lord's doing, and it is marvelous in our eyes ! My soul shall praise him ! ''

CHAPTER V.

Wesleyan University—Professorship in Amenia Seminary—Licensed to Preach.

"I BADE adieu to my beloved parents and friends again to sojourn among strangers." This record in his journal refers to his departure from Darien for Middletown, Conn. With purpose in life finally fixed, with plans for preparation clearly defined, with conscience at rest, and with a glad heart, he set out for his new college home.

At half past four in the morning he took the stage, September 10, 1834. That evening he reached Rochester. His route from there on was to Utica and Schenectady by packet on the canal, by rail to Albany, by steamboat to New York, and to Middletown by Connecticut River steamer.

At Utica he was the guest of Rev. Mr. Paddock over Sunday, hearing him preach and enjoying a class meeting at his house. "Thus Providence threw me in the way of what I most needed. It was delightful after the dissipation of mind attendant upon traveling to join in the songs of Zion. Truly an antepast of heaven!" The trip down the Hudson and a day spent in New York and Brooklyn were a great treat to him. At the Book Room, the scene of his future labors and successes, he met Revs. L. Clark, F. Mason, and Dr. Fisk, President of Wesleyan University. To the latter he presented his letter of introduction from Dr. Luckey. He had also another letter from Dr. Luckey, giving him directions for this his first visit to the metropolis. On account of the names and allusions of historical interest it contains, a few extracts may be ventured. It directs him to go first of all to the Book Room, 200 Mulberry Street, where he will meet the Rev. Mr. Holdich, and adds: " This is quite uptown !" The letter continues : " On entering the city your nearest place among friends will be Mr. Benjamin Mead's, Joseph Mead's father. Joseph will be glad to see you, and the family will make you welcome. They live on Pearl Street, between Whitehall and Broad Streets, on the left-hand side—name on the door. Dr. Fisk usually puts up at Mr. Mark Disosway's, in Stone Street, near Mr. Mead's. Further uptown eastwardly, Cliff Street, near Pearl, you will find the Harpers."

The young student must have overdone somewhat his sight-seeing in the great cities, for in the evening, on the boat going up the Sound, he was not well. " I was very sick, seasick or something nearly as bad. I did not know but the deathly hands of the cholera were on me. I got my berth about eight o'clock, and slept about two hours. I was very near the tremendous water wheels, which gave me no rest, dreamed over the whole train of steamboat accidents, expected every minute the boiler would burst and I should find myself swimming. I spent a very unhappy night." But joy came in the morning with his arrival at Middletown, the greeting of former acquaintances, and the opening of his much loved tasks. He was generously received, and soon felt at home. The warmer cordiality of the professors and students, and the religious sympathy deeper than at Hamilton College, were observed by him. In the same class with him were Davis W. Clark, afterward Bishop, and Henry Bannister, later his associate at Evanston.

At once he plunged into close and continuous application, for he found his classes about three weeks ahead of him. This labor, however, was the rather an exhilaration, and such was his capacity for work that he added to his regular tasks the study of German. During the fall his friend, Mr. Seager, arrived, and they roomed together. He went with him one Sunday to Cheshire, where Mr. Seager preached at the dedication of the new church. They were charmingly entertained by Governor and Mrs. Samuel A. Foote, the parents of Commodore Foote.

Soon after coming to Middletown he conducted a searching self-examination, humbly confessed his unworthiness and instability of experience, and then wrote out the following covenant:

" May the privileges of this year be sanctified to the good of my soul. May every root of bitterness be torn from my heart. May the Christian graces bloom and flourish there. May the infinite perfections of Jehovah awaken a holy emulation to be conformed to his image and assimilated to his likeness. To this end I entreat his blessing upon me in the observance of the following rules, which shall be in force until altered upon the conviction of sound judgment and the enlightening influence of the Holy Spirit:

" 1. To spend two hours daily in reading the Scriptures and devout prayer.

" 2. To watch for and check every rising of self-esteem.

" 3. To use constant and unremitting endeavors to restrain my habitual wanderings of mind both in devotion and study, and acquire a habit of close attention and patient thought.

" 4. To devote two hours, and no more, to each of my lessons.

" 5. To spend one hour or more in vigorous exercise.

" 6. To leave my studies at a proper time at night and rise upon first awaking."

Toward the close of the year he writes : " My outward circumstances here are in every way agreeable. My soul is daily blessed with the love of God and a sense of his forgiveness. I have determined by the aid of my Master to act up to Taylor's maxim, ' Forgo everything else rather than the baptisms of the Holy Ghost.' Blessed Jesus, assist me to perform my sacred vows! Thy service is more delightful than ever, and I hope never to forsake it." On the last Sunday of this year he attended the funeral of a fellow-student, whom he describes as a true Christian, and closes a tribute to his worth with the prayer that his last end may be like his.

He attended a watch-night service for the first time. "Another year is ended," he exclaims, "and I am in the enjoyment of everything necessary to human happiness. Perfect health and opportunities for study give me what I most desire as to earthly good, and the Spirit of the blessed God gives me happiness more substantial than these.

> " ' O, for a thousand tongues to sing
> My great Redeemer's praise !'

" ' Bless the Lord, O my soul, and all that is within me bless his holy name ! ' "

The college year ended July 12, 1835. He made an address at the junior exhibition. His subject was Common Sense. The period had been a very busy one. He had been interested in a theological class conducted weekly by Dr. Fisk, and for this had prepared several papers. He had been a constant attendant at the missionary lyceum, and active in its exercises. He had also spoken at Middletown and the neighboring places on temperance and missions.

"My studies have been pleasant and profitable, and my health has never been better. I have been deficient in no college duties and absent from but one recitation, which was on account of an engagement.

"My peace of mind and joy in believing have been uninterrupted. I have attended upon all the stated means of grace with regularity. I have read the Scriptures more and been more regular in my private devotion than ever before for so long a time. Morning, evening, and at noon I have practiced calling upon God. In connection with my beloved roommate, I have read more or less in the Greek Testament, and by redeeming a little commonly wasted time we have now read about two thirds of it in course. Since the year began we have also followed Stowe's *Guide to the Regular Perusal of the Holy Scriptures*, reading four chapters daily."

The six weeks' summer vacation he spent with his Vermont friends and amid the scenes of his boyhood years. In traveling up the Connecticut valley and about New England, that he might the better see the country in its geological and other features, he made a good share of the journey on foot, and was often both weary and footsore. He visited all the institutions of learning both in and out of his way, East Windsor, Amherst, Dartmouth, Burlington (Vermont University), Middlebury, Andover, and Harvard. A little later

than this he visited Yale College, and at the theological
seminary he heard Dr. N. W. Taylor lecture.   He also
visited and studied the larger towns, being particularly
interested in the manufacturing centers.   Boston was to
him as a great university itself.   At Salem he enjoyed
the museum of the East India Marine Company.

Although this New England trip was profitable to
him, in many respects he confessed that it had been indulged with a loss to his spiritual growth and enjoyment.   "My religious feelings during vacation had been
seriously affected.   By degrees I had seemingly relaxed
the hold of that faith by which I ought to have stood.
Never during my whole religious course had I suffered
so powerful temptations, such painful struggles of soul.
This undoubtedly was owing to insufficient watchfulness
against the evils attending the circumstances in which I
was thrown and which were so different from those in
which I had so long been.   Again, I omitted taking my
Bible, thinking it would be too much inconvenience
when walking, and sometimes I was unable to procure
a copy when I could use it for several days in succession.
The regularity of my devotions was also often disturbed
(seemingly by necessity).   I began to give way to solicitude about the future, to doubt of its being my duty to
preach the Gospel, and even of the truth of religion and
the reality of its sacred joys.   I could from the bottom
of my soul say : 'O, wretched man that I am !'   And
yet the Lord did not forsake me or suffer me to betray
my weakness by outwardly omitting any duty. I found
myself endeavoring to walk by sight and not by faith.
Blessed be God, who again received the returning wanderer, and caused the light of his countenance to shine
upon him ! "

During his last year at college, in November, Mr. Kidder was licensed to exhort by the Rev. Bartholomew Creagh, and the following watch-night, at Middlefield, he delivered his first pulpit address. His subject was " Watching." Of all his studies at this time he most enjoyed his Hebrew Bible. As he must soon leave college and take up his life work, he became intensely interested as to where might be its field. But Providence unraveled all complications and answered all his questions before they grew perplexing. In January he was strongly urged to take the position of Professor of Ancient Languages in Amenia Seminary, at Amenia, Dutchess County, N. Y. He was highly recommended for this chair by the faculty of the university.

This position, besides being a most honorable distinction, would assist toward his support. Yet, it was in response to purely unselfish motives that he accepted it. His only aim was to do good. He writes: " I yielded to a very urgent solicitation to accept the office of teacher in Amenia Seminary, engaging only for the remainder of the college year, thinking that perhaps by extra effort I might accomplish my quotum of study and be of some benefit to others, while in the meantime I might be improving in the knowledge of men and things, and be doing and getting some good in a moral sense. Had I sought my own intellectual improvement or my own ease or gratification, I never should have left my room and privileges in college. I endeavored to decide the question as a matter of duty and not to give self the preference in a case in which the interests of men were concerned."

On Monday, February 1, 1836, he started in company with the principal of the seminary, Rev. F. Merrick, and "passed through Hartford and Farmington, stayed at Bristol, the famous village of clock factories. Tuesday, passed through Plymouth, Northfield, Litchfield, and stayed at a genuine temperance tavern. Wednesday, passed through Sharon, Conn., and reached Amenia, N. Y., in the evening, having had a tedious ride over drifted roads in the most severely cold weather of the winter. The following day I entered upon the duties of the school, which will be laborious. I do not find my situation just as I expected. The school is not in a state of forwardness, to compare with any academy or seminary I have ever attended. But the materials are here, and the wants are felt, which renders labor encouraging and changes inconvenience into a sort of self-denial which is agreeably met. Had I come with any other motive than that of sacrificing my own comforts for the good of others, I should have been discontented; but with this to direct me I found no room for despondency or opportunity to exercise any other than the feelings of the purest benevolence. My classes in Greek, Latin, French, and mathematics were numerous, filling up the working hours of the day. Besides attending to them all in their turn I continued my college studies by improving the early morning hours." After a time he was interrupted. This four o'clock work of winter mornings told severely on his eyes, and they became inflamed. But resting them a while, he went on again and finished his course, presenting himself at the college for examination, passing successfully, graduating with honor in a class of sixteen, August 24, 1836. His commencement oration was on Skepticism, and he was so full of his subject that he says he " wished to go on and speak in favor of the claims and truth of religion."

During the preceding spring vacation he took a trip through Philadelphia, Baltimore, and Washington. In Philadelphia, for the first time, he saw a Methodist Conference in session ; in Baltimore he preached in Wesley Chapel, and at Washington he heard in the Senate the three giants of those days, Webster, Clay, and Calhoun. " Washington as a city has disappointed me. Considering its superior location and advantages, it is positively afflicting to see the want of enterprise and downright negligence which characterize its appearance. The public buildings, upon which many millions have been expended by the government, form a marked exception to this censure. The Capitol, perhaps, as such exceeds my preconception of it. There is a magnificence in its style and extent which charms me. I love to linger among the massive pillars that adorn its domes and arches."

On his way from Amenia to Middletown, for his graduation, he spent a Sabbath in New York, and, the pastor being sick, he was asked to preach in Seventh Street Church, called then Bowery Village. Also, in the evening, in the Allen Street Church, he preached to an audience of near a thousand, " the largest assembly I ever addressed. Dr. Luckey sat in the pulpit and the Rev. S. Marvin in the altar. Notwithstanding these embarrassing circumstances the Lord gave me liberty. My text was John 17. 20 : ' Neither pray I for these alone, but for them also which shall believe on me through their word.'" These were his first pulpit efforts in the metropolis.

His appointment to a professorship at Amenia occurred most opportunely in confirmation of his purpose to adopt the work of the Christian ministry. He had been apparently weakening in his choice of this calling. A

week before he accepted the invitation to Amenia he
makes this record : " I find that for a long period I have
partially let slip the definite object of preparing specific-
ally for the active work of the ministry of the cross,
which on former occasions fired my soul with animation.
I had by degrees taken it for granted that it would be
best for me to enter some situation for instruction, and
perhaps connect its duties with studies and labors as far
as convenient. Anticipation would not be at rest, but
was constantly figuring out the best of circumstances,
and laying plans to secure them. Thus at times a train
of unholy anxieties would rush through the mind, tram-
pling in the dust the humble plant of unwavering and
childlike reliance upon the direction and subjection to
the will of God. I began to think of honors and digni-
ties, and the face of God was often hidden with thick
clouds from my soul.

" In answer to my father, who had written wishing to
know what course I should adopt, I was about to write
and mention some plans which I thought pretty well
concerted. But I concluded first to seek the counsel of
my heavenly Parent. I did so, believing that if any man
lacketh wisdom, by asking of the Almighty he will be
directed. I was conscious of a nearness of access to
which I had long been a stranger, and which brought
peace to my soul. In writing I endeavored to set the
advantages of each course clearly forth so that I might
decide between them. They seemed to preponderate in
favor of preaching the Gospel directly and without embarrassment. And in again looking upon the sacrifices
of the cross, its burdens and its joys, my heart was glad."

God's method in answering his prayer for wisdom was to
call him to Amenia. Here, besides teaching and studying,

he was soon busy with public speaking in missionary and temperance meetings, and what was still more to the purpose in settling the future for him, he was, ere he was aware of it, engaged in leading class meetings, conducting public services, and giving exhortations, speaking occasionally three times in one Sunday, his services being held not only in Amenia, but also in neighboring places. All the while he was disposed to be an honest critic upon himself. " Having endeavored to speak twice I was enabled to make some observations upon myself and my manner that I hope will be of service. One thing must hereafter be regarded as indispensable—*preparation !* And this I hope will remedy repetition of thought and language."

Very early in his stay at Amenia he became engaged in revival work. The meetings were absorbingly interesting. " Seldom and perhaps never before have I felt so deep an anxiety for the souls of others." A list is still preserved of the names of those converted during this meeting. The first names are of two young ladies— daughters in a family who had as little respect for Methodists as had his own friends. One of these afterward became his wife, and the sister went as a teacher in the same mission where he was employed.

Permitted thus to gather seals to his ministry, all his doubts as to God's will concerning his appointed life work were dispersed. Having spoken at one time in the chapel of the seminary on the Commission of the Prophets, he remarks: " I had made preparation with study and prayer, and God was pleased to assist me. If I could always feel my dependence upon him, and have my heart closed to sinful desires, then by the aid of his Spirit I might, by warning the wicked, deliver my soul from their blood. May God ever keep me humble and give me souls for my hire." As showing that there was now in him no thought of variableness on this question of his work, he observes: "I had frequent solicitations to engage in the services of the sanctuary. I did not feel at liberty to refuse. The official members of the church and the preachers took measures to procure me a license in the interval of the Quarterly Conference. In entering thus upon what I had long believed my duty if Providence should thus direct, I found great satisfaction as well as spiritual and mental improvement, for which, as well as his assisting grace, the glory shall all be given to God."

He was duly licensed as a local preacher, March, 1836, by Rev. Ebenezer Washburn, of the New York Conference. The same month he received from Dr. Luckey a letter, in which he strongly counseled him to give himself to the work of preaching rather than that of teaching. The first sermon which he preached after receiving his license was at Sharon, Conn., March 27. The text was Neh. 4. 20, " Our God shall fight for us "—an eager challenge from one who hoped to be a good soldier of the Church militant. He read at this time the *Life of Summerfield*, and was disposed to make comparisons unfavorable to himself: " I was much reproved ; his tenderness of conscience, my callousness ; his devotion to Scriptural study, my indifference." Whatever disposition toward self-flattery he may have had was rigorously suppressed, and as he took the field toward which conscience had been calling him and Providence pressing him, he was determined to recognize only the approval that came down from above.

His license was not to lie in a dormant hand. It had
5

come to him as a sword whose challenge was, " Advance
a step ! " With energies keyed up, with faculties poised,
and with zeal as it were on tiptoe, he strained forward,
waiting for the sign which should give direction to that
step.

CHAPTER VI.

Preaching as a Supply—Joining Conference.

ONE of the preachers on the Amenia Circuit failing in health, Mr. Kidder was asked to take his place, and did so, as a supply under the presiding elder, Rev. Marvin Richardson. He took his turn in visiting the five charges of the circuit, namely, North East, Separate, Oblong, Washington, and Sharon. He had been urged to this work as soon as he received his license, and immediately after his graduation at Middletown he made his arrangements to give himself more undividedly to it. Meanwhile he continued his duties as professor at Amenia until the end of the school year, which was the 23d of the following October, when, as he said and supposed, he "terminated his career of teaching." "It has been a pleasant task," he adds, "and I trust not a profitless one to myself and others." He resigned his chair in favor of his classmate, Davis W. Clark.

He was the more willing to undertake these high duties, even while finishing his course as a student and still occupied as a teacher, for the excellent reasons, as he puts them, that "I find that I shall enjoy superior facilities for learning the usages and becoming acquainted with the institutions of our Church in the place where Methodism has been so long and so prosperously in operation. What is very gratifying, I have the assurance of being cordially received by our people, and of having both their prayers and their cooperation in every effort to do good. Since I have formed the purpose of taking up regularly and exclusively the work of the ministry, I find my feelings in behalf of the work to have gained a pitch and a permanency they have not before had. I feel an ardent desire to be engaged in the labor for souls, and earnestly pray that I may be fully qualified by spiritual gifts for working effectually."

His release from teaching must have been very gratifying to him, for a revival was already prevailing on the circuit, and all his time and strength were needed for his special work. His religious enjoyments were of a high order. He practiced fasting with profit, and was filled with a burning desire for holiness.

During the week in which he met the other preachers on the circuit and gave them his consent to go at once as their colleague and take appointments, he wrote to his father concerning his purpose, and also addressed a letter with a like message to the uncle in Vermont who brought him up. In his communication to his father, besides seeking his approval upon this plan, he asked him for a horse and outfit, so that he might travel his circuit.

While awaiting an answer he received from his father a letter dated a day in advance of his own, containing the tenderest sentiments regarding his approaching twenty-first birthday. " You are now," he wrote, " about arriving at that age in life when custom has made the child in some degree free from the control of the parent, and consequently has discharged the parent from many of his obligations to the child. This age will, I suppose, make no material change to you, yet it is an eventful period to you and to me, one that elicits many hopes and fears. I think much in subsequent life depends upon a good beginning. I am satisfied that I have given myself unnecessary concern on your account, and perhaps injured your feelings, but you will attribute all to good motives and allow me still to continue to follow after you with ardent affection, whatever may be your business or calling. The future is now, as it has been before, fully submitted to you, and I am most of the time quite happy in such a reflection, and I flatter myself that I shall never regret the great sacrifice I have made; most certainly I shall not should you continue respectable and happy. You will avail yourself of an early opportunity to acquaint us with your circumstances, prospects, and determinations for the future."

These affectionate expressions most naturally encouraged the son to look for a favorable response to his request. But, instead, the answer when it did come sorely dashed his hopes, and for the first time his father seemed cold. In part he said: "You will recollect that my advice to you when at Amenia was for you to spend a year or two in teaching after graduating, so that you could supply yourself with library and such other appendages as would be indispensable. This appeared to me reasonable and proper. But in case you could not submit to that course, but must go immediately upon a circuit, I concluded you would come home and I could assist you to a horse and such other articles as would be necessary, without serious inconvenience. But your change of purpose has rendered such an accommodation out of my power, and has subjected me to disappointment, but not to despair. I hope there is some way for you to get along well; but it is hid from me. I have counted the outfit for the first year, horse and equipage, carriage and harness; these will require $250. Your salary of $100 may cover your incidental expenses, but your outfit will bring you immediately in debt without the means of discharging it.   I know of no way I could send you a horse if I had one.   Besides, it is inconsistent to my mind that a society of men should permit a young man that had spent eight or ten years, besides his thousands of dollars, to qualify himself, to labor in their moral vineyard for the mere pittance of a hundred dollars a year!   I look upon it the same as upon a Southern planter who gets faithful services from men without rendering an equivalent.   But I presume you have duly considered all these things and are satisfied that all will be well, and think it strange that I do not view the subject as you do.   I would not wish to dictate to you in religious matters, but I hope that in such affairs as the above you will allow experience to have some weight. My subject is unpleasant to my mind, and I presume will be to you; I will therefore close."

Undiscouraged by this depressing message, the young itinerant, by some means and at his own expense, provided his needed equipment, or, as he styled it, his " rig, horse, saddle, bridle, and martingales," and set out.

But hardly was he fairly under way when he received a letter from his mother, summoning him home on account of the illness of his father.   Making arrangements for the supply of his appointments during his absence, he hastened home.   He found his father better, and, what was most gratifying to him, greatly changed in his views toward his son's course. There was much religious conversation between them, and in a letter written at this time he says: " I have had the happiness, which I did not know would ever be mine, of seeing my father kneel at the altar with me."   The beautiful earnestness of the son, his sincerity, and the quiet enthusiasm with which he described his devotion to duty made a profound impression upon the father, and when he left to return to his work, he was fully supplied with all that he had asked, and more. Quoting from the mother's diary:

"Daniel came to spend a few days with us. His visits are always a period of pleasure, and more especially have we enjoyed his company at this time. He appears to be deeply pious, converses freely with his father, attends to family devotions constantly. He seems like an angel of peace, sent to comfort us in this our day of trial. O Lord, keep him under the shadow of thy wing! We have given him to thee in everlasting covenant. O, fit him for the great work in which he has embarked! So guide him in all his ways, that he may glorify thee in winning many souls to Christ as a crown of rejoicing!" A little more than a week after, she writes: "He said good-bye to us this morning. We have had an excellent visit. We have fitted him out with every article of comfort—horse, buggy, and every appendage thereunto, and he has left us in good spirits, trusting in God. May the blessings of heaven rest upon him!"

Thus furnished, he set out in his own conveyance for his field of work in the east. On his way he stopped at Canandaigua, where the Genesee Conference was in session. Here an event occurred that entirely changed his course. "On going up to the church," where the Conference was being held, he says, "I was met with the intelligence that the day before my name had been presented to the Conference, and I had been received as a member. The air of satisfaction (of some sort) that greeted me on every countenance, as well as their words, told me it was true."

He was astonished and embarrassed, as he had made up his mind to join the New York Conference. In July, after due examination, he was recommended to the Genesee Annual Conference for admission on trial. He also at this time engaged in some correspondence with some of the members of that Conference relative to that step. But afterward, as he supposed, the matter had been dropped. In August, while in New York on his way to Middletown for graduation, he says, " I had proposals made me to take my appointment as a preacher on Long Island—Jamaica and New Utrecht. From the many things brought to my mind by the suggestions of others and my own reflections, I was led to think seriously of uniting with the New York instead of the Genesee Annual Conference. Although I had been within the bounds of the New York Conference for two years, the thought had never occurred, or at least been harbored a moment, of remaining. Nor should I have conceived it at all but through the counsels of those whose judgment I value more than my own. A prophet is not without honor save in his own country. These words may perhaps apply to one who is less than the least of all saints. The principle pointed out by the Saviour is certainly of general application, and ought not to be disregarded by me. That honor alone is to be sought which cometh down from God. I would have before me none other than the question of duty, Where can I be most useful ? not, Where can I enjoy the most ease or mingle most in the society of my kindred ? This question occupied my mind during my whole journey much more than did commencement or anything I saw."

The appointment to the Amenia Circuit coming to him at this time, settled the matter, as he thought, and all indications pointed to his entering the active work in the New York Conference.

The sudden change of field to the west was therefore to him a surprise, and the action of the Genesee Conference threw him into a state of deep anxiety. And yet, in a measure, he had been forewarned; for he found during his visit to his father, that there was a disposition among the preachers in that region to censure him " for not being prepared to stay with them. They had laid a great many plans, expecting my services," he wrote, " and now regard their failure as a disappointment. I trust, nevertheless, that all will yet work for good."

What decision he should now adopt was, for a time, a trying perplexity, and his mind worked with fierce rapidity, as he sat there in the Conference room. " I found myself in a strange dilemma. By some turn in the Conference there had been some speaking and considerable excitement raised in regard to my case from the idea that the New York Conference wished to detain within its own precincts such young men as they chose. I had been recommended by the Quarterly Conference in Canandaigua in compliance with a request to that effect sent to the preacher in August, which I had supposed would not be acted upon, as I had not continued correspondence respecting it, and especially as I had not designed being in the region at all until suddenly and providentially called there. I had but a few hours for making a decision. It was reversing entirely my expectations and arrangements to stay, and to go would be to hazard an excitement which might perhaps injure me, and certainly would the Church and her in-

stitutions. I decided to suffer any inconvenience myself if the proper authorities thought I ought to take the
course and would be responsible for it. The bishop, B.
Waugh, advised me to stay, assigning several reasons,
among which were: 1. The good of our institutions.
2. The belief that I might be more useful in the west.
More remained to be done here, and a more important
theater of action than western New York he did not
know. He believed there would be nothing other than
satisfaction with, and approval of the course, among my
friends east, when the circumstances should be explained.
This he would take upon himself as far as consistent,
and the leading members of the Conference would draw
up a letter to my colleagues and presiding elder, freeing
me from the embarrassment of excusing myself."

According to this promise, a committee was appointed
by the Conference, consisting of Glezen Fillmore, J.
Chamberlayne, A. Abell, Loring Grant, and Wilbur
Hoag, who addressed to his colleagues on the Amenia
Circuit the following letter:

"Dear Brethren:—The design of this communication
is to acquaint you with the circumstances under which
our esteemed friend and brother, Daniel P. Kidder, was
admitted on trial at our Conference. Sometime in
August last he forwarded to Brother Hoag a certificate
of his standing as a local preacher, as a transference of his
membership and standing to Canandaigua, with a request
that he might have a recommendation to our Annual Conference. Subsequently, as we understand, in pursuance of
polite solicitations from you, he consented to engage in
some labor within your Conference, and supposed that
by that means his case would be prevented from coming
to our Conference. This, however, did not result, and

before his arrival here he was actually admitted. Under these circumstances, by our advice and solicitation, he permitted his name to remain here, although he is apprehensive that he will disappoint expectations which he has authorized. This, however, he must do in any event, as we were as confidently expecting his services as you could have been.

"We will add one other reason why we cannot doubt you will approve his remaining here. That is that he originally belonged here, his home and his friends are here, and if his having graduated at Middletown should result in our loss of his services, it cannot fail to caution us against recommending to any more of our young men the Wesleyan University. Anything which would tend to such a result we are sure you would deprecate. We presume that you will blame nobody in the premises, but if you do, blame us, not him."

The Conference adjourned on the day of his arrival, and that evening his name was read off for Rochester, Rev. J. Copeland, his colleague, in charge. In a letter written the following morning, he says : "The Conference adjourned at 11 o'clock in the evening. The preachers are this morning separating to go in all directions preaching their Master. It is an example of the noblest magnanimity to see them toiling through the business of a laborious session, and *ready* at its close to break up any attachment and go wherever the voice of the Church directs. How does this compare with the pride and ease and luxury of a pampered, moneyed priesthood?" Then, referring to his own situation, he adds : "What can I do in the circumstances in which I am thrown? Nothing has been of my seeking or according to my wish. For I have not allowed personal choice to have any influence on my mind. These things are placed—may I not say crowded?—upon me. If by the hand of God, he will sustain me. In his strength alone I trust. The coming year will be one of unremitting labor and of responsibilities greater than I can bear."

Proceeding at once to make arrangements for his new field and future, he sent back to his father the horse and buggy he had so kindly provided, and by more expedi.. tious means he proceeded to Amenia, settled his affairs there, gathered up his effects, shipped his library, and said his farewells.

On Wednesday evening, November 9, at Salisbury, Conn., by the Rev. O. V. Ammerman, he was married to Miss Cynthia Harriet Russell. The wedding trip was a departure the next day to Rochester. Going by way of Poughkeepsie, they proceeded by steamboat to New York, where the following Sunday he preached in Greene Street Church in the morning, and on a sudden call from Rev. Robert Seney, who was afflicted with influenza, preached in the afternoon in the Mulberry Street Chapel, " the second pewed church in New York, and as genteel as any other." The Friday after found them in Rochester.

CHAPTER VII.

First Pastorate.

" IT is natural to pause," he says, " and indulge a few reflections upon an event like this, my first entering upon the more responsible duties of the Christian ministry. I stand in astonishment when I look upon the providences of God, which have placed me where I am. One year ago my present situation was as foreign from my expectation as it could possibly have been. Nor have I since taken a single step which had a design, or, to my knowledge, a tendency to produce it. I had in October, by the advice and solicitation of friends, received a license as exhorter from the Quarterly Conference at Middletown. I did not hesitate to do this when called upon by the Church, inasmuch as the great question of my course in life had been long settled and acted upon. This license was never transcended by a formal attempt to preach until I was called upon by the proper authorities to receive license as a local preacher. In both these capacities I held myself obedient to the service of the Church, in no case occupying any spot until urged to do so on the ground of duty, and never deeming myself at liberty to refuse, or seek for excuse, from any service which thus seemed necessary or proper.

" I had by previous effort secured to myself nearly half of my time during the last college year for extra and private studies. It was with reluctance that I surrendered this, and the delights I had anticipated from it, for

the laborious employment of teaching.   But while I did
so I brought upon myself additional cares equally arduous and more absorbing, namely, those of preparing
often for public speaking.   During the last quarter of my
services in Amenia Seminary, I had taken the place of
Rev. Mr. Ellsworth, and thus had regularly performed
the duties of the circuit.   From the time I first commenced preaching there had scarcely been a Sabbath
vacant of duties, whether at home or abroad.   Now, by
the grace of God, I am what I am, and I trust I may as
truly say, By the providence of God I am *where* I am.

"I find on looking over my minutes that I have
preached just fifty sermons up to the present time.   I
need not comment on this circumstance as a proof of my
inability to occupy the station I am called upon to fill.
Proofs of this stand thick around me on every side, and
it will be happy for me if they produce the proper effect
of making me feel my weakness and cause me to put my
trust in Him who is everlasting strength."

Rochester was a circuit with two preaching places, on
opposite sides of the Genesee River, each having an outfit
of Sunday school, prayer and class meetings.   His first
Sunday, November 20, was a busy one, beginning with a
visit to the Sunday school at 9 A. M.   His first sermon
was from the text, 1 Cor. 2. 3 : "I was with you in weakness, and in fear, and in much trembling."   There was a
sermon again in the afternoon and another in the evening, followed by a prayer meeting with seekers at the
altar.   Something like this was the program of all his
Sabbaths : never less than three sermons, with prayer
meetings and altar services, and frequently after the
morning sermon there was a class meeting.   No matter
how full the day was otherwise, this conscientious young

pastor was always found in the Sunday school, sometimes attending two in one day, and he gave joyfully to this department that attention which showed the just estimate which he placed upon it.

After one of these busy Sabbaths he says: " Thus the day was filled up with labor, and I could wish with usefulness. Lord, hear the prayers of thy servant and people ! "

In common with all ministers he had his dull Sundays. Of one such he records: " A stormy morning, thin congregations, hard work in the afternoon, somewhat the same in the morning. I had all the trouble I would suffer myself to have about it. In the evening I did better. There were five at the altar, and two professed conversion."

Such, however, was his enthusiasm that he was affected but little by depression, and even sickness could not check his ardor. Although suffering at one time with a cold, which disturbed his whole system, he preached to full houses. " In the evening I was aided and blessed particularly in my own estimation and feelings, which were very low in the morning." He chants the vespers of one of his busy Sabbaths in these words : " I seldom ever passed through the same amount of labor with more ease to myself." Here is the order of one of his sample Sundays : " Rose at 4:45 A. M. My mind was clear and devotional. I attended and opened the Sabbath school on the west side and closed that on the east side, preached three sermons, attended class meeting, inquiry meeting, and closing prayer meeting, each about an hour. I enjoyed the prayer meeting better than I have any other on the east side. One soul was happily converted. Many more were at the altar. Throughout this day I was blessed with the presence and aid of the Most High."

During the week also he often preached, sometimes traveling into the neighboring towns. This year he delivered his first Fourth of July and Thanksgiving sermons.

It was with him a rule to make some pastoral calls every day. The sick and the troubled were the objects of his special attention. In his honest purpose to do his work well he slighted no detail. In each family the servants were inquired after, and, if possible and proper, they were brought in to share in the religious devotions with which he closed every call. He writes: " In the afternoon visited nine families, conversed with them on religious subjects, and prayed for them. In several houses I found not more than one professor of religion. In these cases where there is no guarantee for their disposition toward us or the cause we would promote, it is the greatest cross to ask permission to pray with them. Yet, in each of these instances, I had grace to do it, and, I trust to my own profit, if not to that of others."

When he went through a street in the discharge of this duty it was with the thoroughness of a reaper and a gleaner combined. There was no threshold where he did not ask the privilege of saying, " Peace be unto this house." And his loyalty to the obligations of this department of his work took him into many places from which the average minister considers himself excused. His fidelity in thus associating constantly with his people in their everyday life was in part rewarded by the many incidents that came to him furnishing him facts and illustrations from the ever fresh pages of human nature.

He visited one who on his dying bed gave signs of sincere repentance, but afterward, being flattered with the idea of recovery, abandoned his seriousness and went into another world with oaths and blasphemy on his lips. There must have been an accent of prevailing urgency in the young pastor's voice as, with this circumstance fresh in his mind, he called upon sinners to seek the Lord while he may be found. We can imagine, too, how at this time it must have been like an added strand in the cable of his faith to receive the testimony of a dying physician whom he visited, and who said: " I have never seen nor heard of an instance in which the desire for life was overcome but by Christian principle. Infidel philosophy which I have examined and proved is, in many instances at least, a species of self-deception willfully practiced."

Of this part of his work he wrote: " Every time I go out for this object I am impressed with its absolute importance. By this means a minister can make a noble application of the precept of Aristotle, ' Let no day pass without making a friend.' "

His mornings were spent in study and his afternoons were devoted to visiting, but the demands of his pastorate also absorbed his evenings, and there is a record running all along of his attendance upon trustees' meetings, leaders' meetings, Sunday school boards, Bible classes, and singing schools.

Each week, too, finds him in one or more of the class meetings. Having learned while a student the benefit of the band meetings in the development and training of Christian experience, he organized these helps among his own people. He also established and carried on a course of week-evening lectures on biblical subjects, de-

6

signed more particularly for the benefit of the workers in his Sunday schools.

That no moment might be allowed to go to waste he gave to the press the fruit of his busy pen, writing for the *Advocate* and other papers.

Always scrupulously careful in the use of his time, he is now, if anything, more than ever religiously impressed with its proper division and employment. " I am deeply convinced of the necessity of mending my habits, particularly with respect to early rising and exactness in redeeming the time." Rising early meant five o'clock in the morning, for with him the injunction of the Discipline thereto had not fallen into its modern contempt. In order to secure regular and early rising he procured an alarm clock, that strident monitor of easily pricked consciences. The general division of his time was simple, and, as one would think, sufficient: six hours' study, six hours' pastoral duties, five hours' exercise and recreation, seven hours' sleep. Under this arrangement he divided up the several hours of the day by a plan, to which he prefixed the following preamble: " *Whereas*, much of my time has run to waste, and I find habits of sloth and effeminacy ready to fasten upon me to the destruction of piety and all hopes of usefulness ; and, *whereas*, without determined exactness in the disposal of every moment of time the interests of time and eternity are both hazarded ; and, *whereas*, the providence of God has placed me in circumstances of high responsibility, in which without the most vigorous and untiring exertions I am liable to forfeit his honor and the welfare of immortal souls ; therefore, it is incumbent upon me to practice more self-denial than I have ever done, and as far as lieth in me to observe scrupulously these rules. In planning my course of studies I wish to be mindful of present good and future usefulness. Theology in its length and breadth is before me. It will be my object to investigate with care everything which can be rendered of practical service, keeping in view that toward which all other knowledge should point, and at which terminate, the knowledge of Christ crucified. I hope to redeem every moment of time and to make everything tell upon the improvement of the mind and heart. Blessed with every facility at present, if health is spared, it must be criminal to do otherwise than accomplish much in study the coming winter." He laid it down as a principle as nearly inflexible as might be, that for nothing were his study hours to be interrupted.

The preparation of his sermons was a matter in which his conscience urged him to extreme care and an unremitting faithfulness. His method was to study with thoroughness his subject, and then devote Saturday to the arrangement of his skeleton, for up to this time he had never written out a sermon in full. In addition he adopted a little later the practice of writing out during the week, at greater or less length, one of the skeletons from which he had preached the preceding Sabbath. In all, however, he was careful not to depart from his rule of depending entirely upon the Holy Spirit, and he was never negligent in gratefully recording instances of divine help. "Again delivered three discourses and was more than usually assisted by the Lord and his free Spirit." That his preaching might be effective in producing its legitimate results was his special anxiety; he ardently stirs himself up to this end and writes: " I have resolved to amend both in preaching and practice. I fear I have been too easy in preaching, too much disposed to content my hearers with their present amount of religious enjoyment. I hope henceforth to tell the whole truth, severe as it may be." The next Sunday, he observes, " I preached a more plain and pointed sermon than I was ever enabled to do before." A revival was his consuming desire. " Lord, may thy work grow," is the entry with which he closes the record of a Sabbath in which there were sixteen persons at the altar. Finney's *Lectures on Revivals* were read by him at this time, with the comment that "They contain as much practical Methodism, under a garb slightly modified, as any book I have read." The Church in a state of revival, the tree of life changed into a burning bush, was his idea of Methodism.

In the protracted meeting which made his first winter at Rochester full of encouraging fruits, he preached every night of the week except Saturday night, which time he set apart for a converts' meeting, a most happy arrangement, as he found. From time to time he refers to them as " pleasant," " profitable," " delightful."

But he is least of all satisfied with his fullness of service, and often scourges himself round the altar of duty. " Having had occasion to review my own feelings and course of action, I mourn that I have done so little for Christ. From many considerations I have resolved to be henceforth more diligent in my Master's service. My solemn convictions are that henceforth I ought to be studious and more holy." Upon reading Payson's Memoirs, he reflects, " I was enabled to see my own astonishing dullness in private devotion." He also gave a careful reading to Wesley's *Plain Account of Christian Perfection*, in order that he might again preach upon the subject, and that he might enjoy all that God would vouchsafe to one so unworthy.

On the occasion of his first watch night as pastor, he recalled with grateful emotions the fact that just a year before he first ascended the pulpit.

During his first year in the pastorate he preached at Wyoming, where he attended school, and a pious woman at whose house he had boarded, taking his hand, exclaimed, "What hath God wrought!" He visited Brockport and preached three times to a pleasant, attentive congregation. "This place was the scene of my residence and commencement of business six years ago. It has changed but little. But, O, what a change hath God wrought in me! Then I was a thoughtless youth. I recollect once attending the Methodist church as a matter of curiosity, now I endeavored to preach Christ crucified."

A journey to his father's house and a trip to Lima, preaching among his old friends and enjoying the special exercises connected with the close of the spring term, varied the routine of his work. He also visited the Canadian Conference at Toronto. He was introduced to the Conference by the Rev. Dr. E. Ryerson, preached on Sunday, addressed the missionary meeting, and spoke at a tea meeting held in the interest of the Sunday school. On this occasion he introduced two resolutions which were unanimously passed after he and others had spoken to them. Coming from one who afterward rose to be a leader of the Sunday school work in his Church, it may be interesting to read these words, as setting forth his earliest sentiments upon this subject. They were: "*Resolved*, 1. That the magnitude of the work in which we are engaged and the number of difficulties which everywhere present themselves, should lead us to unite our exertions and our prayers with a fixed determination to extend the conquests of divine truth through the whole extent of our land, until all the wanderers in our western territory bow to the authority of our divine Lord. *Resolved*, 2. That the benefits of Sabbath schools which have already resulted, should stimulate us to renewed exertions in this holy cause."

In January of this year he received an invitation to become principal of the Troy Conference Academy, at West Poultney, Vt. The request, from a member of the Committee on Correspondence, was expressed in assuring terms, with glowing allusions to real and prospective attendance, the promise of a full corps of assistants, and description of an ample building in process of erection. The argument was persuasive, and was the first of many pressing calls to a similar work. But he declined it. His heart was fixed and contented in the pastorate. The future in his thought and plan projected no horizon beyond this field. And yet, ere he was aware of it, the curve of duty had swept him into another and widely different orbit.

CHAPTER VIII.

Missionary Life.

DURING Mr. Kidder's earliest reflections upon the ministry, the sacrifice and service of the missionary had been often present as the duty which might after all engross his future. He felt that a call to preach the Gospel embraced this—that his credentials could not be reckoned as genuine unless they included the terms "all the world" and "every creature." Nor did he consider this any hardship. The rather he had always been eager in his yearnings toward the heathen, and the one whom he would love as himself was his neighbor at the uttermost parts of the earth.

To him the cry of distress that broke upon his ears from afar was louder than any call from the favored ones about him. And now, giving up a pastorate rich in the love of his people and fruitful in every sign of prosperity, abandoning the opportunities for study so dear to him, and surrendering the prospects of a growing popularity, he resolved to devote himself to the exposure, toil, and obscurity (as not known in these days) of a Christian missionary.

In keeping with the openness of all his conduct, he took his church into his confidence, and requested their prayers that he might be directed aright.

Early in August, 1837, he received a letter from Bishop Waugh, appointing him as missionary to Rio de Janeiro. "I regret," says the bishop, "your leaving the

Genesee Conference, but I rejoice that you are going to a region where you will be more needed. May the spirit and power of Christ, your Master, go with you and give you great and glorious success!"

A week after he received a letter from his father on what he termed "the engrossing and painful subject of our departure." Only by slow and reluctant stages had the father come on far enough to give his consent that his son should enter the ministry. Of late, however, the prominence of that son, and his growing fame in the pastorate of the largest city of the neighborhood, had quite conquered all parental discomfort and supplanted it with a real and justifiable pride. It was therefore all the more a crushing affliction to dismiss him from home and native land perhaps forever, and let him go forth to confront the hardships of a missionary life under a tropical sky.

His missionary enthusiasm did not render him stoical, and this renewed and deeper disappointment of his father and the separation from his friends caused him unspeakable distress. His mind being, however, made up, he regarded this as a situation in which to love father and mother more than Christ was not to be worthy of him, and he proceeded in his usually calm and orderly way to make the adjustments necessary to a departure for the field where already his heart was gone on in advance. Referring to a good-bye visit from his friends, he says: " We considered ourselves as having parted for a *long, long* time remove. We need not say it is painful and the mind shrinks a little under it, yet we see not reason either to despond or to waver. God is our trust, and shall be our portion forever." In his farewell visit to his father's house he went to his mother's grave. By that low mound he consecrated himself anew to his sacred calling with a devotion that included its holiest, most Christlike sacrifice.

Repairing to the seat of the Conference at Perry, N. Y., he was, under the missionary rule, ordained deacon by Bishop Hedding, in a class of twenty-eight. This was on Sunday, September 24, 1837. The afternoon before he had assisted the bishop in preparing the parchments. "The sermon by the bishop," he says, "was peculiarly solemn and impressive." The following Monday evening he was ordained elder. Of this he says: "Without consulting me the Conference had consummated my election to elder's orders, although I had repeatedly expressed to members of it my own impressions and choice to the contrary. Bishop Hedding said if I declined they would not urge it, but the counsel and judgment of that body fixed it and I submitted, trusting in God to fulfill his righteous designs when I am truly given up to his will." The ordination services took place in connection with the anniversary of the Conference Missionary Society. Dr. Bangs made the regular address, the report of the treasurer was read, then a collection of $200 was taken up toward the prospective missionary's salary. Following this the bishop conducted the ritual. In a letter to his wife Mr. Kidder says: "The bishop took occasion to change some part of the service, adapting it to the special circumstances of the case, thus rendering it, if possible, still more impressive. When it was closed and the bishop had given a parting charge, I spoke a few words to the Conference. The scene of separation was sufficient to melt the heart. I cannot begin to describe the interesting and painful event of parting with that band of noble-hearted brethren who now committed to the care of God the first foreign missionary from their body. You should have seen it to know how deep a concern they take in us—so unworthy." Hastening to Rochester, the next evening he preached a farewell sermon to a crowded house, and " adieus were given to friends who, with tearful eyes, renewed their respects and promised to commend us to God. Scenes of tenderness and power equal to these I have seldom witnessed and seldom expect to enjoy. But they are past only to live in a warm and affectionate remembrance."

Leaving Rochester, the time intervening until he sailed was occupied in visiting friends in New England, in making the necessary preparations and purchases in New York, in diligently seeking information about his new field, and in studying the Portuguese language. He was busy also in preaching and in addressing missionary meetings. In Boston, from which port he sailed, he for the first time administered the communion on the evening of November 5, in the Blossom Street Church.

At length, on Monday, the 13th, he set sail for Rio in the *Avon*, a bark freighted with government stores. There were only nine passengers. Of these, four constituted the missionary family, there being associated with Mr. Kidder and his wife, Mr. McMurdy, also a missionary, and Miss Marcella Russell, sister to Mrs. Kidder, who was sent out by the Board as a teacher. " The parting exercises," he says, " were solemn and appropriate. By appointment, our friends having gathered together, it was found that there were too many to be accommodated in the cabin, so we removed to the steerage, which was filled with persons standing. Rev. A. D. Sargeant addressed the company, expressing with much simplicity and eloquence the objects of these farewell exercises. After singing, Brother Scudder led in prayer. Singing, and the benediction by Brother Knight, of Charlestown, closed the devotional services, when our friends passed up the companion way, taking us each by the hand. In a few minutes came the signal for casting off. The wharf was crowded with friends of the crew and passengers, who stretched their eager eyes as long as they could be mutually recognized. The vessel moved away reluctantly, and while we were still on the quarter deck the captain gave his farewell signal and the crowds began to disappear toward their homes."

January 10, 1838, found the missionary party in the harbor of Rio de Janeiro. The voyage of fifty-six days was for the most part very pleasant, although during its earlier stage there was stormy weather with a very high sea, so that all were more or less affected with the usual *mal de mer*. Mrs. Kidder suffered severely, and on her account there was at one time considerable anxiety. She grew so weak that she could neither go on deck nor be carried there, and "she became emaciated and almost helpless with such unparalleled exhaustion. Some of these were in one sense as dark days as we had ever seen. The gloomy predictions of our friends came up in sad retrospect before our minds. We had, however, expected sufferings, and the only reasonable ground for disappointment was that they were so light. An unshaken conviction of being in the path of duty was infinitely more valuable than an exemption from a little present inconvenience. Our greatest trouble was on the score of apprehension, not knowing when these things might terminate. But we endeavored to confide ourselves in the hand of God, who, we trust, has directed us and will rule all things well." A change in her condition occurring, the spirits of the little party greatly revived, and on Thanksgiving Day, of which he makes note, he says, " We had reason to commemorate it."

At the invitation of the captain he conducted religious services on the successive Sabbaths. The days of the week he gave largely to a study of the Portuguese. The sight of passing vessels, an occasional whale, schools of flying fish, some of which lighted on the deck of the ship, and the catching of a shark diverted the monotony of the voyage. One night the sea was all on fire with a splendid phosphorescence. On December 30 they crossed the equator. One evening, as they were cruising in latitudes where several vessels had recently been plundered, they were alarmed by the sudden appearance of a suspicious looking craft bearing down upon them. All on board were apprehensive, and some to a serious degree. He speaks of himself as prepared to indulge some commotions of mind, as he had just been reading *Conrad the Corsair*, and was in a condition for " imaginations dire." " Nevertheless," he adds, " the ladies preserved the best courage of all, and very sensibly gave themselves no alarm. This was the best course even if the danger had been real. Presence of mind always becomes the Christian. He has less to fear than other men. He knows where his trust is, and there he should rely. He then can discharge his duty like a man, and leave the result with God."

Monday, January 1, 1838, he writes : " Far from our friends we wished them a Happy New Year, the beginning of which we really enjoyed as our bark rode gayly on under the balmy winds of the south, which tempered the heat of the tropical sun."

Before the evening of January 8 land was sighted ;
the third day after quarantine was passed in the harbor
of Rio, and by two o'clock of that day the gentlemen of
the missionary party were in the palace square of the
city. Finding the residence of the Rev. Mr. Spaulding,
the superintendent of the mission, and making the
necessary arrangements, the ladies were brought on
shore before evening. Speaking of his first impressions
he says : " The blacks, the mules, the style of buildings,
and streets, but especially the barbarian cries which fill
one's ears to deafness, were all inexpressibly strange.
But the Gloria was the admiration of all. Its luxuriance
and the exquisite green of its foliage surpassed everything we had conceived. To have been brought thus far
through so many dangers, and kept not only in perfect
health, but in perfect peace, seemed to call for our deepest gratitude. We endeavored to feel our dependence
and give the glory to God."

He and his family were for the time established with
Mr. Spaulding, whose house was charmingly situated
near the Gloria, and the room of the newly-arrived missionary commanded a view of wonderful range, including
fine buildings, streets, the mountains, and the harbor,
with the vessels of all nations riding at anchor. On
January 21, the second Sunday after his arrival, he
preached his first sermon in South America.

Brazil is a land well worthy of earnest, aggressive, and
persistent missionary labor. The religion of the land,
by reason of its settlement from the south of Europe, is
Roman Catholic. From the beginning Protestantism
has attempted to plant a pure Gospel there, it being a
fact well worthy of note that the very first missionary
effort of the Church after the Reformation was from

Geneva to Brazil.   But in modern times the credit of the first mission to Brazil belongs to the Methodist Episcopal Church, which sent the Rev. Justin Spaulding to Rio de Janeiro in 1836.   It is to be regretted that the financial pressure of the times led to the abandonment of the mission and the return of Mr. Spaulding in 1842.

Until he was able to talk with the people, Mr. Kidder busied himself chiefly with the distribution of Bibles and Testaments.   He remarks: " The circulation of the Holy Scriptures in the vernacular of the country was a primary object of our mission.   Hitherto nothing like a systematic effort had been made for the extensive distribution of the Bible in this vast and interesting country.   Although several hundred copies of Bibles and Testaments from the British and American Bible Societies had been previously introduced by means of consignments to gentlemen engaged in mercantile affairs, and although the Bible had never been proscribed in Brazil otherwise than in the usual regulations of the Romish Church, yet in the lack of all effort on the part of the priesthood to give it currency, it was so far as the vulgar tongue was concerned, an effectually excluded and unknown book."

In a record made a little later he continues : " For a day or two there has seemed to be a great interest excited among the citizens in regard to our books or Testaments.   They have been coming for them incessantly. The Salia has been thronged with persons of every age and condition of life, from the gray-headed man to the prattling child, from the gentleman in high life to the poor slave.   Most of the children and blacks brought notes from their masters or parents.   The notes were couched in the most respectful and often in beseeching language.   One or two were from poor widows who had no money to buy books for their children. Among the gentlemen who called were several proprietors and directors of schools, and also students of every age. They wished for French, many of them, and some for English as well as Portuguese. We dealt out the sacred volumes to them according to our best judgment, with both joy and trembling. Such a movement was aston-ishing to Brother Spaulding as well as to us. We were at times disposed to think that it was a concerted plan to get the books destroyed or to get us into trouble, but every circumstance seemed to contradict this, and all who came listened with the profoundest attention to the few broken words we could make them understand about Christ and the Bible. At any rate, judging from the past, we could not suppose that so much divine truth could at once be scattered among the people with-out a commotion being produced by their jealous *padres.* Nevertheless, there was one of that class among the applicants. He received copies of the Testament in English, French, and Portuguese, and on going away re-marked, ' They did not do such things in this country.' Another sent a note in French, asking for *L'Ancien et Nouveau Testament.*" The supply of books, after a little while, gave out, but the messengers continued to come for them until, as he says, "after about two hundred had come within three days, we concluded that about four times as many more had been called for."

For the sake of recreation and refreshment he varied his studies and missionary work by expeditions into the neighboring country. The scenery, the mountains, the rich verdure, the tropical foliage, the rare fruits and flowers, were very interesting to him and furnished many opportunities for the exercise of the vivid powers of description with which he fixed the results of his keen observation.

Part of his work on the Sabbath was a service and sermon on board the United States man-of-war or some of the merchant vessels in the harbor. This was kept up by himself and Mr. Spaulding all the time of his stay there, and developed into a regular Bethel service. By issuing circulars and taking special pains to invite an attendance, the congregation would, in some instances, approach rather respectable numbers. "Nothing," he observes, " could exceed the order and solemnity of the assemblies which gathered together each Sabbath morning on the deck of some noble vessel at whose mainmast the emblem of peace and mercy was floating in the breeze. We generally found the vessel, designated for the time being as the Bethel ship, arranged and decorated in the most tasteful manner, with seats to accommodate all who might choose to come to worship God. How delightful it was to see boatload after boatload of seamen coming alongside for this noble object, men who, but for such an opportunity, would be seeking recreation on shore exposed to all the temptations of vice and the snares of sin! How sublime were the sentiments inspired by such a scene in such a place! The brilliant sky, the lofty mountains, and the swelling ocean could not fail at any time to impress the thoughtful mind; but when, surrounded by these objects, it was our privilege also to witness in a company of seamen the attention of the soul fixed upon eternal things and indicated by the heaving breast, the falling tear, and the unconcealed resolve, ours was no ordinary pleasure." It was also the custom of the missionaries to hold Sabbath evening services at the residence of the superintendent.

CHAPTER IX.

Missionary Life.

LARGE and important as was the work in which he was thus engaged, it seemed hardly sufficient to his aggressive and enterprising spirit. His idea of the duty he had undertaken impelled him to a wider field than Rio, although it was the capital of the empire, and he soon began to plan for a study of the outlying territories in different directions. During the time of his stay in the country he went out on three excursions, acquainting himself with the people in the interior and along the coast, from the Tropic of Capricorn to the Amazon, the first Protestant minister to explore these regions, the Livingstone of South America.

" With the primary object of circulating the Scriptures, in the Portuguese language, the chief cities and important towns were visited, the traveler making himself familiar with the social, civil, moral, and religious condition of the empire, and frequently holding free and full conferences with leading minds of the country."

As a first, or trial trip, he set out on a Christmas expedition with Mr. Spaulding, to visit some of the villages situated on the upper borders of the bay of Rio de Janeiro. This trip occupied him for only a few days and served so to intensify his desire for further quests and wider travels that by the middle of the following January he went alone to the province of San Paulo, distant south from Rio, by the course taken, about three hundred miles. Passing back from Santos, the capital, by the only means of conveyance possible, a horse or mule, he traversed the province, covering more than two hundred miles. In this tour he had reason frequently to acknowledge the providence of God in directing him to persons who had the power and the disposition in a greater degree than any others to advance the object of his mission. In a letter to his father he speaks of this journey to the south as an extremely interesting one in every respect. Although two hundred years had elapsed since the discovery and settlement of the province, and it was one of the oldest parts of Brazil, still he was informed by the people that he was the first Protestant minister that had visited it.

The most important of these expeditions was, however, the last, which he also made alone. It was to the north, and detained him from his family for six months. "My voyage," he says, "along the northern coast of Brazil was undertaken at an interesting and favorable epoch. Up to the year 1839 there had never existed any means of regular and rapid communication between the capital and the extreme portions of the empire, particularly the far north, and not infrequently political intelligence was received at the seat of government, by way of England and the United States, earlier than by direct dispatches. Such, moreover, were the difficulties interposed by the regular trade winds and strong currents that set to leeward of Cape St. Roque, that they could be overcome by no enterprise short of steam navigation.

"To meet so important an exigency the Brazil Steam Packet Company had been organized under the patronage of the imperial government. The *St. Sebastian*, one of the boats of this company, had just returned from her first trip, successful in every way, and had been advertised to leave again for the northern ports on the first day of July."

Provided with numerous and valuable letters of introduction in English, Portuguese, and French, he took passage. In turn he visited the cities of Bahia, Maccio, Pernambuco, Itamaraca, Parahiba, Cerca, Maranham, and Para, stopping a greater or less length of time in each and exploring the contiguous country. At Pernambuco in consequence of missing the regular boat he was detained thirty days over his time. The second day after his arrival at Para, on the Amazon, was the Sabbath, and through the courtesy of the captain it was arranged that he should hold a Bethel service on the steamer. "Some American seamen were present, and several persons came off from the shore. These, together with the ship's company, formed an audience of about thirty, to whom," he says, "I announced the tidings of the kingdom of God. The occasion was very favorable for divine service, and I felt truly grateful for the opportunity, probably the first ever enjoyed by any Protestant minister, of attempting to preach Jesus and the resurrection upon the wide waters of the Amazon." At Para he spent nearly two months, taking in all the points of interest in the city proper and making wide excursions into the interior. His entrance into the river he thus refers to in a letter to his wife: "Yesterday was a very interesting day from the circumstance of our ascending the Amazon. We passed the banks and shoals which lie at the entrance of that mouth commonly called the Para River about ten A. M., just as the flood tide was setting up. The color of the water had already changed to a muddy hue and erelong became quite yellow. The swell behind us was very heavy, and between wind and tide and steam we made nearly ten knots per hour. I came on shore after breakfast and presented my letters to Charles J. Smith, United States consul, who received me with that urbanity and true kindness which I have uniformly experienced at the hands of our countrymen during my travels in Brazil." In this connection it is proper to refer to his generous treatment by our consul at Pernambuco, Mr. Joseph Ray, " who not only received me," he says, " in the most cordial manner, but generously insisted upon my making his house my home; and a most hospitable home I found it during a sojourn of nearly two months in that city."

At Para he preached every Sabbath either on board of an American vessel or in the private house of a friend. Turning his face homeward he made the journey by the regular steam packet line as far as Bahia. Here he remained for about three weeks.

From this point down to Rio he had the opportunity of a trip as unexpected as it was interesting. He received the invitation, and accepted it, of a free passage on board a French ship called *L'Orientale*, a large vessel constructed originally for the merchant service. She wore now a pennant, and, mounting eight or ten guns, had the appearance of a respectable sloop of war. The ship was then on a voyage round the world, having on board a polytechnic school of sixty pupils, who, aided by competent professors, were thus to travel and receive their education at the same time. The enterprise was a private one projected by the commander of the vessel, and conducted on his account, although it had received the sanction of the French government. The pupils were chiefly the sons of the nobility and titled families of

France and Belgium. Many of them also planned to devote themselves to the navy as a profession, and were thus taking their first lessons in seamanship. "It was truly a novel thing," Mr. Kidder observes, "to see counts, viscounts, barons, and marquises knocking about in red woolen shirts, duck trousers well tarred, barefoot, going aloft, standing at the wheel, rowing boats, etc. Some of them, however, did it with an admirable spirit and perseverance, though the majority, I think, make rather poor sailors." Of his experience on board this vessel he says: "I shall long remember the week which I spent as a passenger in her, as one of peculiar incident and pleasure." At night of the 23d of December the vessel came to anchor in the harbor of Rio, and he writes: "So strong were my feelings at the thought of being, after such a scene of wanderings, once more brought back so near to my family, with the hope of meeting them on the morrow, that sleep almost forsook my eyelids. I waited with all patience until the captain was ready to set me on shore, which he kindly did at an early hour, with all my baggage. I hastened home, and in addition to the great joy of finding my own and the mission family well, had the satisfaction of giving them a complete surprise."

The thorough methods of observation adopted during these tours made more than ever clear the imperative need of just such evangelical work as our missionary was planning and had to some extent already carried out. It had been part of his original instructions to make a tour of investigation through the principal provinces of the empire with a view to the introduction of the Scriptures. In executing these orders with his customary completeness, he discovered everywhere a sad want of the Gospel in its enlightening and refining power.

Indeed, in one way of looking at it, it might appear that the people were not capable of an intelligent appreciation of the claims and truths of a genuine religion, for not only were their minds sodden with superstition, but their ignorance also was oppressively dense. In one place there were no schools at all; one gentleman as a matter of favor gave instruction to a few boys. The statement was made by a tabelliao, or notary, that scarcely one person in thirty could read, and although he was a native of the province he had never known of a government school. The region where this information was gathered was in the immediate vicinity of Rio, the capital, the supposed seat of the culture and refinement of the empire. At another place, only six miles from the capital of one of the northern provinces, the missionary held the following conversation with a lad fourteen or sixteen years of age: " Have you any school in this vicinity?" "Yes, one." "Where is it?" "In the palace." "How many attend it?" "I do not know; about three benches full." "Do you go at present?" "No, sir; I finished last year." "Do you know how to write?" "No, nor to read either." "What did you learn at school?" "*Nada!*" (Nothing at all!) The ignorance and stupidity of the priests were, if anything, still more conspicuous, and provoked the sharpest expressions of contempt from the leading men with whom the missionary conversed during his travels.

As might be supposed, the morals of the country were found to be deplorable. Tales of assassination and violence were frequently related to him. One benefit, it was admitted, from the recent wars, was the drafting of the indolent and the vicious into the army. And yet on the other hand, because of these same wars, it came to pass that in some of the provinces both life and property were especially insecure. A common question every morning was, " How many were stabbed last night?" The answer usually was, " Five or six."

More desperate, however, and deep seated than even the spirit of violence and murder, was the licentiousness that everywhere prevailed. This Mr. Kidder described as the abomination of desolation in this land, and it was so prevalent that to a great extent it had lost in the minds of the people its heinous character, so that he had difficulty in making clear its sinfulness to a cultivated gentleman with whom he was talking, and this person expressed the greatest astonishment when at the missionary's request he read Rev. 21. 8. At the foundling hospital in Rio from thirty to fifty infants were received every month. These unfortunate little creatures were to a large degree the children of female slaves. Their masters did not want the trouble of bringing them up, and perhaps wished the mothers to serve as wet nurses. Fully two thirds of these victims of lust died shortly after they were brought in, and one of the physicians declared the whole affair to be " one great butchery !"

The worst feature was that the clergy, by their example, served rather to encourage than to check this corruption. Their reputation for licentiousness was notorious. In one village was found a priest with a growing family of at least five children. A gentleman occupying a prominent position as an educator, a Portuguese by birth, and a Catholic, said : " There are three hundred padres in Rio, and probably not more than a dozen good ones among them." By this he meant men of good moral character. A French gentleman present at the same time said : " Here the padres have no shame. When they enter a store or any public place they speak no other language but that of obscenity. They openly have large families, and do not hesitate to provide publicly for their children every necessary article. Such things are done in Europe, but under cover." A native said that he did not allow his children to go to confession; he had a daughter seventeen years of age who had never yet confessed to a priest, and should not till the eve of her marriage. The greater part of the padres were so immoral that instead of fulfilling the proper designs of their office as ministers of religion, they perverted their opportunities of privacy to instill into the minds of young females ideas which they ought never to learn. Another Brazilian said in the presence of this gentleman that his children were brought up to confess annually, for which purpose he sent them to a confidential priest. "Ah!" said the former, "you are a fortunate man if you have found a confidential priest!" Yet another gentleman of culture, who had frequent and free conversations with the missionary, had begun to study and prepare for the priesthood. But he turned aside and took up instead the law, lest in entering the ranks of the discredited clergy it should be said to him, "Physician, heal thyself!" This person was strong in the impression that the clergy should have the power to marry, for they were, *de facto*, much worse than married, with immense scandal to religion.

There was but little in the teachings of the Church in Brazil to correct, and much the rather to confirm, this state of moral degradation. One friendly critic, being himself a Catholic, insisted: "There is no religion here at all. Nothing affecting the soul; it is all for show!" The religious services were largely of the processional order with banners and fireworks, turning the Lord's Day into an opportunity for gross sensationalism. In a letter Mr. Kidder says: "You would hardly credit my words were I to attempt to picture the glaring abominations which here prevail under the name and cloak of religion, but which destroy morality and degrade human nature itself." And another, a business man from abroad, who had spent many years in that country, writes: "I am anxious to get once more into a Christian country, where images and idolatry are abhorred, and where people are educated and not mere animals. One living among a set of superstitious idolaters is apt to turn heathenish himself. I have much need to go north to recover from the baleful influence of bad example."

What preaching there was rendered the pulpit a rostrum from which to sound the praises mainly of the Virgin Mary, and from a typical sermon were gathered such sentences as these: "The glories of the Most Holy Virgin were not to be compared with those of creatures, but only with those of the Creator." "She did everything which Christ did but to die with him." "Jesus Christ was independent of the Father, but not of his mother." The sermons were commonly delivered *memoriter*, and the speaker did not scorn the offices of a prompter, who in turn did not hesitate to stand, manuscript in hand, in full view of the congregation.

"A large part of the object for which the churches are built seems to be the display of images. Frequently in front of the churches platforms were erected for the particular exhibition of decorated idols. In sickness or drought prayers were offered to them, and there was published in the country about this time a long list of saints who presided each over a different part of the body and mind, and who were to be sought unto in any case affecting these special organs or faculties. The beautiful Indian names once spread over the country had been nearly all driven out by the names of the saints, and one of the priests insists that it was of the devil that the land was named Brazil and not called, as once proposed, the Holy Cross. As it is, the provinces, cities, towns, villages, estates, forts, batteries, theaters, streets, etc., are called after the saints, and every person, black or white, must be baptized in the name of at least one saint. There was a kind of rivalry or party spirit among the saints, some persons having great confidence in one saint and some in another. In praying to these saints for help or healing it is customary among the lower classes to promise a candle or something like that in case the prayer was heard. When the result was recovery or a fortunate issue the saint was supposed to have wrought a miracle.

" The people, too, have great confidence in wonder-working medals which are distributed in large numbers by the priests and preaching friars. This low form of superstition is not limited to the ignorant, but the cultivated are also careful at once to adorn and protect their persons with these miraculous toys." Talking at one time with one of the most intelligent of the gentlemen whom he met, Mr. Kidder asked him if he had any confidence himself in these medals, and he answered: " The fullest; I carry one with me constantly; I put it under my pillow at night and kiss it every morning. Moreover, I am taking some of them home as the choicest presents for my family."

A religion intellectually and in other respects so low down, had in it, we may be sure, no lifting power of any kind. It could not even hold the people where they were but their morals steadily sank, and they were, moreover, burdened with a depressing unbelief. " It is not to be concealed," he writes, " that a large proportion of the thinking people are already infidel, and that from the very fact that their honesty leads them to despise the useless ceremonies in which they have been educated, and they know of nothing else which can be called religion." There was really no regard for the faith as it was presented to them. The people generally assented to the dogmas of the Church, but seldom complied with its requirements except when obliged to do so by their parents, in the case of the young, or prompted by the immediate fear of death. Infidel books were common, and at the auction sales of books which were frequently held in the cities, the works of Voltaire, of Volney, and of Rousseau were offered to the highest bidder, and bidders were always found. In a conversation with a thoughtful and conscientious padre, Mr. Kidder asked him if things were growing better or worse. " ' Worse,' he replied, ' worse continually!' 'What means are taken to render them better?' ' None. We are waiting for the interference of Providence.' I asked him what report I should give to the religious world respecting Brazil. ' Say that we are in darkness, behind the age, and almost abandoned.' ' But that you wish for the light?' ' That we wish for nothing. We are hoping in God, the Father of lights.' "

Beautiful beyond compare to our exploring missionary was this land in all its natural features. He claimed that one must roam wide to find its equal in loveliness and variety of scenery. But he mourned its moral darkness and deformity, and cried out: " How infinitely would be

augmented the charms of a land like this were it the seat of
a stable government and a pure religion, were it the abode
of justice, peace, and righteousness!   It avails nothing to
say that the people are honest and know no better.   The
time has come when they must know better or do infinitely worse.   The land was literally covered with
crosses, crosses set up by Portuguese explorers, crosses
in front of churches and where religious ceremonies have
been held, crosses to decoy Indians into captivity, crosses
to mark the spot where a murder had been committed,
crosses as a protection against wild beasts, and crosses
whose origin must be left to conjecture, so that as Henry
Martyn said, 'Crosses there are in abundance, but when
shall the doctrines of the cross be held up?'   Indeed, it
is a spot over which the angel spirit of that faithful missionary might sing with the same propriety as when he
paid it an accidental visit on his voyage to India:

> 'O'er the gloomy hills of darkness
> Sit, my soul, be still and gaze!'

O that the day were come in which as Martyn seemed
to anticipate some happy missionary should be instrumental in turning this people to the pure and faithful
worship of the living God!"

CHAPTER X.

Missionary Life.

IF there was not moral character enough in the priest-hood to correct this infidelity and vice there was at least malicious energy enough to oppose the missionary in his work for a reformation and the revival of a pure religion. He writes: "A formal league was organized to counteract our influence. Into it a great many were initiated, particularly of the old Portuguese, and every means was used to excite their alarm and inflame their prejudices." The Jesuits were so stirred up that they became pious in self-defense, and, as one instance of their abnormal zeal, they opened for public worship a church which had been closed for seventy or more years.

The confessional was set to work under high pressure, and within its professedly sacred precincts the priests were directed to inquire of the subjects who presented themselves whether they had been corrupted by the Methodists, and to warn the faithful, and on pain of non-absolution to swear man, woman, and child to an eternal enmity against reform. By reason of an episcopal circular, preaching to the natives was rendered for the time impracticable. At one place Mr. Kidder was presented with a copy of a document issued by one of the archbishops, " for the warning of the people against a noted heretic who, as it appeared from the name repeatedly given in Italics with particular notices of an index hand on each side, was no other," he writes, " than my humble

self.   Said person is represented as a daring adventurer
come to disturb public order, to trample upon the laws,
insult the religion, abuse the hospitality, disdain the
civilization, and offend the dignity of the nation.   Voluminous reasons are given why he should in no way be
tolerated; and not only the authorities of Church and
State are challenged to be on the alert against him, but,
as the circular states, one writer volunteers to lead a
crusade against his person."

This was not the only threat of personal violence.   At
one place it was intimated that if he landed he should not
come off alive.   The intelligence of this plot was not
communicated to him until after he had visited the perii-
ous locality, completed his work, and gone elsewhere.
Upon his being informed of the conspiracy he concluded
that possibly its dangerous plan might be carried out
when he returned to that place as he contemplated.
"And what then?" he asks.   "Am I to shrink from
duty?   Even were it certain that a cowardly and igno-
minious assassination were planned for me, what have I
to fear?   Cannot God deliver me from the snares of the
wicked?   But if it please him that I become their victim
it will still be well and in some way will promote his
glory.   I have reasons to thank him that I have been
delivered from the fear of death."   The president of one
of the provinces that he visited issued an order for his ex-
pulsion addressed to the resident United States consul.
This was couched in terms of due and formal emphasis, as
follows : "Most Illustrious Sir !—I have complaints that
the American citizen, the Rev. D. P. Kidder, recently
arrived in this city, has manifested intentions of gaining
proselytes and of instructing its inhabitants in religious
principles different from those which are generally fol-

lowed in it and in all Brazil, and I am even told that
he has already distributed some small tracts which, be
their contents what they may, demonstrate those intentions; and as the quiet of the province, whose late dis-
orders had religious opinions as one of their causes, requires that any individual should be separated from it
who may give a pretext, and above all a religious pretext, for their renewal, it is my duty to declare to you,
that you may make it known to the said Mr. Kidder,
that I will cause him to leave the province immediately
if these facts shall be certified to me on evidence by the
police through whom I order them to be investigated."
This was carrying repressive measures a little too far, and
the governor was apparently ashamed of his action, for no
process toward the carrying out of this order was issued.
The missionary remained in the province prosecuting his
work two whole months, and, upon departing, received
without difficulty from the same governor a passport.

Concerning this whole question of menace and mach-
ination he writes: "Of all the intimations of danger
and threats of violence which I have so repeatedly heard
during this voyage I can say that none of these things move
me. Conscious of pursuing a course approved of God
and honorable in the sight of all men, why should my
life be dear unto me if it be required either as a sacrifice
to the wicked jealousies and manifest alarms of a corrupt
priesthood, or as a testimonial to the truth and power of
these principles by which I have through divine grace
been actuated? God forbid that I should swerve to the
right hand or the left from the path of duty, let men do
what they may! Death shall have no sting and the
grave no victory, thanks be to the Lord Jesus Christ,
who giveth *us* the victory!"

As a reinforcement to the arm of the law the resources of the press were summoned to the fray. Not only was the archepiscopal circular already referred to widely scattered and conspicuously posted, but the newspapers were enlisted. Mr. Kidder says: "A series of low and vile attacks were made upon us in a certain newspaper, and in immediate connection a periodical was started with the avowed object of combating us and our evangelical operations. It was an insignificant weekly of anonymous authorship." Through the columns of these and other papers the authorities were loudly called upon to see if the conduct of the missionaries was not culpable under the criminal code of the country. It was declared that the distribution of Bibles and tracts would work for the destruction of Catholicism. Other charges still more virulent were brought, and in one case the old accusation against the apostles was revived against the missionaries, that they were drunk!

To submit tamely and in quiet to these slanderous attacks was too much for the courage which is born of the truth, and so, paying for his communication at the regular rates for advertisements, he inserted an article in reply and exalted the advantages to be derived from the reading of the Scriptures. This, however, did not end the controversy, but provoked a rejoinder hotter and more intemperate.

In its opposition to the spread of the truth, more obstinate, if not more demonstrative, than the hostility of the priests and the attacks of the press, was the prejudice of the people. What training they had received seemed to render them incapable of attaching any idea of sacredness to the Bible. In their minds it seemed to bear no evident connection with the religion which they had been taught. He writes: "You would be surprised to hear a man speak of the Bible as a *new* book. Yet such was the reason which a gentleman assigned for his making repeated applications to us for one, and *he* a public functionary, and a person of as much apparent intelligence as I have seen. This fact shows something of what the case must be with the great majority of the people. Hundreds of them never heard of such a book. What, then, can they know of Christ, and what sort of Christians can they be?" Biblical training, it was also given out, was dangerous, as it would turn the children into Jews!

Three several times Mr. Kidder was disappointed in his efforts to have some of his writings put into the correct Portuguese idiom, because those to whom he had committed the task feared lest they might do wrong if they thus assisted in the spread of Protestant doctrines.

It was an imbedded and current opinion, even in the minds of the educated among this people, that no matter in what religion a man might be born he should remain in it and die in it. One of the best informed and most liberal of the natives remarked to Mr. Kidder, that " it is a very dangerous thing to change religion or government. Religion is like a vast river ; it is perilous to stop it or alter its course." On the other hand, as a rare exception to the incorrigible prejudice of these people on religious matters, he met a young Brazilian who seemed to give a true measure of the capacity of his countrymen for the reception of the Gospel truth when he said, that " it was his decided conviction that missionary operations would be of little or no use in this land unless promoted by the colonization of Protestants."

In all this dismal recital, and much more like it that

8

might be dealt out, there was large reason for the discouragement of the ardent and enlightened missionary, and his feelings came forth in the following strain: " How feeble is human force toward removing such a mass of error even were there no other obstacles than the perversity and blindness of the human heart. But now that a powerful influence is exerted to sustain the love of error and the practice of false principles, who can foretell when righteousness shall here flow as a river?"

The impression, however, would be not only unfortunate, but also unfair, if only the above facts and inferences were left to tell their story, for in one sense they are the background whose somber shade serves all the more to emphasize the bright and encouraging colors in which the picture proper is to be presented.

The opposition which he met with, as well as the low state of morals and the corruption of religion, made it clear that there was great need of a reformation and the spread of a pure Gospel. So far, therefore, from being discouraged by the gloomy outlook, he was the more nerved as by the call of an unrelenting necessity. He writes home to his father: " The longer we stay here the more plainly are we convinced that we have been sent of God and have a work to do, which, although it may bring persecution and opposition of the bitterest kind, yet is one in which angels would delight." In addition to this he found encouragement to duty and even to heroism in the fact that above and beyond the animosity displayed in some quarters the people of all classes, the ignorant and the well-informed, the masses and the officials, cheered him with their hospitality and inspired him with their liberality. Of one place he says : " I met with a reception as cordial as I ever received among

strangers at home." Again he says : " I have been everywhere received in the character of a Protestant clergyman with the utmost kindness of manner and liberality
of feeling." At times he was almost encumbered with
the warmth of his welcome and the profusion of his entertainment. In one place his letter of introduction was
addressed to a Catholic priest, and he remarks : "It affords
me unfeigned satisfaction to say that the hospitality
which I received in his house was just what the stranger
in a strange land would desire." In one of his letters he
makes the statement: "As to boarding houses, I have
not been in one since I left, but have in every place received the generous hospitality of those who would have
felt injured by the idea of compensation for any kindness
shown me."

In all he was gratified to observe the most friendly
opinion of his native land. At one time when he was
presented as an American, the response was, "*Ah boa
terra !*" (A good country!) A native of the northern
province exclaimed : " Ah, what would not Para be if it
were in the hands of those North Americans!" Everywhere and without hesitation they gave him the *entrée*
of their homes and apparently of their hearts.

He enjoyed the greatest freedom of conversation, and
his surprise was certainly no less than his gratification
to find on the subject of religion a widespread and pronounced independence of thought and almost a reckless-
ness of expression. This it must be admitted was in
keeping with the toleration of the constitution. Although it made the Roman Catholic apostolic religion
that of the State, yet it allowed all other forms of religion to be held and practiced save in buildings " having
the exterior form of a temple." To quote his own

words: "I will here state that in all my residence and travels in Brazil in the character of a Protestant missionary, I never received the slightest opposition or indignity from the people. A few of the priests attempted resistance, but the fact that they were unable to excite the people showed how little influence they possessed. On the other hand, perhaps quite as many of the clergy and those of the most respectable in the empire manifested toward us and our work both favor and friendship. From them, as well as from the intelligent laity, did we often hear the severest reprehension of abuses that were tolerated in the religious system and practices of the country, and sincere regrets that no more spirituality pervaded the public mind." From San Paulo he writes: "I have been furnished unhesitatingly with official documents respecting all subjects, civil or ecclesiastical, concerning which I had curiosity to inquire, and have been presented to some of the most distinguished men in the place, including some who may be considered as holding high positions in the empire, as, for instance, the ex-regent." In this province also he was introduced to many members of the Legislature. "From all of them," he says, "as a Protestant clergyman I received warmest expressions of civility and kind wishes." A young Brazilian lawyer, while declaring himself a Catholic, regarded Protestants as Christians and brethren, and confessed that they were generally more actuated by the spirit of Christianity than those of his own Church. Another rejected the idea that there was no salvation out of the Church, scouted the dogma of the real presence, and thought that the cup was an essential part of the sacrament, and yet all the while he insisted that he was a firm Catholic. Still another declared himself halfway between Catholics and Protestants. Although he did not approve of the Bible being used as a universal book, he thought that the practices and religious exercises of the Protestants were the best. This man also claimed that there was a great deal of actual idolatry in the worship of the images which is winked at by the priests. One of these independent thinkers, who was hearty in his accord with the plans and work of the missionary, volunteered to interview the bishop. He corrected certain erroneous views which the bishop entertained of the missionaries, assuring him that their object was good, being only to preach the Gospel, which every minister ought to do. One priest refused to wear the full canonical dress, and another pronounced against the persecutions and intolerance of past ages. He said that the unlimited power of the *pontifex* originated in the fanaticism or idolatry of the people. He laughed at the idea of the pope's infallibility, and said that no Catholic would assert so absurd a thing, else what the need of councils?

The press, too, after a time, seemed to show a better temper, and the paper in whose columns had appeared the attacks on the missionaries agreed to open its pages to a defense of Methodism and the work of spreading the Scriptures. Another editor, whose paper had been the most violent, informed Mr. Kidder that there would be no more attacks from that source against the Protestants or their principles. He also stated that the writer of the offensive articles, who was an emissary from Rome, and whose communications had made the paper ridiculous, had now dissolved his connection with their office. These articles had certainly brought the paper that published them into disrepute. There were many who gave

expression of their contempt for these effusions, and one
gentleman, a lieutenant in the national navy, having
called to obtain a Portuguese Bible, expressed great satisfaction that no attention had been paid to " the trash
of a paper which had been publishing articles against
their distribution. He thought it must be an unprinci-
pled man who would endeavor to disparage such a book
or hinder its circulation, especially in a new country like
this, where so much depended on the diffusion of correct moral principles and religious knowledge."

After all, the most significant index of the encouraging temper of the people was the avidity with which
they received and even sought for the religious literature which the missionary furnished. Only in one case
was a tract refused ; priests and nuns even accepted
them, and the former were in some instances seen reading them as they walked in the streets. In one of the
larger cities he visited on his northern tour he was desired by the directors to furnish a quantity of tracts for
distribution as premiums at an anniversary which was
celebrated with great splendor in the most flourishing
college there. As already related, Bibles and Testaments were immensely popular, and the opposition to
their circulation only rendered them the more sought
after and widely read, so that, as Mr. Kidder writes,
" The truths of inspiration found free course to hundreds
of families and scores of schools, where they might be
safely left to do their own office upon the minds and
hearts of the people." Wherever he went the distribution of these sacred books, both by gift and sale, was his
chief occupation, and his only embarrassment in spreading them abroad was the limit of his supply. There
were cases where persons seemed to be almost desperate

lest they should be overlooked. Often there was what might be called a " rush " for them. In one of the out-of-the-way places, having seen a Portuguese Bible, he asked the owner if he liked the book; he answered: " O, yes; I am very fond of reading it, it is so instructive and consoling; but the trouble is I cannot keep it at home. My neighbors love to read it, too, and they are continually borrowing it from me. I have loaned it to go great distances in almost every direction; but now it is at home, and I think I shall not let it go any more." The missionary gave him a new copy on the condition, to which he agreed, that this one should continue its good work of traveling around among his neighbors near and far.

One of those who expressed gratification upon the receipt of a copy of the Scriptures was the ex-president of the province and a member of the legislative assembly. This man, the ex-president of another province, and others equally distinguished favored the spread of the Scriptures all over the land, and announced themselves as glad to distribute books and tracts, not only in their own towns, but in the regions beyond, where religion was still less thought of. The observation was made that if Brazilians once understood the object of the friends of the Bible, they could not but appreciate them in the most grateful manner. On all sides he found those who were willing to assist him in the dissemination of the word of God. Even priests were among these volunteer colporteurs, and one who had been trained to serve at the altars of the Church accepted the agency of this work and expressed the hope that he might some day become an evangelist. This instance of generous and efficient aid coming thus unexpectedly filled our missionary with the warmest gratitude, and he broke out: " I was overwhelmed with the goodness and providence of God in thus showing himself better than our fears, and directing my footsteps to the person, perhaps out of hundreds, best calculated both by circumstances and disposition to promote our great work."

Going beyond the gift or sale of the copies of the Scriptures to individuals, Mr. Kidder conceived the idea of introducing them into the public institutions. The hospitals accepted them gratefully, and his offer to make a donation of Testaments to one of the schools having been gladly welcomed, he entertained the plan of having the Bible distributed as a reading book in all of the schools of that province. In one of his letters he says: " We are encouraged to know that there is a general desire for an acquaintance with the Scriptures. The Bibles and Testaments have been introduced into scores of schools as reading books, and the priests have no authority to prevent their circulation to any extent whatever." He was agreeably surprised on account of the favor with which the scheme for a general distribution was received. Prominent men, the members of the Legislature, and the Bishop of Rio gave it their warm approval. The President of the Assembly said that it caused him happiness to reflect that their province might be the first to set the example of introducing the word of God to its public schools. A bill for the purpose was presented in due form to the Legislature of the province directing the teachers of the schools to receive the books for use. Immediate action on the bill was prevented by the discussions which the sharp political differences of the period provoked, and which consumed all the time of the session, but the prospect of its adoption at the following session was full of hope and encouragement. This expectation, however, was disappointed through the machinations of a busy English Catholic priest, so that the proposition was reported unfavorably, although to the credit of the province it is to be said that it was never formally rejected.

CHAPTER XI.

The Sad Return Home.

ALTHOUGH Mr. Kidder was thus interested in his work and thoroughly given up to it, he was all the while severe in his self-criticism.

> "A silent court of justice in himself,
> Himself the judge and jury, and himself
> The prisoner at the bar."

In one of his accounts of self-examination he charges himself: 1. With the want of a greater sense of the responsibility and infinite importance of the work of God, and consequently of greater devotedness to it. 2. Too great a delight in worldly studies to the disparagement of the pure and holy word of God. "How little have I understood and practiced my ordination vows!" 3. Too great a neglect of a careful and laborious preparation for that awful place—the pulpit. "I have offered the Lord what has cost me nothing and my ministrations have been unblessed!" 4. Too little of the spirit of fervent prayer and constant devotedness of heart to the glorious service of my Master. Again he says: "I have recently had some painful, but not to be mistaken, evidence of a partial decline in spirituality. Among the long-continued efforts necessary (and I fear sometimes too much prompted by ambitious feelings) to acquire the languages of the babbling earth, I have been too neglectful of the language of heaven. My prayers have become languid and formal, and, O! where shall I stop were I to enumerate the inconsistencies of Christian character of which I am conscious? How many more are marked by Him who knoweth the thoughts of the heart! I have been for some time resolving: 1. To give more attention to a devotional reading of the Scriptures, my present reading being too much for the sake of the words of the language [Portuguese] and not the meaning. 2. To let no day pass without reading more or less in some work calculated to promote practical piety. I must now add, 3. To give more time to my regular periods of private devotion and precede them, certainly at morning and noonday, with one or both of the above kinds of reading. How little meditation has preceded, how little reflection has followed these exercises which of all others ought to be considered the most solemn and important! I will endeavor to consider I am going into the presence-chamber of the King! what gifts can I carry, what offerings can I make which he will deign to accept? Thy sacrifices, O God, are a broken heart and a contrite spirit. What am I in need to ask at his hand? Is it not that pride, my besetting sin, may be removed from my heart? that fear and love of the world may be removed? that sinful tempers may be subdued? that wandering thoughts may be repressed? that every root of bitterness may be extracted, and that love, perfect love to God and man, may fill and rule my heart? My expressions in prayer are too general and unmeaning. I am persuaded that much of what I am lamenting has grown out of endeavors to redeem my time. So prompt is evil to come out of good! Lord, have mercy upon me!" At the opening of the year in which he conducted the last of these missionary expeditions, he writes: "I hope to be more diligent, more active, more believing, and more prayerful during the year to come, or any portion of it which may be mine. While faithful I have the most confident trust in the guidance and blessing of Him whom I serve. Let this, then, be my great business, to prove faithful, and all will be well."

In these ingenuous disclosures we are permitted to view the inner life of one whose whole object was to study to show himself a workman approved of God that need not to be ashamed. Returning to his home after his long absence, coming back to his young family who sadly missed him, he had a right, doubtless, to bring with him the reflection that he had fully covered his work, and yet it was his conscience and not his conceit that listened for the "Well done, good and faithful servant!"

The work which he accomplished in these expeditions was not such that it could be displayed in a table of statistics. It was, in the main, as it was intended it should be, a prospecting excursion; or, as it might be styled, a reconnoissance, important, indeed essential to the after attack and invasion; an attack, an invasion which should be the more certainly successful for Christ and his cause because through the information thus gathered it would be intelligent.

And yet he understood his task to be one also of seed-sowing, and diligently prosecuted it in this direction. "All providential openings for doing good were gladly embraced, and arrangements were made to establish the Scriptures on sale, with tracts for gratuitous distribution. It is to be presumed that the numerous copies of the Scriptures and scriptural publications thus furnished to the reading community have not failed to exert a most happy influence in promoting general tranquillity and the practice of virtue." Nearly ten years after it was reported that these methods for the spread of the Gospel were still at work.

Summing up the results of these expeditions, he says: "We now had correspondents along the whole coast. During my tour I was enabled to put in circulation many copies of the Holy Scriptures and about sixty thousand pages of religious tracts. Besides this I left Scriptures for sale and tracts for distribution in the principal places. Thus by the establishment of depositories in the maritime towns where the Scriptures could be procured by persons from every part of the interior between San Paulo and Para, a great step was taken toward offering the word of God to the entire nation, and inviting the inhabitants generally to receive it."

Brief as was Mr. Kidder's stay in South America, his influence was long felt, and permanent good followed the evangelical journeys which he made. Fifteen years afterward a missionary of another denomination "became acquainted with a prominent Brazilian gentleman, whom he found was an experimental Christian, his life exemplifying the Gospel teachings, which he sought everywhere to diffuse, and who, when asked what had produced this great change in his character and creed, answered, 'I owe it all to a Bible left with me by *Padre Kidder* many years ago.'"

Having completed these important missionary tours, gathered the information essential to a wise prosecution of his further work, and set in train operations and influences which he justly judged would be lasting and far-reaching in their benefits, he settled down again to an earnest prosecution of the tasks immediately at hand in the missionary headquarters.

On his first Sabbath at home he preached on board an American vessel to a congregation of eighty seamen. About this time he organized a temperance society among the seamen, and was greatly encouraged by its immediate popularity and rapid growth.

Right in the midst of his unceasing labors he was brought to a check by an attack of severe illness. His pain was violent and he was prostrated with extreme debility. "Thus it seemed good to Him who has kept me as in the hollow of his hand during a long period of exposure and peril, now when least expected, but at the same time when I am best prepared for it, to send on me this light affliction." The evening before he was taken sick he had gone to the place of worship, having made preparation to preach from the text, "Cut it down; why cumbereth it the ground?" He adds: "I desire to kiss the rod, and take it as a most solemn warning that I am the cumberer of the ground, and that the ax has been most justly laid at the root of the tree!"

In a little less than two weeks he was ready again for duty and preached twice, in the morning on the Bethel ship, and in the evening on shore.

His wife, whose spirit all through was that of the consecrated missionary, now became urgent that he should give more especial attention to his work among the people in their own tongue. He was already a good reader and writer in the Portuguese, and had read the Bible through in that language, but he had not yet attempted to preach in it. He writes: "After some conversation with my dear wife on the subject of our calling and duties, I feel deeply impressed with the necessity of devoting my time and efforts more exclusively toward a preparation for evangelical labors in the Portuguese language, inclusive of preaching. I fear that I have been too indifferent to this subject and have given my personal studies and engagements too much of my time, for surely I have not often been unemployed, or triflingly employed.

"Incessant occupation the first year with the Portuguese language; the second, with traveling and the necessary preparations, have prevented me from giving that attention to my theological studies which I would desire and which the Church reasonably exacts. On my return from the north I was disposed to give them greater prominence, and they, together with the necessary writing which devolved upon me, filled up my whole time. I have made no special efforts toward preparing tracts or sermons in Portuguese. This, however, must be the order of every day, and I must let nothing divert me from the speedy and perfect acquisition of a tongue through which nearly all efforts for the spiritual amelioration of this country must be made. I must lay aside all ambition to be a theologian and delight to be in all things a faithful missionary, in which may God help me!"

During this period he received from his father a letter commending his course in choosing the self-denying service of Christ. He wrote:

"My dear Son:—I cannot tell you how thankful I now am that you have followed, undeviatingly, your convictions of duty, without turning aside for any objections made by me."

This letter contained also another message, which awakened a still deeper joy. It told the news (good news, indeed) that the father had become converted. The son's personal pleadings had not been for naught.

His prayers had been answered. The father had found the pearl of great price. In this intelligence there was for the missionary an added incentive to earnestness. It came like a new girding of his purpose.

But alas! the zealous young missionary whose spirit was constantly urging him to fresh endeavors for Christ, whose enthusiasm was all the while moving him to minify the value of his past labors, was now, all unknown to himself, walking into the depths of a shadow whose chill fell like a frost upon his budding plans.

Sunday, April 5, 1840, he enters in his journal this simple line: " Mrs. Kidder was not well enough to be present at the evening service." This was the beginning of sore trials, the collapse of all his missionary hopes.

Her disease was at once met with medical treatment —the best that the science of the time and place could afford was generously appealed to. Several physicians were in consultation, and the duties of nurse he assumed himself. " I gave up my whole time to her from the first, thinking it little enough that I should make every possible effort for her comfort, only regretting my extreme incapacity for the delicate and soothing attentions requisite for a sick bed.

" These times of trial are those which show us how much our hearts and happiness are bound up in those we love. But of all other priceless blessings which we enjoy on earth, what can be greater than a virtuous, affectionate wife, or a fond and devoted mother! What a bereavement the loss of their society even by sickness, how much more by death! But yet our stronghold is the Almighty. He knows what is best and can give us grace to acquiesce in his holy will."

With one fugitive passage of improvement in her

symptoms she grew steadily worse. The faithful watcher at her side during the long nights began to be tortured with the thought of her possible death. "It was during these anxious hours," he says, "that I first seemed to realize that I could lose her. I had thought of it as a mournful possibility. I had apprehended it from the frank and timely warning of the physician, but to think that it would be so I could not, until the glassy eyes, the fixed and vacant stare, the faltering nerve, and the wandering mind convinced me that, except by a miracle of divine mercy indeed, it must. Bitter and frequent were the tears shed over her during the hours of that restless night. Her thoughts seemed to dwell among her kindred, several of whose names she mentioned, besides those of her children. Thursday, the 16th, about four o'clock in the morning, she turned over, extending her arms toward me as if to embrace me, and said in her own sweet and affectionate manner, 'My dear husband!' These were among the last intelligible words she uttered. Remaining quietly, as if in a sleep, for about three hours, at a quarter past seven in the morning, her spirit fled without a struggle or a groan or the least indication of her great change, save that she ceased to breathe!"

Here now was trouble for the widowed husband, left in charge of two young children. His crushing sorrow broke forth: " How impotent is language, how incapable of describing the anguished feelings with which a husband must behold a scene like this, the partner of his joys and hopes, the mother of his children, the dear object of his dearest earthly affections separated from him at once and forever! But it is done, the silver cord is loosed, the golden bowl is broken, the pitcher is broken at the fountain, and the wheel broken at the cistern, and the dust is made ready to return to the earth as it was, but as the consequence of this the spirit has returned to God who gave it. 'The Lord gave, and the Lord hath taken away'; blessed be the name of the Lord!' O, that he would enable me to think of the infinite gain and glory which her ransomed spirit has acquired by being thus early set free from the cares and sorrows of this unsatisfying world, and not to repine at my unspeakable loss, or sorrow as others without hope." In another place he writes thus of her death: "She was cut down in the midst of a field of usefulness, for which she had become peculiarly qualified. Her willing and faithful services in the work whereunto she was sent were suddenly and fatally checked by the unlooked-for approach of death. But she died as she had lived, a humble, devoted Christian, and in her final hour triumphed over the last enemy by falling asleep in Jesus—that Saviour

'For the light of whose smile in the heaven of love'

her warm heart continually aspired. Her precious memory will be long and fondly cherished upon earth, but her record is on high."

Friends were not failing in their attentions, and the remains, lovingly cared for, were, according to the custom of the country, removed the same evening. They were taken to a house in the English cemetery to remain until the burial. "O, the loneliness of that lonely night!" was the cry of his heart. "I slept soundly, perhaps from fatigue, till midnight, when I arose and thought of walking out in the still and lovely moonlight, but concluded not to forsake the place rendered doubly dear to me by sorrow. I, therefore, walked my room for about two hours and again sought rest."

At four P. M. on Good Friday the interment took place, and although the place was somewhat remote and an opportunity had not been afforded for an extended notice, still there was a large number of friends present near a hundred, including Americans, English, German, French, Portuguese, and Brazilians.

The burial service was read by his associate, the English clergyman, the German minister also being present. "When the cold earth was heard to rattle upon the coffin," he adds, "we turned away and sought our homes in silent grief. In parting, however, most of the company came one by one to give me an affectionate shake of the hand.

"The next day I remained at home in my room. It was Hallelujah Saturday, the termination of Lent, the day of rejoicings, the hanging of Judas, etc." His soul kept no holiday. The day following, however, the Sabbath, delaying not his Master's work to build an altar to his grief, he attended the Bethel service, and, as he describes it, "attempted to preach from Amos 4. 12 : 'Prepare to meet thy God.'"

It being plain that his work in this field, for the present at least, was at an end, he began to make preparations to take his motherless children to their friends in the United States.

"This bereavement," he writes, "like the untimely winds of autumn, swept many tender blossoms of hope and promise forever away. It imposed upon me the imperious necessity of a speedy embarkation for the United States as a hopeful means of preserving the life of an infant son. The great change which has come over all my prospects, and indeed everything which relates to my future life, fills me with astonishment and unutterable emotions. I do not endeavor to banish the thoughts or feelings to which, connected with this subject, my mind constantly recurs. No, it is not with regrets, but with fondness, that I cherish the remembrance of my lamented partner both in her life and in her death. Thus will I ever cherish her sacred memory and our plighted love, believing that her angel spirit will closely accompany me through all the varied windings that remain before me."

The following Sabbath Rev. Mr. Spaulding preached the funeral sermon from 1 Cor. 15. 26: "The last enemy that shall be destroyed is death." "The room was never before so crowded with hearers. The most profound attention was observed, and it is to be hoped that good and lasting impressions were received by many."

During the interval that was occupied with the completion of his preparations for embarking, he was also continuously busy with his regular duties, preaching on the Sabbaths and holding meetings during the week. Attending their services at this time was a Lieutenant Foote, son of Governor Foote, of Connecticut, an officer of the American sloop of war then in the harbor from a cruise around the world. This young officer took part in the meetings, and, from his account of the various mission stations he had visited, he greatly cheered and refreshed the spirits of these toiling and sorrowing heroes of the cross.

At length the hour of departure arrived, and he embarked on board the ship *Azelia*, Saturday, May 9. "After the children were at rest I had leisure to walk the deck of the vessel in silent meditation. I gazed upon the starlit canopy above, upon the giant mountains, the great city, the enchanting scenery still more lovely under the mellow light of evening, and upon the hushed waves and glassy waters around me. But all these failed to soothe the anguish of my heart. I could but contrast my condition with what it was a few months before, when, returning from a long voyage, we lay at anchor near the same spot. How high then did my heart beat with expectation when I saw myself after perils by sea and by land so nearly restored to the bosom of my family. How anxiously did I watch for the flight of hours till morning came, when I could leap on shore and hasten to the embrace of my wife and children! But alas, what a change has come over me and mine! My wife is no more, and my children are orphans! I am again embarked, it is true, but the laden vessel only awaits freedom from her anchorage and the spreading of her canvas to bear me far, and perhaps forever, away from the dear remains of her who has been the partner of my joys and the solace of my sorrows. She sleeps in a foreign grave, no more to hear the voice of affection from husband or child. But her spirit, freed from earthly clogs, will follow us— me, indeed, to the land of our birth, but our offspring to a land of strangers!"

The nurse he had engaged being brought down at once with seasickness, he was obliged to begin the voyage by taking care of the little ones himself. The passage was unusually rapid and prosperous, and within less than thirty-four days out they cast anchor at Staten Island. He reported promptly to the Missionary Board. A resolution was passed, approving of his return as "necessary and expedient." He was requested to hold meetings in the interest of the cause in the principal towns and cities through which he should pass during his visits to his friends, and he was directed to return to the same field after a due interval.

Reaching the home of his wife's parents in Connecticut his sorrow broke out afresh. "O, what bitterness and grief are caused by the tender associations which hallow this spot. But the loved one is no more to return. The children can never supply her place, but still they will ever remind me of her, and I hope may live to remind me of her virtues as strongly as they will of her person."

But stronger than his grief was his loyalty to duty, and his sorrow was not as sacred as his obedience to the command that called him to be again about his Master's business. Breaking away from his little ones, forgetting the things behind which clung so to his heart, he began at once to take up the task which the Mission Board had assigned him, of presenting the cause of missions in the various Conferences and to as many congregations as he could reach. In this way he made a tour of New England and eastern New York, and in the fall started for the far West.

At Middletown he was elected on the joint Board of Trustees and Visitors of the University and received his degree of A.M. The following Sunday he preached in New York at Willett Street. That week, upon invitation, he went with a party to Staten Island. Rev. George Peck and Rev. Charles Elliott, of Cincinnati, were in the company. The object of the excursion was to make observations and collections in various departments of natural history.

The second week of September, 1840, he attended the session of his own Conference at Lyons, N. Y. "The Conference was opened with the usual solemnities. The scene overwhelmed me with inexpressible emotions, especially when we sang the hymn,

> " ' And are we yet alive
> And see each other's face? ' "

Having passed the required examinations he was admitted to full connection in the Conference. He helped to organize a literary and theological society, drafting for it a constitution and reporting it to the Conference.

A flying visit to Darien, the home of his youth, followed this.

The Mission Board having concluded for the future to maintain but one missionary in Rio, he reported to the bishops for further direction. He was transferred from the Genesee to the New Jersey Conference, and stationed at Paterson, June 2, 1841. Hastening east for a brief visit to his children, he entered again upon his work as pastor.

CHAPTER XII.

Pastorate at Paterson.

DR. LUCKEY having declined the office of Missionary Secretary, to which he had been elected, Dr. Charles Pitman was chosen. He was at the time Presiding Elder of the Trenton District, and Rev. D. Parish was taken up from Paterson and appointed to the district; Mr. Kidder, as has been related, was assigned to Paterson.

The account of this pastorate might be styled, The Story of a Great Revival. The church was in a state of continual fervor and growth, and each of the two winters he was there, there were protracted meetings of the old-fashioned type, continuing in each case until the time when the happy young pastor must hasten to report the good news to Conference.

This was not accidental, but the result of well-considered and faithfully applied means. His method and success intimate a close attention on his part to the Rules of a Pastor, given in the Discipline, and emphasize the fact that a Methodist church operated as a Methodist church is of necessity warm, aggressive, and prosperous. From the outset he began, and without relaxation to the end, he pursued the work in hand with his characteristic zeal, enthusiasm, system, and thoroughness. His church was his kingdom, his world. Every part and department came under his constant supervision, his personal activity was a pressure felt upon its entire machinery. He showed also the faculty of inspiring others with his own passion for labor; he multiplied himself in the willing contribution and fruitful efforts of many hearts and hands.

His first Sunday was June 13, 1841. He preached morning and evening, and held a general class in the afternoon. "This first Sabbath in my station passed pleasantly, and I trust profitably. We have here a fine church and most interesting congregation. O Lord, render thy servant useful to all for whom he shall labor in thy name!" Of his second Sabbath he says: "I visited the Sunday school twice, met one class and preached twice, enjoying the duties and labors of the day much through divine assistance and grace."

All his Sabbaths were thus filled up. The Sunday school is never neglected, and there are always three services besides. His first communion was July 4. "I administered the sacrament to nearly four hundred." A shepherd faithful to so large a flock as that had need to measure himself clear across the full meaning of the "instant in season and out of season."

These busy Sabbaths were the boundary lines for laborious weeks. Besides his study and regular pastoral work, as a sample of the manner in which his time was taken up, he mentions for one week's engagements, a funeral, two class meetings, a prayer meeting, one evening given to a lecture, and one to attendance upon a temperance meeting. This weekly temperance gathering was established when he reached Paterson, and found in him at once and always an interested worker. He delivered frequent addresses, and assisted all he could in its special labor of reforming inebriates. Sunday school board meetings, leaders' meetings, official board meetings, and the weekly prayer meeting left but few evenings to himself. Even these he would not appropriate to that quiet and study which he would have found so profitable and congenial, but gave them up to the service of the Church, so much so that in arranging a division of his time into periods and tasks, he entered opposite to his evenings, " Meetings." Having found Thursday a free or open evening in the schedule of the church, he set it apart for special instruction and preparation of the Sunday school teachers for their work. " I delivered a lecture in the church and organized a class of thirty-five persons, teachers and others, interested in the objects of the Sunday school instruction. I propose, if duly encouraged, to continue a series of lectures with a view to calling out the talents and enlisting the energies of the youth of our congregation." He found opportunity also during the week evenings to visit the classes in the church, which he did with fidelity and regularity. One evening he led one class and dropped into two others. He had also each week on Wednesday afternoon a pastor's class.

During all this time he was constant and thorough in his pastoral visiting from house to house. " I distributed the various families of my charge into twelve pastoral districts according to the streets, to promote convenience in visiting." This arrangement, with the names of the streets and the names of the families written out in his neat style, is still preserved among his papers. The sick were the objects of his particular and loving attention, being visited by him two and three times a day. Pious and beautiful deaths made a profound impression upon him. Coming away from a home where a young mother had just departed leaving two children unconscious of their loss, he writes: "O, that scene of grief was but too much the counterpart of mine own so vividly remembered!"

In all the above we can readily see some of the subsoil plowing and seed-sowing which resulted in the revivals he had, phenomenal even for those times. From the outset he expected such results as legitimate if not necessary. As early as August he began having prayer meetings after the Sunday evening sermon. On one evening he notes with regret that a visiting brother occupying his pulpit preached so long that the prayer meeting was crowded out. The first Sunday evening in September there were penitents at the altar, and so from that date on.

As the season advanced his sermons became more and more intense and urgent. Having preached on Repentance and Regeneration, he followed these up with a series of sermons on Future Punishment, which were delivered to crowded evening congregations.

At length, when all seemed ripe for the desired and quietly contemplated forward movement, he adopted the wise plan of consulting the officers of his church in the matter. "At our leaders' meeting I proposed the question whether we should engage in an extra effort for the conversion of souls. The answer was unanimously affirmative. We also agreed to observe Monday as a season of special prayer for a preparation of heart and a blessing from the Lord." The Sunday following he relates: "The question of an extra meeting and the pledge of concert in prayer for it, as well as the promise of an attendance upon it, was proposed to the society. It met a unanimous response." This was in the morning. In the afternoon a love feast was held, and at night the altar was at once filled with penitent seekers of salvation, one or two of whom found the pearl of great price.

Thus was the revival sprung upon them, and every night (except Saturday nights, which were reserved for special conversation and prayer with young converts and penitents) from New Year's until March the work went on with marvelous power.

The second Sunday was a great day. "I had liberty of speech when addressing the people in the morning on the 'Convenient Season.' In the afternoon at half past one the classes met, and at three o'clock a general prayer service was held at which several lay brethren from New York were the principal assistants. The evening was a time of power; about forty persons knelt at the altar and seats in front. Several professed conversion." Every Sunday morning during the progress of the meeting he gave opportunity for the new converts to join the church, and at each invitation new names were added to the list of probationers. Frequently he was disappointed during the week nights in not receiving promised help from his ministerial brethren. "But," he adds, "the Lord continued with us and great good was done in his name."

On the Sunday which closed the first month of the meeting the house was full both morning and evening. His subject for the evening was The Judgment. "Just as I was concluding an alarm of fire was started near the door, which threw the congregation into excitement for a moment. I endeavored to turn the circumstance to as good account as possible, but fear the enemy got some souls by the trick. The altar was again filled and three or four found peace."

At this stage of the meeting he formed a society among his members for the distribution of tracts, starting off with a hundred names. Through their aid he sent abroad into the community a large quantity of this kind of religious literature.

Having preached one Sunday evening from the very opportune text, " Do thyself no harm," he says: " The penitents came to the altar without inviting."

These continued and exhausting labors were at the expense of great fatigue, and, writing of one of his busy Sabbaths, he says: " I preached twice, attended a funeral, and also a general class meeting. I found myself completely worn out, but my heart was cheered by witnessing the conversion of four souls. To God be all the glory!"

This remarkable revival, closing his first year, added to the church one hundred and twenty-two probationers.

From the very outset of his second year the impetus of this great spiritual movement was felt. The Sunday following his return from a camp meeting in the neighborhood he records: " I had wonderful liberty in preaching. The love feast in the afternoon was deeply interesting, and promised so much good as to induce the appointment of extra meetings on Monday and Wednesday evenings which were well attended. The Spirit of the Lord was manifestly present." This was in August, and as in the preceding year, so again in September at the prayer meeting after the Sunday evening sermon, there were seekers at the altar.

Branching out in his evangelical zeal beyond Paterson, he established a Sunday school in a neighborhood two miles distant called Oldham, and opened a Sunday afternoon preaching service, " with a prospect of good." He

also held protracted meetings for two weeks every evening except Saturday and Sunday evenings, at a place
several miles away called Red Mills. He had already
organized there a class of six persons. The meetings
were held in a new barn. " In this neighborhood a similar effort in behalf of perishing souls had never before
been made. Prejudices were understood to be numerous
and strong against Methodism, but they gradually gave
way, and a most happy influence is believed to have been
exerted upon the community in general. On the whole
the spirit which pervaded this meeting was a most delightful one. I trust that the fruits of the labor will be
seen in a coming day. The immediate results, although
not as great as we could have wished, were perhaps
as great as under all circumstances could have been expected."

The troublesome tide of the Millerite excitement
now rolled in his direction. " Mr. Miller's tent having
been in Newark, some of our people went to hear the
lectures on the Second Advent of Christ. Opinions appeared to be as various as the prepossessions of the visitors. Three lectures on the subject involved in the theory
were delivered in the Free Presbyterian Church on as
many week evenings." This unhealthy sensation, however,
instead of being a diversion of himself and church from
the one commanding work to which they were called,
was so wisely seized upon by him, as that it was made
to contribute toward the spirituality of his people and
the salvation of souls. Under date of November 12 he
says : " Having reflected fully on the subject I believed
it my duty to take up the subject of Prophecy, and give
the result of my investigations in a series of discourses
to begin the next Sabbath." Accordingly he began on

that morning by preaching on the Example of the Prophets, and in the evening his topic was The Burden of Babylon, with an introduction to the course. " The church was filled to its utmost capacity, and probably contained fifteen to seventeen hundred persons." The prayer meeting following was full of interest. In due order followed the sermons on the Jews, The Messiah, The Destruction of Jerusalem, The Second Coming of Christ, The Kingdom of God, Boast not Thyself of To-morrow, as applied to the Second Advent of Christ, and The Judgment. This last one in the course was preached on watch night. Of this service he has left this record: " The work of the Lord which was already begun in power seemed now gloriously to widen and extend. The altar was no longer large enough to contain the penitents. Benches were placed in its rear, and the first row of seats were cleared all around to make room for the mourners in Zion. Many souls were blessed. The prayer meeting continuing until near twelve o'clock, the entrance of the new year was awaited in silent prayer. The church remained crowded to the last.

" The work of the Lord so gloriously begun continued in mighty efficacy for a series of weeks, devolving on me such an amount of labor and care in endeavoring to seek the lost and keep the found, as I never sustained before. The labors although responsible and arduous, nevertheless abounded in the sweetest consolations. Many incidents of deep and thrilling interest occurred. One characteristic of this revival was that a large number of its earlier subjects were men, of whom I have received a greater number into the church than were members of it before. Great pains were taken to enlist their zealous efforts to bring in their friends and companions which the Lord enabled them to do with marked success." Among the names of those mentioned who assisted him in pulpit labors is that of the late Rev. William P. Corbit.

In a letter written this spring he reports: "Our extra meetings commenced on Christmas and continued till March, almost three months, every night. As a part of its fruits I have received about three hundred on probation. The pastoral visiting necessarily due to these, besides the originally large numbers of my flock, has been sufficient to require all my time save the fragments I could snatch for preparing sermons. You can scarcely form an idea of the glorious scenes witnessed within and around our altar for weeks in succession. From sixty to one hundred were seen kneeling nightly, imploring pardon for their sins, and scarcely a night during the whole meeting was undistinguished by the conversion of some souls."

He closes this letter with the following views on the subject of Millerism: "I have always considered the scriptural doctrine of the Second Advent as divinely calculated to do good to the souls of men, but I am constrained to deprecate the presumption by which many have of late pretended to fix upon those 'times and seasons' which God hath put in his own power. And all honest people deprecate the prevarication with which these teachers change from time to time their calculations when compelled to do so by their disappointment. I do not believe the Gospel of Christ needs any adventitious aids or improvements, and with us the results have so proved. From all the discourses delivered in this place by Millerite lecturers we do not know of a single conversion, whereas, through the old-fashioned way of preaching Christ and him crucified, there have been added to the different churches some four or five hundred souls."

Continuing the story of the revival in his journal, he says: "Among the results of these wonderful meetings were increased efforts in some of the sister churches, which resulted in many accessions to their several communions.

"Among those added to our membership was a class at Acquackanonk [now Passaic], where the work of the Lord broke out through the instrumentality of a few private individuals without a single sermon being preached. A Methodist lady from New York came up to visit her sister, a young lady lying at the point of death, but unconverted. Hearing of a pious young man, a member of my charge, who had recently moved into the place, she sent for him to pray with her sister. The young lady was converted and died happy. The neighbors had been present, some had become awakened, and the meetings continuing, a few became converted. At this stage of affairs I was applied to to take charge of the meetings, which I did by sending leaders to conduct them. A class having been organized, it was immediately proposed to build a church in the place, there being none save two Dutch churches. A neat small chapel, worth about $1,000, was all that was needed, and I was instructed to head the subscription in behalf of Mrs. Holsman, one of our members residing near, with $500.

"About the same time a successful subscription was put in motion to build a church at Red Mills. The land was given at both places, and it is proposed to have the corner stones of both laid before Conference.

"Our congregation, moreover, had so much increased
10

in Paterson that it became very desirable to have a second church, which no doubt would have been immediately undertaken but for the heavy debt still resting on the present edifice, and the very great difficulty of raising money by any means or for any object at this juncture. We have filled up the old classes, and organized four new ones, in some cases with very promising members."

Of these three months he says: "They cover the most important and happiest period of my life thus far. My health has been perfectly good, and I have been greatly prospered and blessed of the Lord in every relation I have sustained whether to my family, the Church, or the world."

On his last Sabbath he preached in the morning, Psalm 137. 5, 6, "If I forget thee, O Jerusalem," etc. In the afternoon, he says, "We held an extra general class meeting at which the lower part of the church was crowded with church members. In the evening I preached on the Final Judgment."

The fruitfulness of these two years appears in that they added to the church four hundred and sixty-five probationers. As an incidental result of the spiritual strength and healthfulness of the church there were certain temporal improvements, such as the refitting of the Sunday school room and the substantial reduction of the oppressive church debt. No wonder the impressions of this remarkable pastorate left a glow that lingered long after in his heart. As late as 1861 he makes this entry concerning it: "The period of my pastorate in Paterson is vividly remembered as one of constant labor and encouraging success. Throughout its continuance I was brought into close contact with the people of a manufacturing town.   They represented various nationalities, but affiliated agreeably with each other and the church. It was my custom to visit indiscriminately and often all the members of my congregation. I thus became greatly identified with them, and secured a warm place in their sympathies and affections. All such advantages I endeavored to use diligently and earnestly for the cause of Christ, and I am thankful to say with most encouraging results."

His duties in this interesting church were not, however, so absorbing but that he found time to pursue as a sort of mental relaxation those literary employments in which he took such a delight. Indulging a conscientious purpose to redeem his time, he carefully divided each day into schedule periods. " Having made a trial of my new division of time and arrangement of study," he says, " I am persuaded that it will work well. The twenty-four hours are divided into three equal portions. The first is devoted to study, writing, and reading, occupying the earlier part of the day. The second, occupying intervals together with the latter part of the afternoon and the evening, is set apart for devotion, exercise, recreation, pastoral visits, and religious meetings. The third, as nature requires, for necesary rest and repose. If health and the divine blessing enable me to carry this arrangement into effective operation during the year, I may reasonably anticipate that great advantages will result not only to myself personally, but also to the work in which I am engaged."

In addition to his regular theological reading he gave Bunyan's *Pilgrim's Progress* a careful perusal, and took up Wesley's *Journal* for a thorough study. "I have commenced reading Mr. Wesley's *Journal* in course.   I have not only found it interesting, but deeply instructive on several points of the greatest practical importance concerning which I have long felt the need of information without knowing where to seek it. I have also re-commenced Watson's *Life of Wesley* to keep pace with his own diary. O, that I might follow him as he followed Christ!"

During this interval he was also quite generously occupied in delivering lectures and addresses. He spoke on Female Education and repeatedly on Temperance. Before the Lyceum Education Society, of New York, he delivered an address on the Moral and Literary Aspect of the Empire of Brazil. There was present in his audience Mr. Robert H. Morris, the mayor of the city.

Current events, however, turned his attention at this time more particularly to the subject of Mormonism, and we have records of his having spoken on this topic frequently and with telling effect in different places. At one of these appointments a circumstance occurred which has an interest of its own. "According to previous invitation and arrangement I went to Little Falls to lecture on Mormonism. I gave the facts respecting that system of delusion for about an hour and forty-five minutes. At the close a Mormon preacher who was present asked if he might speak. I replied that I had no objection, but the people hissed him down two or three times in succession. It was very evident that his work was done in that place."

CHAPTER XIII.

Pastorate at Paterson—Pastorate at Trenton.

IN all these exacting engagements, putting every moment of his time at a premium, he did not forget his obligations as a parent, and from the hills of Connecticut he felt the tug upon his heart of two little motherless children. He made flying visits to clasp them in his arms and freshen his desolate spirit with their guileless love. He always found them contented, well, and happy in the tender care of their mother's parents. But every time the parting was more painful to him, his heart, too, was hungry for a home. He would have a refuge where the excitements and exactions of the pastorate might not enter to weary and wear.

Accordingly toward the close of March, 1842, he hastened away for a long journey, as it was then, to the West, and reaching Worthington, O., was there married, April 6, by the venerable Jacob Young, to Miss Harriette Smith, Principal of the Worthington Female Seminary. This was for him in every sense a most fortunate alliance. His orphan children fell into hands loving and competent, and as time went on she added to his household three children of her own—two daughters and a son. She still survives, having tenderly ministered to his comfort in his failing years, and having added to the usefulness and luster of his active life by the grace and dignity with which she brightened his home, the genial and generous manner in which she entertained strangers, and the uncommon faculty she displayed of transacting affairs. A masterful soul was hers, often asserting itself over a feeble body, dragging uncomplainingly the heavy chain of pain as she hastened to the delights of self-sacrificing tasks. East and West the circle of her acquaintances is large, esteem for her readily ripens into love. All who know her will be happy and hearty in their indorsement of the following tribute : " She was a lady whose remarkable talents, great executive abilities, and genuine Christian hospitality have rendered her 'a helpmeet' to her husband to a degree rarely seen, even in our favored times; and whose tireless philanthropy has linked her name to institutions which will hold her memory in grateful reverence long after she has closed her beneficent career."

The return from Worthington after the marriage was made according to the fashion of those times by modes of travel remarkable for variety if not for speed, carriage, canal packet, stage, steamboat, and railroad. A passage in this itinerary cannot fail to be interesting, as reciting in detail and with fidelity of description the manner in which they crossed the Alleghenies a half century ago. " From Pittsburg," he says, " our course was by the Express and Pioneer Line on the Pennsylvania Canal. Our route lay up the streams tributary to the Allegheny, which at various intervals afforded slack water navigation. The ordinary rate of travel is only three miles per hour in the canal, but in the streams is five. We passed under one very large hill by a tunnel eighty feet in length. The course was continually ascending by locks. At Johnstown the western section of the canal terminates. Here both freight and passengers are transferred to a railroad. This is composed of eight inclined planes with respective intervals extending to Hollidaysburg. Up and down the planes we were moved by a stationary engine, and in the intervals by locomotives and horses. Thus 'the mountain was made a plane and the crooked places straight.' On these mountains we passed through another tunnel nine hundred and one feet in length. The last four miles were traveled by the simple force of gravitation. At Hollidaysburg we took another boat of the eastern section of the canal, in which we were excessively crowded. Reaching the junction of the Juniata River with the Susquehanna, we crossed the latter by means of a towpath on the side of the long bridge on which the horses passed. Before this we had crossed the Juniata by a rope ferry. Daylight of the fourth day out from Pittsburg found us at Harrisburg."

The close of this deliberate and variegated wedding tour brought them to Camden in time for the session of the New Jersey Conference, at which he was returned to Paterson for his second year. A month later the children were brought on, and the parsonage was lighted with the glow of a completed and happy family.

No part of the return trip was more enjoyed than the stay in Cincinnati. They were actually taken into the arms of that hospitality for which the Queen City has been ever famed. But this visit was memorable in the history of the Church as leading directly toward the founding of the Cincinnati Wesleyan College, the first institution of a collegiate grade in our denomination north of the Ohio and west of the Alleghenies, and the first chartered college for women in the world.

During an evening spent by Mr. and Mrs. Kidder at the residence of Dr. Elliott, Editor of the *Western Chris-*

tian Advocate, a conversation upon the higher education of women made so strong an impression upon Dr. Elliott's mind, that in the morning he greeted his guests with the announcement that the one place to plant such an institution was right there in Cincinnati, with its three thousand Methodists, a city with advantages in healthfulness, central location, and attractive features unsurpassed. Besides, Cincinnati having been selected as the place for the publication of the *Ladies' Repository*, had already become a sort of emporium for female literature.

The matter was at once presented by Dr. Elliott to the ministers and representative laymen of the city, and secured their immediate and hearty concurrence. Mr. and Mrs. Kidder were pressed to assume the charge of the enterprise. He replied that he would give the proposition favorable consideration, intimating that he would be free to take hold of the movement in the ensuing spring.

It must be admitted that he was warmly inclined toward it. He says: "I have hitherto uniformly refused all such applications, but such are the peculiarities of the institution now contemplated, such is the demand for its existence, and such apparently will be the field it will open for both myself and wife to be useful, that I have thought best to make the experiment, if Providence shall so direct. In connection with the pastoral charge of the pupils I shall have opportunity for preaching and general usefulness in the city. Whatever I may be able to do in writing will be in close connection with the *Western Advocate* press; and at Cincinnati, more than any other place, I think, an individual may do something for the great valley of the Mississippi. Teachers need to be raised up there. The moral and religious character of women needs to be better developed and more thoroughly trained. Perhaps the present scheme will enable me in some good degree to subserve these various and important interests. One thing is sure, I have never been acquainted with any that promised fairer. I have in no way sought it out for myself, and my constant prayer shall be that God will direct me there or elsewhere according to his own will."

He was particular, however, to stipulate, as a condition of his acceptance, that the Cincinnati people should proceed at once to put up the necessary college buildings. With a foresight that after events literally fulfilled he claimed that they could raise the money for the buildings much more easily while the need for the school was felt, and he predicted that if they began the work of the institution in rented premises, it would be twenty-five years before the college proper would be built.

This was the very mistake made. Upon his return to Paterson he was in receipt of newspapers giving an account of public proceedings in Cincinnati with reference to the Female Institute. Communications were also sent to him, one of them signed by Bishop Morris, L. L. Hamline, and William Neff, as a committee, informing him that a building would be rented, and asking him to accept the presidency, and come on in the fall to open the school. Such a departure as this from what he considered the fundamental conditions of success changed, in his judgment, the whole outlook of the experiment, and he declined, saying that in any event it was not possible for him to leave before the coming spring. "I replied that it was inconsistent, in view of many reasons, to leave my present appointment until its time regularly expired, and signified their freedom to make choice of any other principal."

For the present at least his heart was manifestly taken up with the work of the pastorate. In November of the year preceding he declined an invitation to the presidency of the Wesleyan Seminary at Albion, Mich.

At the close of his second year in Paterson three of our leading ministers of that day, among whom was Bishop Janes as he was after known, requested him to become agent for the American Bible Society for the State of New Jersey. This also he declined, and presented himself again at Conference to accept gratefully the uncertain (as it was then) but always hopeful future of the Methodist itinerant.

His next appointment was at Greene Street, the only Methodist church at that time in Trenton. Upon his arrival some of the officers of the church met him at the station with a carriage, and he and his family were driven to the home of Mr. Richard J. Bond, with whom they were to remain for a few days. Some of the members of the church kindly assisted him in unpacking his goods. The parsonage, which he describes as excellent and well situated, was deficient in furniture, but at a meeting of the stewards it was agreed that if he would purchase the necessary articles, they would take them off his hands as soon as they could. Upon these generous terms he was happy in seeing his family soon comfortably settled.

"My first Sabbath," he says, "was agreeably spent, and from the appearance of the large and attentive congregation I was convinced that my lot was in the midst of an ample field of duty, if not of usefulness." He is affected, however, by different emotions on the occasion of his first communion. He writes: "I was surprised and grieved to see so small a number out of so large a membership partake of that holy ordinance." But this discovery was not allowed to discourage him. Instead, with his characteristic disposition to strive at once for the correction of every evil which stood in the way of the prosperity of the church, he made this neglect the subject of a sermon, taking for his text, "This do in remembrance of me," and he adds: "I had the happiness of seeing the sacrament of the Lord's Supper attended by a much larger number of persons (perhaps double) than partook of it last month."

One sermon that he preached during this year caused quite a flurry of excitement, although without any such purpose on his part. His entry is as follows: "Preached to a crowded house on religious exclusiveness, especially that of (apostolic) succession. This circumstance produced a great commotion in Trenton, as there happened to be (quite contrary to my knowledge or expectation) a large number of High Church people present, some of whom thought proper to get angry and say very hard things. This feeling, moreover, was aggravated by the satisfaction which others saw fit to express at the event. Another minister in the place invited me to repreach the sermon in his church, but I did not comply with the invitation."

His relations with the pastors of the fraternizing churches of the place were most interesting. Having at one time exchanged pulpits with the Presbyterian minister, he adds: "This exchange of pulpits was the first that has taken place in Trenton, and it is mutually hoped will be introductory to a kinder state of feeling among Christians of different denominations."

Millerism obtruded itself also into this field, and he felt it his duty again to give attention to it. "The Millerite lecturers having started some excitement with their wild theories, I found it necessary to preach to our people on their duty to the Church. The effort appeared to be owned of the Lord." Some time after this, finding that these disturbers of Zion had been busy among his people and had made some impression upon a number of persons in a little community near Trenton, where some of his members lived, he again preached upon the subject with much plainness, showing in three sermons their errors respecting the Kingdom of God, The Times and the Seasons, and The Practical Tendencies of the System. "As the result," he says, "two or three left us, but the rest were cured."

At the very outset it was plain to him that he had come into a field where the most thorough and unsparing labor must be laid out upon the pastoral department. Within the first month after his arrival, besides all the work connected with putting the house and grounds of the parsonage into a proper condition, and providing many needed articles of furniture, he adds, "I have copied out the entire Church Record in a manual form, and have obtained the statistics of sixteen classes, so that I now know the situation in life and the residence of a majority of the church members. I expect next week to commence visiting in order and in earnest. Thus alone shall I be able to accomplish what duty will require toward the flock over which the Holy Ghost has made me overseer. I find considerable differences between the customs of the people here and of those whom I have left. There are also equal differences in our circumstances in many particulars. These differences, however, balance themselves, and leave on the whole but little to choose. We have whatever we desire as essential to comfort and improvement and, we trust, the means and the disposition to be useful."

In his arrangement of time and work he gave three hours each during four afternoons a week to pastoral visiting. Closing one week he writes: "I have visited ten to fourteen families per day since Monday. Having promised to visit all the families in the society if possible during the first six months, I found it necessary to double my diligence in order to get through in time. I moreover concluded that it would be much better for my health to abandon books for a while and give myself up to visiting the people. I found them much scattered through Trenton, Lambertville, Morrisville, and the surrounding country. I was enabled at the second quarterly love feast to report myself as having gone through the society once to the best of my ability, having visited during five months, notwithstanding sickness and absence, about two hundred and seventy-five families."

In November, thinking the field ripe for definite and continuous work in the effort to save souls, he began to hold "extra meetings." His first movement was in the outlying neighborhoods, where were some of his members and a few of his classes.

On Christmas he opened the revival services in Trenton, commencing his first meeting at the unusual but Wesleyan hour of five o'clock in the morning. The experiment was a great success, for the attendance completely overflowed the basement of the church. The protracted meeting thus begun continued for more than five weeks, and forty persons joined the church on probation.

During February he had the joy of preaching the dedicatory sermon of the new and beautiful church at what is now known as Passaic. This church was part of the fruit of the revival at Paterson. It was also his great pleasure to be at Paterson and witness the reception into full membership in the church of one hundred and fifty of the converts of that same great revival.

He took a trip to Rochester, planning to enjoy a little rest and refreshment among the many friends of his first pastorate, but he was taken seriously ill, and ended his visit in just sufficient strength to reach home.

Being appointed by his Conference a member of the Visiting Committee for Dickinson College, he reported accordingly and found himself the only member from three Conferences present for the examinations, so that the labor of preparing the report fell to him, although the other members came on in time for the commencement exercises. During this year also he made the address before the trustees and visitors at the annual exhibition of Pennington Seminary.

The close of the year finds him busy in making preparations for the entertainment of the Conference which met in his own church. He describes an experience often duplicated when he says: " I had but little difficulty in finding the requisite number of lodgings for the preachers, but to arrange them all satisfactorily for both parties was something of a task. However it was accomplished, and a complete list published." He was returned to Trenton, and was furthermore appointed on the committee to print the *Minutes,* an office, he adds, " which devolved on me about a week's work."

Preliminary to the session of the General Conference of 1844, the bishops held their meeting in Mr. Kidder's

house. This was their last before the division of the
Church. There were present Bishops Hedding, Waugh,
Morris, and Soule. Bishop Andrew did not report.
Bishop and Mrs. Soule were the guests of Mr. and Mrs.
Kidder.

Under date of June 10 he makes this entry in his
journal: "Mrs. Kidder arrived from New York in company with several delegates on their way home, bringing
news that the General Conference had adjourned late
Monday night, and also that in their afternoon session
they had elected me to the office of Editor of Sunday
School Publications and Tracts, an office newly instituted
for the especial purpose of improving and enlarging our
Sunday school literature.

"This intelligence was very unexpected to me, and
seemed to excite considerable commotion among our
friends in Trenton. As, however, I have never disobeyed
the voice of the Church, but always counted it joy to
enter upon her hardest service, so now I do not feel at
liberty to shrink from the duty to which she has assigned me, although I am well aware that it will be more
laborious and responsible than any I have hitherto undertaken. May I not also hope that in attempting to
provide for the mental and spiritual instruction of the
five hundred thousand children of our Church, I may be
more than ever useful. I will trust in God for this result,
and use my best endeavors."

At the close of the month he writes: "I now consider
my pastoral labors here brought to a close, although I
have resolved to remain in Trenton over the fourth of
July on account of a Sabbath school anniversary which
has been appointed for that day. Having had the training of the scholars, I thought it best to conduct the ex-

ercises, that they might have the better opportunity to do justice to themselves and their undertaking."

Reviewing his pastorate in Trenton, he says : " I have now filled this station fourteen months. During this period the Church has enjoyed general quietness and prosperity. During the revival of last winter about seventy were received on trial. The finances of the church have improved in every department. The Sabbath school has grown greatly. A fine infant school of seventy to ninety pupils has been fully established in connection with it, and in fact no single wheel of our machinery has stood still. I have enjoyed great peace almost without interruption, and in preaching the word have often found sweet comfort applied to my own heart. On the whole, I can never expect to enjoy myself better in any situation in life than I have almost uniformly done as a pastor of the Church of Christ. If I can be more useful in any other relation, I will be content."

It must be granted that this election threw a grave responsibility upon one who had but lately passed his twenty-eighth birthday.

CHAPTER XIV.

Secretary of the Sunday School Union.

THE twelve years (1844-1856) spent by Mr. Kidder in the service of the Church as Editor of Sunday School Publications and Tracts, and Corresponding Secretary of the Sunday School Union, have been described by another writer as " of a value that it is hardly possible to overestimate."

The Sunday School Union, which had been established in 1827 and reorganized in 1840, and the Tract Society, which had been founded 1817, had practically to be remodeled ; the *Sunday School Advocate*, as to its literary excellence, its mechanical execution, and the extent of its circulation, must be conspicuously improved ; Sunday school libraries, as to the number, the variety, and the merit of the books, must make a wide departure ; Conferences must be visited, Sunday school conventions and institutes held ; the Church must be roused and informed concerning the religious instruction of the the young, and permanent sources of needed and enlarged revenues must be opened—in short, the young secretary and first General Conference officer of this name and grade must signalize his appointment, must emphasize the wisdom of his selection by the accomplishment of a task that should of itself mark an era in the history of the Church, and by its very success fix at once the permanence and growing importance of his office.

11

It was during the week beginning July 7, 1844, that he assumed his official duties in the Book Concern, then located on the historic spot, 200 Mulberry Street, New York.

It soon became apparent to him that a large share of his work must be done elsewhere than before his desk ; he must go out into the open field of the widely scattered Conferences, and distribute by personal presence and address such information concerning the mission and needs of the Sunday School Union as would rouse the inspiration and quicken the activities necessary to the prosperity of his department.

He began by visiting all the Conferences in New England and those about New York city, going as far west as the Genesee, holding its sessions in Buffalo. Here he was the guest of Hon. (afterward President) Millard Fillmore. He was a busy man during each one of these visits, addressing the Conference, speaking at the Conference anniversary of the Sunday School Union, meeting with the Sunday School Committee, and assisting them in the preparation of their report. In the interims of the Conferences he visited different places, speaking and preaching in the churches and assisting the pastors in taking their Sunday school collections.

Laborious as these journeys were, he found them to be of great advantage to his work. " My visits to the Conferences and churches in different sections of the country have given me opportunity for learning the actual state of Sunday school education and the means necessary to be provided for its more general promotion."

One of these trips took him out to Galena, Ill., to attend the sessions of the Rock River Conference. At that time this was not the holiday excursion it is now.

There was a measure of relaxation and exhilaration in these expeditions, these opportunities of feeling the throb of energy, the thrill of enterprise in these new and far-off countries, and, as a rule, he returned refreshed and keyed up for yet more vigorous work. But he found always (to his dismay had he been less courageous and systematic) a mass of accumulated matter piled up for him to dispose of. To this, he says, "I now addressed myself with a good zest and a determination to put all to rights in due time." At another time of protracted absence for a like reason, he writes on his return: "I found at the office that an immense amount of labor had collected, requiring my individual and most strenuous efforts for a long period. I set about the task I had to perform with industry and zeal. A vast number of letters were on hand requiring answers, and the miscellaneous business needing attention was greater than I had had at any previous period." Taking into account his labors in conducting his correspondence, revising and editing books, reading manuscripts for new books, editing the *Sunday School Advocate*, writing circulars, preparing addresses for Conferences, and composing his annual report (this alone cost him always many days of painstaking labor for weeks), we need not be surprised to read often in his diary such entries as these: "Hard work," "Full day's work," "Overwhelmed with business."

And yet, with all this press of public and office work, he always attended the sessions of his own Conference and took part in its deliberations, performing all the labors belonging to it, besides representing the interests with which he was officially charged, and, as a rule, writing out for the Conference its Sunday school report.

Added to all his other obligations he was also regular in his attendance upon the meetings of the Book Committee, and in the monthly and often special meetings of the Board of Managers of the Sunday School Union.

During a portion of this period he was a good deal embarrassed by frequent and sometimes severe attacks of illness. It would seem that the new style of life, the frequent and wide journeys, and the interruption of the regularity of his habits hitherto maintained, as well as the anxiety pressing on his mind in the development of what was really a new department of Church work, told heavily upon his strength and for a while periled his health. But the vigor of his constitution and the superior nursing of which he was the fortunate subject, always brought him through, and becoming more and more adapted to his work, he continued and increased in his labors.

It soon became apparent to all the observing that Dr. Kidder (for about this time McKendree College, in Illinois, honored him with the doctorate, and a little later his *alma mater* complimented its discernment in the same way*) was the right man in the right place, and that the new departure which the Church was then exploiting would under his conduct reach the consummation of a marked and abiding success. He was seen to be a man of broad views, original ideas, and aggressive methods, while his careful attention to details left scarcely any margin for mistake, and his fidelity to labor shaped all plans into performance.

Addressing the Church in the opening of his first annual report, he grasped at once the scope and pur-

---

* During the latter years of his life the degree LL.D. was conferred upon him by the U. S. Grant University.

pose of the organization he represented. "The Sunday School Union of the Methodist Episcopal Church," he writes, "is an institution peculiar in several of its features. It is not an isolated and independent organization; but a part and parcel of the Church herself. Like a wheel within a wheel, its proper function is to act under the auspices of the Church, to move in the same orbit, and to promote the same great ends. In our Sunday school work heretofore our exertions had not been so systematic and well directed as was desirable. There was no common center around which we could rally, no visible bond of attachment connecting our efforts, no agency for receiving contributions for this cause and distributing their avails to the destitute, no provision for collecting and arranging statistics, and, in fine, no authorized and efficient organization designed to deliberate upon the great interests involved in this department of Christian labor or to devise means for their promotion. To supply these obvious and manifold deficiencies the Sunday School Union was called into being by the unanimous voice of the Church. Its organization was such as to embrace all existing Sunday schools as auxiliary members of the Union without formality or delay.

"A publishing institution it was never intended to be, but was the rather to aid the Book Concern in making proper selections for this department, and also in giving currency and circulation to its books, while at the same time its patronage should tend to reduce the prices. But its great and peculiar office was to listen to the calls of the destitute and supply their wants."

These objects, thus comprehensively and clearly stated, he claimed were with any enlightened Christian a sufficient argument in proof of the necessity of this

Union.   For the Church to neglect the purpose aimed at by this organization was "to neglect the means of her own establishment and perpetuation, and to leave souls without number in the road to death."   Furthermore, he urged, " We have hundreds of ministers and many missionaries engaged in toilsome and self-denying labors at home and abroad, who need nothing so much as Sunday school books for the children and people to whom they are sent.   Strike this Union out of being, and they have no institution to which they can go with any claim for relief.   Support it liberally, and it is competent to supply all their wants."

All these considerations he strengthened with these closing words: " Nor is it now optional with us whether to act or not.   The demands of the time are imperative. We must go forward, or surrender all claims to spirituality and enterprise.   In self-defense and in defense of our holy religion we must act, and we must act efficiently."

Feeling justly that the importance of the cause he represented was such that all that was necessary was for the people to have the needed information concerning it, and they would gladly and generously rally to its support, he took all pains and spared no expense to secure the distribution of this information.   Although postage was not the matter of moderate charge it is now, still he regularly mailed two copies of his annual report to each charge, one for the pastor and one for the superintendent, recommending that portions of the report be read in the Sunday schools of the Church.   Besides this, when he found that his office duties were such that he could not make his regular visits to the Conferences he sent a carefully prepared circular, giving the most recent facts in full, thus among other excellent results making the work of the Conference committees on Sunday school adequate and satisfactory.

He was also particularly urgent in the matter of the holding of anniversary exercises of the Sunday School Union in connection with each session of every Conference. And in a circular still extant, over his own signature, addressed to the pastor of the church where the Conference is to be held, he says:

"I take the liberty of requesting you to see that arrangements are made for an anniversary meeting in behalf of the Sunday School Union of the Methodist Episcopal Church, to be held during the approaching session of the Conference. Various circumstances combine to render it desirable to have timely arrangements made in advance. The object which this institution has in view in asking for public anniversaries at the several Conferences is not so much the raising of funds as the awakening of a deeper interest and a more active and enlightened zeal in the practical work of Sunday school instruction. While, therefore, a collection may be taken to accommodate all who wish to give we desire that the arrangements be planned with more especial reference to diffusing information respecting the character, designs, efficiency, and claims of our Sunday School Union, and arousing the conscience of both preachers and people to more earnest and self-denying labors in behalf of the children of the Church, the nation, and the world."

In another place he says: "That such anniversary exercises, including the addresses delivered, and the action taken have already done much toward diffusing and increasing the spirit of the Sunday school enterprise throughout the land, we have conclusive evidence. We therefore express the hope that henceforward a Sunday school meeting will be considered an indispensable part of the public exercises of each Annual Conference." History was being made in these words. They were an exhortation and a call to a practice that has long since settled into a custom, and the fulfillment of the hope above expressed has, with the regularity of the recurring sessions, found a place on the program of every Conference of the Church.

Spreading, as our Church was in those days, over large tracts of sparsely settled countries, it was constantly confronted with the question whether it should join with other denominations and establish what were termed Union Schools, or husband what resources it might have in any place, and found a school that should be entirely its own and under the control of its Discipline. This problem the secretary discusses in the following terms: " Shall the Church surrender its identity? Should it merge its individual responsibility in some general arrangement with others? We wish emphatically and once for all to say that we cordially approve of union efforts wherever they are called for. We would always hold denominational preferences in abeyance to the grand principles of Christian charity. We would always and everywhere enjoin upon our friends to cooperate freely with Christian brethren of whatever name in all efforts that promise the greatest good. Having said thus much we are prepared with equal emphasis to say that we do not feel called upon to abandon a good and efficient school or the prospect of one among ourselves, even though it be small, to accommodate the views of a few individuals who would prefer to unite with us temporarily on another plan." In much more that is strongly and well said he calls attention to the fact that under the best of circumstances there is in these union measures a tendency to instability, if not to uneasiness and dissatisfaction; a suspicion springs up that one class of workers is gaining an undue advantage, or it really happens that one sect or class of sects gains control of the organization, and what was designed for the promotion of a true catholic union moves with a long stride toward sectarianism. So that his conclusion is: "With our own proper flag floating over us we launch our vessel upon the widespreading ocean, to succor every wreck of humanity and pick up every sinking soul that may be reached by our lifeboats. And in pursuing an independent course we claim to be respected not only in our rights, but in our choice." We can fancy the influence these ringing and sensible utterances must have had in those times, and Methodism has had half a century of phenomenal growth and covered the great West with establishments as stable as they are numerous, largely because under the guidance of such counsel as this she founded her own constituencies and was saved from frittering away her energies in spasms of sentiment.

Discovering with an acumen of which he wished always his Church to have the first fruits, that the permanence of our Sunday schools in any place, and their growth eventually into a church membership, depended largely upon the care and system with which they were organized, and that our connectional system called for uniformity in this important matter, he devised and published a form of constitution defining the duties of officers, teachers, and scholars of Sunday schools. This constitution has remained in force ever since, and, with modifications of greater or less value, is still the organic law of the thousands of schools of Methodism.

In still further bringing his department to that completeness of outfit and work for which it has since been so justly celebrated, he felt it his duty at the opening of his administration to call the attention of the Church to the need and the great importance of a thorough and uniform method of collecting statistics. In his published report he says: " Hitherto there has been but little uniformity in the reports of different Conferences respecting their Sunday schools. In hope of promoting greater uniformity and also of securing more complete returns on several points, the Union has drawn up a new form of report and submitted the same to the Annual Conferences. The new form has been everywhere approved." This blank form was sent to all the preachers through their presiding elders. " The necessity of some formula to aid in the collection of our statistics has long been felt, and we are now gratified with the belief that the very thing wanted has been fixed upon." This we of these modern times can believe, inasmuch as it is the same form, with but slight changes, that has been ever since in use and at present prevails throughout the whole Church.

There was need not only that an exceptional and comprehensive form should be adopted, but there was also, as he found, a task before him in educating and influencing the preachers and others concerned to give attention to this matter and take pains to fill out these blanks. He says with urgent earnestness: " We are deeply anxious to avoid every neglect or lack of effort which can possibly occur to mar our statistics, and we would like to impress on the mind of every preacher and every Sunday school secretary the fact that an omission on their part to report faithfully does inevitably affect the aggregates of the Conference to which they belong and finally those of the whole Church.

" In collecting statistics an omission to count one causes an error just as great as an overcount of one. Both errors should be avoided.

"Accurate statistics, connected with the benevolent enterprises of the day, no less than with commerce, agriculture, and general education, are becoming more and more valued. In no department of Christian benevolence can they be of more importance than in that of the Sunday school. Yet up to this time in the whole history of our enterprise, there has been a great lack of well-authenticated statistics. Nothing like a general exhibit of what is going on or has been done in England or the United States, for example, can anywhere be shown. Some prominent Sunday School Unions make no efforts to collect statistics, others are so limited in their operations as to render their aggregates of but little general use." This seems a surprising statement to us, made familiar as we are with the fullness, the system, and the accuracy of the figures gathered in every department of government, trade, and religion. Quoting further, we read: " In these circumstances we are called upon to be more careful and persevering, in order to carry ours to the highest state of perfection. Our system is fully competent to this, and if all will do their part we doubt not that the body of statistics we shall be able to publish will be more complete than any hitherto offered to the world." This prediction has been to the letter fulfilled. The exceptional and justly enviable fame of our Church in these matters has long since been established and undeviatingly maintained. It holds an acknowledged precedence in the good opinion of those whose duty or convenience it is to study and collate statistics. It is for us, therefore, gratefully to remember those whose genius devised and whose patience pressed into popular use those plans which have made possible our present satisfactory position in these respects. And we are not likely to do violence to our nobler emotions by forgetting the tribute due to him whose methods, as we have seen, have not only the merit of priority, but the still greater worth of a perfection in detail struck out, as it were, at one blow.

CHAPTER XV.

Secretary of the Sunday School Union.

IT was part of the work of the Sunday School Union to assist new and struggling schools by grants of books and other supplies. At that time there was no home missionary work more pressing in its call than this. A young nation was being molded in those Sunday schools. Large outlays of money could alone meet the demands. Funds were wanted in regular flow and generous amounts. One of the earliest tasks laid upon the secretary was the perfection of a plan by which the needed income might be secured. It was necessary also that this plan should be advertised throughout the whole Church, and urged with a fervor and wisdom that should rouse a general movement toward a much needed benevolence.

He writes: " It is a circumstance no less mortifying than true, that our actual receipts from all sources during the five years of the existence of this Union have been less than $700. It is difficult to assign satisfactory reasons for this slow progress. The Sunday school cause does not indeed contain those elements of excitement and romance which give eclat to certain other topics. But it is none the less important on this account. On the contrary, its intrinsic importance appeals to the faith, the hope, and the charity of every Christian."

This inadequate support of the cause of the Sunday

school by the Church was one of the reasons which moved the calling of a convention of Sunday school workers and friends in the city of New York just before the session of the General Conference that created the office of the Secretary of the Sunday School Union and elected Mr. Kidder. In his first report he thus refers to this convention: " The deliberations and resolutions of that body had an influence on the action of the General Conference which was in session at the same time, and may be said to have resulted indirectly at least in two important disciplinary changes. The one provided for the appointment of an Editor of Sunday School Publications and Tracts, who was to reside in New York for the specific purpose of superintending these departments of our literature. The other established periodical collections to be taken up in all our Sunday schools wherever practicable, to aid the funds of our Sunday School Union."

The convention alluded to had recommended the General Conference to " direct that each preacher having charge of a circuit or station make a collection at each of his appointments once a year, for the general Sunday school cause, and transmit the same to the Treasurer of the Sunday School Union of the Methodist Episcopal Church, to enable the Board of Managers of said Union to supply needy and destitute places with Sunday school books." The General Conference saw fit to modify the recommendation by assigning the collection specially to the Sabbath schools.

This was narrow and short-sighted, based largely upon the idea that prevails now in some churches, that the Sunday school should be supported financially by those who are already giving their time and labor to its conduct and maintenance. Dr. Kidder saw that this was a mistake, but he was loyal, and accepted the plan. He hoped that it might " have a fair trial," and said, " Experience will doubtless demonstrate whether this was the wisest arrangement that could be made." Experience did its work punctually and after its usually thorough fashion. Another and wiser General Conference adopting the suggestion of the convention aforesaid, put the collection where in all reason and right it belonged, on the church and not on the Sunday school.

Meanwhile in every way he pressed the claims of the Union upon the attention of the Church.

Quoting again from his first annual report: " This Union is dependent for funds upon voluntary subscriptions and donations. It has no salaried collecting agent whatever. It casts itself with its claims upon the sympathies and liberality of the Church and her members, and the Church has seen fit to recommend quarterly collections to be made in its behalf in all our Sabbath schools, not that the Union is to be dependent upon the slender means of children only, but that beginning in the Sunday schools, we should teach our children to do right—a task which would be ill discharged unless we gave them a consistent example.

" Our cause will probably be always subject to embarrassments, owing to carelessness and lack of interest on the part of those who ought to be its active friends. What we particularly solicit is that the subject be not overlooked, but that every school will at least do something."

In a circular addressed to the Church by a Committee of the Board of Managers of which he was chairman, he says: " In the past, instances often occurred of small and feeble schools belonging to our Church, in vain making application for aid to any institutions we had, and consequently going to other Unions for assistance. It is but just to say that in such cases other Unions promptly and liberally rendered the aid required. While we thank them for so doing, we appeal to our friends and brethren throughout the land to save us from such indebtedness in the future. We do not attempt to conceal the mortification that a Church having more than a million of members and ability second to that of no other in the land, ought to feel in being dependent upon sister denominations for the relief of one of her Sabbath schools. We assert that it is wholly unnecessary, and therefore radically wrong. True it is but recently that we have had a proper organization for attending to this work. And we believe it would be better still to have no such organization than, having one, that it should be sickly and insufficient.

" We should be unfaithful to the trust confided to us if we could consent to give the Church rest until she does what she may and ought to do, by placing this Union upon an elevated and permanent basis. There can be no excuse for neglect. We are doing nothing for ourselves or for the world that can justify us in indifference to this enterprise."

About this time, in answer to many pressing invitations to perform pulpit service in various directions, he issued a card in which, after alluding to the absorbing nature of his office duties, he expresses his hearty willingness to accept all such invitations wherever feasible, but suggests that his acceptance of such appointments must be contingent upon the service to the Union which he may be permitted thereby to render. One of two objects he states he would like always thus to cover. "The first is the increase of the subscription of the *Sunday School Advocate*, and the other is the collection of funds for the aid of new and destitute Sunday schools, or in other words to replenish the treasury of our Sunday School Union. Either a pledge of one hundred new subscribers or the offer of a collection for our Sunday School Union under favorable circumstances, although of no personal interest whatever, yet would be a consideration so congenial and so weighty in itself as always to assist materially in deciding upon what ministerial engagements it will be consistent to make." There can be no question, judging from these words, that here was a Church officer thoroughly taken up with his department, his vision covering but little besides or beyond its obligations and opportunities, and making its growing duties the beginning and the end of all his exertions.

The steady, though never sufficiently expansion of the receipts for this cause, showed that these and other appeals had not been without avail.

Not only was the rapid spread of the Sunday school throughout the land uppermost in the mind of this aggressive secretary, but also, as of equal importance in his thought, the advance of its rank as a teaching institution, and the improvement of its methods of instruction.

He argued strongly for the principle of graded schools, the separation and arrangement of the schools according to the ability of the scholars. "There should be regular gradations of advancement from the simple teachings of the infant class to the higher walks of biblical study. Scholars of every age should have some-

12

thing before them to invite onward their most active progress." The present distribution of the members of the school into the three departments, now so universally adopted—primary, intermediate, and senior—is, in the words just quoted, set forth in a shape more definite than a suggestion.

His was also the early call to a systematic and thorough study of the Scriptures. "Instead of being content," he says, "with a partial and confused idea of Scriptural truth, the scholars should be induced to seek and aided to acquire a comprehensive knowledge of the Bible." Herein we have a foreshadowing of that connected and course study of the word which has since been dignified by the names Berean and International.

But he saw still further and was clear in his impression that it is the teacher that gives character and standing to the school. "The office of the Sunday school teacher must be more highly appreciated. The public mind is not habituated to a more glaring and absurd mistake than that of placing a low estimate upon the dignity and importance of the services rendered by Sunday school teachers. That an unworthy estimate of the character of these services quite too generally prevails is proved by the fact that a deficiency of regular and competent teachers is the GREAT DIFFICULTY with which our cause has to contend. Sunday school teaching requires the best talents, the highest attainments, and the most devoted piety of the Church." Feeling deeply these truths which he thus put so vigorously, he was constant and emphatic in pressing upon the Church the importance of a special training of teachers for their work. He would have this a business, to which one should be educated as for his life work, making it, so to speak, one of

the learned professions. "Teachers must be educated
and trained for their work. Several years of instruction
and practice are thought necessary to learn the art of
making a shoe, a hat, or a coat. How absurd, then, to
suppose that the art of instructing the young in things
pertaining to the kingdom of God can be taken up at a
moment's warning, or even tolerably performed without
some special instruction in the duties of the office and the
best method of performing them! The Church should
provide every necessary means for enabling teachers to
secure the best qualifications. Among the first of these
means is a suitable teachers' library. Another is a
teachers' Bible class. A third is an annual course of lectures upon topics of special interest to teachers. The
best results may be expected where teachers with a sincere desire for improvement have access to the proper
means of securing it."

In his second annual report he speaks with such a far-
sighted wisdom on this subject, that his words (of rare
historic value) may be quoted at length: "In addition
to the means hitherto employed to advance the cause of
the training of teachers we think it time to ask whether
a system of *Normal* Sabbath school instruction may
not be established. Schools thus designated have been
founded by several States of this republic, for the express purpose of training and qualifying teachers for
common schools. Besides the regular institutions
founded and supported by the States, voluntary organizations called Teachers' Institutes have been formed
with a kindred object in many of the counties, especially of the State of New York. At these institutes,
which are of only brief duration, the time is devoted to
mutual improvement by means of lectures, reviews, ex-

aminations in different branches of study, and explanations of different modes of teaching and governing.
Such meetings of teachers, if judiciously conducted, can
hardly fail to be profitable ; and they give occasion to
ask why Sunday school teachers may not have similar
means of improvement ? Perhaps a basis for them is already established in our district Sunday school conventions and in the courses of lectures often delivered to
Sunday school teachers.

" Why may not these be rendered more practicable and
consequently more interesting? Even if all the teachers
of the district could not meet during a sufficient length
of time to take a complete series of lessons on the best
methods of Sunday school instruction, those who could
if representatives of the different schools, might return
and impart the knowledge they had received to their
several associates. In cities, if the spirit of the enterprise sufficiently prevailed, normal classes of Sunday
school teachers might be organized whenever the services of a competent person could be secured to conduct
them. Who can tell what an amount of good might be
accomplished were some dozens of our most successful
and competent laborers in the cause of Sunday schools
to devote a portion of their time annually to training
teachers on the plan now suggested ? Could they succeed by such means in elevating the general character of
Sunday school instruction ; could they give a new impetus to one of the greatest benevolent movements of
the age ; could they by moving upon the minds of some
hundreds of teachers influence the hearts and characters
of thousands of children, would they regret any sacrifices
necessary to accomplish such glorious ends ! "

In these utterances the observing will recognize the

predictions of a seer and the proclamation of a herald, announcing as near at hand those Sunday school institutes and various Chautauqualike movements, which have since attempted if not entirely fulfilled his ideal. Even in that early and incohate day he saw more than the Church has since built. And even now we must take up his lament of nearly fifty years ago : " We confess that we fear that the day is distant when the Church will occupy as high ground on this subject as that already assumed by several States of this Union, *namely*, that in order to promote general education most effectually, institutions must be provided for the special instruction and training of teachers." Evidently his was a mind large enough to comprehend the magnitude of the enterprise which he was championing, and equally was he clear to see that the Sunday school must at once ally itself with the forces which were beginning even then to urge the march of improvement into its present quickstep. " Why shall we not everywhere aim at the highest results and spare no efforts to accomplish them ? Availing ourselves of the enlarged experience and the multiplied facilities which are constantly accumulating in connection with this enterprise, why may we not in our efforts to do good keep pace with the spirit and improvement of the age? What might not be done if every Christian competent to do the work would heartily engage in it, and everyone engaged in it were emulous to excel ! "

By the terms of his election, Dr. Kidder was made responsible for the reading matter furnished to the Sunday schools, including the fitting out of the Sunday school libraries. His ideals here were at once pure and progressive. He proposed, if possible, to protect as well as inform and interest the minds of the young, and to this end asked the cooperation of the authorities of the various schools. "Of what use," he asks, "will it be that the best authors are employed to write, and that unwearied pains are taken to secure all real improvements in the publication of Sunday school books, if officers of Sunday schools, instead of appreciating these results and availing themselves of these advantages, are disposed or persuaded to fill their libraries with other books! Other books can be found of more showy exterior, and of more amusing contents; since those who publish them feel at liberty to address the vulgar passions, if by so doing they can promote their own interests. Who is to guarantee the moral and religious character of their contents? Evidently the purchaser cannot. It is with him but the work of half an hour to buy an amount of trash and error that will not have been purged away from the minds of its readers when half a century will have passed away.

"A large class of books and reading may be good and appropriate for secular purposes, but not at all adapted to teach religious truth.

"There is no place in which a book of bad or doubtful character can do more harm than in a Sunday school library.

"The guarantee of *substantial* truth should be required both in the publication and purchase of Sunday school literature. This rule is a liberal one. It does not rigidly or superstitiously insist upon literal fact when unimportant substitutions or combinations are called for. It does not exclude imaginary illustrations, allegories, parables, or dialogues. It opens a door wide enough to admit an ample variety both in subject and style. It will enable us to use books of biography, history, natural history, mission miscellany, and narratives of fact and travel.

" A little reading calculated to promote thought and mental discipline is much more likely to be useful than a library of books which merely occupy the time and please the imagination, exciting the emotions, but enfeebling the intellect.

" Departing from this ground we strike down the last barrier between a religious and healthful literature and that rising flood of trashy, corrupting issues of the press which threatens to deluge even the sanctuary of the living God. Although this may rage around us let us stand firm upon the rock of truth, let us inscribe truth, substantial, eternal truth, upon our banners, and we may yet live to prove that ' truth is mighty and will prevail.' "

A glance over the early catalogues of the Sunday School Union's publications will show that all the books offered by it were safe and instructive. The healthful in entertainment and the reliable in fact were abundantly furnished, but obliquity in morals and slang in diction were rigorously shut out.

The steady increase of the demands for the publications of the Union showed that both the spirit and the practice of the secretary and editor met with the approval of the Church. The sale of books rose from seventeen and a half millions of pages in the first year to more than seventy-nine and a half million pages in the second year. The happy idea of a five-dollar library, containing fifty volumes at an average price of ten cents each, which was originated at this time, and which has been continued ever since in one shape or other, also largely enhanced the bulk of the sales.

CHAPTER XVI.

Secretary of the Sunday School Union.

AS editor of the *Sunday School Advocate* he felt the pressure of his responsibilities and also the quickening influence of his inspiring opportunity. His election was in contemplation of a purpose to elevate this editorship to a rank equal with that of the other organs of the Church.

The first entry in his journal upon his taking possession of his desk was: " I found but little doing in the department of Sunday school books. That together with the editorship of the *Sunday School Advocate*, although nominally under charge of the editors of *The Christian Advocate and Journal*, had been for a long time confided to the management of an assistant in the office."

The subscriptions to the *Advocate* numbered at this time 10,000, and, what to him was not a very cheering fact, he discovered that by the regulations of the publishers the most of these subscriptions would be discontinued at the end of the current volume, in two months.

In his salutatory he said in part: " Whatever may be expected by some of his friends, the new editor has no disposition at this time to enter into a discussion of his plans and prospects. It will be enough for him to say that he enters upon his duties conscious that they are vastly responsible and at the same time difficult satisfactorily to discharge. These duties, however, were allotted to him without any desire or expectation of his own, and he finds placed before him the alternative of doing the best he can to fulfill them or of doing what he never yet has done, namely, shrink from any requirement the Church has made of him.

"It will not be without embarrassment that he can bid farewell to his personal identity by assuming the editorial WE, but as this must needs be done hereafter, he takes this occasion to speak a word for himself and express to his readers of all classes an anxious desire to serve them acceptably and profitably. Errors and mistakes will doubtless be associated with his best endeavors, but whenever they shall be made known to him, it will be his chief pleasure to correct and avoid them."

The modesty of these words is as impressive as their sincerity, and the conduct of the paper during the three quadrenniums that it was under his control showed no departure from the temper and purpose with which he assumed it.

The improvement of its patronage was the immediate task that confronted him. By the action of the Sunday school convention already alluded to, it had been recommended that the price of the paper should be reduced. This measure was resolved upon at a joint meeting of the editors and the Book Agents. Also, as a fruit of his visits to the Annual Conferences, he states that "arrangements have been made for the more extensive circulation of the *Sunday School Advocate*." But the improved make-up of the paper itself both in appearance and matter was the cause mainly of the rapid growth of its subscription list. Frequently was he encouraged by spontaneous words of approval that came to him from all quarters. One writer said: "Its circulation has diffused a new life in our Sabbath school." Another writes:

"The best encomium which I am capable of bestowing on this excellent periodical is that the subscribers say that it grows better and better." Another: "Our excellent *Advocate* is very highly appreciated in our Sunday school in this place. I scarcely know what we should do without it." Another still: "You have the thanks of many, both old and young, for the useful and interesting variety with which you fill up the *Sunday School Advocate*." And to quote from yet one more: "Your *Advocate* is just what we want. We find it positively, comparatively, and superlatively good!"

The growth of the patronage began at once, and one of his earliest entries for this period was the statement: "The increase of subscribers to the *Sunday School Advocate* is very encouraging, exceeding the most sanguine expectations." During the first eight months the rate of increase was 5,000 per month, and in two years the constituency of this periodical had expanded from 10,000 to 85,000.

There was here great cause for thankfulness; coincident with it was the growth also of the membership of the Sunday schools of the Church. In his annual report, issued January, 1847, he announces that as compared with the statistics of April, 1845, there had been an increase of 1,103 schools, 13,728 teachers, and 81,682 scholars.

After a little more than a year of labor he expresses himself in the *Advocate* as follows: "We are grateful to be enabled to say that during the past year the cause of Sunday schools in our Church has been decidedly prosperous. New zeal has been manifested, and new efforts have been put forth in various places, and they have been crowned with encouraging success. From the statistics of almost every Conference a handsome increase in the number both of teachers and scholars is apparent. The amount of good reading, both in the form of books and of Sunday school periodicals, that has been put in circulation is greater by three or fourfold than what was sent out from our press during any previous year.

"On the whole, we look forward to the labors of another year with confident hopes of more enlarged success. We have an immense work before us. We have only begun it as yet and no time is to be lost." An entry during the same time in his journal gives us an insight into his private emotions with regard to his work and its conspicuous prosperity. "I feel greatly encouraged," he wrote, "and deeply humbled with a sense of God's goodness in enabling me to be in any degree useful in my present responsible position."

With such plans and such results—results encouragingly suggestive of further and yet more notable success—the secretary closed his first quadrennium in office. Two General Conferences, that at Pittsburg and that at Boston, by a unanimous vote, gave him the indorsement of a reelection, and for eight years longer he was continued in this congenial, inspiring, and yet laborious field.

He was a delegate from the New Jersey Conference to the General Conference held at Boston. It was for him a busy session. He was on three Standing Committes: the Sunday School Union Committee, the Tract Committee, and the Committee on the Book Concerns. The reports of the two former were prepared and presented by him.

By the action of the General Conference held at Pittsburg he was to a large degree released from the labor and the consumption of time involved in the visiting of the Annual Conferences. He was thus left in the enjoyment of more freedom for the attention necessary to carry on the work of his office, which was steadily growing both in detail and importance. About this time he refers to an immense amount of labor in his office which would require his undivided labors for a long period. He adds: "I set about the task I had to perform with industry and zeal." His correspondence was large and increasing, and, as he says, "the miscellaneous business needing attention was greater than I had known at any previous period." His department was taking on the proportions of a vast machine, and its operations were impressing the whole Church, so that his fidelity, instead of relieving, increased his burdens, made his duties more toilsome, and called for yet greater diligence. Only by following the bent of his mind and adopting a rigid system in the pursuit of his work and the division of his time was he able to cover his tasks.

His order for October, 1848, was as follows: 1. Periodicals read and marked; 2. Manuscripts on hand to be examined; 3. Descriptive Catalogue to be prepared and published; 4. Tract list to be revised; 5. An edition of new tracts to be published; 6. An edition of Sunday school tracts to be published; 7. Sunday School Union Report to be prepared and published; 8. Sunday school circulars to be issued; 9. English books to be read and revised as they arrive. There were no crumbs to be swept up under the table where this omnivorous industry indulged but never cloyed its appetite.

Early in his second quadrennium he received instructions from the Book Agents to decline all manuscripts and other publications which were not essential to his department. "This," he says, "is the first real check that has been laid upon my working *ad libitum* in the preparation and issue of books. I confess it is a relief, and yet, although it may lighten a certain class of my labors, will still leave me enough to do."

During this period the scope and work of the Sunday School Union took on such proportions that it was extensive enough to engage the entire attention of one man, and therefore he presented a memorial to the General Conference of 1852, for the reorganization of the Tract Society. His suggestions were adopted, and a new and separate tract organization was created. He was thus left free to apply all his attention to the demands of the Union, his special and chosen work.

Unwilling to be so bound to his desk that he should be out of the mind even if he was out of the sight of the ministers of the Church, he adopted the expedient of issuing circulars addressed to the several Conferences as they came up to their annual sessions. "Experience," he says, "has taught me that whether I can visit the Conferences or not, it is important to communicate with them directly on the great interests of the Sunday school enterprise. The official circulars of the secretary become then, as a matter of course, Conference business and are referred to committees to whom they suggest important courses of action."

His anxiety to be in touch not only with the pastors, but with the Sunday school workers all through the Church, prompted him to undertake the herculean task of preparing a post office directory of all the Sunday schools under his care.

" By means of this," he says, " the moment any document is published we can send it out simultaneously to every part of the country with confidence that it will find its way into the right hands. The Union would then be able to advise its auxiliaries of the best methods of conducting their operations, of the issue of valuable books or tracts, and in short of everything necessary to their keeping pace with the times and with the onward progress of this great enterprise."

He was unwilling to be isolated from the host of workers out in the field, who were carrying forward the plans which had originated in his fertile mind. He seized eagerly upon every scheme that could establish a connection between them and him. The remotest members of this great body were made conscious of the throb of the heart and the pulse of the brain that were in sleepless action for them.

As far, too, as he could find release from his editorial duties he continued his visits to the Conferences, journeying from Baltimore to Illinois and Michigan—the distant West—enduring the inconveniences and fronting the dangers which in those days constituted the romance of travel.

In 1852 he carried out a purpose which he had been maturing, namely, a trip abroad. His entry is as follows: "Having resolved to make, in accordance with a plan for some time cherished and already officially recommended by the managers of the Sunday School Union, a tour of observation upon Sunday schools in Europe, I began to make preparations in various ways." With his characteristic carefulness he left no item of his official duties unprovided for. "It was arranged that the publication of Sunday school books should be in great measure suspended till my return, save that of reprints which I might send duly edited across the Atlantic. The plan of the new volume of the *Sunday School Advo-*

cate was duly fixed upon, and several numbers prepared in advance. The principal parts of the ensuing annual report were prepared, and everything in the office anticipated as far as possible for months to come."

This tour occupied him from October until the following June, and comprised a thorough study of the points of interest in the principal cities of England and Scotland, France, Italy, and Germany.

As a representative of Sunday school interests and the officer of a great and growing Church in the wonderful Western world, he was cordially received and was plied with invitations, particularly in England and Scotland, to attend Sunday school and temperance meetings, where his words were listened to with interest and appreciation. Many facts and points pertaining to his work at home were noted by him for future suggestion and application, while a description of his trip in detail enlivened the current columns of the *Sunday School Advocate.*

One object aimed at by his trip abroad was to make provision for the future supply of his Sunday school libraries. He secured contributions from many accredited writers of the Old World.

The high estimate which he put upon the influence of this share of his duty moved him to such contagious zeal that an increasing number of authors of talent were stirred to activity also in this country, and his embarrassment was the necessary choice among a multitude of rarely good manuscripts.

In 1848 Sunday school books were printed also in German at Cincinnati. The next year there was issued what was styled a Descriptive Catalogue of the publications of the Sunday School Department. It was an octavo pamphlet of 183 pages, and contained a classified list and description of everything issued from the Book Concern designed for the use of the Sunday schools. About the same time steps were also taken to establish depositories for the distribution of Sunday school books and supplies at different points and distant from the few centers where up to this time they could be found. These intelligently aggressive measures began at once to show their good fruit, and in the next year the sale of Sunday school books was larger than any previous year, amounting to $60,000.

He urged again the grave importance of carefulness in the selection of books for the Sunday school libraries. His words even in this day would be recognized as timely: " A frothy flood of light and fictitious literature is deluging our land, and thousands of minds are becoming so corrupted or enfeebled by it that they have no longer any relish for reading what is solid or useful. Even in Sabbath school libraries works of a more than doubtful character are beginning to be common. Persons actuated by inferior motives may succeed in other kinds of authorship, but it is doubtful whether a strictly good Sunday school book was ever written by a person whose ruling motive at the time was anything less than to glorify God by enlightening, instructing, and blessing those who might read. We would encourage no person to write a line for this department who would not consider it a high and honorable achievement to produce a good Sunday school book, and who would not be willing to labor long and hard toward the attainment of such an end."

CHAPTER XVII.

Secretary of the Sunday School Union.

IN addition to the publication of the books that enter properly into the composition of the Sunday school library, four important works were undertaken and accomplished during this period. They were a Condensed Commentary, a Sunday School Manual, a Sunday School Hymn Book, and the compilation of a new Catechism.

The Condensed Commentary grew out of a series of Question Books on the various books of the Bible, which had been prepared for the systematic study of the Scriptures. In referring to the need of such a work he says: " It is indeed not a little remarkable that in the whole history of Sunday schools up to this time there should have been so little comprehensive study of the Scriptures, the very kind best adapted to the wants of the masses. According to the usual plan of studying the books of the Bible, few pupils, if any, have time to pass through the sacred volume, and consequently most of them fail to secure connected and comprehensive views of sacred history, and of the complete record of inspiration. The first great object these books are designed to secure is the consecutive reading of the word of God, with such attention on the part of the reader as may enable him to pass an examination upon the subject and language of each section as he progresses."

Enjoying as we do in these favored days the prepara-

13

tion of Sunday school helps which carry the student entirely through the Bible within a given time in a systematic course and with intelligent and thorough-going methods, we may be happy in the gracious duty of feeling and expressing our gratitude to him whose foresight opened the first approach to the path at present so pleasantly and so generally traveled.

The Sunday School Manual was a volume designed, as he says, for general circulation among the ministers of the Church and others. Its title was, *A Brief Exposition of the Character, Operations, and Claims of the Sunday School Union.* It embodied all the most important information respecting this institution. It was his desire to place this in the possession of every teacher and every family in the land, interested to peruse it and act upon its suggestions. The principle upon which he proceeded was that the heartiness and activity of the people in this cause would be in proportion to the amount and clearness of their information upon it. He therefore thought no labor or expense ill applied that was given to the business of furnishing them with facts.

The General Conference of 1848 having directed the preparation of a new Church Hymn Book, he was appointed a member of the Committee on Revision. An entry in his journal reads: " In addition to my usual engagements I was occupied for a week or two in the revision of the new Church Hymn Book in connection with the other editors." The beginning of the following month he writes: " Met with the editors and Book Committee in joint session upon the Hymn Book. As a subcommittee we selected fifty hymns for youth and children, to be inserted in the appropriate place in the Hymn Book, in addition to ten or twelve placed there by the committee." The next day his entry is as follows: "Spent the day in the same labor of revision, and the evening to a late hour in discussing the propriety of introducing the children's hymns, that measure being strenuously opposed by the Hymn Book Committee." Continuing the next day, he writes: "A compromise was agreed to, committing to me the preparation of a Supplement for Sunday Schools, and Youth, and Children."

Two or three months after this we find the following: "A portion of my time was occupied in a correspondence with Dr. McClintock respecting the arrangement of the Sunday school hymns in the new Church Hymn Book, the Hymn Book Committee having refused to surrender the few hymns which they had originally reported to be placed in the Supplement. I demanded those hymns for the Supplement on the score of congruity and of right, and also on the ground that they had been voted to me for that use by the bishops. Unfortunately Dr. McClintock was away, the bishops were gone, and the Hymn Book Committee, having the direction of the printing, had the book set up as they wished and an edition printed, before the error was discovered. The correspondence was protracted, and the delay likely to grow out of it so long, that the Agents saw fit to take the responsibility of going on with the work before the question of difference could be officially decided. I had some doubts whether under such circumstances I ought to furnish the Supplement for publication, or be in any way a party to such a manifest perversion of propriety and of the expressed will of the proper authorities. The Agents, however, pledged themselves to print the Supplement in all the forms of the Hymn Book, so that it might be furnished to all who might desire it as a part of the Church Hymn Book proper. By this means the desideratum for which I had contended was sustained, and the incongruity of having two sections in different parts of the book devoted to Sunday school hymns was left chargeable to those who caused it.

"This affair, as a whole, caused me no little labor and anxiety. In the outset I never dreamed of opposition to my request in behalf of the 400,000 children of our Sunday schools, that they should have a suitable portion of hymns provided for them. And when the question came to an issue I had the satisfaction of having my views corroborated by the bishops, editors, and Book Committee generally. Two members of the Book Committee, who unfortunately represented the whole committee, opposed the addition of more Sunday school hymns than they had originally reported, until their opposition threatened the veto of their whole report. Finally, having assented to a compromise, they were unwilling to give up the paltry collection (only six hymns for children) even to allow them to be transferred to their appropriate place in the book! The result was that in the end the Hymn Book was made to contain nearly ninety hymns for youth and children, whereas I and those whom I represented proposed in the first place to be satisfied with fifty inserted in the body of the book." Later still a distinct hymn book for the Sunday school was prepared by him.

In congratulating the Church upon the preparation and issue of this collection of hymns for the Sunday schools in connection with the regular Church Hymn Book, he said: " It was always deemed proper that the children should become familiar with the standard hymns, both as helps to devotion and as a means of instruction in Christian doctrine. By the double use, therefore, of this issue in the school and church, our children are fast becoming familiar with the very hymns they will sing in mature life and in old age.

"Such matters may appear insignificant to some; in fact, all our efforts in behalf of the young are despised by many on account of the small importance they assume in comparison with the bustling events of the world. Persons, however, who consider youth as the period in which character is formed, who know the controlling power of early associations, and especially the influence of music and devotion on the tender susceptibilities of childhood, will never deem it unimportant or an ordinary occasion that allows of furnishing the right kind of hymns to hundreds of thousands of the children of the Church. If the character of nations is influenced by the patriotic songs taught to their children and sung by them in after years, surely the character of a Church and the welfare of her membership will be improved by having the songs of Zion made familiar to her children and taught again to her children's children.

" Nor is the fact of uniformity to be overlooked. It is desirable that our children in the East and West, the North and the South, sing out of the same book and have the same hymns." According to the way in which some observers describe the present condition of Sunday school singing, there is need again that some words of an intelligence and clearness like to these just quoted be given the force of an official utterance.

The great work, however, which he accomplished during this period was the preparation of a new Catechism in three parts, of advancing grades. January 17, 1849, he writes: " The Book Committee met, and I submitted to

them the business of revising the Catechisms of the
Church." In his report for that year he says: "The
General Conference having directed the revision of our
standard Catechism, that work is now in progress. The
Catechisms hitherto used among us were compiled many
years ago for the Wesleyan Methodist Church in
England. Although correct in doctrine, they have not
been found well adapted to the use of our people,
chiefly on account of containing many hard words and
phrases not easily remembered by children. It is
now proposed to revise these. Some of the most venerable and distinguished divines of our Church have
been invited to cooperate in the preparation of this
Catechism."

At intervals, as he could command the time, this work
occupied him until the next General Conference. One
of his entries is: "I find this a heavy task, but one of
great interest." Again he writes: "Dr. McClintock, by
my invitation, very kindly assisted me in this important
matter. After due consideration it was seen that no
mere revision would answer the important purpose designed. The *Wesleyan Catechism No. 2*, which had been
prepared by Rev. Richard Watson, was found on careful
analysis to be little more than a recast of the *Westmin-
ster Catechism*, with such changes of phraseology as
would conform its teachings to Wesleyan views. With
all their excellencies neither of the above-mentioned
Catechisms was prepared in such a view of the tastes
and wants of the young as had been clearly suggested in
later years by the Sunday school experience of the
Church. Hence it was determined to write out the
whole with the greatest care." This he did.

Having completed the work so far as to submit it to

the judgment of those prepared to pass upon it, he repaired to Poughkeepsie, N. Y. "The principal object of my visit," he says, "was to submit the draft of the new Catechism to the venerable Bishop Hedding for his criticism and approval."

Speaking of the bishop, he adds: "Although in feeble health, his mind was active and his judgment both profound and acute. He seemed quite equal both to the theological and the literary questions involved in such an examination, and it afforded me no small satisfaction to find that my labors upon the Catechism in the main, if not in every particular, met with his hearty approval as well as official sanction. Two hours of close conversation on these topics exhausted his strength so far in the morning that I took leave to allow him to rest, and returned in the afternoon to complete our task. I left him at evening with a deep consciousness of having been privileged above the common walk of virtuous life in having enjoyed a day of rich communion with a Chris. tian patriarch quite on the verge of heaven."

Afterwards to Drs. Olin and Bangs, members of the Committee for the Revision of the Catechism, " I submitted the same matter that had been read carefully to Bishop Hedding, and with a similar result. Both these great and good men were in health and vigor, and gave personal and continuous attention to the matter in hand. At the close of their examination, in connection with Dr. Holdich, they cheerfully signed the recommendation of the work to the General Conference and the Church. Finally, at the proper time, I met the Book Committee, to whom I submitted the action of the Committee to examine the new Catechisms, and was instructed by the former to present the same to the ensuing General Conference."

This body having also approved of the work, the fruit of his long-continued and painstaking labors was issued the following July (1852). In a subsequent report he speaks of the "revised Catechism of the Church" as "containing not only the form of sound doctrine which our children and youth should be taught, but also the covenant virtually made by Christian parents in behalf of their children at baptism, and which in due time they should be taught to make their own. Thus whatever zeal may be awakened on this subject need not die out for lack of a proper direction. Indeed, the more general study of the Catechism in our Sunday schools and families is one of the most hopeful indications of the present period." Even with this encouragement, however, there was yet apparent to him such need of improvement in this direction that he was constrained to continue as follows: " The custom of infant baptism is very general, not to say universal, in the Church. But what proportion of those parents who consecrate their children to God in this holy ordinance follow up the act of consecration with faithful and conscientious instruction and training, in the idea that as they have been initiated into the Church in infancy, so they are obligated to be Christian children, and to spend their lives as consistent members of the Church of God? The answer is that very few thus teach and train their children.

" Let it not be supposed that parents only are at fault. If the question is asked, What proportion of ministers who admit the children of believing parents to the ordinance of baptism fully and solemnly explain to those parents the nature and extent of their obligations to train up those children in the nurture and admonition of the Lord? the answer must again be, Very few. Scores of baptisms take place without any allusion to these practical matters."

After referring to the salutary rule of the Discipline on this subject he adds: " The truth is, we are less in need of rules than of practice, and yet it may be safely said that some pertinent exposition of the full duty of ministers, churches, parents, and children, with reference to this important subject is greatly needed." Yet further amplifying the subject, he dwelt upon the importance of an early association of the baptized children as probationers in the Church, the arrangement of them in classes under the care of " leaders skilled in discerning character and imparting appropriate instruction to the young."

Under such intelligent direction and urged by such energy, it was to be expected that the Sunday School Union would prove at once one of the most progressive institutions of the Church and, in truth, its advance in usefulness and power was a wonder, conspicuous even among the many marvels that marked the growth of the Methodist Episcopal Church. Its only serious embarrassment, that which alone checked its progress, was the old difficulty which has all along hindered the work of the Church, namely, the lack of funds.

Although the receipts had grown annually, the increase part of the time having been sixty per cent and the resources of the society in every way steadily advancing, still the income was far from sufficient to meet the demands which the vigor and aggressiveness of the Union had itself created, and a debt was soon the consequence.

Often the collections in the churches were depressingly small, and frequently they were not taken at all. "Year after year," he says, "passes by and *large* NUMBERS of our ministers and churches report absolutely nothing at all to aid the Sunday School Union."

This debt was cleared away before his term expired.

In discussing the economy of the Sunday school in one of his reports he claims: " This year we have not devoted fifteen cents, or the price of a medium sized Sunday school book, to each scholar. In any possible light in which it may be regarded the Sunday school is one of the most economical as well as the most efficient means of promoting evangelical influences, the good of communities, and the salvation of souls. The unparalleled cheapness of Sunday school education arises from the simple but glorious fact of gratuitous teaching. If our hundred thousand teachers were to be paid for their services at the rates of common labor, say at the average of a dollar a week, our Sunday school would cost us the additional sum of FIVE MILLIONS OF DOLLARS per year. Not only do Sunday school teachers make this immense donation of time and labor to the cause of God, but in many cases they, to a very great extent, meet the expenses of the schools by giving generously of their money."

The Iowa Conference in 1853 availed itself of a provision of the Discipline, and appointed an agent who traversed the entire State, carrying in his wagon books and other requisites for the establishment of schools, and in one year he organized one hundred. We may find in this movement one cause of the preeminence of Methodism in that State.

The lack of means was particularly trying to the secretary, because he was not only alert to seize every advantage, but also acute to discern the thinnest shadow of an approaching opportunity.

He saw that the political revolutions of 1848 in Europe would occasion an increase of emigration to this country. "Emigration from the Old World to the New has been rapid for years past. It is now likely to be more rapid than ever before. Herein may be seen the importance of the Sabbath school enterprise in the economy of God's providence, and also the important relation we sustain to it. If this country is to be filled up with a people who know not God and read not his word, better were it that America had never been discovered. But we hope for better things. Agencies are already instituted for the evangelization of both our native and immigrant population. Among these agencies the Sabbath school, little as it may be known to many who are aiming to control human events, is to be regarded as by no means the least powerful."

Again he says : "We want to make Sunday schools as free to the poor as the air they breathe! We designate the following objects as calling for systematic and general effort: The multiplication of Sunday schools, and the increase of teachers and scholars in schools both new and old ; the better qualification and greater efficiency of teachers ; a more complete supply of the best kind of text-books, reading books, and periodicals ; a more general attention to scriptural study, and the knowledge of the Bible as a book ; the conversion of souls.'

CHAPTER XVIII.

Secretary of the Sunday School Union.

ONE of the plans adopted to encourage the formation of schools was the offer of a premium of five dollars' worth of books to every new school organized. Not only, however, to increase the number of the schools, but also to improve their grade, was a fixed purpose of the Union. The secretary never for a moment wavered in his conviction, already and early proclaimed, that the rank of the school was in every case determined by the average intelligence of the teacher. And in one year out of fifty-nine titles of tracts issued twenty-six were for the benefit of the teachers.

He insists: " The most pressing demand now in the Sabbath school is for intelligent and faithful teachers. The Sabbath school teacher must as necessarily fit himself for his office as the minister of the Gospel, and for the very same reason—success and souls depend on it."

Impressed with the importance of a thorough training of the teachers, he returns to his recommendation of normal schools, conventions, and institutes. These last mentioned " are neither more nor less," he says, " than an application to the Sunday school of the idea taken from that of the common school teachers' institutes as known in the States of New York and Massachusetts. These institutes are neither more nor less than meetings of the school-teachers of a county, held at some convenient place for periods varying from one to three weeks.

The object of the meetings is mutual improvement. The means employed are lectures, recitations, discussions, examinations, essays, criticisms, etc. Such meetings when judiciously conducted have always proved profitable, so much so, indeed, that the States alluded to have appropriated sums of money to aid in defraying their expenses. In our report of 1847 we asked, Why may not Sunday school teachers adopt similar means of improvement?"

With regard to conventions he writes: "We are pleased to see that our favorite idea of Sunday school conventions is extending and becoming popular in all directions. In addition to city, county, and district conventions, we are beginning to have State conventions, in which all denominations are represented."

Addressing himself again to the topic of normal schools, he asks: "Why should it be thought a thing extravagant if we were to urge that a great Church like ours ought to have at least one well-located, well-established school for the particular object of specially and thoroughly training persons for the great work of Sunday school teaching? Several States of our Union have founded normal schools, at great expense, for the purpose of training and qualifying teachers for their common schools. Are common schools more important to the State than Sunday schools to the churches?

" Again, having already numerous colleges and seminaries in successful operation, why might not some or all of these institutions open Sunday school departments, with lectures upon the theory and experiments upon the practice of Sunday school teaching, in addition to suitable instruction in biblical science?"

As an echo of the above sentiments so urgently and

logically put, the following, signed by the present secretary of the Sunday School Union, is interesting and apposite:

"NORMAL TEACHERS AND SUPERINTENDENTS.

"The demand is imperative for better teaching, and hence for better equipped teachers, in our Sunday schools. There is but one way whereby this demand can be met, and that is by the establishment of normal classes for the training of Sunday school teachers. We propose, therefore, the more complete organization of the normal department of the Sunday School Union. The registration will begin on January 2, 1893."

Dr. Kidder also originated a scheme to secure from the colleges and seminaries of the Church a body of educated and consecrated youth to man the Sunday schools of the Church. "Recently," he says, "some experiments made in visiting institutions of learning, and presenting to the minds of students in a direct form the claims of the Sunday school cause upon their personal co-operation and service, has led to the issuing of a circular to the presidents and principals of all colleges, academies, and seminaries under the patronage of our Church."

In this circular he remarks: "The great desideratum of the Sunday school enterprise at the present time is a sufficient supply of competent and persevering teachers. In my inquiries as to the possible methods of enlisting and qualifying the requisite teachers, my attention has rested with peculiar hope upon our literary institutions. I therefore venture to address you, as the official director of one of those institutions, a few suggestions and inquiries.

"Could you not deliver, or cause to be delivered, one or

more lectures calculated to fix the attention of your students upon this subject, and to exhibit to them at once their privileges and their duties in connection with this promising mode of doing good? Can you not establish and maintain normal Bible classes in which both by-example and precept your students will be taught to teach religious truth? Can you devise and experiment upon any other plan calculated to accomplish the object proposed and communicate the results for the benefit of other institutions? Will you be kind enough to write me freely and fully your views and impressions upon this subject, informing me whether in your judgment there may not be and ought not to be some general and concerted action in our literary institutions designed greatly to increase the number and efficiency of Sunday schools in all parts of the country?

"There can be but one opinion as to the great desirableness of interesting as extensively and as deeply as possible in the promotion of Sunday schools the increasing and influential class of educated youth."

The strengthening of the element of culture, important as it was, never for a moment obscured his vision of the spiritual purpose and mission of the Sunday school. In the tables of statistics no item gave him so much enjoyment as the figures reporting the conversions.

"On reaching the topic of conversions in the schools no Christian can fail to pause with devout thanksgiving for such an evidence of the divine favor." And yet he is not satisfied, and no wonder, for great as the number was, and in one report double that of the previous year, he noted that the average was only two conversions for each school!—about one for every ten of the teachers! "Where are the nine?" he asks. "When compared with the whole number of scholars, the total number of conversions indicates that less than one in forty have been the subjects of converting grace." He closes this study of results with the appeal, "Let us attempt great things for God and expect great things from God!"

"We recommend every Sunday school within our bounds to devote one session per month to the exercises of a prayer meeting. We recommend all our churches and congregations to observe the second Monday evening in every month in a concert of prayer in behalf of Sunday schools, and for the revival and extension of the work of the Lord in and by means of them."

The anniversaries of the Sunday School Union were great occasions, held in different cities and commonly in the spring or fall, although the one held in Wilmington, Del., made the wide departure of selecting as its date July 3 and 4, and the arrangement proved a success. The one held in Cincinnati, the first west of the Alleghenies, was opened with a parade of the Sunday school children of the different Methodist churches. They marched to Wesley Chapel. "Though this is the largest church in the city it could not contain the thousands of scholars which crowded every seat, aisle, vestibule, and stairway, leaving no room for spectators, hundreds of whom went away being unable to obtain admission." The Rev. Dr. (afterward Bishop) Simpson was called to the chair. The first address was by Dr. Kidder, who was introduced as the Corresponding Secretary of the Sunday School Union. Considering the scene before him, his theme was most happily chosen, "The Sunday School Army," and with fitting illustrations and impressive figures, he showed it was an "army of defense, of invasion, and occupation."

This meeting of the children was followed by the opening of the anniversary proceedings proper in the afternoon of the same day. At this session the corresponding secretary spoke again. In the evening was held the meeting for the general public. This time the secretary spoke to the topic, " A General Exposition of the Plan, Adaptation, and Power of the Sunday School Union of the Methodist Episcopal Church."

His labors did not end here. These Western people made him do heroic service the following Sunday. He spoke at six different Sunday schools, being kindly conducted, as he says, from one to the other by Dr. Simpson in a buggy. In the afternoon he preached to the children in Wesley Chapel, and at night in the Ninth Street Church he preached to the Sunday school teachers.

The anniversary at Boston occurred during the session of the General Conference in that city. The children's meeting in connection with it was held in Faneuil Hall. In his address Dr. Kidder began with some allusions to the hallowed and patriotic associations of the place and proceeded to show that the bulwark of our national safety and the true glory of our country were the practice and maintenance of public virtue, strengthening his argument with numerous facts and illustrations. The necessity of the Sunday school as a means to this great and desired end was well illustrated by comparing its infancy with the original size and beginnings of Faneuil Hall, in which American liberty was born. As the nation progressed the hall became enlarged, till at the present moment it was of the most extended dimensions. So in regard to the Sunday school, the institution is now in its infancy, but with God's blessing it was destined to spread its influence and auxiliaries all over the world.

14

In conclusion, he commended the cause to the labors, the prayers, and the fond expectations of all who would see this world made purer and better.

All his addresses on the great theme that fully occupied his heart, delivered both to children, to teachers, and to preachers, at anniversaries, conventions, institutes, and Conferences, although uttered with a conscientious regard for propriety and a rigid ruling out of everything that might smack of sensationalism, were instructive and impressive, and the testimony of one of his listeners may be properly introduced here: "I wish especially to thank you for a speech which you made some years since. I have sometimes thought it was that speech which made me an advocate for the Sunday school cause, or if I was already prepared for the work, and waiting with those outside the vineyard because no man hath hired us, yet it seemed to need your voice to speak with authority to my heart, saying, Go ye also into the vineyard.

"By the memory of that blessed hour, I expect to recognize you, my brother in Christ, when we meet in our Father's house. I never expect to see you on earth, but I hope to have the privilege of sitting down beside you in the kingdom of God, and telling you the thoughts and feelings of my heart while listening to your appeal in behalf of the Sunday school, and also of the blessed effects which followed the teachings of that hour. The Sabbath school has seemed like a charmed place to me since that day."

Thus in labors more abundant the happy years sped away. With the approach of the session of the General Conference of 1856 he decided not to present his name for reelection.

Without detriment to any interest of the Union he could now retire. Every department was in working order. His labors had established this institution. It was carried beyond the experimental phase. It was as much a fixture, a member indissoluble of the body of the Church, as the Missionary Society itself.

The steady growth of the Sunday school under its guidance had reached the outer edge of the continent, and the people everywhere touched by its beneficent and active spirit had come to recognize its worth.

A brief summary in figures of the results during his incumbency, while it can give no adequate idea of work done by him, is in place. The collections for the Sunday School Union during the five years preceding his first report, as already noticed, amounted to less than $700. But from the report issued January, 1857, we learn that these collections had during his last year amounted to more than $12,000.

The number of books published rose from a beginning hardly worth counting to nearly 1,000 separate volumes, edited or revised by him personally, printing more than 70,000,000 pages that year, and binding nearly 2,000 volumes each working day of the year. The schools had increased in this period from 5,000 to more than 10,000; officers and teachers from 50,000 to more than 114,000; and the number of scholars from 300,000 to more than 600,000.

The *Sunday School Advocate* continued up to the last of his editorship to expand its well-earned popularity. The attention and labor with which he addressed himself at the outset to its improvement never flagged. Merit in matter and taste in appearance were his constant thought. The heading, at first severely plain, was changed three times, the last being the most attractive in design and finish.

Each bound volume had a different picture on its title-page, either a copy from sacred geography or a historical scene from the Bible, or an allegorical representation of some truth.

A study also of the other engravings scattered over its pages, as they appeared in the successive numbers, would prove an interesting history of the progress of that art. In every respect the management, while accepting first ventures, was persistently bent upon reaching and appropriating last results.

The Rev. Dr. Elliott, Editor of the *Western Christian Advocate*, Cincinnati, a most discriminating critic, bestows this generous estimate upon the Sunday school organ: "After comparing our *Sunday School Advocate* with all the most valuable issues of the press of like sort, we are led, honestly, to conclude that the *Sunday School Advocate* stands clearly at the head of the whole list, and is superior to them in many respects. The number published, and the great advantages of the Methodist Book Concern, have placed this periodical at the head of its class."

Not only did this periodical call forth high praise from our own people, but it was also a valued visitor to an outside constituency. In one year fifteen thousand of its subscribers were of other Churches. And the retiring secretary left it with a subscription list of 105,526.

In the last number edited by him he addressed to his readers the following farewell: "At the end of twelve years' service in the department from which we now retire, it becomes us to take official leave of our numerous readers and Sunday school friends. And, first of all, we have to express our sincere acknowledgment for the kindness and charity with which our humble efforts have been received. Next to the gratitude due to God for the prosperity with which he has deigned to crown the cause in which it has been our lot to labor, we cherish a sense of obligation to the Sunday school public of our Church for the unvarying kindness and Christian regard which we have experienced in the prosecution of our duties. Wherever we have gone throughout the bounds of the Church, we have been welcomed as the representative of a favorite interest dear to the hearts of ministers and people, old and young.

"We have done what we could to advance that interest, and have often regretted our inability to do more. Nevertheless, we have not been without encouragement that our labors have not been in vain in the Lord.

"Although connected with the Sunday school department of the Church at a most important period with reference to its literature and system of operations, yet ours has been chiefly a work of faith and not of sight. Whatever of fruit has been manifest, we trust that still more will be apparent hereafter, and especially in another world.

"In the many millions of pages which we have been instrumental in placing in the hands of the Sunday school scholars and youth of America, we are not aware that there is a single line which,

"'Dying, we would wish to blot.'

Indeed, we trust that, when we shall have passed away from earth, those immortal pages will be speaking to the hearts and consciences of generations that shall live after us."

But the most gratifying feature in this final review of his work was the steady growth of the number of conversions in the schools, the total falling but little short of the entire addition to the church membership for the same period, the proportion being as six to seven.

The General Conference, at its session in 1856, passed the following resolutions: "*Resolved*, 1. That we highly appreciate the services of our respected brother, Rev. Daniel P. Kidder, as Corresponding Secretary of the Sunday School Union of the Methodist Episcopal Church during the last twelve years, and that the prosperous condition of our Sunday school work is largely indebted under God to his valuable labors.

" 2. That we hereby tender to Brother Kidder our sincere thanks for his services and our earnest wishes for his future welfare."

At the July meeting of the Board of Managers the following resolutions were unanimously adopted:

" The Board of Managers of the Sunday School Union of the Methodist Episcopal Church deem this first meeting of the Board after the retirement of the Rev. Dr. Kidder from the office of Editor of Sunday School Books and Corresponding Secretary of the Sunday School Union, a suitable occasion to record their sense of the valuable services which he has rendered to the Sunday school cause in connection with our Church during the period of his official connection therewith. Therefore,

" *Resolved*, That the Rev. Dr. Kidder, in the exercise of a discriminating judgment and an enlightened enterprise in the publishing of Sunday school books, has placed the publishing department of our Sunday School Union in a position of great importance to the Church, and of usefulness to the Sunday school cause.

"*Resolved*, That by his untiring energy and zealous devotion to this department of Christian effort he has largely contributed to draw toward it the attention and sympathies of the Church, and to establish it in the important relation which it now sustains thereto.

"*Resolved*, That the thanks of the friends of Sunday schools are eminently due to the Rev. Dr. Kidder for his services in their behalf, and we hereby tender to him the assurance that, as members of this Board, we cherish a lively sense of their value and importance, and that our best wishes will follow him into whatever field of future usefulness he may be called to enter.

"WILLIAM TRUSLOW, *Recording Secretary*."

The Christian Advocate and Journal of that date had the following announcement: " Dr. Kidder has labored during several years as Secretary and Editor of the Methodist Sunday School Union. He may indeed be considered the founder of that important department of the Methodist Book Concern. It has grown up vigorously under his care, and will be a permanent monument of his ability and usefulness."

About this time he received a letter containing an extract which may be quoted as expressing doubtless the feelings of many with respect to his retirement: " May I not tell you how sorry we are to see the last *Advocate* which will be sent out by you. For ever since our eyes were opened to discern spiritual things we have been indebted to you for spiritual help through its columns. Tears will come thick as I write the little word Goodbye! May the God of heaven be with you always!

Good-bye!" And from across the waters were these words of affection and appreciation: "Allow me to express my regrets at your retirement from an office for which you seemed so admirably fitted and in the discharge of which God made you so eminently useful."

Thirteen years after, Dr. (now Bishop) J. H. Vincent, then Secretary of the Sunday School Union, wrote to Dr. Kidder in the following cordial strain: "No Sunday school worker on the continent has such a record as yourself. I am brought face to face with your work every day in the Union. Its foundations, broad and deep, were laid by yourself, and to you is due the preeminence which our Union enjoys to-day. I think and speak of this fact often."

CHAPTER XIX.

Professorship in the Garrett Biblical Institute.

ALTHOUGH engrossed with the exacting details of his office, Dr. Kidder never for a moment lost his interest in the other enterprises of the Church, particularly that of education. As secretary, his enthusiasm was due largely to the fact that he considered the Sunday school an educational institution of vast power and unlimited capacity. The thirst for knowledge which took him from his home when a college course was not the fashion that it now is, and his enjoyment in teaching, not only remained with him, but grew with his years of diligence and observation.

His awakened attention never slept or dozed ; he was always on the lookout for new ideas and studying the work of established institutions. His thought was busy sifting the practical from the theoretical, and seeking the fittest for his Church. As opportunity offered he visited model public schools. He comments on a call he made at Union College, where he was entertained by Dr. Nott. He made an address to the students. He spent a Sunday at Wilbraham, as the guest of Dr. Raymond, listening to Gilbert Haven, the pastor, and adds, " I was much pleased with the privilege of visiting this first of our Church academies, ever associated with the memory of Wilbur Fisk."

Called by his official duties to frequent and wide travels in the Northwest, he saw at once its strategic positions for educational enterprise. As early as September, 1852, he speaks of an interview with Dr. Hinman, at Niles, Mich., concerning the educational interests of the Northwest—an interview which he calls "important." In this conversation some of the details were discussed with regard to the founding of a university at or near Chicago, for which the charter had been recently obtained. A few days after, Dr. Hinman wrote to Dr. Kidder respecting a meeting he had held with the projectors of the enterprise in which he says, "Your plans were generally carried out." Also at this time letters passed between him and Judge Goodrich with regard to the plans for the necessary buildings. At his request Dr. Kidder furnished him with a sketch of the arrangement thought to be desirable. A little later the judge informed him that the university project was "booming."

Dr. Hinman, the first President of the Northwestern University, located at Evanston, Ill., died in 1854. But without a halt the plans moved on to maturity, and in 1855 the classes were opened. Dr. (now Bishop) R. S. Foster was president from 1856 until 1860, and for nine years thereafter the institution was under the efficient management of Professor H. S. Noyes, A.M., acting president.

But Evanston was to be honored also as the seat of ministerial education in the Northwest, and in this foundation the unobtrusive but effective activity of Dr. Kidder was an originating and determining factor. At Chicago, September 17, 1853, while representing the Sunday School Union at the session of the Rock River Conference, he was questioned by Judge Goodrich as to the best direction of the property which Mrs. Eliza Garrett was then planning to devise to the Church for educational purposes. The doctor's answer was prompt. "I suggested a biblical institute as the grand desideratum of our educational enterprises in the West." A specially trained ministry, he thought, was a need that called for provisions which should be no longer delayed.

At that time he went out to take in the situation at Evanston, known then as the site of the Northwestern University, but "occupied," as he says, "by the original inhabitants." Returning to Chicago, he had by appointment a further interview with the judge respecting the drafting of Mrs. Garrett's will, she being present.

Mr. Garrett had died in 1848. It was some time before she came into possession of her property. She obtained it by setting aside his will, he not having allowed her what was her right under the law. As soon as she obtained it she determined to use it to promote the interests of the Church in some of its departments. It was her thought to turn the gift into some of the educational lines of the Church. Dr. Kidder, having remarked that the Church was already aroused to the importance of providing schools and colleges, but not awake to the necessity of ministerial training, urged that this was the greatest need of the hour.

Judge Goodrich was prepared to know in advance that this would be the advice of Dr. Kidder, for a year before this he had written to the judge recommending the founding of a theological school coincident with the establishment of the new university, although, as he expressly stated, it should be under the care of a distinct corporation and with a separate charter.

One month after the above interview with Mrs. Garrett, the judge wrote to Dr. Kidder inquiring about particular features of the will and the chief provisions of the charter.

"Would it not be right," he asks, "to have it called 'The Garrett Theological Institute of the Methodist Episcopal Church?' How many trustees ought we to have? What particular provisions in the will or charter would you suggest? Please make any suggestions which may occur to you." In reply the doctor affirmed again his judgment of the wisdom of a separate charter, and suggested that the name be "The Garrett Biblical Institute." He advised nine as the best number for the trustees, "a fair medium," he observed, "between too large and too small a body of trustees." He then adds: "As to special provisions of the will and charter, the most important matter will be to secure *sufficient general powers.* It is impossible to foresee many contingencies that will be likely to arise in the future. Hence our confidence must be in the good sense of those whom the Lord will raise up to direct interests designed for his glory. In some of the foundations of English colleges it is expressly enjoined that beer shall be made and furnished the students. Many other awkward arrangements of the olden time the corporations manage to get around or improve upon. I allude to such matters as illustrating numerous changes that may occur in the conditions and habits of society which it is useless to attempt to anticipate or prevent.

"Besides the founding of theological institutions is a new thing with us, and the whole subject should be gravely and cautiously studied by a competent board of trustees and faculty, endowed with ample powers to adopt such regulations and means of usefulness as they may determine by inquiry and experiment to be best adapted to the great objects in view."

Matters had thus far progressed, a theological institution had been determined upon at Evanston, the will of Mrs. Garrett was being drawn with reference to it, and the charter was in process of formation, when Dr. Dempster passed through Evanston on his journey farther west to establish a like institution at Bloomington, Ill. The projectors, however, of the educational foundations at Evanston told him that not Bloomington, but Evanston, was the place for such a plant, and the objections to the former place and the special advantages of the latter were set before him with such clearness and earnestness that he needed only a trip to Bloomington to render him a thorough convert to their views.

Dr. Dempster's return to Evanston, was, as had been predicted, with the conviction that Evanston rather than Bloomington was the place for the future theological school. And now that Mrs. Garrett's will had been made (although the fact had not yet been announced, nor were any of the funds likely to be available for some time) the projectors of the enterprise felt encouraged to persuade Dr. Dempster to begin his school in Evanston.

They made arrangements with him to that effect. The building was erected in 1854, and early in the following year the school was opened. Dr. Dempster, after his return to Concord, wrote to Dr. Kidder, expressing the hope that he might have him as an associate in the enterprise just arranged for at Evanston, and observed further, that his counsel in the movement would be important, and that he would deem it a special favor to have any suggestions from him.

In the matter of the charter for the Garrett Biblical Institute Dr. Kidder and Judge Goodrich were in constant communication, and the document was the product of their joint labors.

At the time Mrs. Garrett's will was drawn she was not yet fifty years old, and in good health.   Of course she might change her mind in regard to the disposal of her property, so no extensive financial responsibilities could be assumed on such a basis, but in November, 1855, she died suddenly.   Judge Goodrich, writing of the event to Dr. Kidder, says: " Her personal mission is done, but look away down the track of time and see what an immortality on earth she has.   How her influence or the influence of her beneficence will widen and widen until it shall circle and pervade the earth.   Consider this providence and your connection with it, and see what ought to be done or you ought to do.   I suggest this to you with more freedom because you made the suggestion to me to try and induce her to make this disposition of the estate God had given her, although God had likewise put it into my heart and she had previously proposed to do so. So many minds meeting upon this subject at about the same time, it seems to me that God intends some great results from this event."

The death of Mrs. Garrett called for the immediate action of the trustees, and Judge Goodrich was in continual correspondence with Dr. Kidder, consulting him as to the disposition of the property, the question of the president and faculty, the character and location of the building, and asking him on all other subjects connected with the enterprise to favor him with his views and suggestions.

The institute becoming now an established certainty, the matter for consideration next in importance was its proper recognition by the representatives of the Church at the General Conference meeting in May, 1856.   Dr. Kidder and Bishop Simpson had already had more than one interview in regard to it, and were in happy accord as to its organization and the best manner of gaining its indorsement at the General Conference. Under date of April 13 he writes: "Bishop Simpson took tea with us and spent the evening with me. We talked over at length the affairs of the Garrett Biblical Institute. A principal object of the consultation was to make a judicious plan for securing the recognition of the institute in a fitting manner from the ensuing General Conference. As the result of our conference I prepared and sent out several documents bearing on the subject in the course of a few days following."

He also drew up the memorial to the General Conference, and meeting the Chicago gentlemen at Indianapolis, he was actively and influentially engaged with them in pressing these proceedings to a successful conclusion.

Thus does Dr. Kidder appear as an initial feature in all these important movements. The project maturing at Evanston dwelt constantly in his mind, taking on many of the proportions of its great future. Its frame and order were molded in the interims of his office work, and in his home, both with the members of his family and the visiting representatives of the Church, it was the absorbing theme of conversation.

Furthermore, as a sign of his belief in the rectitude of the undertaking and his confidence in its success, he bought large quantities of land in the vicinity of the university grounds. The trustees had assumed as much responsibility as they dared, but they wished to have the adjoining property in friendly hands. For this reason their agent, as he could get hold of the small farms of the old settlers, purchased them, Dr. Kidder agreeing to take them.

For some time his thought had been shaping toward the conviction that he should terminate his office as Secretary of the Sunday School Union and devote his future to the cause of ministerial education. When he was entering upon his third quadrennium he had been approached in a confidential note relative to his taking charge of a theological department about to be opened for one of our growing Western universities. Toward the close of the year 1854 he writes: "During the past year I have had a strong impression upon my mind that it may hereafter become my duty to devote myself to the enterprise of ministerial education. I have been in circumstances to observe that there is a growing desire on the part of the Church for higher qualifications on the part of her ministry and in many young ministers and candidates for the ministry a desire for better opportunities of study and special training. Conjointly with these things is the natural interest I feel in the result of the movement to found a biblical institution near Chicago, concerning which I was consulted at an early moment and have been in correspondence ever since.

"Now while I shall calmly and patiently await the openings of Providence with reference to any duty of this kind that may hereafter devolve upon me, I am disposed in conformity with my personal tastes and my obvious duty as a minister to improve any opportunity I may now have for more enlarged study. I therefore propose to renew my old habit of a division of time, and as far as possible to redeem four hours each day for biblical studies and systematic reading.

"I now find myself in my fortieth year, a period of life in which I can no longer consider myself, as I have always hitherto felt, a young man. Having been enabled by the divine blessing already to accomplish sundry important objects of life in the several capacities of minister of the Gospel, missionary, editor, author, Sunday school secretary, and traveler, I can now with propriety devote myself, with the hope of less interruption than heretofore, to those studies and labors which are in accordance with my taste and with the grand and settled purposes of my life. With these intentions and a confident trust in the divine blessing and guidance, I commit myself to God and the future, fervently hoping that his glorious will may in me be fully done."

With the opening of the year 1856 he received a letter from Judge Goodrich in which he said : " I do not know as the Church will be willing to release you from your present position or as you would feel at liberty to retire from it. Although your present position is one of immeasurable importance, yet cannot some one be found who could fill it who yet would not possess the same requisites for this place as yourself? There can be no doubt of your election if you are willing to accept. All the trustees desire it."

Many of his trusted friends were opposed to his leaving the Sunday School Union, among them the veteran editor of the *Advocate*, Dr. Bond, who said to him : " The Father will whip you if you give up the Sunday school work." Nevertheless his mind was finally decided, and at the proper time he sent the following note to the General Conference : " Dear Brethren :—Having been thrice elected to the office of Sunday school editor and secretary without solicitation or urgency on my part and without competition on the part of others, and having at the end of twelve years' service strong inclinations to enter a somewhat different field of labor (not within

15

your appointment), I take occasion respectfully to inform you that I prefer not to be considered a candidate for any office."

This conclusion to accept the unsought opening at Evanston was not reached by him until after many balancings in his mind as to whether, after all, it might not rather be his immediate duty to enter again the pastorate. With his customary carefulness and thoroughness he traverses the whole subject in the following paper:

" I. Shall I enter the Biblical Institute at Evanston?

" 1. I feel, and have for some time felt, a strong attraction to such a work, an impression that such would be my ultimate duty.

" 2. I am thoroughly convinced that the future welfare of the Church depends in no small degree on the thorough and appropriate training of our rising ministry.

" 3. I think that such a field of labor would be highly congenial to my tastes and habits, and that I should find great delight in pursuing the studies and engagements appropriate to such a calling.

" 4. My acquaintance in the West and familiarity with its customs and wants are not unfavorable to the arrangement.

" 5. The providential connection I have had with the founding and early history of the institution indicates a propriety in my devoting to it my labors if not my life.

" II. Granting that I ultimately purpose going, should I go now or after one or two years in the pastorate?

" 1. Having been a long time (12 years) out of the pastorate it would be useful to me to renew my pastoral habits and get on the ministerial harness.

" 2. The studies and cultivation which would be appropriate to me as a minister would be in direct line of preparation for the other field of labor, and the experience I should acquire would be valuable.

" On the other hand, 1. While in the pastorate there would necessarily be much time and labor spent in local duties that would not be preparatory, although they might be useful.

" 2. By delaying and being otherwise occupied I might afterwards less easily adapt myself to the work of a teacher.

" 3. By going now I may devote myself at once to special preparation for my future duties.

" 4. I may have an appropriate influence in organizing and modeling the institution.

" 5. Some person must do the work of organizing, and perhaps in this direction I have some special gifts."

At this juncture some words from those whose counsel and judgment he particularly valued determined his mind toward the field at Evanston. Dr. Hannah, one of the visiting delegates from the British Wesleyan Conference to the General Conference, said to him that he thought that it would be just the thing for him. The same day that he received the official tender of the professorship Bishop Simpson expressed himself in opposition to his thought of taking a pastoral relation and argued for the necessity of his going immediately West. The day following, in an interview with Bishop Janes, he was unequivocally advised to accept the chair offered to him. In this connection he adds: " The more I reflect upon this call and consult with my friends respecting it, the more it appears like a providential opening for my future labors! "

At length, having gone on to Evanston to inquire

personally into the state and prospects of the institution, and having had an interview with the trustees, in which he proposed certain radical changes in the organization, and these modifications having been adopted so that all was arranged to correspond with his views, he accepted the chair of Practical Theology, to which he was unanimously chosen, and began to make his preparations for removing to Evanston.

That he was the right man to be officially and efficiently identified with the opening of this scheme so important to the Church may be gathered not only from what has been already recorded, but also from the contents of the following paper drawn up by him six months before his election:

"A biblical institute for the Methodist Episcopal Church—What it should be and require

" 1. It should be eminently practical. It should be so planned and conducted as to forestall competition in all the West, in our own Church at least. Thus alone may we avoid the evils of subdivision so sadly seen in our college operations.

" 2. It should be organized after no existing model, but in view of the wants and circumstances of our Church, with due reference to the experience and mistakes of others.

" 3. It should provide for the wants of those who have had few advantages as well as those who have had many. And why may it not plan its courses of instruction so as to secure other pupils than those of our own Church, and thus aim at influencing the whole theological character of the Northwest?

" 4. It should make a thorough examination of the wants and qualifications of each candidate, and seek to make its instructions specific in small things as well as great.

"5. Its standard of graduation should be high. And yet its facilities should be freely offered to suitable persons who could not take the full course.

"6. It should instruct by study and thorough drill, more than by the superficial plan of lectures.

"7. Every effort should be made to keep the students warm and active in the enjoyment and practice of religion.

"8. Also to instruct them in all the details of ministerial duty, such as Sabbath schools, missions, tracts, etc.

"9. They should be examined on the state, economy, and agencies of the Church.

"10. Every effort should be made to guard them against effeminacy of body, mind, or heart, and to cultivate the *esprit du corps* of the itinerancy.

"11. Great attention should be paid to manners, system of life, habits of study, etc.

"12. Where text-books of the right kind are not in existence they should be prepared."

CHAPTER XX.

Professorship in the Garrett Biblical Institute.

THE 18th of September, 1856, found him and part of his family established in the home of Professor Noyes at Evanston. Here he remained during the winter, his own house being in process of erection.

Under date of September 22 he writes: "I had my first official meeting with my associates in the faculty." These were Dr. Dempster, Dr. Bannister, and Dr. Johnson. It was the policy of the trustees to elect no president; Dr. Dempster, as senior professor, was acting president.

September 24 the institute opened. "Owing to the inorganic conditions of affairs," he writes, "recitations were dispensed with." The number of students was small, "and many of them but poorly prepared for an enlarged course of theological study. The faculty, however, sought to adapt their efforts to the necessities of the case and to lay a good foundation for the time to come." Two o'clock, September 25, he heard his first classes in elocution and Church history. His record is: "Not finding any class prepared for my department proper, I volunteered to take a class in elementary rhetoric and another in ecclesiastical history. An elocution class I assumed as belonging properly to me, and by arrangement gave a course of weekly lectures to the school." Under the date last mentioned he writes further: "We have been one week in Evanston, a week of anxiety and labor, but nevertheless a pleasant one. We all think the place beautiful and are pleased with its scenery. As to my prospective duties, they appear pleasant to me and I have now before me a more inviting outlook of study than I have enjoyed before for years. Reviewing the intellectual pursuits of former years is especially exhilarating to me, and also the opportunity of extensive collateral reading."

The last day of this month he refers to a meeting of their faculty, held that date, in company with the faculty of the Northwestern University, to consult respecting the establishment of a reading room. On the 7th of October he gave his first lecture to the students. It was delivered extempore and was an exposition of the rules for a preacher's conduct.

At this time, in keeping with his anxiety to do all he could for the benefit of the students, he instituted a Bible class for them, conducted by himself each Sunday morning.

The following month Dr. Dempster was called to New York, and, both his remaining colleagues being sick, Dr. Kidder had sole charge, and in one day, besides his own recitations in rhetoric and ecclesiastical history, he heard three classes in Greek and two in Hebrew. All this time, too, he was superintending the building of his house. Of this he says: " My studies during the autumn of '56, as well as for some months following, were somewhat interrupted by the necessity of taking measures to build me a house, which enterprise, in the absence of a sufficient number of competent mechanics and all the conveniences of a larger place, devolved on me no little care and expense.

" During the first year the duties of the faculty to the

students were not heavy, but no inconsiderable amount of time was necessarily spent in planning a course of study for the future and making such arrangements as were necessary for the proper organization of the institution. The closing year finds me in the enjoyment of excellent health and of unnumbered blessings, for which I desire to record my sincerest gratitude to God the giver.

"On a review of the present year I see little to regret, except the loss of time incident to the changes in my circumstances and the necessity of so much contact with the world and its cares and business.

"I have felt conscious of intellectual and spiritual loss as the result of so much diversion from my more congenial employments, but I have submitted to it only as an unavoidable necessity against the effect of which I have endeavored both to watch and pray. I have all along been cheered with the promise of 'grace sufficient for the evil day,' and also with the hope of greater advantages following.

"As to the great change in my manner of life and public engagements, it may be too early to form a correct judgment. Nevertheless I rejoice to be still clear in the conviction of providential guidance and support. My mind and feelings for some time in advance had been undergoing a preparation for my present position and duties for which I cannot account on natural principles. I trust that it, as well as the change itself, is of the Lord. Indeed seldom during my life have I had more clear and satisfactory convictions of duty with reference to an important change in my course or position.

"I regard the institution with which I have become connected as a great and hopeful experiment connected

with the urgent wants and dearest interests of the
Church. What good I may be able to do in connection
with it I know not, but I am impressed with the conviction that I have a most responsible work to perform
here. Not so much indeed with reference to the present
moment as to the future.

"I see clearly, and have done so from the first, that
it is to be a work of faith, and that years must elapse before we can reasonably expect the complete establishment of such an institution as the Garrett Biblical Institute ought to be. In order, however, to such a result,
distant though it be, some persons must zealously and
faithfully labor and plan.

"To this work I have in my mind freely consented,
and surrounded as I am by worthy colleagues, I find
much satisfaction in laboring on in hope.

"We have at present only some twenty-five students,
and many of them but poorly prepared. Still they are
generally laborious and hopeful, and what we do for
them seems to be appreciated.

"The studies which I have in hand give me a fine opportunity for review, and the comparative leisure which
I enjoy gives me occasion to prepare for future duties."

A later extract from his journal reads as follows:

"In the early part of 1857 the result of the deliberations of the faculty was embodied by myself as a committee in a pamphlet entitled *A Manual of Information
Respecting the Garrett Biblical Institute.* As our numbers only reached thirty-seven in the aggregate, we published no catalogue but issued the Manual in the stead
of one.

"The first anniversary occurred on June 23 of this
year. Some of our students of the more advanced

grades delivered orations on the occasion. Our greatest embarrassment during this year arose from the irregularity in the attendance of our students, but few of whom remained with system through the year from beginning to the end."

During the vacation he moved into his new house. Shortly after he was taken severely ill with a disease that resembled cholera and which brought him, he says, "very near the unseen world." He was sufficiently restored to visit the Rock River Conference, to which this year he was transferred.

The second year the institute was opened with a senior class of six. "I was consequently called upon," he says, "to teach in the studies properly belonging to my chair. But in addition to them I taught a large class in Angus's *Handbook of the Bible*. This year we were encouraged with a large number of students, fifty-three in all, and with a more regular attendance upon their duties in the institution; also in finding our plan of studies and the general management to work satisfactorily. The second year passed by in a remarkably noiseless manner, with fewer incidents of note to mark its flight than any other that I can remember. We had become accustomed to our position in the West, and remained quietly to enjoy it, yet fully occupied with useful labor."

September 22 the third year of the institute opened with fifty students, and only three in the senior class. The class in homiletics was, however, enlarged by the addition of several students of the partial course.

The anniversary sermon this year was preached by Dr. Kidder. His theme was "The Enemies and Arms of Christianity." The *Northwestern Christian Advocate*, in its report, described it as "an able sermon, full of noble thoughts and worthy utterances. It was eminently a sermon for the times."

In the fourth year, in addition to his regular work, he took a class in Hase's *Ecclesiastical History.* He delivered also a series of lectures on bibliography and a general course on homiletics.

During this year a change was made in the arrangement of the term, so that the long vacation would occur in the winter months instead of the summer. In the summer Evanston was not only a beautiful place on account of its undisturbed growth of forest trees, but, because of the cool lake breezes, was also most enjoyable. As a consequence of this new adjustment of the school year, the students would be saved the expense of fuel, the item for lights would be reduced, and the winter would be left open for them to accept opportunities to teach country schools, and thus make necessary provision for their expenses. The plan was an admirable one, and deservedly popular; the school year was from March to November.

The year 1860, he says, " opened under fine auspices." As his extra work he gave a course of lectures in oratory and enlisted the school, dividing it into classes which he met for the most part in the church.

The school year of 1861 he described as " one which as a whole proved quite the most interesting and satisfactory of any thus far spent in the institute. The number of students was eighty-five, well proportioned among the classes. The senior class, being large and well qualified, claimed my most hopeful labors in a more complete course of homiletical lectures than I had before given. I had a class also quite as numerous in ecclesiastical history. The number of students having increased, I necessarily had increased labor in attending to their elocutionary and written exercises. This year more than before we were able to realize the full design and power of the institution, the former years' labors having been preparatory to this result. Although troubled with some absences and irregularities in attendance, yet this class of drawbacks was fewer in number than heretofore. There was also developed this year a plan whereby the arrangement for the work of the students in the home missionary field of Chicago was brought to perfection.

"The anniversary for this year was held in Clark Street Church, Chicago. The day, October 31, proved fine, the audience was good, and the exercises seemed to interest and, indeed, to delight the people generally. Many and unequivocal were the expressions of satisfaction made by our friends, and we all felt at the close of the services that an important epoch had been reached in the history of the institution. Of our class of seventeen graduates, fifteen were already admitted to Conferences and had received important appointments to which they went forth immediately."

One of the faculty being absent at the beginning of the next year, the remaining professors had each about an hour a day of extra work. "Notwithstanding the excitement and partial interruption," he says, "caused by the terrible civil war with which our country is desolated, the scholastic year has been, on the whole, a successful and happy one, for which I feel truly thankful. A class of fourteen was graduated, who entered at once upon the work of preaching the Gospel in five or more different Conferences."

The latter part of November, 1863, Dr. Dempster died. "This unexpected event threw no little gloom over our community, and made it necessary to devise new plans with reference to the institution." Dr. Kidder became senior professor and acting president.

At the opening of the school year they had an encouraging number of students, and as usual from widely distant parts of the country. By an especial arrangement Dr. Bannister and himself conducted all the classes. This pressure was relieved by the election and arrival of Dr. Raymond in the latter part of July. He says: "Having surrendered to Dr. Raymond logic and Angus, I was enabled to accomplish more satisfactorily my instruction in ecclesiastical history and my own proper department." About this time the work on homiletics which he had prepared was introduced as a text-book, and he remarks that he found it a great practical convenience to himself, and apparently a great help to the students.

Until the very last of his stay at Evanston he continued his practice of doing much work that belonged really outside of his department. Church history was almost continuously in his hands, and he carried on without interruption a course of lectures on various topics.

As the centennial year of 1866 approached, attention was turned toward making it the occasion for the enlargement of the facilities for the work of the institute. Circulars were sent out to the Conferences of the West and Northwest, and as a consequence more ministers were present from the patronizing territory. The need of a new building for dormitory and recitation purposes was very much felt, and steps were taken to secure the necessary funds. An agent was appointed to take collections. An association of ladies was also organized in the latter part of 1865. In the fall of 1866 Miss Frances E. Willard, the corresponding secretary, being called to Lima, N. Y., Dr. Kidder's daughter, Kate, was chosen to her place, and performed constant service until the building was finished and furnished. This society raised $30,000. As the structure was an adjunct to an institution which had its foundation in a woman's gift, it was properly determined to name it Heck Hall, after the woman who gathered the first Methodist congregation on this continent, Barbara Heck.

The claims of the institute, the doctor adds, " seem to be well received, and its friends cherish lively hopes of its more rapid and successful progress in the future, although well content with its usefulness in the past." At length " the plans of a new building having been duly canvassed and determined on, ground was broken in June of the year 1866, and the next month the corner stone was laid with appropriate ceremonies."

Further on he relates : " As our centenary building approached completion it devolved on me to devote considerable thought, time, and effort to suitable preparations for a public dedication on the fourth of July, 1867. Through the divine blessing, that event occurred under most favorable and encouraging auspices and with pecuniary results that astonished everybody. Money was pledged for the furnishing of the building in amounts practically sufficient, and with an enthusiasm that was most opportune."

" The last week in October," he writes, " witnessed our anniversary, which was well attended by visitors from abroad. The examinations were spirited, and the graduating class of twelve contained young men of excellent promise. By appointment I delivered the anniversary sermon. The subject was, 'The Responsibilities of the Christian Ministry.' By request of the joint board of trustees and visitors the sermon was published first in the *Northwestern Christian Advocate*, and afterwards in pamphlet form for free distribution particularly among young men. Its practical suggestions proved useful to many, and the demand for it continued during my connection with the Garrett Biblical Institute."

The school year of 1868 opened in the commodious appointments of the building dedicated the summer before. During the vacation the doctor had revised and republished the rules of the institute, with a students' pledge attached.

During May of this year he attended the sessions of the General Conference in Chicago, being a delegate from the Rock River Conference.

On the 23d of May the General Conference visited the institute and held an enthusiastic meeting in front of Heck Hall.

The two following years in the history of the institute were uneventful, but full of work. But in the year 1870, one of the professors having returned from abroad, discussions arose in the faculty meetings in reference to a proposed change of terms and vacations, the project being in Dr. Kidder's judgment unduly pressed. October 12, at a trustee meeting held in Chicago, a change of term and vacation was urged and finally carried, as he says, against his earnest protest.

It early became a part of the doctor's regular duty to travel about over the patronizing territory and visit the Conferences in the interest of the institute. Concerning these trips he says frankly: "I find less pleasure in visiting Conferences than I once did, perhaps owing to a greater fixedness of studious habits. Yet it seems to be at least an occasional duty to go abroad and represent our institution and confer with the ministers of different sections of the country." Instead of finding it an occasional, it became an increasingly frequent duty, occupying much of his time and carrying him over large tracts of territory. Besides his regular professional employment he also did a great amount of clerical work for the institute. Preliminary to the centennial year he was busy and spent a considerable time with architectural plans. His entry under this head is as follows: "Throughout the year, in addition to my regular duties in the institute, I was more or less occupied in perfecting plans for the purpose of building, together with improvements on the original building." The preparation and sending out of circulars in the interest of the institute seemed to fall entirely to him.

As acting president it was laid upon him to preside at the commencements, address the graduates, and confer the degrees. This task he always performed with the quiet grace peculiar to him. His last address as reported was, in part, as follows:

"The doctor said that he had chosen the motto, 'Be Representative Men,' from which to address them. He congratulated them on the successful issue of their studies, and spoke eloquently of their future mission. Men like them would always be wanted. The Conferences had thrown their doors open wide to receive them, and they were all now under appointments and had authority as pastors of churches. They would go to five different Annual Conferences and to four of the great Northwestern

States, where they would be brought into contact with hundreds of ministers and thousands of people. They were, therefore, now called of God to be representative men. All ministers were in a sense representative men. They would be severely criticised and meet with many obstacles; but he urged them not to shrink from the responsibility of being representative men, and to recognize it in all they should be called upon by God to do.

"In conclusion, he spoke some touching words of farewell in such affectionate terms as to move the audience to visible marks of feeling."

Dr. Kidder was not so much an acting president as that he was any the less a careful and painstaking professor in his special department. His feeling was that he could not be honest with himself unless he was honest with his pupils. One of the Conference visitors writes: "I will speak first of Dr. Kidder's department—'Homiletics and Pastoral Theology.' The young men possessed a correct knowledge of these branches that are so important to a Methodist minister and showed that they had carefully studied the Discipline.

"At this examination the class, with remarkable unanimity, commended extemporaneous preaching. Dr. Kidder is thoroughly Methodistic and will never contribute to the bondage of the pulpit by favoring the practice of reading. Careful preparation was urged as essential to successful extemporaneous discourse, and special prominence was also given to the fact that our most efficient ministers are those who go from their closet to the sacred desk. If all our young ministers could receive instruction in this department of theological study they would be more useful in their pulpit ministrations."

Dr. Kidder sought also to promote in every way the

16

religious standing of the institute and encourage the spiritual growth of the students. At the time that theological schools were in their formative state in our Church one of the stock objections was that the improvement of the young men in intellectual training would be at the expense of their piety, and the ministry would receive its accessions in the shape of well-adjusted mental machines without the requisite spiritual motive power. But thanks to the godly men who stood about the cradle of the Garrett Biblical Institute, this charge, so far as it is concerned, has never had the vantage ground of fact. The religious services regularly maintained by the students, always encouraged and often attended by the faculty, and especially the love feast which was held at each anniversary, showed that the old fire had not died out and also kindled afresh its flame.

The love feasts were particularly memorable, recalling the incidents that made Pentecost famous, and lingered like a rare illumination in the recollection of those favored with their enjoyment. One present writes:

"Many conscientious persons in our Church, while admitting the intellectual advantages of theological schools, claim that they send out ministers who seldom have the divine unction. This may be true in some instances, but the defect is in the individual and not in the influence of these institutions. If these objectors could have been with me in the annual love feast of the students, held in Heck Hall on Tuesday evening, their prejudices would have disappeared. Nearly all the young men spoke, referring to their present religious experience and their views of the holy office to which they had been called. The testimony of each was clear and scriptural and was given with such warmth and power that the large audience responded with shouts and amens. It was a real 'old-fashioned' Methodist class meeting, and among the happiest of the throng were the professors and other prominent ministers."

To this may be added the testimony of another:

"The spiritual side of student life in the Biblical Institute, as indicated at the students' love feast, is full of promise; it is healthy, individual, hopeful, and aggressive. And if there is any charm in old familiar terms— it is evangelical life; it is 'old-fashioned Methodism;' it is 'full salvation,' in doctrine and experience."

CHAPTER XXI.

Leaving Evanston—Professorship in the Drew Theological Seminary.

THE residence and service of Dr. Kidder in Evanston, so delightful, so abundant in labors, and so fruitful in results of good to the Church, was now about to close. Many reasons readily appear why it should have continued until the paralysis of death (nothing less) should check the busy toiler, but it might not be so.

It will be remembered that the terms of the institute year were so changed as to throw the long vacation into the summer. This Dr. Kidder thought to be a mistake, and for the disadvantage of the students, but still contenting himself with his protest expressed in the proper way, he yielded to the majority vote of the trustees and faculty. But scarcely had the school year of 1871 opened, when another event occurred, which not only surprised him, but resulted in the dissolution of his official connection with the institute.

This he recites in the following terms: " About the middle of April the faculty was called to Chicago to meet with the trustees and a committee of the trustees of the Northwestern University, to consider a scheme for the unification of the two institutions, the most striking feature of which appeared to contemplate the *subordination* of the Garrett Biblical Institute. On calling a meeting of the faculty at my library, on the evening of the second day after, I found my colleagues so far committed to the scheme referred to as to indicate that they were the abettors, if not the authors of it. From such a state of things I at once perceived that some decisive steps were necessary to prevent the consummation of a serious injury to a great interest of the Church.

"Two courses appeared open to me: either (1) to hold my position and contest the contemplated project; or, (2) defeat it by a flank movement which might be an easier and a more effectual mode of showing the bearings of so ill-judged a scheme.

"Feeling ready and prepared for either course, I nevertheless sought not to be guided by impulse, but rather by the spirit and providence of God. My first wish, therefore, was to ascertain whether I might not be needed in some other equally important field of labor. Having about that time received a catalogue of the Drew Theological Seminary from Dr. Foster, I thought proper to write to him inquiring as to a candidacy for the vacant chair of Dr. McClintock. So cordial was Dr. Foster's answer that I assented to become a candidate for the post at Madison, and on the 16th of May I received a telegram announcing my election to it."

In accordance with this situation, on the day of the anniversary for that year, June 29, his resignation was presented to the trustees and accepted by them in a series of resolutions. The letter of resignation and the resolutions were in the following terms:

"GARRETT BIBLICAL INSTITUTE, EVANSTON,
June 29, 1871.

"*To the Trustees:*

"Dear Brethren:—For reasons that seem to me to be weighty, I hereby offer my resignation of the professorship of practical theology, to take effect on the 1st of August next.

"Although called to another field of labor, you may well believe that after fifteen years of close personal identification with this institution I shall not cease to cherish an ardent desire for its highest welfare and largest usefulness in all time to come. Yours sincerely and fraternally, DANIEL P. KIDDER."

The trustees adopted the following resolutions:

"In accepting the resignation of D. P. Kidder, D.D., as professor, in this institution, of practical theology, we cannot suffer the severance of his official relation to this institution to occur without expressing our sincere regret and our high appreciation of his earnest devotion and faithful labors for fifteen years, and since its chartered existence, to promote the usefulness and elevate the character of this institution; and also our acknowledgment of his cordial and efficient cooperation with the trustees, and successful efforts in prosecuting and carrying out all their plans for the welfare of the institution and the elevation of ministerial character and education.

"*Resolved*, That we tender to Dr. Kidder our most ardent wishes for his usefulness and success in the new and important post to which he has been called in a kindred institution and field of labor, and pray he may be equally and more abundantly a blessing to it than he has been to the one he is now leaving."

This year there was an unusually large number of the alumni present at their general reunion. Suitable resolutions were passed by them expressive of their appreciation of his very efficient services as their former instructor, and of the loss to the institution in his resignation.

" A step so important in my history," says the doctor, " seems entitled to a brief note of personal explanation. For the general principles by which it was governed I can refer to several paragraphs in my work on the pastorate, written in the advocacy of the itinerancy and in the tenor of my long-established convictions. When writing those paragraphs I did not specially think of their application to myself, having for a considerable time, more particularly since the death of Dr. Dempster, regarded myself providentially called to remain in the post I held in the Garrett Biblical Institute.

" The first serious thought of leaving as a possible duty was suggested by the circumstances already related. The almost immediate and striking coincidence of an official call to a professorship identical in character with my own in a section of the Church to which I had strong attachments and where I believed that my field as a preacher of the Gospel would be greatly enlarged, made a deep impression on my mind. In fact, never in my life had the vocation *interna* and *extera* been more strikingly correspondent. According to my former belief the usefulness of this institution for some time to come is likely to be diminished by an arrangement adopted against my protest and with which I cannot co-operate heartily. Not feeling in any way responsible for a diminution of interest forced upon me by measures which I resisted conscientiously, but could not control, I nevertheless felt a great sense of relief in being providentially excused from continued work under their depressing influence. Corresponding with this there sprang up in my mind a new ambition to be useful by a legitimate use of my talent and experience as a teacher of young ministers in a section of the Church where formerly I had done so much preliminary work as a preacher and Sunday school editor.

"With these views and feelings my course was plain, and when properly comprehended did not cause me a moment's hesitation. I moreover had the satisfaction of being confirmed in my own impressions and judgments by the disinterested advice of all, or nearly all, the intelligent friends with whom I thought proper to consult on the subject. While they uniformly expressed regret to have me leave, their judgment seemed as uniformly to correspond with my own. Indeed, I had my own regrets at the idea of leaving, especially at the thought of becoming severed from my long and agreeable associations with Judge Goodrich, with whom I had acted so pleasantly and hopefully in the foundation and development of the Garrett Biblical Institute from the day when its idea first dawned upon the mind of Mrs. Garrett. Nevertheless, as that association must some time be severed, I believed that occurring now and in the circumstances it did, it would strengthen the judge and his associate trustees in taking measures for the future good of the institution, perhaps even more than by my continuance as heretofore. In this belief I became fully confirmed before leaving Evanston by various circumstances, not the least significant of which was the entire abandonment of the project of making a common president of the Northwestern University and the Garrett Biblical Institute. Corresponding to this was a well-defined development in the minds of the trustees of the latter of a purpose to elect their own president hereafter, and thus set at rest various sources of agitation and irritation."

Distance, however, did not diminish his love for his first field of professional labors. Shortly after his departure the institute suffered its great loss by the Chicago fire. The income was reduced $7,000. In response to the call for assistance he promptly reported by a generous subscription.

Drew Seminary opened in November of 1867. For some time before this Dr. Kidder had been in correspondence with Dr. McClintock, answering his inquiries as to the ends to be accomplished in such an institution and the means of attaining them. In a letter still preserved, dated March 18, 1867, Dr. Kidder argues strongly for the elevation of the standard of scholarship requisite to an entrance upon the curriculum to the seminary. In part he says: " Our ten and one half years of experience in this institution [Garrett Biblical] have been a continual struggle to elevate the standard of preparation for theological study in our Church. For a long period the great majority of students seeking the advantages here offered were not only nongraduates, but very indifferent academic scholars. They supposed that a short course of study in a theological institution was all they needed —a supposition encouraged by the flattery of injudicious friends, often by the urgency of presiding elders, and sometimes by persons of still higher positions in the Church. The same class of advice, seconded by the influence of many college officers, operated to urge graduates of colleges directly into Conferences without previously studying theology.

" Against all this we have succeeded in establishing a fine *esprit du corps* in favor of collegiate graduation prior to entrance upon our regular course, so much so that many who thought at first that they could only take a partial course have paused in the midst of it to make up a collegiate course as essential to graduation in the Garrett Biblical Institute. Thus it happens that a large majority of those we have catalogued under preparatory studies are now actually pursuing a college course at the Northwestern University and other colleges.

" I dwell upon this point because it was only after considerable experimenting that we found it to be the key of our difficulties. By the course we are now taking we strengthen the colleges and have a right to demand their hearty cooperation."

His interest in Drew Seminary from the very beginning of its history, and the fact that he was called to occupy the chair of his lifelong friend, Dr. McClintock, rendered his coming to the seminary a matter of gratification to him. His welcome was assured and warm. Dr. Foster, the president, wrote him: " I need hardly say that it gives me great pleasure to congratulate you and the seminary on your election." Dr. Strong wrote: " I need hardly repeat what you have already learned, that we are all highly gratified at your appointment here. Let me ask that you will bring your family directly to my house, until your own arrangements for housekeeping shall be completed." This offer was accepted gratefully.

He first met with his fellow-professors on the evening of September 13, 1871. " This meeting," he says, " was suggestive of excellent promise. I am greatly pleased with my associates, their evident competence, their friendly spirit, their earnest purpose."

The year proved to be one of solid work and no little interest. His department required organization and received it. The classes were not large, but contained some men of promise who appreciated their advantages.

"I had occasion to prepare some new lectures, but as the topics had been well studied the labor was not taxing. Professorial life in a theological institution is necessarily one of routine. That routine, however, always had for me a charm. I can truly say that the quiet years spent at Drew Theological Seminary were to me as full of interest as they were of work.

"In addition to my regular tasks I also, by special request of the trustees, took charge of the library and did no little work in arrangement, classification, and cataloguing. Later on I incorporated the library of the late Dr. McClintock with that of the institution."

In 1872 there was a change in the presidency, Dr. Foster being elected bishop. In 1876 occurred the failure of Mr. Drew and the cutting off of the resources of the seminary. "This calamity," he adds, "gave the faculty no little anxiety and extra work."

To Dr. Kidder there fell the special labor of taking charge of the accounts of the Janes Memorial Professorship. He conducted all the correspondence for this fund, prepared and sent out the circulars, receipts, and certificates. This taxing labor was continued by him through four years. At this period, too, much of his time was occupied with the correspondence that usually falls to the president.

He also, with the other members of the faculty, took the president's classes, so that he might be free to travel about in the interest of the crippled endowment. In addition to this he transacted with the students the entire loan business of the seminary, disbursing the funds of the Board of Education, the New York Educational Society, and the McClintock Association.

Without question he allowed himself to be overworked.

His zeal for any task laid upon him by his Church, his loyalty to duty which made it instinctively impossible for him to shirk, and his unwillingness to decline the tax always imposed upon ability—all this conspired to heap upon him labor so great that there was left to him but a remnant of time and strength for the preparation necessary to a proper appearance before his classes, and had he failed in the least in his attendance, attention, or thoroughness as an instructor, there would have been an adequate cause.   But he did not.

It was not made known to him directly or even by intimation that there was the least dissatisfaction with either his methods or the results that appeared in his department.   Indeed the rather, when at one time a measure was mooted that might have disturbed the tenure of some of the faculty, he was confidentially informed that the scheme was not at all aimed at him.   So far as he knew, or had any opportunity of knowing, the students, the faculty, the trustees, and the friends of the seminary were pleased with his work.   As well as he could judge from word or sign he rendered competent service.   Had it been otherwise, had he been favored with the least hint that his work did not meet the established test of usefulness, his prompt resignation would have relieved the trustees of the necessity of an act which is sufficiently characterized in its recital.

Under date of June 8, 1880, Dr. Kidder makes this entry in his diary: " I received a startling piece of news!" This was nothing less than the communication to him of a plan arranged in secret, whereby a majority of the Board of Trustees had committed themselves to the purpose of displacing him at their approaching annual meeting and electing his successor.   Outside of the faculty there were four gentlemen, who afterward attained to the episcopacy, who took a position or expressed an opinion with regard to this act. One of them conveyed to Dr. Kidder the information of this plot, which otherwise would have burst upon him with all the surprise designed to crush an unsuspecting victim. Another, giving personal attention to the animus and details of the movement, wrote to him that " the work of disaffection had been well done." A third, in a manner yet more public, visited the whole affair with his unsparing strictures. While yet another, over his own signature, quoted the sentiment of a high official of the Church to the effect that the action of the trustees was " an outrage."

Seven days after the first announcement to him of this " startling piece of news," Dr. Kidder sent the following note to the Board of Trustees : " Brethren :—I hereby respectfully tender my resignation as Professor of Practical Theology, to take effect on the adjournment of the New Jersey Conference in March, 1881, or sooner should a duly elected successor be desired to occupy the chair."

He continued his instructions in the seminary as before until the opening of the following spring. " Early in March, 1881," he writes, " I closed my lecture courses and instructions in Drew Theological Seminary and proceeded to meet the New Jersey Conference, at the adjournment of which my resignation of the chair of Practical Theology had been planned to take effect. I thus rounded up a full quarter of a century of continuous service to the Church as a theological professor."

CHAPTER XXII.

Secretary of the Board of Education.

ON leaving Drew Seminary it was Dr. Kidder's expectation to enter again the pastorate. But his career as a public official in the Church was not yet closed. On November 9, 1880, he was unanimously chosen Secretary of the Board of Education. He accepted the office with the intention of performing its duties gratuitously, so long as he held his chair at Drew.

Within a week after his election he took possession of the papers of the Board, and by an arrangement with the Book Agents, he was provided with desk room at the Book Concern, 805 Broadway, New York.

His choice for this position was widely hailed as one of the fittest that could be made, and the spirit and system with which he began his duties showed that it was his intent that this interest, in some respects the most important which he had been called to serve, should be favored in every respect with a healthy stimulus and a thorough improvement. A correspondent wrote thus to one of the Church papers: " During our recent visit to New York we had the pleasure of meeting Dr. Kidder, Secretary of the Board of Education of the Methodist Episcopal Church. We were greatly pleased to find him entering upon his new field of labor with zeal and purpose to accomplish more through this agency than has been done heretofore. He is making himself familiar

with the details of the office, and good results may be
expected from his labors.   There are more demands
upon the Board for assistance than its present resources
will meet, but he hopes to devise means by which additional aid may be obtained.   Dr. Kidder will make himself felt in this neglected department of Christian labor."

About this time he was chosen one of the eighty delegates to represent the Methodist Episcopal Church in
the Ecumenical Conference to be held in London the
following September.   But burdened as he was by labors
in two important fields, judging, too, that it was not best
to absent himself from his new office, he declined.

His first work of a public character was to prepare for
the Church *Manual* such matter as belonged to his department.

"From this time forward," he says, " my leisure or unoccupied time was diligently employed in correspondence,
circular writing, and other duties of my new and congenial office."   It was congenial, it may be added, in
large part, because he felt toward the Board of Education the interest the father has in his child.   His efforts
toward the systematic assistance of young men preparing
for the ministry—efforts dating back to the beginning of
his incumbency at Evanston—were really the inspiration
and origin of the association of which he was now so
properly the active officer.

Under the title "Board of Education," Bishop Simpson's *Cyclopedia of Methodism* has the following : "The
General Conference of the Methodist Episcopal Church
of 1860 appointed a special committee to report and determine a plan for an Educational Board.   No action was
taken until 1868, when the Committee on Education reported a plan for the organization of a Board to consist

of twelve trustees, six of whom should be ministers (two of them bishops), and six laymen, of which number five should be a quorum." This is interesting, but it is not sufficient. It is history, but not ancient history.

In his letter to Judge Goodrich, laying out the needed plans for the proposed institute at Evanston, Dr. Kidder says: "It must be projected on a large yet practicable scale, and be made as strong as possible to aid indigent young men who are called to preach. Thus alone can it compete with the urgency of presiding elders who hurry young men into the field prematurely." This was in January, 1856.

Two years after this, under date of July 5, we have this interesting entry in the doctor's private diary: "I spent my morning in a faculty meeting, in which action was taken in favor of organizing a Ministerial Education Society." The latter part of the same week he writes: "I met on a committee to form a constitution for a Ministerial Education Society." Ten days later he reports another meeting for the same purpose. The work of writing the constitution fell to him. On the following day he enters, "I devoted the morning to the preparation of the constitution for the Ministerial Education Society;" and the day after his record is, "I finished the constitution." Four days after this it is noted, "I read the life of Cornelius and gathered some valuable hints for our Ministerial Education Society." On the fourth of August following there was a convention in Chicago in behalf of ministerial education which he attended, and describes as passing off "hopefully as well as pleasantly." The third day after this he says: "I met in Chicago the committee on constitution for Ministerial Education Society. We had a pleasant interview and unanimous action was taken agreeing to call a convention at the time and place of the next session of the Rock River Conference." The next item of interest in this connection is to the effect that he prepared an article on this subject for the *Northwestern Christian Advocate.*

The convention above referred to was held at Waukegan, Ill., on the afternoon of August 27. This he attended, and he observes that it resulted in the organization of a society. That evening, he says, " I spent in writing a circular to the Conferences concerning this society." The next day at 8 A. M., he adds, " I met the Board of Ministerial Education Society." These early allusions contain yet another reference to the circulars prepared by him for distribution to the Conferences.

Thus fully ten years before the organization of the Board of Education as related in the Cyclopedia, a strong Western movement in the same direction was developed and launched. It had been born also to live and grow, and in the year 1867, during the summer, Dr. Kidder writes: " I gave my personal attention and no small proportion of my time to the inauguration of efforts to raise funds to aid worthy young men called to the ministry in prosecuting their education. For this object I accepted the Corresponding Secretaryship of the Ministerial Education Society, of which I had been a director from the first, wrote and printed circulars, visited several Conferences, and advocated the cause by my voice and pen as extensively as opportunity offered. Notwithstanding somewhat serious obstacles in the way, good results followed directly and became a hopeful augury for still greater success in the future." The next year we find him again engaged in the same work, and in the follow-

17

ing year, in the report of the Garrett Biblical Institute, he speaks strongly and at length on this subject, as follows: "The only thing now lacking to the complete success of the enterprise committed to our charge is an adequate provision of funds to aid worthy candidates for the ministry and missionary work who need assistance to enable them to accomplish the requisite studies promptly and thoroughly. Up to this time the educational benevolence of our Church has been chiefly directed to the establishment of institutions of learning of various grades. Now that this object is so far attained that we have a complete system of seminaries, colleges, and theological schools, it would seem that we ought, as the next object of connectional effort, to provide means for enabling young men among us moved of the Holy Ghost to preach the Gospel, however poor, to have access to the full advantage of our entire system of Church institutions. We would not in any case recommend aid to an extent that will render personal exertion unnecessary. But knowing that many worthy young men feel compelled to abandon their studies prematurely, and that many more think it impossible to commence a theological or even classical course for lack of means, we would plead with the Church to come to their aid. We would stimulate their own highest exertions by timely encouragement given in so generous a manner as to cement the affections of struggling young men to the Church which needs their services and yet promises but a limited pecuniary reward. The activity and liberality of most other churches in this matter is a wholesome example to us." These words were addressed to the General Conference which, as related at the outset of this sketch, organized the Board of Education of our Church.

This action of the General Conference was the outgrowth of the movements set on foot during the year 1866, the centenary year, commemorating the hundredth anniversary of the introduction of Methodism into the United States. Dr. Kidder had been appointed a member of the committee to arrange for a proper celebration of this event. "Toward the end of January, 1865," he writes, "I was occupied with revising and printing the by-laws and general scheme of the Ministerial Education Society, so as to have it in readiness for the consideration of the Centenary Committee, of which I had been appointed a member."

Two sessions of this committee were held, one in February in Cleveland, one in New York in November, 1865. He attended both of these meetings and reported, "They were full of interest and responsibility, involving very earnest discussions, but resulting in a harmonious plan for the exercises and efforts of the centenary period."

In the General Conference of 1868 he was a member of the Committee of Education. As already related, this was the committee which reported the plan for the organization of the Board of Education.

The peculiar gratification he felt may then be imagined as he took into his hands the activities of an institution whose urgency he had been one of the first to voice, whose germ he had helped to plant, whose growth had been under his fostering attention, and whose completion into a connectional department reported in conspicuous lines the shaping impress of his thought.

"In January, February, and the early part of March, 1881," he writes, "I did double duty, (1) in completing my year's instruction and general work in Drew Theological Seminary, and (2) in preparatory work in behalf of the Board of Education. Neither branch of effort seriously interfered with the other. With the duties of the first I had become familiar during twenty-five years of consecutive experience. For those of the latter I had been in some measure prepared by my twelve years of connection with the headquarters of the Methodist Episcopal Church as Sunday School Editor and Corresponding Secretary of the Sunday School Union and Tract Society, and also by my experience in organizing the Ministerial Education Society of the Northwest, which, in point of fact, led directly to the organization of the Board of Education. Furthermore, my extensive and continuous correspondence and intercourse with candidates for the ministry from 1856 downward, had enabled me especially to appreciate the circumstances and wants of the youth of the Church, who are and ought to be aspiring to qualifications for public usefulness.

" In such ways, if not by natural tastes, it seemed to me that I had been providentially prepared for the new and responsible duties to which I was at this period called. I therefore gladly, if not efficiently, devoted my leisure to the preliminary work which was found to be necessary to a proper development of an interest of the Church which up to this time had not received the attention it deserved."

In March, 1881, having finished his engagement at Drew Seminary, he writes, " I commenced an active term of service as Corresponding Secretary of the Board of Education, adding to my previous and preliminary work the visitation of Annual Conferences for the purpose of publicly explaining the claims of the Board and enlisting efforts in its behalf."

The next month he began the preparation of his program for Children's Day. This was a new departure in the arrangements for that important and increasingly popular anniversary. Heretofore the Church had issued no official program, and as a consequence many enterprising publishers had entered the field with the effect of selling large numbers of Orders of Service, each one with independent views. There was, therefore, no unanimity of thought, no one plan was carried out, the meaning of the day was obscured, its mission was not presented at all, or in an insufficient or distorted manner. The performance left behind no impression that was of special value to the Church.

Thus was the day in many quarters diverted from its appointed purpose, and its pecuniary results with increasing volume were flowing into channels outside of the treasury of the Board. The failure to correct this must not be longer tolerated, so Dr. Kidder thought. Not, however, by advising, lecturing, or scolding his constituency did he attempt a remedy, but by the better method of a substitute—an improved program, with the imprint of the Church. In this way it was his aim to emphasize the object of the day, explain the mission of the Board of Education, and recommend its work, giving in an attractive form such facts and figures as would make the occasion a memory of information and inspiration, and secure for the cause it represented the hospitable thought and cordial support of all the lovers of Christ and Christian education. These official programs at once became popular; they were a new strand in the connectional bond that united a great Church.

On the same day all over the world the young united in the same service, were taught in the same beautiful and impressive manner the same lessons. The Board of Education became at once one of the best known institutions of the Church, although one of the youngest, so that even the Missionary Society, that had contentedly jogged along in its dignified conservatism, gave incohate indications of desiring also a special day and a prepared program! Beginning with this his first year, these programs were continued during the entire period of Dr. Kidder's incumbency with improved features, and resulting from the first in enlarged collections.

Their preparation cost him a vast amount of thought as well as labor. He sent out and asked for information and hints for the coming Children's Day, and more than six months in advance he would examine this correspondence in making up the forthcoming Order of Service.

He labored with the problems involved in the theme to be developed (for each program had a special subject or title which it unfolded, in songs, addresses, and representations, leading in each case up to the central purpose of the Board and its work), the matter to be used, and the character of the music. This task grew to be with him each year more serious, for the reason that he wished in each case to make the past a point of departure, going on toward something better. Thus we read in his diary: " Engaged most of the day in perfecting details of the program which in view of its objects and the numbers to be printed, I am seeking to make as perfect as possible." Again we read : " I grappled with the task of preparing my program, which I find by no means an easy one on account of the high standard I wish to maintain."

With his usual fertility in expedients he conceived, during the summer of 1883, the plan of having a medal struck off both in silver and in gilt in commemoration of the approaching centennial of Methodism. These medals were to be distributed as a feature of the next Children's Day services. He concluded that the sale of this medal would bring in large returns to the Children's Day Fund. Upon consulting with Bishop Simpson and others, the project was approved. At once he set about its preparation, and the circulation of information concerning it. In due time the medal appeared. The program for that year also brought out the centennial feature of the epoch, and both went everywhere, until the medal became as familiar as current coin, and the centenary of organic Methodism in the United States was imbedded as an imperishable record in the minds of millions of the young. Financially the project was a success of phenomenal proportions, the receipts amounting to an excess of $56,000, making the income of his office since he took it $116,000. Conceiving that a second crop was possible for the Church from this fervid soil, he issued announcements of the sale of the medals for Christmas of that year. Concerning these he reports that there was a great demand. In short, the medal abides still as the sensation of that period, and is of itself a monument to his quiet but effective genius for doing good.

The original idea of the projectors of the Board of Education had been to create a fund from the income of which all loans and gifts should be distributed. Dr. Kidder was convinced that this was not the best way, that the people who furnished the collections would be better satisfied, and the more certainly could be trusted to continue and increase their annual gifts, if they saw that the entire amount each year, after paying legitimate expenses, was disbursed to relieve the largest number of worthy students. This opinion urged convincingly by him prevailed, and became the practice of the Board.

Although he was now approaching a time of life when travel had lost for him much of its exhilaration, and home and the undisturbed opportunities for reading and study were proportionately attractive, still he never relaxed his practice of visiting the Conferences in the interest of his work. He recognized the fact that the society he represented was not only comparatively young, but that there was not a clear view of its objects and plans among the preachers and churches. He therefore traveled widely through the bounds of our Methodism, addressing the preachers in Conference session and the people at the anniversaries, besides meeting with the Committees on Education, and assisting them with facts and figures and points in the making up of their reports. Every spring and fall during his term of office he made these tours throughout the connection.

Thus it came to pass when he let these responsibilities fall from his weary hand this society was one of the best understood in its mission and method.

The composition and copying of his annual reports was very laborious. Besides this his pen was all the time busy in contributions to the *Manual*, in the preparation of circulars to bishops, presiding elders, to Conferences, to pastors, to Sunday school superintendents, circulars for collections, Children's Day circulars, letters to the children—all written out by his own hand, and proofs personally revised. So also were the Children's Day programs in almost every case. The toil of these tasks and the weariness of their details he was willing to endure, being convinced of the value of this kind of work in advancing the popularity of his cause with a reading public.

There were besides letters to be written in great numbers. This was a task of unceasing pressure. A large part of this correspondence related to the proper distribution of the annual appropriations for loans to students. "While some of the duties of the office," he writes, "especially those of receipting and accounting for funds paid could be appropriately transferred to assistants, I never felt at liberty to surrender to anyone the investigations necessary to determining to whom loans should be made and in what amounts. Besides I found the loan accounts in so chaotic a state, that I saw the necessity of personal experiment and study as a means of devising and perfecting some easy yet effective system of accounts specially adapted to the nature of the business to be transacted, including its relations both to individuals and to institutions."

His disposition to be scrupulously correct in dealing with the money of the people given for a special purpose was not always generously seconded by those holding responsible positions in the Church. He had difficulty in securing the statistics necessary to make a complete task of his reports and estimates under this head. With all his press of other work he was compelled to write more than once to those in charge of our educational institutions, sometimes to as many as fifty at a time. We can readily imagine the annoyance such looseness and carelessness must have caused him, accustomed as he was to consider accuracy and promptness architectural lines in the structure of conscience.

At the very beginning of his taking office he was encountered by an evil practice that was rapidly sapping the vitality of the society, and making the hope of its usefulness a vanity. The situation may be best stated by one who gave the unpleasant facts to the open air of public print. He says: " The Children's Day collections which find their way to the treasury are inexplicably small, amounting to less than a thousand dollars. Where collections are taken year by year, they are in most cases retained for the purposes of a particular school or applied to some local institution." This practice of mis-appropriating in whole or part the funds raised on Children's Day, this pious pilfering from a sacred trust, pained Dr. Kidder like an affliction, and by circulars, communications in the Church press, consultations with the bishops, by addresses at Conference sessions, and urgent appeals in the Committee of the General Conference, he opposed it. His success in his office made this resistance yet more necessary, for as the fund under his management rapidly increased, it became proportionately popular, and was eagerly plucked at by those who (to be charitable) forgot that by explicit legislation these moneys were dedicated to a given and connectional object, namely, the assistance of young men preparing for the ministry.

The corresponding secretary never relaxed his vigilance nor slackened the vigor of his opposition to these spoliations. And although one of the champions of the sectional and exigent theory charged him with " undisciplinary proceedings," his victory was finally complete. This very one, who embellished his speech with Italics, acceded to the wisdom of accepting a revised position, and these perversions of the Children's Day Fund became as unpopular as they were illegal.

As at the beginning of his term of office he met with a practice which periled the usefulness of the Board of Education by the misappropriation of its funds, so at the close he encountered a proposition which in his judgment menaced its future by abolishing its individuality.

This was a plan styled " The Unification and Consolidation of the Church Benevolences." It contemplated the combining together of some of the societies and the practical absorption of others, the Board of Education being merged into the Freedmen's Aid and Southern Education Society, and the office removed to Cincinnati. This scheme he regarded as worse than wild, and fraught with untold mischief to all the great benevolences of the Church.

Being appointed by the General Conference (1884) a member of the commission to consider this plan, he prepared a paper expressive of his views. By those who read it his argument was pronounced complete, sweeping, and irrefutable. This document was passed into the hands of his successor in office, and was unfortunately lost. A loss indeed! as otherwise some of its facts and reasonings might be profitably quoted as an antidote against any future symptoms of a like dementia. However, the plan with a sonorous title perished in the process of incubation, and is not likely to disturb the future with anything more substantial than its memory.

It was in the latter part of 1886 that he prepared this paper, and it was the opinion of his friends that the effort of its composition, added to incessant labors long continued, was too much for his strength. The indefatigable toiler, unsparing of self in the service of his Church, began to show signs of breaking—signs that even his brave spirit was constrained to recognize.

Restless nights following days of relentless work hindered the needed repair of brain and body.   From frequent entries in his diary, brief but significant, it was plain that all the horrors of insomnia were upon him. He maintained the unequal conflict as long as he could. With a purpose unflinching, but with a trembling frame, he held himself up to his task, until he found that it was not worth while to mount guard any longer over a treasury empty of force and effect.   The dreaded time had come.   His office as held by him no longer represented full service wrought, and he resigned in July, 1887.

CHAPTER XXIII.

Literary Work.

DR. KIDDER became early a writer of books. His record in this department parallels well his work as professor, secretary, and editor.

Upon his return from Brazil and while traveling through the West, he fell in with Joseph Smith, the prophet of Mormonism. His attention was thus turned to the study of this superstition, and the result was his first book, in 1842, entitled *Mormonism and the Mormons; an Historical Review of the Rise and Progress of the Sect Self-styled Latter-Day Saints.* The press notices of this book from every quarter were unvaryingly favorable. "This book is better adapted to check the progress of Mormonism among those who read it than any other publication which has hitherto met our observation." "All who desire to know the truth and the whole truth with respect to Mormonism will find it here condensed into a volume lucidly written and carefully compiled. This is by far the best work we have seen on the subject of which it treats, and hence we commend it to our readers without reserve or qualification." "The author shows himself fully competent to the work he took in hand, and has embodied in these pages that kind of information which should be disseminated through the churches far and wide." "A searching and vigorous exposure of the blasphemies, impostures, and evil practices of the Mormon leaders, and of the absurd infatuations of their deluded followers." " The author has given us a full-length likeness of the Mormon monster in the West, knowing that to be induced to shun the father of lies we have only to see him in his detestable deformity." These, selected from among testimonials of different denominations in and out of the country, are specimens of the general approval of the author's object and the complimentary estimate of the manner in which he had executed his purpose. This work was quoted as a standard up to the date of its last issue, 1882.

During his residence in Brazil he came across a work which he deemed of sufficient importance to give to the larger patronage of an English reading public. He therefore published it in 1844, under the title, *Demonstration of the Necessity of Abolishing a Constrained Clerical Celibacy; exhibiting the Evils of that Institution and the Remedy. By the Right Rev. D. A. Feijo, Senator and ex-Regent of the Empire of Brazil, Bishop-elect of Marianna, etc. Translated from the Portuguese, with an Introduction and Appendix, by the Rev. D. P. Kidder, A.M.* " A bold but unsuccessful effort was made soon after the organization of the present form of government in Brazil to abolish clerical celibacy. The author of the work before us took an active part in this endeavor and published this treatise, for a translation of which we are indebted to the accomplished Editor of the *Sunday School Advocate*. It is a production distinguished for its force of reasoning and extent of authorities cited, and discusses boldly the very important question of clerical celibacy in the Roman Catholic Church." This extract is from one of the many notices given of this book by the press of that time. Another states: " The book was printed for private circulation and would probably have been lost to the world had not the Rev. Mr. Kidder, a missionary of the Methodist Episcopal Church in the United States, during his residence in Brazil become acquainted with its author, and received from him a copy, from which he has made the translation before us. 'The Roman Catholic,' says Mr. Kidder, 'will here find a frank and fearless discussion of an important branch of his Church polity, substantiated at every step by venerated names and acknowledged authorities.'" By a subcommittee, appointed to examine the work, it was warmly recommended for publication to the Book Committee of our Church. From all directions, in the most emphatic terms of approval, this work was received by a light-loving public. All the religious papers of different denominations noticed it favorably, and in many and warm terms Mr. Kidder was commended for his enterprise in issuing the book.

The next year our author gave to the press a work entitled *Sketches of a Residence and Travels in Brazil;* embracing Historical and Geographical Notices of the Empire and its several Provinces; in two volumes, 8vo, with illustrations. In the preparation of this work he drew not only upon his own observations in South America, but was also furnished with documents by the Brazilian consul in New York, and consulted original sources at Washington.

This was a new field of labor, not only for the pen of of a Methodist preacher, but also for an American author. "No book was more required by the wants of the age than this." So says one enthusiastic reviewer. He continues: "Here we have two volumes replete with well-assorted facts, giving a distinct view of the origin, history, and present condition of the empire of Brazil. The whole is absorbingly interesting, and we take pleasure in recommending the book to the attention of others." In a like strain and with lengthy comments it was noticed and reviewed by the religious press on both sides of the ocean.

All the New York papers gave it prominent consideration, some of them, like the *Commercial Advertiser*, in more than one issue, and with extracts, comments, and complimentary notices that filled more than a column. The leading journals of other American cities heartily indorsed it. In the first year after its issue it went through three editions. It was the subject of the leading article in the *Princeton Review*, covering twenty pages; the *Methodist Quarterly Review* gave it nearly thirty pages; and it was discussed in two succeeding papers in the *United States Magazine*.

Its reception in England, however, was, if possible, even more friendly. *The London Critic* noticed it with four pages closely printed. *The London Athenæum, The Journal of Belles-Lettres*, and *The British Quarterly Advertiser* all followed suit. *The London Atlas* said : " It is the best work we have on Brazil." By the *Spectator* it was welcomed as an addition to the British Library. The Brazilian minister at Washington was particularly pleased with the work, and so expressed himself in an autograph letter to Mr. Kidder.

None of the good things said about the work so much pleased the author as the following remark in a review in the *Religious Spectator* by Dr. Sprague: " It is fitted indirectly to be an efficient auxiliary in the great cause of truth against error, holiness against sin." In reply to this Dr. Kidder wrote to Dr. Sprague: " Had I not intended to give my work such a character I should not have been justified in writing it. Had I failed in my design the book might have pleased certain critics more, but in my judgment had better never have seen the light."

As to the literary merit of the work, it may suffice to quote the closing words in the *Princeton Review* : " In point of style the work is highly meritorious. The natural transparency of the diction presents nothing to interrupt our easy progress ; and on some occasions the author rises with his subject to what we consider the best manner of simple narrative. The book is worthy of a place among the more elevated productions of our national literature." The illustrations in this book, it may be added, were nearly all from original sketches by the author.

An edition in reduced size was issued for the specific object of supplying the district school libraries of the State of New York. This was done in answer to a request from those prominent in charge of them and who urged upon the publishers the importance and feasibility of such a venture. The Superintendent of Common Schools for the city and county of New York wrote : " I take pleasure in recommending this as a work well adapted for introduction into our district school libraries, where it will be sought after by the multitude of our youthful readers with avidity and read with entertainment and instruction." From the office of the State Superintendent of Common Schools at Albany came these words : " I have perused with great interest and pleasure your valuable *Sketches of a Residence and Travels in Brazil,* and most fully concur in the commendations which it has received from the periodical press of every class in our country. The character of the work in all respects is such in my judgment as to render

18

it a valuable accession to any library." Still further. The well-known Josiah Holbrook expressed himself in the following glowing terms : " From fifteen to eighteen years ago I wrote much and spoke more to give an impetus to school libraries, and am hence interested in everything respecting them, especially the selection of books. The deep interest and rich instruction I have received from perusing and reperusing *Sketches of Travels in Brazil*, by Rev. D. P. Kidder, have impressed me with the entire fitness of this work in subject, spirit, and style, for this important class of libraries. I would most gladly contribute my small mite to give this excellent work a place in all such collections through our country."

The work was superseded only by itself in a different form. In 1857 the author was associated with Rev. J. C. Fletcher, a missionary of the Presbyterian Church, in the preparation of the book under the title of *Brazil and the Brazilians*. It had a large sale, and went rapidly through successive editions until the ninth, in 1879, revised and brought down to date. "It is regarded as the best authority extant upon the subject. Much of its contents is embodied in one of the Blue Books of the British Parliament."

A year or two of instruction in his department at Evanston convinced Dr. Kidder of the great want of a compact and comprehensive text-book on homiletics, and he says :

"According to a plan I have for some time meditated, and which has been encouraged by all whom I have thought proper to consult on the subject, including some of the bishops and book agents, I at this period commenced the systematic preparation of a text-book on homiletics. I found that the task was highly agreeable and directly in the line of preparation for my regular duties in the institute."

This was in the winter of 1859–60, the first winter vacation of the institute, and he spent it for the most part in New York, busy in the Astor Library, the libraries of the New York and Protestant Episcopal Seminaries, and the library of the Book Room, consulting authorities and collecting material. He spent a day some time after this with Professor Fisk, of Chicago, listening to a rehearsal of Fitche's lectures on homiletics, and in conversation on kindred topics.

He had many interruptions, and was forced to confess that " bookmaking does not proceed rapidly."

It is finished at last, and we can imagine the thrill of gratification with which he made the following entry: " Having by hard and constant labor up to the middle of February (1864) completed my manuscript, I thought it best to go to New York and attend to at least the commencement of its publication."

It was favorably received by competent critics on both sides of the water. Among the English comments may be quoted the following: " This is a systematic work, embracing every branch of the subject, and is without exception the most thorough treatise we have ever met with."

Another: " In the work before us the author appears to us in a new character, and to greater advantage than before. The examination of it has given us a satisfaction almost amounting to delight. It is both Christian and scholarly ; without pretense, and without ostentation, solid but not cumbrous, and full without being tediously minute."

From the American comments: " In its plan, spirit,

and execution we know of no better treatise on preaching than this. The author has clearly enough maintained his own individuality as a thinker, and therefore we find in this useful treatise very much that is fresh, not a little that is new, and some reflections of a practical character worth more than any theories however beautiful."

Another says: " Suggestiveness is the controlling feature of this work. You are in a state of wonderment, when once through it, at the immense field traversed, with gratitude inexpressible at the grand views in regions beyond, to the verge of which you have been delightfully led by a hand so loving. On sermon-making proper, the author is a Saul among all the giants. The sixth, seventh, and eighth chapters are worth all the Claudes, Sturtevants, etc., gone before. If with this book the main difficulties of preaching do not disappear, it were wisdom for anyone to retire to private life."

Dr. McClintock wrote: " The preface to this book modestly gives as its aim ' to aid clerical students and junior ministers in preparing for their life work.' Considered with reference to this proposed end, I know of no rival to the book, nor indeed any that approaches it in excellence. It exhibits all the essential requisites of a good text-book for students: simplicity of arrangement, comprehensiveness of outline, directness of statement, and fullness of illustrations, along with necessary brevity and compactness. The young men of this generation who commence their study of the art of preaching under the guidance of this book have greater advantages than any generation of their predecessors. But Dr. Kidder has far transcended the modest aim of his preface. His book is not only an admirable text-book for students, but it is also one of the most complete historical, scientific treatises on preaching that have appeared in any country. He has thoroughly mastered the subject, not only in its nature, but also in its history and literature, and has digested his ample material into a compact and pregnant treatise, covering both history and practice. This commendation may seem very strong, but I think I am fully entitled to use it. Some years ago I contemplated the preparation of such a book, and gathered and studied all the leading writers on the subject. The opinion which I offer is, therefore, not a random judgment. I trust that Dr. Kidder's book will find its way not merely into the hands of students, but of all our ministers."

Some years later, when Dr. Kidder had removed to Madison, during one of the lecture courses at Drew, Dr. William M. Taylor, of New York, spoke on the " Best Methods of Preparing a Sermon." In the course of his remarks he said that in his judgment the most satisfactory work on that subject yet written had been prepared by one of their own denomination, Dr. Kidder. At once the audience broke into a storm of applause, led by the students. Dr. Taylor did not know that Dr. Kidder was at that time a professor in Drew Seminary, nor that he was then, with the other members of the faculty, sitting behind him on the platform.

On being introduced to Dr. Kidder at the close of the lecture, Dr. Taylor stated that the unusual vigor of the applause which greeted his remark, and which surprised him at the time, was now explained, and he felt sure that his praise of the Homiletics would be regarded all the more sincere, in that he was not aware, when he spoke, of the presence of its distinguished author.

Nearly thirty years after the work was first published an editorial in our leading Church organ observed that this book "was when issued, and still remains, according to the discriminating testimony of such men as the late Leonard Bacon, the best work on homiletics in the English language."

Dr. Kidder found that still another text-book was needed, and accordingly he set about its preparation. On November 14, 1868, he writes: "I commenced systematic work on my proposed book on the pastorate."

The book appeared in the spring of 1871. It was entitled *The Christian Pastorate*, and so rapid was its sale that in July of the same year he was called upon by the publishers to prepare for a new edition.

Like his other books, it called forth many and favorable notices. A few may be cited.

"Dr. Kidder is well known as a successful author, preacher, pastor, and teacher. Out of the wells of his large and rich experience, and from the abundant stores of his reading and observation, he has drawn the materials for this excellent treatise. It grasps many themes with a strong hand, and will hold the attention of a thoughtful reader to its hot and earnest words." Another writer observes: "This contribution to our literature is of peculiar interest from the fact that it presents not the views only, but the actual methods of the author's own pastoral work, and is, more truly than any other of his writings, a reflex of his habits of study and labor." Yet another critic remarks: "It is a work of rare excellence, thoroughness, and simplicity. Every thought seems to fall into its proper place, and to be clothed in the most fitting words. There is no attempt to appear profound by reason of obscurity. Depth of learning and thought are there, but as the ideas of the author are clear and definite, so also is their impression on the mind of the reader. Above all, a spirit of Christian devotion pervades the whole, and every truth is shown to be founded on Scripture and experience."

While he was finishing his work on the *Christian Pastorate* he writes: "I conceived about this time the plan of another book, to be entitled *Helps to Prayer*." At this date, however, he did nothing more than to sketch briefly its plan. Quoting from an entry during his first year at Drew, he says, " I made some beginnings of preparation for my intended *Helps to Prayer*," and in July, 1874, he writes, " I so far completed my book as to place the manuscript in the printer's hands."

In the title it was described as "A Manual Designed to Aid Christian Believers in Acquiring the Gift and in Maintaining the Practice and Spirit of Prayer in the Closet, the Family, the Social Gathering, and the Public Congregation."

The following are some of the kindly notices it received: " This is a precious volume, a treasure, a jewel. Such books of devotion are worth their weight in pearls." " It contains a plain, methodical, and scriptural treatment of the subject." " It is full of suggestions, and may be a well-chosen companion for the daily devotions of the pious."

The author received many letters thanking him for giving this work to the public. Among them was one from his ever-loved friend, Judge Goodrich, of Chicago, in which he said :

" I am sure your book will tend to promote the habit and spirit of prayer, especially of family prayer, which is so much needed. I hope it will have a wide circulation, and be the instrument of abundant blessing to many hungry souls."

Dr. Kidder was a voluminous writer for the periodical press, beginning with a communication to *The Christian Advocate and Journal* as early as his seventeenth year. His teacher and friend, Dr. Luckey, observing his faculty in this direction, encouraged him. He continued his contributions to the *Advocate*, discussing with spirit and intelligence various topics, including scientific. When but twenty-one years of age a series of six articles from his pen does much credit to his mental furnishing. While pastor at Rochester he wrote often for the *Auburn Banner*. Throughout his life current topics were treated by him in the religious press.

Nor were the secular papers neglected. During the latter part of 1861, pending the excitement occasioned by the capture of Mason and Slidell, and the threatened rupture with England, he sought to allay by his writings any outbreak of ill-timed zeal. He says: "The period was full of heat and absorbing concern respecting a threatened war with England. To aid in calming the public excitement, I wrote several articles for the press which practically anticipated the action our government subsequently adopted."

He took part in several controversies, the most notable of which was his discussion with some members of the Committee on the Revision of the Hymn Book, in reference to the second line of the first verse of Hymn 246. He sought, as he had tried many years before, to have it read: "Everlasting King." His opponents preferred to retain "Galilean King." The debate, with the impressions made by the arguments, *pro and con*, belongs to history. It resulted as most of those tournaments do, with both riders still in the saddle, at least in their own opinion. And inasmuch as the committee had what counted for more than arguments, namely, votes, the hymn stands as it does.

In the preparation of his *Annals of the Methodist Pulpit* Dr. Sprague was assisted by Dr. Kidder, who collected much valuable material for it, and also wrote two of the biographical sketches contained in it. When the work was published, he prepared an article on it for the *Methodist Quarterly Review*.

In Kiddle and Schem's *Cyclopedia of Education* he wrote on Sunday Schools and Theological Education. For McClintock and Strong's *Cyclopedia* he prepared the articles on Homiletics, Leaders, Leaders' Meetings, Local Preachers, Logic, Lay Preaching, Missions, Ordination, Pastor and Pastoral Theology, Polity, Sacrament, Sermonizing, Sunday Schools, and Tracts and Tract Societies.

During the interval from 1845 to 1856 the literary labors of Dr. Kidder were chiefly those of editor of books for Sunday school libraries, writer of editorial and other matter for the *Sunday School Advocate*, and writer of tracts. Besides he had the preparation of his annual reports, which together filled almost one thousand four hundred pages octavo.

As editor of Sunday school publications, besides numerous question books on different parts of the Bible, catechisms, lesson books, and catalogues, there were of bound volumes (exclusive of tracts and books in paper covers) nearly a thousand, all revised and edited by him.

Concerning the rule governing the entrance of his name upon the title-page of these books, he says : " I have never allowed my name to be placed on any book as editor which I have not personally examined, and actually both revised and corrected, sentence by sentence, as occasion required. I have not supposed that I could secure the objects of my appointment by the General Conference with less labor than this; and my only fear has been that too many mistakes would occur after I had done the best I could to prevent them."

Many now in middle life will doubtless appreciate the impressions so happily expressed in the following extract: "I don't know how far back in the century your life race was begun, dear reader, but it was at a period now dismally remote if the name of D. P. Kidder fails to awaken pleasant memories.

"To me they are the 'open sesame' to more Sunday afternoons than you could string on the whole circle of the year. How plainly I can see the garden seat under the fragrant cedars! How pleasant the awakened memory of silence and impenetrable shade, twin charms of my dear 'forest home,' the drowsy hum of Sabbath-breaking bees, the cow bell's idyl, from the tranquil pastures by the river bank, and in my hand a book brought home from Sunday school in a town three miles away, and 'revised by D. P. Kidder!'"

There was less renown perhaps in literary work of this kind, laborious as it was, than in that of writing books that should make his name famous, but his fidelity and patience in these modest undertakings have proved incalculably fruitful for good. They have affected with an influence of abiding power the lives and works of scores of preachers and writers who are giving eminence to the closing years of the century.

In February, 1880, he engaged to prepare a weekly discussion of the current International Sunday School Lesson in the *Golden Days*, an illustrated weekly paper for boys and girls, then for the first time introduced to the public by Mr. James Elverson, the publisher of Philadelphia, who, when a boy in the Sunday school at Newark, had often seen Dr. Kidder and listened to him with impressions lasting and helpful. This was an opportunity to preach Christ and salvation to a vast and increasing congregation of youth, which any lover of children such as he might well covet. For seven years (during which time his comments ran through the entire Scriptures) he failed not to appear with attractive, instructive, and animating words to the young and eager listeners that ranged themselves each week before his invisible pulpit. He enjoyed and gave expression often to the reflection that no sermons were addressed to so large a congregation as his, and few could challenge the expectation of so great results.

This was a fitting termination of the literary labors of one whose earliest official occupations were in the interest of the young, and whose affection for childhood and youth had never ceased to grow and glow.

CHAPTER XXIV.

Interest in Missions.

SPEAKING of our work in China, Dr. J. M. Reid, in his book, *Missions and Missionary Society of the Methodist Episcopal Church*, says: " In April and May of 1835 the Missionary Lyceum of the Wesleyan University at Middletown, Conn., had been discussing the propriety of establishing a mission in the interior of Africa, which led to a discussion of a broader question, ' What country now presents the most promising field for missionary exertions?'   The Chinese empire was warmly advocated, and the Lyceum resolved that the Methodist Episcopal Church should send missionaries and a press at once to that field.   A committee, consisting of B. F. Teft, D. P. Kidder, and E. Wentworth, were appointed to prepare an address on the subject to the Church.   This paper appeared in *The Christian Advocate* of May 15, 1835, occupying three columns with a very full exhibit of the field and its claims."

It was written by Mr. Kidder, who was one of the original members of the Lyceum and its corresponding secretary.   This document produced results.   China became the absorbing topic of missionary meetings, and Christian gentlemen, enthusiastic and generous, subscribed funds for an immediate beginning.

This was not Dr. Kidder's first public effort in the interest of missions.   In December of the previous year

he had delivered an address before the Lyceum upon the
" Character of the Christian Missionary."

Speaking of this Lyceum he says: " I have attended
it regularly. I have acted as corresponding secretary.
The duties have been laborious, but pleasant and advantageous." Under the same date we have this entry in
his journal: " Lord, here am I, send me! if it be thy will.
But nothing, Lord, but thy grace can be sufficient for
me. The love of country, of home, of friends, of *study*,
and a thousand other attachments which seem to have
entwined themselves into my very existence, rush into
my mind and plead indulgence. This struggle of mind
has, I trust, taught me something of my own heart. I
feel now perfectly resigned and can say in sincerity, Lord,
thy will be done. May I ever feel this calm submission,
and when the moment for action comes, be found girded
for the conflict." His miscellaneous reading, at this
time, he speaks of as including subjects connected with
the missionary enterprise.

While he was still a student at Middletown there
appeared another communication in the *Advocate* from
him. It was entitled " A Dialogue Between a Christian
and Self on the Duty of Becoming a Missionary." Self
argued the case with strong pleadings, but the final conclusion of Christian was that reason, Scripture, and conscience left him no refuge, the inexorable " Go " was
upon him. This " Dialogue " was a disclosure of his own
convictions and struggles.

In 1837, running from April to August, he published
in the *Advocate* a series of eight articles, averaging each
a column and a half, over the signature Palermo, entitled
" Means for the Conversion of the World." Concerning
these another has said : " They present a singularly clear

and comprehensive view of the Gospel plan in its various applications to the greatest work of which humanity is capable."

As the time drew near for his departure to a mission field he says : " I sent a letter to Rev. Dr. Bangs inquiring respecting the wants of our missions in South America and intimating a willingness to go if needed. While worldly enterprise of every stamp is leading men to the ends of the earth, I cannot endure that the enterprises of the Gospel should linger for want of anything I can devote to them."   At this time Dr. Fisk wrote to him : " I am glad to find that the missionary spirit is still glowing in your heart.   I hope and pray it may prompt you to go into that door, wherever it may be, that Providence shall open for you."   Dr. Luckey also wrote him : " Your missionary heroism I cannot but admire, and hope the God of missions will open your way and make you a great blessing to the Church and the world."

Concerning his wife (who was to fall an offering upon this altar) he writes : " She has been as ready as myself, and we have tried to keep our minds prepared to meet any sacrifice.   Our friends remonstrate not only with the protest of strong and authoritative affection, but also with arguments which we cannot answer, at least to their satisfaction.   All we have to wish or say is, May the Lord direct ! "

It would appear that these feelings, his decision, and departure all found their immediate cause in a communication that he read in the latter part of May in this year (1837), from Rev. Mr. Rule, Wesleyan missionary at Gibraltar.   He writes of this : " Our *Advocate* brought a Macedonian appeal for missionary aid in behalf of Spain from W. H. Rule, Wesleyan missionary at Gibraltar.

My mind seemed peculiarly open to impression. Having the previous week had my attention directed to southern Europe, and the many dependent upon the languages of those countries for instruction in things relating to another life, and those languages destitute of Christian books and almost destitute of Protestant teachers, I felt my spirit stirred within me in behalf of the many now without the Scriptures and suffering under the superstitions of monkery and the withering influence of papal dominion, I therefore determined immediately to say to Dr. Luckey, editor at New York, that if there were none more worthy offered, I would respond to the appeal. The same being the disposition and desire of my wife." Later still, when his decision had been reached and his preparations were being made for sailing, he wrote his acknowledgments to Mr. Rule in the following terms: "I have in a number of instances read letters from you which have been published in this country. Immediately on the perusal of your later appeal to American Christians in behalf of Spain, I offered myself to our Board to go to Gibraltar. They do not see their way clear to commence operations on the Peninsula at present, but have given me a destination somewhat similar on the Catholic soil of South America. I am directed by an official letter from Bishop Waugh to repair to Rio Janeiro as soon as practicable." This message to Mr. Rule he signed as his "affectionate though unworthy laborer for the conversion of the world."

When he was in Brazil he did not forget the Lyceum at Middletown, which had been of such benefit to him while a student. He maintained his interest by letters and by sending contributions of curiosities for its museum.

The crushing providence which suddenly and effectively closed his personal labors in the field he had entered with such high hopes, and where he had prosecuted his work with such judgment and enthusiasm, did not in the least quench his zeal for the cause to which he considered his life dedicated. His interest, if anything, seemed intensified, particularly for the country which he had just left.

And such was his ardor that the Board appointed him to make a tour through the country and stir up the Church. Beginning in August, 1840, he canvassed some of the Eastern States, and leaving Buffalo in the latter part of September he came on to Detroit, by the way of the lakes, and traversed Michigan.

Crossing Lake Michigan by steamer, he reached Chicago. From there he went to Rockford, then to Beloit, Wis. Next we find him in Dixon, Ill. Thence his course brought him to Fulton city, which he describes as a small village on the banks of the great Mississippi, which " I here saw for the first time."

Davenport and Rock Island he speaks of as delightfully situated, and promising to become large towns. Passing the confluence of the " two mighty rivers of the West, Missouri and Mississippi, a scene," he says, " combining the grand and the picturesque on a magnificent scale," he reached St. Louis at four o'clock in the afternoon of the eighth day of his trip down the river!

Closing his mission in St. Louis, he proceeded down the river, passed Cairo, and entered the Ohio. On the boat, at the request of the passengers, he gave an address on Brazil, for which he was warmly thanked in written resolutions drawn up by a committee appointed by the audience. After a stop at Louisville he passed on to Cincinnati. Giving attention to his commission here,

among other opportunities he addressed an immense
mass meeting in Wesley Chapel. He then proceeded
to make a thorough canvass of the interior towns of
Ohio, with long and difficult rides by stage, the only
mode of conveyance.

Leaving Ohio, he met with Rev. E. R. Ames, then
Western missionary secretary (afterwards bishop), at
Wheeling, and held missionary meetings with him at
this place, at Pittsburg, and at Allegheny City. Parting
with Mr. Ames, he came on East, stopping at various
places until Baltimore was reached. At Washington he
spoke with Dr. George Cookman at the missionary anniversary, and after paying his respects to President Van
Buren, and hearing some of the great ones of that day
in the Senate and House, he went on to Philadelphia
and, with a run by rail from nine in the morning till
three in the afternoon, he reached New York, January
30, having been occupied with his tour nearly six
months.

" On reviewing, step by step, the long and interesting
journey which I have accomplished since last August, I
cannot forbear to record my devout sense of gratitude to
the great God who has guided my footsteps and
brought me thus far safely through many wanderings and
not a little running to and fro, that knowledge might be
increased. I was everywhere received with Christian
courtesy and with a kindness I can never forget, while
by the circumstance of forming personal acquaintances
with the residents of most places I visited, I had the
best opportunities of learning all that was interesting and
important concerning the regions through which I traveled. In my tour I have been in some portion of fourteen
States, two Territories, and the District of Columbia. I

19

have traveled 3,424 miles, preached 50 sermons, and delivered 40 missionary discourses and addresses ; $2,320.05 have been collected and pledged at different missionary meetings, and 27 persons constituted life members of the Parent Missionary Society. During the whole period I have scarcely suffered an hour's illness."

It was at this period he conceived of the plan of contributing annually for the Christian education of a heathen girl and boy. This project he carried out sometime afterwards, and although now the giver is dead, his works do follow him, and the boy grown to manhood and bearing his name is accomplishing success as a Methodist preacher to his own people in India. His presiding elder, in a communication appearing in the *Advocate* a year or two since, writes:

"I have just visited one of Brother D. P. Kidder's schools. These schools are doing great good. Kidder is one of our best workers, true and faithful. He plans his work, and does it equal to any man we have."

So deeply were Dr. Kidder's services to the cause of missions appreciated, and so valued by the Board were his counsels, that in his appointment to the pastorate, instead of being sent to Bordentown, as it seemed he might be, he was located at Paterson, in order to have him nearer the headquarters of the Missionary Society.

The time having come for the founding of our mission in China, he was asked to take charge of it. "I have been repeatedly spoken to on the subject of going to China to superintend the commencement of a mission in that empire. Although I trust I have lost neither the spirit of missionary effort or consecration, yet I have not felt it my duty to offer for this work, chiefly owing to the relations I sustain to my aged parents and my three young children. Still I take a deep interest in the establishment of that mission, and hope to be able to do something toward its promotion."

On the 16th of December, 1846, he writes: "I attended a regular meeting of the Missionary Board. I introduced a resolution recommending the bishops to appoint two young brethren as missionaries to China, reserving the future appointment of a superintendent of more mature age, if that shall be recommended by the General Missionary Committee. After a fair discussion, the resolution passed unanimously."

He was appointed chairman of the committee to arrange for the opening of the Chinese Mission, and to collect information concerning that empire. With thoroughness he studied all available authorities, and reported as the conclusion of his investigations that Foo-Chow was the point most advantageous for the location of the mission. His report was accepted, and this place was chosen.

In May, 1847, he says: "I was in attendance upon the sessions of the General Missionary Committee, and made it my special business to vindicate the claims of India and China."

In October of this year he writes: "On the 4th I accompanied our friend and brother, George Loomis, out to sea on his embarkation for Canton as seamen's chaplain, an appointment I had been instrumental in procuring for him."

Two years after he prepared a memorial to the bishops on "The Superintendence of Missions," which was approved and signed by the officers of the Missionary Society. He was appointed a committee to look up a principal for the Oregon Institute. The next year the

health of Dr. Pitman, the missionary secretary, declin-
ing, he wrote part of his annual report, particularly that
relating to China.

The resolutions relative to the resignation of Dr. Pitman, and presented by Dr. Bangs, were also prepared
by Dr. Kidder.   At a following meeting he had the
pleasure of nominating his old friend and college chum,
Dr. Seager, as one of three candidates for missionary secretary.

He seemed to be the special confidant of the missionaries, had a large correspondence with them, and their
letters, carefully preserved by him, are a treasury of
pathos and trust, disclosing the freedom with which they
recited to him their wants, their difficulties, and their
sorrows.

In this connection it is appropriate to quote from a
communication furnished by him some time before to
the *Advocate*, in which he urges Christians at home to
write often and regularly to the missionaries abroad.   It
is entitled " Reasons Why the Correspondents of Missionaries Should be Punctual."   Among the reasons
given are :

" Because justice as well as friendship requires it.
Because by so doing only can correspondents fulfill
the golden rule.   Because their failing to be punctual
often subjects those in question to an involuntary expense of feeling, which ought never to be called for, and
which exerts no happy influence over the missionaries
or their work.

" By punctuality is not meant *waiting* to answer letters, but writing regularly and upon fixed times, whether
an opportunity of forwarding is known or not, and
whether anything unusual occurs or not.   In waiting for

opportunities many are lost, and at length a long course of events is generally chronicled as, ' nothing remarkable.'

" If one were called upon to specify what more than anything else is capable of aggravating the pain of separation from country and friends, it would not be the impossibility of intercommunication, for that could be borne ; it would not be the receipt of unhappy tidings, for whatever comes from the hand of God is to be acquiesced in with thankfulness ; but it would be ' hope deferred,' suspense protracted, and final disappointment in expectations based upon friendship or religion. Reader, if you have a friend far absent on the errands of his heavenly Master, ask yourself, first, have you been faithful in your remembrance of him and his work in your closet ; and, secondly, if you ought not to endeavor to hold up his hands and cheer his heart by friendly and frequent communications.

" Recollect, moreover, that unless your letters are *directed aright and the postage paid*, they will seldom reach their place of destination."

At the time of his going to Evanston he was desired for the superintendency of our mission in Central America. It was felt, too, that it would be a loss to the working force of the home office to have him removed from its councils. One closely and officially associated with its operations wrote him as follows : " Dear Brother :—If it seem presumptuous in me, you'll somehow dispose of the matter and try to believe that I intend all for the best, when I say that I do not see how you can be spared from the missionary work."

But his going to Evanston did not by any means imply that his interest or activity in this department should cease, or in the least decline. The rather, he appreciated the increased advantages he would have in important directions for the encouragement of this cause. He would be in direct contact with young men preparing for the ministry with a view to the possible sphere of missions. It would be his rare privilege so to guide and instruct them as that no mistake be made, and that the inspiration in the case of those certainly called to this field should not wane through lack of proper counsel and fostering care.

During his first year in the Garrett Biblical Institute the students were organized by him into a sort of home missionary society, preached regularly, and held meetings for evangelization in the suburbs of Chicago and within a radius of twenty miles about Evanston. There was need of it, for when the institute was opened there was not in the whole distance of thirty-five miles between Chicago and Waukegan and the distance of twelve or more miles westward from Lake Michigan, a single Protestant church or a regular ministry. Of this organization Dr. Kidder was the president, and he gave one morning of each week to inquiries and reports respecting the labors of the foregoing Sabbath and to practical remarks.

Early in the history of the institute there was a definite proposition of the trustees made to the General Missionary Society, looking toward the special education of missionaries at the institute on terms of a most generous character.

Shortly after this the bishops visited the institute and conferred with the faculty and trustees respecting its interests, and especially respecting the education of missionaries. "Following the episcopal visit," the doctor writes, "several of our students were appointed missionaries, three being set apart for India, namely, J. Baume, J. R. Downey, and J. W. Waugh."

In June of this year, 1858, he writes: "I participated in the services of a Missionary Sabbath in Chicago and preached in the evening the last sermon in the brick church of Clark Street. Before the next Sabbath mechanics had commenced taking down the building preparatory to a reconstruction in the form of the Methodist Church Block, for which on the 4th of August I was called upon to lay the corner stone."

At the session of the Rock River Conference in the fall of 1861 he preached the Conference missionary sermon.

In June, 1869, he addressed a communication to the editors of *The Missionary Advocate*, as follows: "Dear Brethren :—I have just read your recent article asking, 'Where are the young missionary men of the Church?' and expressing the painful apprehension 'that the missionary spirit and zeal of our young men of talents are abating.'

"It has fallen to my lot within the past twelve years to have personal knowledge of the experiences of some three or four hundred young men believing themselves called of God to the ministry, many of whom are now in the ministerial office.

"Of these I may safely affirm that a goodly proportion had the foreign mission field early and definitely associated with their first impressions of ministerial duty. A certain other proportion would readily have devoted themselves to the foreign work had a specific call of the Church been made to them at a proper period of their education.

" Presuming that these cases of my acquaintance are fairly representative of others in greater numbers throughout the Church, I feel free to express the opinion that any lack of qualified laborers for our mission fields results more from a want of system by which proper candidates fail of encouragement and training at the proper time, rather than from any abatement of the missionary spirit among our young men.

" If the Church is in earnest about missionary work she must know that missionaries will be wanted from year to year during a long period to come, and she must be not only willing, but anxious to have competent and devoted young men in ample numbers constantly studying to prepare themselves for foreign fields. On this plan, whenever the want may arise, trained and tested candidates are on hand at a short notice. No skillful general goes into action without a *corps de reserve*, and it is bad generalship on the part of the Church militant to omit timely and far-seeing provisions for her future service abroad.

" This is a warfare on which no man goeth at his own charges, and hence the Church has no moral right to require instant service without previously giving suitable notice and encouragement.

" For lack of this, two classes of embarrassments arise : 1. Many young men, in every way suitable candidates for foreign missionary labor, become disheartened in the effort to acquire a thorough education, and fall short of the just requirements of the Missionary Society; while others who persevere unaided, having to devote years of valuable time to earning means to complete their courses of study, become, while doing so, too old for the successful acquisition of difficult spoken languages.

" 2. Many worthy and devoted brethren whose highest early aspirations were to be qualified for the missionary work and to be employed in it, not having been suitably encouraged, turn their thoughts to the home field, make corresponding plans and engagements, which cannot be disrupted on sudden emergencies.

" In view of such facts I think that the lack of candidates is to be attributed to our own lack of provisional arrangements in reference to this very matter, rather than to any defective action of the Holy Spirit or insufficient zeal on the part of our young men. Hence I am, as I have been for some years, anxious to have suitable measures adopted to prevent similar results in future."

This article produced an impression. Dr. Durbin replied : " We have received your communication on the subject of ' Training Missionaries for the Foreign Work,' and have read it with deep interest. We thank you for it. It indicates a zeal *with* knowledge."

Dr. Durbin then asked some questions bearing upon the matter and said : " The more plainly and the more frankly you write to us on this subject the more we shall be gratified, for we wish to serve the Lord Christ." In answer to this Dr. Kidder wrote at once and with such satisfactory statements and explanations that Dr. Durbin responded as follows : " I have carefully reread your letter and am satisfied that it ought to be published, and I propose to give it in *The Missionary Advocate* or issue it *in tract form*, and send it privately by mail to the preachers, bishops, and seminaries. If you have any preference in regard to one of these two modes of publishing, please advise me."

In going to Drew Seminary his undying love for this work went with him. He writes : " Beyond the particular duties of my chair, I was charged with the special responsibility of counseling the young men in reference to missionary enterprise and duty. As a result, more or less direct, of what I said and did in that line, the year 1873 (the sixth year since the opening of the seminary) was marked in the history of the institution as witnessing the first departure of missionaries from its halls to foreign lands, two to Japan and one to China—forerunners of a greater number in following years."

What, therefore, could be more appropriate, and what to him more gratifying, than that in his last official position he was permitted to be especially helpful to this cause, to which in the beginning he had dedicated his life? It was his duty, but still more his pleasure, as Secretary of the Board of Education to dispense moneys for the assistance of young men studying in preparation for mission fields. Thus through him the Church carried out the desire and plan he himself had suggested more than ten years before in his letter above quoted to the Secretary of the Missionary Society, namely, that provision should be made so that young men would not be required to devote years of valuable time to the earning of the means necessary to carry them through their courses of study. The loving Master rewarded his servant by giving him the joy of working out his own scheme.

Disastrous as seemed the calamity that called him back from his chosen work on a foreign shore, one may well conclude, after a careful study of his life, that, after all, Dr. Kidder's services in the cause of missions have been far more valuable than if his entire life had been spent in distant lands.

CHAPTER XXV.

Characteristics.

FROM the amount of work done by Dr. Kidder, and well done, it might be readily judged that he was a man of large and vigorous physique. But such a conclusion would be a mistake. He was slightly built. The following description is from one who saw him at Drew Seminary: " In form he is tall, slender, and erect. His features are of classic mold, clean cut, and incisive, aptly typifying the character of his mind; the lips are thin and compressed, expressive of decision and firmness; his utterances are somewhat rapid, but distinct; his mind is literal rather than ideal, practical rather than speculative. His manner is grave and dignified, but at all times affable and courteous."

Although his attention to duty was never interrupted by any long-continued illness, still in the latter part of his life he was subject to attacks which not only took him suddenly, but rendered him at once unconscious. Other men with this ailment might think themselves invalid and proportionately excused from serious activity, but he kept himself in tone and at the working point by careful observance of an appropriate diet and the systematic practice of exercise.

In his attention to this latter he never relaxed. While a member of the General Conference at Boston he purchased a ticket for the gymnasium, and spent a part of each day in practicing on its bars and rings. It was his rule also to have some simple apparatus for athletics always in his study. Out-of-door exercise, however, he greatly preferred, and when permitted by the weather he was either working in his garden, riding horseback, or taking long walks. His Evanston and Madison friends will recall him dashing along on his pony, riding with the ease and grace of a courier. When living in New York it was his custom to walk one way each day between his office, Broadway and Eleventh Street, and his boarding place, West Fifty-fourth Street. Frequently he would lengthen this trip by a saunter through Central Park. He was never weary praising the beauties of this loveliest of public gardens. Almost daily he reported with delight the discovery of unexpected paths and nooks.

He sought by all legitimate means to keep himself in trim and pose for the fullest of successful endeavor. He considered himself consecrated to unreserved diligence in the cause to which he had joyfully dedicated his life. His industry was a passion. Work was his habit. Time was his eagerly seized opportunity. It was husbanded and righteously appropriated. Each day was portioned off and its hours allotted. Each evening justified the satisfaction that belongs to the review of work well done. He operated his life by a schedule. His will, quiet but firm, was the train dispatcher of duties that left on carefully determined headway—duties that without collision came through to accomplished tasks. Because his method was to " plan his work and work his plan," he was never in a hurry although he was always busy.

His effectiveness was not due to the fact that he wrought only on old lines. He was aggressive, inventive, venturesome. No preconceived notions nor conservatism served to chill the welcome with which he entertained new schemes and new systems. Yet his plans were wise, they were thought out with patience. His enthusiasm was not so rash as to disturb his deliberation. And as his projects were treated always by the tests of honest work they expanded from theory into results, and remain still fruitful in benefits to the Church.

His record is that of an original and wise builder. He was the right person to be in at the beginning of things. He was beforehand with the idea of the *mission* to China.

At the date of this writing (the latter part of 1893) a communication, a column long, from the president of one of our Western colleges has appeared in the New York *Advocate*, pleading for the endowment of a lectureship on "Christian Missions" in his college. More than thirty years ago, in a paper formulated by Dr. Kidder and addressed first to the Missionary Society and afterwards to the bishops, the Garrett Biblical Institute offered to provide such a department for the Church free of expense. Again, in 1869, Dr. Kidder addressed a communication to the missionary secretary urging substantially the same arrangement as that now proposed. The college president says: "Is it not remarkable that while American colleges are training men and women for almost every vocation in life, while Harvard boasts even a department for the training of veterinary surgeons, there is not in any American college any suitable provision for training men and women for this most important field of Church activity, for this highest work in Christian civilization?" This reproach would not to-day lie against Methodism had the far-seeing wisdom and repeated appeals of Dr. Kidder prevailed.

As Sunday school secretary he made the Catechism an available text-book, provided the schools with their own hymnal, developed the system for raising funds for the support of the Sunday School Union, simplified and systematized the method of gathering statistics throughout the Conferences. By his graduated question books he opened the way for the uniform lessons now so generally adopted. The Sunday school convention and institute were elevated into commanding ideas by him. The normal school was from the beginning his earnestly advocated thought, and a Sunday school library, carefully revised and steadily growing, is one of his gifts to the Church.

Three years before the Garrett Biblical Institute took form it was his uttered conception, and his urgent and intelligent counsel must not be forgotten when we are seeking to discover the guiding minds which gave direction to the timely beneficence that made the project possible.

It is to the unpretentious entries of his diary we must go to find the early shaping of the idea of the Board of Education. Afterwards, as its secretary, he was on hand in time to rescue its accounts from chaos. By his thorough readjustments he made its bookkeeping practicable. His suggestion that the volume rather than the income of the collections should go direct to the beneficiary work of the Board, made it at once a growing power for good. The introduction by him of the official program of service for Children's Day is one of the longest levers in the hands of our boasted connectionalism. When he resigned from this office Bishop Ninde wrote to him: " I am sincerely glad and grateful for the invaluable work you have accomplished during the past six years. You have succeeded in making the Board of Education a power whose influence is felt for good throughout the whole extent of our beloved Zion. I have been honored with a somewhat intimate knowledge

of your feelings and plans, and am thus the better fitted
to appreciate your great service to our educational work.
I have sought to second your efforts as opportunity
offered and am glad to know that your policy is so
thoroughly established that it will continue to bear
beneficent fruits even if the hand that shaped it is laid
aside."

He has left his generation in possession of results as
permanent as they are beneficial. The monuments still
stand, and are likely to remain, which testify to the fact
that the Church did a good thing for herself when she
captured the love and gained the services of that quiet,
earnest, thoughtful, and diligent young man of western
New York. ·

He was modest. Sufficiently affirmative and aggressive for the cause he had in hand, he was retiring when
his own advancement was contingent. He showed none
of the talent for seeking office. He withdrew and gave
space to others when the strife for eminence was on. A
place to work was his definition of position, and in his
thought usefulness was fame. He strove the better for
his Church because for himself he never strove at all.

Loyalty to duty was his escutcheon. Obedience to
the nobler calls was his inspiration. He could conceive
of no dignity higher than faithfulness. Integrity was his
method, accurate business habits and attention to details
he reckoned among the credentials of honesty. It would
cost the effort of a difficult, if not impossible, argument
to persuade him that carelessness was not criminal.

He never unbraced his resistance to the encroachments
of intellectual feebleness. He was determined to preserve if possible to the end his mental agility. He observed that the drift of officialism was toward narrowness

and dullness. Such a consequence he counted a calamity.
He would not degenerate into a functionary, but purposed
to hold himself to the steady upward movement of a
student. He said: " Even in vacation, if you lay down
the sledge, be sure and keep the little hammer always
going." This was his practice. Music was always spurt-
ing from his anvil! " Seize the moment of excited
curiosity for the acquisition of knowledge." This aphor-
ism he often urged upon the attention of his students.
It had proved profitable in his own case, and aided him
in the formation of the habit of gaining information, as it
were, on the wing, for the pressure of his professional and
official duties often robbed him of the delights of quiet
and connected study. But when he could earn a respite
from these engagements his one indulgence was his
books. For these he never lost his relish. After he had
been working ten years in his office of Sunday school
secretary, with no time for anything outside, he writes:
" I have been toiling away incessantly at my official duties
as in the preceding years, scarcely giving myself any
leisure even for private reading or study. As this year
has advanced, however, I have found so many of the
heavy duties of my office disposed of, that almost without
expecting it I am in possession of considerable time for
reading. All such time and opportunities I intend to
turn with God's help to good account the coming year.
On even a slight indulgence I find my long-cherished
fondness for books to revive in great strength, and I
begin to be more than ever sensible how much I have
denied myself during the last ten years in devoting my
time so exclusively to the hard work of my office."

So anxious was he to husband every moment that he
adopted the practice of reading in the cars in his many

journeys at the risk of his eyesight, but with the result of covering many important books. While living in New York toward the close of his public career, he kept up his studious habits, was constantly attending lectures on astronomy and other sciences at the Cooper Institute and elsewhere, visiting picture galleries, and reading books, both new issues and the standards. Among the last books he read, or rather reread (for often during this period he read over again some book that had been among his favorites when young), were *Pilgrim's Progress* and *Paradise Lost*—good books those for a pilgrim who was so near to his paradise regained!

Thus almost up to the end did he keep his mental force unabated. Long after fifty was passed the "dead line" for him was not yet in sight. At sixty-six he wrote concerning the establishment of a theological seminary on the Pacific coast, outlining a plan, suggesting methods, and giving counsel with a clearness and fullness that showed his perception to be as correct and his judgment as trustworthy as when he was communicating his valuable advice in the matter of the founding of the Garrett Biblical Institute. He was past sixty when he conducted his famous controversy with regard to Hymn 246, and whatever may be the views of anyone as to the merits of the question involved, all will agree that logic and rhetoric were no dull blade in his hands, and whoever may have been the Pyrrhus, he was no aged Priam. In his seventy-first year, traveling among the Conferences to an extent that would weary a young man, and making addresses constantly in the interest of the Board of Education, he was particularly complimented in one instance by the presiding bishop upon the fullness, point, and force of his speech.

20

This same year he preached before the New Jersey Conference his sermon in commemoration of the fiftieth anniversary of his entrance into the ministry. His theme was, " Fifty Years of American Methodism." He kept himself out of sight in the glory of his Church, although with truth he might have said, " Part of all these things I have been." The sermon in its arrangement of facts and figures, and its generalizations, showed that it was the product of a mind to which the years had brought ripeness, but as yet no frost. By request it was repeated in Philadelphia and New York, and was published in *The Christian Advocate.*

Rev. Dr. J. A. Roche addressed him the following :

" Dear Brother :—I write to express my personal thanks for the noble tribute you pay to Methodism in your sermon on ' Fifty Years of American Methodism.' It is comprehensive, minute, and just. The facts furnished, the reasoning indulged, and the conclusions reached ought, I am sure, to give it a more permanent place in the literature of the Church."

Dr. Kidder was very fond of preaching, and never declined an invitation. Often was he called upon to deliver special sermons, as at dedication and commencement occasions, Conference and missionary sermons, memorial, centennial, anniversary, and watch-night sermons. In his earlier day scarcely a week passed in which he was not filling some pulpit in the neighborhood of his home. Sometimes he would preach as often as three times a day. An entry in his journal alludes to his weariness in preaching so often, but he adds that he is comforted in the hope that good may be done.

In Newark where he resided while Secretary of the Sunday School Union, he took charge of a movement that grew into the organization of the Central Church. For some time he served its pulpit every Sunday. While at Evanston he enjoyed an opportunity for a partial return to the pastorate. Rev. J. H. Vincent was pastor in Rockford, Ill. Leaving for Europe and the East, he engaged the doctor to take his charge in his absence. He says: "I found the Court Street Church a pleasant and promising field of labor, and that I could attend to its Sabbath duties regularly with nearly as much convenience and with little more loss of time than the miscellaneous appointments I have been accustomed to fill. By going out Saturday mornings I gained most of the afternoon for visiting among the people, which I immediately commenced on a systematic plan, and so far accomplished in a few weeks as to feel at home among the principal members of the church and congregation.

"The resumption of the pastoral relation, even in a modified form, after an interval of many years, proved agreeable from the first, and induced me to put forth extra efforts to accomplish duties at once so promising and congenial. While I have good hope that this arrangement will prove advantageous to the cause of God in the interesting town of Rockford, I also hope to derive benefit from it in view of my responsibilities to the young ministers under my instruction in pastoral theology. I trust that by renewed practice I may make my department more *practical* than ever."

In the fall, as the institute year drew toward a close, and his labors were in consequence increased, he writes: "Between the duties at the Court Street Church and the institute, the month of October was a very busy one, requiring all my time and energies. But God gave me strength and fine health to meet all the just requisitions made upon me, including those of our annual examination and anniversary."

During two months of the following winter vacation he lived with his family in Rockford. "By this arrangement," he says, "I was able to identify myself thoroughly with the pastorate and people, and to labor more for the religious good of the community." Revival services were held at the church. He had expressed himself more than once as regarding "the simple work of the pastor to be, after all, the grandest and most pleasant work in which any minister can engage." We can imagine how he relished this taste of his old-time joys.

Practicing as a rule what he always recommended in his class room, the delivery of the sermon without a manuscript, he showed a readiness in preaching when unexpectedly called upon. At a District Conference in Kingston, N. Y., he thus took the place assigned on the program to one of our best known ministers.

According to the average standard Dr. Kidder was not a taking preacher. His sense of the proprieties of the pulpit was a conscience, and served to check that freedom in illustration, expression, and action commonly depended upon to furnish a current popularity. In his thought, as a condition of his preaching at all, his manner as well as his matter must be truth. If in listening to him the object sought was entertainment, the rousing of emotions, deep perhaps but evanescent, then without doubt disappointment was the hearer's usual reward. But if to open the mind of the Scripture, display doctrine with a clearness that was itself an argument, define duty with such plainness that one might carry it away like a memorized formula, and, with a warmth too honest to be extravagant, to so urge that duty that the hearer was uncomfortable if he did not carry it away—if this be the office and mission of the sermon, then Dr. Kidder was a successful preacher.

At the great meeting in international assembly of the Evangelical Alliance in New York city, he was appointed to read a paper on " The Best Methods of Preaching." His place on the program came in between Dr. Joseph Parker, of London, and Henry Ward Beecher, who also discussed the same subject. A facetious writer, furnishing a report of the occasion, observes:

" No contrast could possibly be stronger than that between the style and delivery of our excellent Dr. Kidder, and that of Parker before him or Beecher after him. On the printed page Dr. Kidder is at no disadvantage with his contemporaries of the hour, and his work will profit by comparison with that of either, whether it be in the matter of breadth, order, or finish. But in the matter of delivery and popular effect, I conjecture the doctor felt very like a mill pond between two cataracts! But let him be content; there's safer swimming, broader sailing, and deeper fishing in the mill pond than in both the cataracts together; though thunder and rainbows are scarce there, likewise, happily, shipwrecks, which cannot always be said of cataracts."

Furthermore it may be noted, that while the cataract represents force, the mill pond represents resource. The cataract will soon clatter itself dry unless it can lean back upon the mill pond or its equivalent. To take the depth and dimensions of the mill pond, is to measure the usefulness of the cataract. And usefulness !—all there is in preaching outside of that ought to be locked up in a parenthesis !

Dr. Kidder was unwilling to intrude himself into the

phenomenal opportunities of this distinguished program
unless with the assurance that whatever other qualities
his paper might lack, it should not be found wanting
when measured by the standard of usefulness.

Upon the mind of a thoughtful listener Dr. Kidder made
the impression that he was a deeply religious preacher.
He was willing to undertake the sermon only with the
assurance that he was divinely aided.   Among his
private papers are some prayers written out by himself
for his own particular profit and guidance.   There is one
entitled " Prayer for aid in selecting subjects and in
preaching the Gospel."   A few extracts will show his
spirit in approaching this solemn duty : " O God, I thank
thee that unworthy as I am, thou hast not only called me
from darkness to light and made me partaker of the
grace of salvation, but hast commissioned me to preach to
my fellow-men the unsearchable riches of Christ.   Once
more the duty devolves upon me of standing before the
people to proclaim thy word of truth.   O forbid that
with languid indifference I should content myself with
the mere formality of preaching ; rather may I rise to the
highest conception of the greatness of the responsibility
and of the eternal interests which ever depend upon the
right and faithful discharge of so momentous a duty.   O
give felicity and power of thought, readiness and force
of utterance, convincing speech and the demonstration
of the influence of the Holy Ghost.   Deliver me, O Lord,
from wanderings of thoughts, from the intrusion of worldly
interests or cares or influences, but especially from all
vanity of mind or the slightest disposition to seek the
applause of men.   When I enter the sacred desk let
thine overshadowing presence be round about me, and
let me and the people feel that God is there."

CHAPTER XXVI.

Characteristics.

THE cultivation of his religious life, to which he gave so much attention in the early part of his experience, remained until the last a carefully cherished habit. The honest searching of his heart was his frequent practice. His self-examinations were not only strict, but at times severe. Never resting in present attainments, he was constantly stirring himself up to higher stages. Laying down for himself rules for better living, he promised to be more diligent and devout, that he would speak and write more for God, and would commit more Scripture to memory.

He particularly enjoyed the social meetings, in all weathers he was at the weekly prayer meeting. He was also one of the old-fashioned sort that attend public worship twice on Sunday. At Evanston he organized a class meeting, chiefly of students, to meet at his house. Of this he says: " The attendance upon and conduct of this class proved an interesting and profitable exercise."

His expressions of thankfulness in closing up the year, in noticing his birthday, and in returning from his frequent journeys, have always running through them a strong devotional trace. " I would here record," he writes, "a devout sense of obligation to my heavenly Father for the providential care which he has extended over me amid the uncounted exposures of travel by land and water during a series of years. Thus far, in every variety of circumstances, I have been mercifully preserved from either suffering or witnessing an accident to life or limb."

On his fiftieth birthday he was presented by the students with a handsomely bound copy of Webster's Unabridged Dictionary. In alluding to this in his journal he makes it the occasion of appropriate reflections. "On opening the services of the institute I was surprised by an address on the part of the students and a present commemorative of my fiftieth birthday, of which they seemed to have become aware before I did myself. My attention having been called to the fact of my having crossed the line of half a century of human life, I found it suggestive of many and impressive reflections. Up to this time I have considered myself young. To-day I cherish the feeling that I am not old, and yet I see myself passing the meridian of my earthly life. May I be more diligent to redeem the time and apply my heart unto wisdom!"

One of his entries at the close of the year is as follows: " I feel thankful to God for an unwavering confidence in the great atonement and for a constant witness of the Spirit that I am a child of God. O that I may grow in grace and the knowledge of the Lord Jesus Christ!" These annual reviews are to him particularly gratifying when he is permitted to consider work well done—service faithfully rendered.

" I closed up," he writes, " a healthful, a laborious, a happy, and, I trust, a useful year of my life." Again his entry reads: " On reviewing the year now closing I perceive clearly that the goodness and mercy of the Lord have followed me from the beginning to the end. I have been able to do full service in every department of effort to which my responsibility has extended. I hope I may yet be able to do good and effective work for my divine Master during the year about to open."

With him life was worth living so long as Christ and the Church wanted his work. To be happy only as useful was in his view the Gospel in practice. In all that came to him as duty he sought to deliver his goods in honest weight rather than in decorated forms. As a preacher he was anxious for the hearer's soul, not his applause. At one time, delivering his message among his old acquaintances where he knew that the larger number were not in sympathy with his straight-edge views, he writes : " Nearly all the families were present and many old neighbors, and heard, I trust, truths they will remember with profit."

The work he could put into life, not the enjoyment he could get out of it, was his motive. Visiting in the East, the place of his childhood, he observes: " I spent several days among the scenes and friends of my boy-hood, an occasion this for grave and profound reflection. Such, however, is the pressure of practical duties that I have time neither for poetry nor sentiment, save the sentiment of deep gratitude to God for enabling me to live and strive to be useful, while others are dead, or sickly, or, what is worse, worldly-minded."

This dedication of his powers to well-applied endeavor continued clear across his active years. As with his mental vigor, so with his working faculty, it suffered no abatement from old age. On his seventieth birthday he writes : " I occupied the day and evening with meditation on the goodness of the Lord in bringing me so favorably to this advanced period of life and still prolonging my capacities of work and enjoyment in the cause to which my days have been consecrated. The theme is both vast and pleasing, and the gratitude it inspires is immeasurable. Yet I trust it may find at least partial expression in future activity in the cause of Christ." Dr. Kidder's one object, unbroken by any considerations of self, unfretted by any ambitions for place and honor, was to do good, to be of service to his Church, or to benefit some person. In one place he writes: "Nothing is so grateful to me as to be exclusively devoted to my one business." His duty was savory to the degree that it was salted with self-sacrifice. With a quietness that ruled out all affectation, a goodly proportion of his best activities were for the profit of other people. An entry in his diary reads thus: "Intensely occupied all day at my office, with various duties of my own and other people's." In another place he speaks of his own work being delayed "on account of doing the duties of others." It would seem that he had on hand nearly all the time some case of need which he was managing with patience and kindness to work out to helpfulness. Strangers were sought out in the hospital and cared for, beneficiaries were for months at a time the inmates of his house, and others were rescued from difficult situations and assisted at school.

One whom he had aided in business writes in the following grateful strain : " I cannot allow this opportunity to pass without endeavoring to express in some slight degree the deep sense of gratitude which I entertain for the many exhibitions of kindness toward me on your part, and for the manifold interest which you have ever taken in my welfare, from the period when you so generously extended a fostering care to a comparatively new beginner up to the present hour. From my present standpoint of temporal prosperity I look back upon the past and recognize yourself as one of the chief instruments under Providence in enabling me to arrive at my present successful position in life. I find no language at my control which can express my gratitude."

Among his letters are many from those whom he had in various ways favored, and from parents abroad whose sons he had assisted to acquaintance and position in this country.

To those contemplating the ministry he was eagerly and promptly helpful, and he was always ready with his friendly counsels. Many a young man has been saved to a cultured ministry in the Church through the weight of his advice in competition with the pressing arguments of presiding elders and even bishops. His word in substance always was: Take time, tax every endeavor to gain high intellectual attainments, and resist quietly but resolutely that influence from whatever quarter it may come which would urge you to a plunge into the pastorate so premature as to doom your future to mediocrity if not failure, to obscurity if not depression."

To one who is now a successful missionary he wrote: " It is highly important for all young men designing to enter the holy ministry at this period in the world's history to lay a broad foundation of general knowledge and of mental cultivation preparatory to the more especial study of theology." To another, who is now a bishop, but who then was struggling with the problem, " Shall I continue in the pastorate, or go to the theological seminary?"—a problem complicated by counsel coming from the highest quarter and advising against the seminary—Dr. Kidder wrote: " I return you herewith the letters of your friends which are in the highest degree affectionate and consistent with *their* views. I doubt the propriety of my giving you any specific advice, since I could hardly do so without arraying advice *versus* advice.

" If I were to advise it would be on the basis of opinions honestly entertained, but which are entitled to no weight on account of their honesty unless they be also correct.

" It seems to me that the whole series of arguments in the oldest of the letters you sent me, although plausible, is fallacious. It proceeds on the idea that human characters are fixed quantities, and that Wesleys, Whitefields, Summerfields, etc., are called of God *as such*, whereas, when called of God, they were inexperienced young men, and only became what they ultimately were by *long years* of effort, study, prayer, and labor. I doubt not that scores having as good natural talents as they, and as true a call from God, have buried their talents by indolence and remained in insignificance and narrow spheres of usefulness, when they might have done much more for God and the world.

" In your case, I think you should yield to no despondency. For my part, I do not see why you have not as good reason to suppose that your intense longings for improved qualifications for the ministry are as much prompted by the Holy Spirit as your desire to enter the ministry at all. Hence I have still good hope that a way will open for their gratification in such a manner as both you and your friends shall ultimately acknowledge to be of the Lord."

How like a fresh breeze to one all but fainting in an unfriendly atmosphere was this prudent and encouraging letter!

His students, remembering his patience in deliberation and wisdom in advice when they had occasion to confer with him, and recalling also his kindness of heart toward them, always felt free after they had gone out into their fields to communicate with him respecting any difficulties in their work, or any personal or family troubles. And such loving words as these from one of them, " I always feel as if you stood in a very close relationship to me *spiritually ;* I have never forgotten the kindly interest you manifested in me during and after my stay with you," might be repeated in substance from many other like sources.

So much did Dr. Kidder feel under obligation to promote the welfare of his fellow-creatures that he never yielded to the tendency of the student and professional man to become a recluse. He was public spirited. He was active always in forwarding movements that looked to the social good and the religious improvement of his times.

He was present at the initiatory meeting of the Evangelical Alliance in New York, was appointed one of the committee to draft a constitution, and became some time later one of its officers.

As might be expected, he never lost his interest in the prosperity of the Sunday school. He writes that he took much pleasure in cooperating with his friend, Rev. J. H. Vincent, in the establishment of Sunday school institutes.

December, 1874, he says: " I participated in the exercises of the joint anniversary of the Sunday School Union and Tract Society. The three only secretaries those societies have so far had were present, namely, Drs. Wise, Vincent, and myself." His sermon on that occasion, "A Reading and a Working Church," has been published as a tract.

He felt it his duty, wherever he lived, to contribute as he might to the advancement of the place. At Newark he became interested in the establishment of the Newark Wesleyan Institute. For this he gave a great deal of time, traveling, as he could find leisure from his office engagements, to solicit stock for the building and endowment, meeting with trustees and committees night after night, studying plans, arranging courses of study, and selecting teachers, visiting the school often during its sessions, attending always its examinations and commencements. For eight years he was president of its Board of Trustees, and had the reward of seeing the institute become one of the most flourishing schools in numbers, influence, and grade in the State, one of the most cherished objects of the city's local pride. It was his ambition that it should become " the grand central, model academic institution of the Church." So completely, however, was it dependent upon his originating and organizing faculty, and the presence of his tireless and well-guided energies, that even his absence in Europe crippled it sadly, as he found to his grief upon his return, and his departure for Evanston was coincident with its collapse as a Methodist institution.

At Madison he served as an officer of the Morris County Temperance Alliance. To this he says he devoted considerable time. In Evanston, stirring with the pulse of Western enterprise, every forward step taken found him efficient in encouragement and aid. Another describes him as " actively bearing his part in the varied public enterprises of the new and thriving community." His services unselfishly rendered were often at the expense of serious breaks into his literary duties. During one of his vacations his principal occupation was work upon one of his books; "subject, however," he adds, "to many interruptions from claims upon me in connection with the new church enterprise and various local matters from which I cannot well detach myself."

To the new church here mentioned he gave freely of his time and thought, being a trustee and a member of the Building Committee. He also made a generous subscription. He had the satisfaction of seeing it well along before he left Evanston. On his last Sunday there he preached in the old church, and the following evening the grateful citizens gathered in the new church to give him a farewell reception. As a current report describes it, "Evanston turned out *en masse* to testify respect and regard for one of its most estimable families about to leave for another field of labor. L. L. Greenleaf, Esq., made a farewell speech, and presented to Dr. and Mrs. Kidder on behalf of their townsmen an elegant clock of Italian marble and bronze, with vases to match. Dr. Kidder replied, dwelling on his past life here, and observed that wherever he might go his affection for this ' town of towns ' should be unchanged."

To this may be added the tribute of Judge Goodrich, Dr. Kidder's friend from the first, who could not be present at the reception : " No one entertains a higher respect for Dr. Kidder than myself. No one appreciates more fully the inestimable services he has performed for the Church, or more sincerely regrets the loss the institute will suffer in the severance of his connection with it."

In leaving Evanston a matter of concern with Dr.

Kidder was the disposition of his house. He had fourteen years before built it with a taste, an elegance, and a convenience that made it at the time the finest residence in Evanston. And with all the wealth and improvement that have lifted the incipient village into the ambitious city, the house does not find comparison odious. It has needed no outside changes to sustain its architectural standing alongside the many stylish houses since erected.

It faced west, was two stories high with a broad veranda extending along the entire front. The grounds were cultivated to the highest degree, abounding with selected fruit in bush and tree and vine.

Here the doctor wrote his books and prepared his lectures, working at his standing desk in the northeast corner of the large study and library built around with glass-covered bookcases. Opposite, on the south side of the ample hall, was the parlor. Here one daughter was married, the doctor celebrated his silver wedding amid a host of congratulating friends, and often had it been thronged at receptions and commencement reunions. Above, on either side of a central hall, were the guest chambers and family rooms.

Sunday evenings were spent in Christian song in the cheerful sitting room back of the parlor, with bay window opening south, and back still of this was the dining room, with long table always full. For the doctor and his accomplished wife had the very soul of a courtly hospitality, and welcome was the presiding genius of the house. Bishops, college presidents and professors, secretaries, missionaries, and representative men of the Church, native and foreign, were among the constant stream of guests.

Also, in the beginnings of the population of Evanston, it was a practice with the doctor and Mrs. Kidder to invite every newcomer and every family that settled in the place to spend an evening with them. " Be not forgetful to entertain strangers," was written on the doorposts.

But a feature of this hospitality which the young men since scattered in all lands have carried away and treasure among their happiest recollections, was that whereby they were made to feel at home. He originated and maintained the custom of inviting the students from the various classes in companies of a number convenient for accommodation at the table, to take supper and spend an hour or two in pleasant social converse with the family before proceeding to their evening studies. Thus the professor was also the friend. Homesickness was a malady impossible, and the influence of this practice seemed to pervade the entire community, so that cordiality to strangers and especially students became in the primitive Evanston a fine art, rendering it in this respect honorably peculiar among college towns.

Dr. Kidder had a particular fondness for young people. Among all his guests none were more cordially received than the young men and young women who had sought Evanston as the shrine of culture, and who were then carrying on the unnoticed but critical battle with poverty and obscurity. One who is now enjoying deserved fame on both sides of the ocean thus expresses herself:

"Across the way from the snug cottage where I write, almost concealed by clustering trees, is a commodious mansion—Dr. Kidder's home. As my eye follows the winding gravel walk that leads to its hospitable door, my heart stirs at thought of all I owe to those who dwell

21

there, who welcomed me, a lonesome schoolgirl to their fireside years ago.   It was of incalculable benefit to us, whose opinions were then forming, that the Kidder home, with its large library lined with well-filled bookcases, its roomy parlors, and its broad piazza, on which we delighted to promenade when summer nights were fair and sweet, brought to our young hearts the conception of Christ and Christians as a social force.   From some of our hearts, at least, the heavenly vision has never faded, and no 'society,' after the stratified regulation pattern, has ever had one charm for us since then."

In short, here was a house which had been from the beginning the home of a typical Christian family. On its altar the flame of a simple worship had never died out. Refinement, comfort, rest, peace, congenial labor, and happiness were its pervading atmosphere.   Sorrow here was decent, tempered with grace, and enjoyment was pure, unmarred by extravagance.   It had been blessed with the presence of Christ, and the doctor could not tolerate the thought of surrendering its ownership into irreligious hands.   He says: " The question of leaving Evanston having been determined, I thought it best to offer my homestead for sale, and deemed myself fortunate, after comparatively little effort, in finding a purchaser.   Our whole family and many of our friends had felt anxious to have a house which from the first had been consecrated to the highest forms of religious sociability occupied by a family that loved the Church and its institutions.   In this also we were gratified."   The title passed into the possession of a Christian gentleman, who at this writing still resides in the house.

CHAPTER XXVII.

Characteristics.

LIKE his home in Evanston, his residence in Newark was also delightfully situated, surrounded with cultivated grounds, and was abundant in the ministries of hospitality. It was the stopping place of missionaries. They made it their home while fitting out for their departure or recuperating on their return. What he wrote to one missionary he said in substance to all, " Come directly to my house and bring your company with you."

The house was seldom without a guest. Many of the notables of the Church were at some time under his roof. Bishops and others held important meetings in his parlors, and there were social gatherings of ministers and their families. Nor were his associates in the Book Room overlooked. The employees in groups were from time to time invited out, and so also were the book agents, editors, secretaries, and their wives.

In cherry time the heads of all the departments and their families spent an afternoon and evening with him. The fruit was unusually plentiful and luscious. The guests took possession of the grounds, climbed the trees, and helped themselves at will. Supper was served. Toasts and speeches followed, and the not-to-be-forgotten ice cream closed an entertainment which is still talked about by those that remain.

Among those who enjoyed the hospitality of the

Newark home was Mr. Elie Charlier, just arrived from France. He established in New York a boys' and young men's French school, and continued it for twenty-five years. Terminating his connection with it on account of failing health, he wrote to the doctor to be present at its closing exercises, and said : " My dear Dr. Kidder :— Thirty-three years ago I spent a happy summer under your roof. Now I am going to quit public life. I should be glad if you would be with me. Come if possible. Yours as ever."

At Madison an open house was again the rule. When the Rev. Dr. J. F. Hurst (now bishop), the successor to Professor Nadal, came on from Germany, Dr. Kidder gave him, his family, and attendants a cheerful accommodation until the house selected for him was put in readiness.

At Drew the residences of the professors are part of the general outfit, and are within the grounds of the seminary. Dr. Kidder was assigned to the house formerly occupied by Dr. McClintock, the first president, he taking Dr. McClintock's chair in the faculty.

Dr. Kidder says : " There need not be (if there could be found) in this world a place more perfectly and agreeably adapted to rational and Christian living.

" In all my surroundings I am constantly reminded of my lamented predecessor, whom I had known as a dear friend for many years, and with whom I was intimately associated for eight years—1848 to 1856—when we were both editors in the Book Room at New York. From the period of his call to organize this institution, he had repeatedly consulted me by letter. In the spring of 1870 he passed away. Little did I then think that I should be called to be his successor in this particular sphere of labor. But so it is, and I sincerely hope that I may be enabled ever worthily to fill the chair vacated by his death."

The place having been unoccupied for about a year the grounds had suffered much from neglect. But with his customary attention to such matters, at considerable expense and with labor in which he did not hesitate himself to take a share, he had in the course of six years brought the garden and orchard to a high condition of forwardness, and was indulging the just expectation of a prolonged and uninterrupted period of returns. But in 1877 he was informed that the house and grounds were wanted for the president. Dr. Kidder had read, " Follow the things that make for peace." He had read, " In honor preferring one another." And venturing, at a modest distance to follow Him who "pleased not himself," he moved out, exchanging houses with the president.

Dr. Kidder never failed in the cheerfulness with which he took the long and repeated journeys in the interest of the causes he was appointed to represent. Those who saw him starting off with springing gait and quick step, carrying his old-time leather traveling bag, will ever recall him as one who, though weary often, as well he might be, was none the less happy in his tasks. But when he was thus going away, his heart was always traveling back on itself and hovered still about the circle at home. In one of his letters he writes: " Thus far the time has passed rapidly and pleasantly, for I have been much engaged, and yet my mind has wandered homeward hour after hour toward the dear objects of my affection. My anxieties for you and the children are strong beyond expression, but my confidence in our almighty Protector is unwavering, hence I leave you calmly in his hands."

When his long circuit was completed and he was back again with his family his joy was as exuberant as that of a child, and his expressions of thankfulness to God for the safety and health of his loved ones during his absence were unbounded and repeated.

He found relaxation from his public obligations in the entertainment and instruction of his children. He assisted them in their studies, particularly their Latin and French. His Sunday afternoons and evenings were given up to them in Scripture study, religious counsel, and the singing of hymns. Along in his late years one of his children wrote to him: "I wish I could give expression to my feelings as I think over all you have been to me, in childhood so tender and loving, in my wayward youth so patient and so lavishly kind, in my maturer years never ceasing in your care and attentions, and always ready to help and advise. You have been a perfect father! I often feel deeply that I am not worthy of you and of all you have bestowed upon me, but I hope you will overlook my shortcomings in the abundance of my love."

In sickness he was a faithful, untiring, and competent nurse, and when, out of repeated and serious attacks, his wife was marvelously brought back to health his heart labored with inadequate words of praise. One of the eminent ladies of Evanston's former day writes: "I have a heart full of grateful memories of my kind and faithful friend—most kind and generous when I most needed kindness. In my family for ten months, and my neighbor for fourteen years—later having my only home in his family—I never heard an unkindly word or saw in him aught but cheerful, considerate kindness for all the inmates of his house."

In the same line are the beautiful and earnest words of another : " It would be doing violence to the spontaneous admiration with which one prominent trait of his character has ever inspired the present modest biographer, were that trait to be passed over in silence. Unhappily it is not of such frequency in those whose exhausting mental pursuits are, perhaps, an apology for their proverbial ' nervousness,' as to divest its mention of a quite refreshing novelty.

" I refer to the sweetness of manner and of disposition that characterize the home life of my honored friend. To those brought nearest him by ties of blood or sympathy, those most dependent on him for encouragement and help, he unvaryingly displays a gentleness of manner, of word, and of deed, that command the loftiest esteem of all who are cognizant of them. There are deeds recorded of him in the secret annals of living hearts, as well as of those that have long since ceased to beat, which for gentleness and delicacy might shame the knights of old, and, after all, it is such memories as these that shed a sweeter fragrance than the widest fame."

One of the early entries in the doctor's diary runs thus : " As a family we are highly favored. Our circle has remained unbroken for a series of years. We enjoy as a rule excellent health. All at home." But this was not always to be. Twice in his lifetime was the circle broken, death carrying off two daughters, the eldest after a lingering illness, and the other, his youngest child, the beautiful Eva, "rare and radiant," many years after snatched away with startling suddenness. These strokes he endured with his characteristic fortitude, but the iron, especially in the last case, went deep into his soul.

He never forgot a grief; even to the last he recalled

with pain the fierce blow that struck down his young wife at his side in a mission land. Forty years after he writes to a brother missionary bereaved in like manner: " Having been similarly afflicted while in a foreign field, I know too well the bitterness of the cup you are called upon to drink to think of attempting to mitigate your grief by any other consolations than those afforded by the glorious Gospel of our risen Lord. But I rejoice that such consolations abound to the faithful in Christ Jesus in the deepest bereavements through which they are called to pass."

Dr. Kidder's erect bearing, quiet dignity, moderate tone in speech, and manner of deliberation and reflection, doubtless made upon many the impression that he was reserved and cold, that he held himself so well in hand that he was undisturbed by his own sufferings and that the troubles of others did not move him. But those knew better who knew him better. Although as to outward expression, both concerning himself and others, he was surrounded by a shore line of decorum, yet he was all the while approachable, sympathetic, responsive. The sorrows and difficulties of others made immediate and large drafts upon his pity. He loved to touch his fellow-men, and when permitted to touch, he clung. No one was fonder or firmer in his friendships. He never lost a friend. He never disappointed confidence; he never wounded affection. Carefully right, he was not painfully rigid. If you admired correctness you would like him, if you were pleased with gentleness you would love him. He was a good man. This was the impression he made upon his friends. When he was leaving his associations in the East for his new life in the West, one who had been closely connected with him in church work and for years had had his office near his, wrote in the following tender and quaint style: " I part with your presence with regret. A good man's example is never removed, having once been known, and his personal presence must be valuable alike to all sections of the country. I am gratified that you are Jesus Christ's man wherever you go, and therefore there must be to you ever, as I desire and pray, good luck in the name of the Lord."

When the news of his election to Drew got abroad he was cheered by many words of greeting. " I rejoice," wrote one, " to learn that you have been elected to so important a chair. By all means accept. Your many friends in the East will give you a cordial welcome. The Lord be with you and yours!" He was invited to join the Philadelphia and Newark Conferences, and was affectionately welcomed into the New Jersey Conference, to which he presented his transfer. Speaking of the agreeable change in coming East he says: " I was able to preach not a little, and took pleasure in revisiting places and churches where I had officiated in former years, and also in visiting old friends in new places."

While visiting the Conferences in the interest of the Board of Education he was gladdened by meeting here and there his former students, now doing valuable work in the pastorate. At one time it was his pleasure to assist in the ordination of some of those who had sat in his recitation room.

These were those to whom he had given his best when he was at his best. Their appreciation of his services as a teacher, and their love for him as a friend, had intensified with the years since. Whenever they met him they enjoyed talking over the days spent at Garrett and Drew—days of confidence, fellowship, and affection.

While he was still at the seminary one of the Conference visitors wrote: " Though I was present but a few days, I learned to understand and share the feelings of his students, who showed their deep love and respect for him as a man and a Christian brother as well as a faith-ful teacher."

When he came to leave Drew, and his work as a theological professor was to end forever, this devotion of the students took on an expressive form—a farewell meeting, with the faculty and the students, and a pre-sentation from the latter.   His own allusion to it is brief and unassuming.   After referring to the addresses of the members of the faculty, he writes: " M. E. Ketcham, in behalf of the students, made a fine address, presenting me at the close with an elegant and costly study table. The whole occasion put my modesty to the severest test, and my hoarseness prevented my making much reply."

The event in detail was thus described in the local newspaper: " After the usual chapel service at Drew Sem-inary last Tuesday morning, at which all the students, the faculty, and their families were present, the president of the seminary, Dr. Buttz, announced that an hour would be devoted to, as he termed it, .' a love feast,' on the occasion of Dr. Kidder's leave of the seminary, according to the terms of his resignation.   He particularly referred to Dr. Kidder as a paternal counselor to the students. Dr. Strong said that it is difficult to fill the chair now made vacant by the resignation of him who has elevated the department of practical theology to the high posi-tion it occupies in the Methodist Episcopal Church.

"Dr. Miley said that he felt like congratulating Dr. Kidder in his high appointment; and that likely no other man, unless it be Bishop Simpson, had held a General Conference appointment for so long a time—thirty-seven years.

"Dr. Crooks referred to Dr. Kidder as an eminent example of fidelity and thoroughness in every position the Church had honored him with.

"Rev. C. R. Barnes, pastor of the Methodist Episcopal church in this place, said that when but an errand boy he called on Dr. Kidder in Mulberry Street, New York, related to him how that he felt he was called to preach, and how he received advice and consolation which did much to influence his course in life.

"At this time the students sang the familiar hymn:

> "'Blest be the tie that binds
> Our hearts in Christian love,'

after which they presented Dr. Kidder with a handsome study table.

"Mr. M. E. Ketcham, of the senior class, spoke in part as follows: 'We shall ever associate your name with acts of warmest sympathy and cooperation in all that was for our interest, and with many worthy works for the Church and for the good of mankind. We desire to evidence our real sentiments of regard toward one who has been so true a friend to us. I have, therefore, the honor, in behalf of the students of Drew Theological Seminary, of presenting you with this study table. While it may remind you of pleasant scenes at Drew, and of the warm friendship here formed, we trust that it may also be of practical service to you in your new work, and that you may have occasion to use it for many pleasant years.'

"In response to this, after referring to the words of the other professors, Dr. Kidder said: 'I accept this present, not so much for its intrinsic worth—beautiful

and valuable as it is—but as an evidence of the good will
and kind regards of the students who have so generously
given it.'   He alluded to the pleasure it had given him
and Mrs. Kidder to entertain the students at their house
from time to time.   He was now entering upon a new
work; it had opened up very unexpectedly and seemed
to be in the line of duty.

" Dr. Buttz said, in closing, that Dr. Kidder, by his books
and teachings, had virtually founded the department of
practical theology in the.Methodist Episcopal Church. He
said that while in the Protestant Chapel in Paris he met
Dr. William M. Taylor, of New York, who told him that
in preparing his Yale lectures on preaching, Dr. Kidder's
book on Homiletics had been of more service to him than
any other."

Rightly had the genial Dr. Buttz styled this episode
a "love feast."   It was a festival of hearts that had
ever been true to each other—hearts that might be
locally separated, but never spiritually divided.   Although the honored guest of this banquet of souls has
departed, the students still talk about him in their old-
fashioned way, the "love feast" is prolonged, and in
the following chapters we are invited to enjoy yet more
of it.

CHAPTER XXVIII.

Words from the Students.

WHEN the present work was under contemplation, circulars were addressed to as many of those who had been under the doctor's instruction as could be reached, asking them for any letters from him they might be willing to lend, and also a brief statement of such incidents and impressions as they might think fit to communicate. The response was generous. Much valuable matter was sent, for which grateful acknowledgment is herewith made. The utterances, too, of affection were so warm, and the estimates of character were so honest and discriminating, that no valid explanation could justify the omission of copious extracts. They are given without name, without regard for order of date, and without note or comment.

" In Garrett Biblical Institute I was a student under Professor Kidder. As a teacher he was painstaking and thorough; his scholars must not only understand, but remember; he was a driller.

" He took a personal interest in the students. They found him approachable, self-denying, judicious, brotherly, almost fatherly; and, let me add, they found also in Mrs. Kidder a fountain of Christian sympathy and practical encouragement.

" I occasionally called on Dr. Kidder in his study, looked through his large library, and asked him concerning his methods of indexing, arranging papers, and saving knowledge, and I found him one of the most orderly of men."

"In my course of five years at Drew Seminary, these, among other excellent features, in the character of Dr. Kidder attracted my attention particularly:

" 1. His thoroughness in everything he undertook.

" 2. His unswerving fidelity to duty. Faithfulness in his office, turning neither to right nor left by fear or favor.

" 3. His wonderful facility in remembering and calling by name the large number of students, even those who had been upon the grounds but a short time.

"Dr. Kidder impressed me as constantly toiling in sight of an immortal, *invisible* crown, with an eye single to the glory of God, and not as a man pleaser."

"Dr. Kidder impressed me as a minute and laborious worker. He had a pigeonhole for every article in use, every line of thought or branch of business which fell within his range of work, and he knew where to find it. His wide range of reading made it possible for him to give instantly most reliable and valuable advice to one in the selection of books, either for a general library, or on special subjects. Nine years' experience on the mission field has shown me that his suggestions as to the kind of books, bindings, etc., to be chosen for use in Asiatic countries were equalled by those of no other.

"One always felt in the presence of Dr. Kidder that he was a thoroughly dignified Christian man. He was never caught off his dignity, never stooped to rehearse anything of doubtful propriety in speech or thought, in order to make lecture or conversation agreeable to a certain class. He was not repulsively formal in his dignity, and could enjoy the humorous, but that humor must be intelligent, manly, and clean.

" As I look back upon Dr. Kidder's work there comes prominently the feeling that he was preeminently a *safe* man. The interests of the Church were safe in his hands; so were those of the individual. By many he will be lovingly remembered when the dashing, vociferating teacher has been quite forgotten."

" He was one of nature's gentlemen, intensified and brightened by the power of Christianity, who was ever intent on fulfilling his obligation to God, the Church, and the world."

" I had the great privilege of spending two years at Drew while Dr. Kidder was still professor, and during that time enjoyed his instructions. He it was, perhaps more than any other man, who turned my thoughts toward the missionary field. I have the most fond and loving remembrance of him."

" For three years I was permitted to share the benefits of his instruction at the Drew Theological Seminary. My recollection of him as a teacher is that he was always imbued with a sense of his responsibility; nothing in his department showed the slightest tendency to carelessness, but all his work manifested completeness. I remember that at times there was a desire to criticise his method of instruction as rigid and exacting, but maturer reflection revealed the wisdom of his course. He was the representative type of men who unite in

them the ennobling powers of scholarship with the graces
of a truly Christian profession.   No one could doubt the
deep sincerity of his piety ; it impressed me day by day.
It was not of the impetuous, enthusiastic character, but
more of the steady shining of the sun, the mild and
gentle flow of the clear, placid stream which ever glad-
dens and beautifies the plain.   The impressions in recalling the repeated hospitalities I enjoyed at the home
of Dr. Kidder are of the most exalted character.   He
was a true friend, a wise counselor, a good man in the
broadest sense."

"It was to Dr. Kidder among the first to whom I confided the fact that I believed myself called to mission
work, and at all times I found him a safe confidential
adviser and a sympathetic friend.   He had a thorough
knowledge of all literature bearing upon the subject he
taught so many years in Evanston.

"He was a good financier, and the Garrett Biblical
Institute owes much to his wise management in this respect.

"He was a good administrator, and while always genial
and kind commanded that respect which insured obedi-
dience."

"My memories of Dr. Kidder, dating back to my first
acquaintance with him, are clear, vivid, and, I trust, permanent.   Certainly there are no memories of him that I
should wish to forget ; they are all pleasant, and all of
an edifying character.   When I entered Garrett Biblical
Institute I found Dr. Kidder the first to receive me and
advise me as to my best course to pursue.   I think every
student who entered the seminary can attest this fact,

that it was from our revered and beloved Professor Kidder that we all received our first hearty welcome and our first valuable suggestions, and subsequent instructions, regarding our course of study as well as our plan of life."

"There were no compromises with negligence on the part of a student, and absolutely only *true merit* availed anything in the classes of which he had charge. Knowing this, the students always had a high motive for study.

"He lived for genuineness, usefulness, not the imaginary, but some tangible good."

"I knew him in 1859–60. We students were a rough set of diamonds, and, whether of the 'first water' or not, we needed the polish Dr. Kidder was eminently fitted to give. Whether in his hospitable home, or riding on his horse up to the old institute building, or sitting in his chair before us as teacher, he was always the same faultless and lovable man."

"He hated shams, and fearlessly denounced wrong of every kind. In more instances than one he rebuked conduct in students which he felt was unministerial or ungentlemanly, but in such a way as not to incur enmity.

"He was also quite ready to notice and to commend excellences which he discovered in men, and to use them to good effect as occasion offered. As a particular friend to the married students who were struggling along financially, or who had sickness in their families, his kindly deeds will long be remembered. He went about doing good.

22

" He was a man of great dignity of bearing, which was sometimes interpreted as egotism.   This impression soon disappeared upon closer acquaintance.

" He was never so reserved or so much occupied that he could not courteously and kindly listen to any appeal for assistance made by any of his students, whether relating to books, to preaching, or to financial matters.

" He was very careful not to overencourage ambition in students when he felt that there was a lack of capacity behind the ambition, but instead of discouraging one he would suggest such lines of procedure as he felt assured were safe to follow, and by such advice many men have succeeded fairly well who by adopting the other course might have ignominiously failed.

" There is no doubt that Dr. Kidder had the most intense hatred of rum and tobacco, as every class under him can testify.

" I well remember a day when the class waited in expectant silence for some startling revelation, as indicated by his face soon after he entered the room.

" He laid down his usual armful of reference books, arranged and rearranged them on the table before him, adjusted his glasses, looked up at the class and then down again upon the table, drew out his handkerchief, suppressed a slight cough, arose and opened the window as though suffocated with impure air, and began his remarks to the class with an apology for taking the time of the class, and proceeded to give a dissertation upon the filthy use of tobacco, finally startling the class, especially those nearest to him, by the remark: ' My olfactory nerve is so extremely sensitive that I detected the presence of tobacco almost as soon as I entered the class room, and it is now so very near me as to be positively offensive.'

" Then followed a kindly exhortation to the brethren to repent and sin no more, intimating that he could never conscientiously recommend to any position any brother who was addicted to the habit of using tobacco. There would be but two or three perhaps in a whole class of thirty who had previously acquired the habit, and to their credit be it said that most of them abandoned the habit before graduating from the seminary."

CHAPTER XXIX.

Words from the Students.

"NO man I ever have met impressed himself more fully upon my life than Dr. Kidder. His influence was gentle and kind, and yet very deep. No man in his generation did more to elevate and ennoble the ministry than did he."

"It was especially difficult for me to build the outline of a sermon, so when we came to that part of homiletics I asked him to allow me to continue submitting outlines to him for correction, and he did. On one outline he wrote: 'You show marked improvement; this is as good as any you have made.' I was *much pleased*, but in a few days he wrote on another outline: 'Any verse in the Bible would have fitted this sermon as well as the one you have used.' This brought me down to my level again.

"He, however, gave me a good outline for the text I had used, which proved very helpful.

"I could not help but notice how perfectly self-possessed he always was. In the winter of '74 and '75, I think Dr. M—— was pastor of the Methodist Episcopal church in Morristown. There was a great revival in progress. Some of us students went up to hear the doctor preach one Sunday A. M. Dr. Kidder was in the congregation. During the singing of the first hymn the pastor spied him, and coming to his pew invited him into the pulpit. Dr. Kidder offered the prayer, the pastor read a Scripture lesson, and after the second hymn announced that owing to the fact that he felt himself greatly weakened, having spent the previous night in prayer, he had asked Dr. Kidder to preach in his place.

"The doctor then arose, and without one word of apology or explanation, delivered a most masterly sermon, full of historical facts and dates, as well as numerous quotations of poetry.

"It was a marvel to us all how he could have done it, not having any manuscript with him and no warning that he was to preach."

"Dr. Kidder took me often into his own home, showed me the consideration which won my lasting gratitude, and inspired me with confidence that patient fidelity to duty would compel success.

"I came to admire him for the versatility of his talent and the thorough consecration of his life. Nothing which he undertook was slighted, but he did honest, thorough work in a very wide range of service. To have known him and loved him, I prize among the treasures of memory."

"He was untiring in his efforts for the welfare of the students while under his care, and none the less interested in their success in the work after leaving the school.

"He set in motion influences for good which are destined to live for all time and bear much fruit in eternity."

"During my student days it was my privilege to enjoy a more than ordinary degree of intimacy with Dr. Kidder.

On my arrival in the country he had been kind enough to receive me into his house and treat me as a member of his family. I had become much attached to him, and felt very thankful for the kind consideration and Christian courtesy with which he always treated me. Some of the best lessons of my life I learned while in his society. One was to utilize time and so systematize my life as to make the most of the opportunities granted me.

" Dr. Kidder took a warm interest in those who were preparing for work in the mission fields. Missionaries in many lands have reason to remember with gratitude the sympathy and help received from him."

" I wrote a letter to Dr. Kidder telling him my wish to be a student at Evanston, to prepare for the ministry. He sent me a kind reply, encouraging me in my purpose.

" When I met him he made me very welcome. He always had a pleasant word of recognition for the youngest student.

" He was very particular about etiquette—but he had reason to call attention to the subject in those days—and yet his reminders were administered without hurting anybody's feelings."

" It was my pleasure to recite to Dr. Kidder for two years—the last he spent at Drew. He was a friend to all the boys, and specially so to those who found it necessary to borrow money with which to complete their course."

" I have the recollection or the impression of a man with a kind heart and much interested in the welfare of the students.

" He was in the best sense of the word ' a man of the world,' and his hints and suggestions were of much value to young men who had not seen much of life. He lived so completely by method, that I doubt whether he ever did an uncharacteristic thing in his life."

" I sometimes found myself approaching him timidly, and was invariably put at ease as soon as I began to speak to him. He was emphatically the students' friend, and his influence gave shape and character to the lives of many under his charge. I cannot express the reverence which I now feel toward him."

" He took a special interest in students from foreign countries, inviting them to his house during the Christmas vacation, and trying to make their stay in the seminary as pleasant as possible. I have received many acts of kindness from him which I can never forget."

" I hold Dr. Kidder next to my own father as a teacher and friend. My acquaintance with him began when I entered Drew. In the summer he was forced to exchange residences with the president of the seminary. But he quietly and gracefully submitted.

" I was at the seminary without any apparent way of meeting the expenses of further schooling, and in no small distress over the fact, and he at once entered into a series of plans and operations which completely relieved me of all embarrassment.

" Three marked characteristics of Dr. Kidder were especially impressed upon my mind: 1. His patient, forgiving spirit. 2. His painstaking industry. 3. His remarkable conscientiousness.

"The first was most conspicuous in the above-mentioned exchange of houses. The good doctor, without a murmur, to my knowledge, stepped down and out. Not only was he patient, but he was forgiving and obedient to the dominant party, for all the next year, if not longer, he did gratuitously the seminary correspondence which belonged to the president.

"With reference to his industry it may safely be said that scarce ever was Dr. Kidder seen but he was either on his way to work or hard at it. When he took special exercise, which was almost daily, it was usually in some garden or household toil.

"The secret of Dr. Kidder's excellences, I think, lay in his remarkable conscientiousness. All he did was just as near right as he could do it. So prominent was his conscientiousness that it overflowed into conscientiousness for others. I once wrote and handed him a caustic essay on hypocrisy. He suggested that it might be taken as vindictive, and that I had better tone it down. My chum had an ungainly swing in his walk. The conscientious doctor called him aside one day and so explained and illustrated that my chum was cured instantly. Who would not have been horrified to have seen the dignified Dr. Kidder affecting awkwardness? Chum said it nearly killed him. But since he only had to take one dose he survived and has ever since been the better for it. Dr. Kidder had withering sarcasm when perfectly proper for faults, but never for people. Surely, no one ever heard him denounce any person, living or dead.

"Dr. Kidder was a good, cheerful, thoughtful, unselfish, zealous, friendly man of God. His memory to to me is fragrant and ennobling."

" His life was eminently serviceable to his Church and his generation, and not the least part of that service was the merit and sincerity of his Christian character. He was never at his best in his service at Drew. There was too much of the administrative work put upon him in the absence of the president."

" Dr. Kidder was the most considerate, inspiring, and delightfully remembered instructor of all my early years. I always found him the same cheerful, noble-spirited follower of his Master."

" He always set before his class a higher standard than that of becoming learned pedants. He sought rather to impress upon them a high ideal of *manhood*. The students always believed in him—to them he was the impersonation of a true man. His instruction was a benefit, his example an incentive, his approval a benediction, and his memory a delight."

"My student life at Drew Seminary, as I look back upon it to-day, is a picture of beauty and happiness. My life there was an ideal one, and Dr. Kidder helped to make such a life a blessed reality. He has enlarged and ennobled my life, and I bless God that it has been my great privilege to sit at the feet of this beloved teacher of Drew."

"It seems to me that too much stress cannot be laid upon the fact that for the truest *Christian courtesy* Dr. Kidder was justly noted. It was not the courtesy which so often passes current for that grace—not the veneer which comes of familiarity with artificial rules of etiquette—but a profound consideration or considerateness of others, in which alone true courtesy consists.

"I cherish his memory as of one who impressed me with his sterling goodness of heart as well as his great intellectual balance."

"Dr. Kidder was ever on the watch for opportunities by which he might secure the interests of the Church. My own case is in point. I was employed in a store in Pittsburg. At one time Dr. Kidder made a brief visit to the family of my employer, a former New York friend. I was present. By my name he recognized a former Conference relationship with my father.

"Soon he had drawn from me a sketch of my life, and learned my convictions of duty concerning the ministry.

"His kindly spoken truth and exhortation fell as from heaven upon my heart, and I was moved to promise that if any way should open before me to the ministry of the Church, I would look to God for help to enter the open door. The door opened in due time, and Dr. Kidder presented the offer by which I was enabled to begin a course of study at Garrett Biblical Institute.

"I will ever remember his words of encouragement and his wise suggestions as I toiled for success, and my thankfulness is ever alive with praise to God that a completion of the courses of study was at last chosen instead of the partial course which had been thought of.

"In my humble opinion the Methodist Episcopal Church never had among her sons and fathers a more diligent and sincerely devoted servant, or one who with more of uniformity secured the success of the interests of the Church which were committed to his care. In all his career he gave greater prominence to his work than to the workman, so that while his work has ever been most valuable for the welfare of the Church, the man himself has to a very great degree been hidden from sight.

"I wish not to accuse the Church of unworthy partiality for more highly favored men, but yet I think that careful consideration of his life and service will show that none have been more worthy of honor and praise, and also that few have toiled on to the last with more heroic consecration to the work at hand, unaffected by the fortunes of honor and praise. And yet I cannot but think that the worth of Dr. Kidder has not been appropriately appreciated by the Church to which he gave the toil of a long and useful life."

"He took great delight in aiding any student in his work who showed any appreciation of such help, and he possessed remarkable facilities for doing so, far beyond what anyone had any idea of who neglected to avail themselves of his assistance.

"He was always ready to preach for the students at their appointments, and his sermons were always interesting, and often wonderfully comforting and inspiring.

"He preached a sermon for me from the text, 'But now we see through a glass darkly,' etc. I shall always remember it, and it is talked of to this day by the people who heard it."

"One year after I had graduated from Garrett Biblical Institute, and had joined Conference, Dr. Kidder visited our Conference and was taken very ill.

"When the news reached me I went to his room, found him very sick, but quiet and restful in spirit.

"After other friends had left I remained with him for some time, during which he experienced another and severer attack of the disease, and seemed for a few minutes to be sinking.

"When, in response to his request to raise his head from the pillow, he whispered, ' If I should go now all is well,' this gave me anew the assurance that his life was always witnessing that he lived ready to depart and be with Christ."

"As a humble but heartfelt tribute to the memory of Dr. Kidder, permit me to say that the blessed fruitage of his pure, thoughtful, methodical, and consecrated Christian life will abide and increase, and never be fully measured until the great day of God's final reckoning. The two years at Evanston under his tuition will ever remain in memory as the most sacred and helpful of all my life."

CHAPTER XXX.

At the Last.

DR. KIDDER, seeing that his work was done, that he must pass the remainder of his days, be they many or few, in retirement, yielded reluctantly, although gracefully, but not until he had put in one more stroke on the side of good works. His library, after certain selections had been reserved, he gave—in number about two thousand volumes—to the Gammon School of Theology at Atlanta, Ga. There was also a large number of valuable pamphlets.

After several attempts at restoration by repairing to health resorts, he concluded, in the fall of 1887, to make his home in Evanston. Here reminiscence would itself be like a bracing atmosphere, and here even after nearly a score of years there survived many of the friends of the early and heroic days. The local paper noticed his arrival in these words:

" Dr. and Mrs. Kidder have come back to Evanston, and we hope to claim them long as neighbors in the growing suburban city that was but a hamlet when they knew it first, and owes to them as much, certainly, as to any other single force, the more celestial aspects of its life."

Although he had withdrawn from the field of his honorable activities, and could lay no claim by his services to the contemporaneous notice of his Church, yet he was not forgotten. The General Conference of 1888 made him Honorary Secretary of the Board of Education. His brethren, too, in one way and another gave him evidence of their unfailing and grateful recollection. Dr. Merrick, of Delaware, O., who had known him ever since the days at Amenia, wrote: " There comes to me in these days a wonderful reviving of early friendships. Toward yourself and your dear companion I feel especially drawn.

" The good Father may see it to be best that we be called aside for a time from our ordinary vocations that we may give the more thought to whatever of further preparation may be needful to fit us for our new and higher mode of being. I trust we shall all sweetly acquiesce in whatever he appoints, assured, as we must be, that he doeth all things well."

Rev. Dr. R. S. Maclay, first Superintendent of the Mission to China, wrote : " You were so intimately associated with the establishment of our China Mission, and have always taken such a deep interest in the entire work of our foreign missions, that your absence from 805 Broadway is especially noticed and regretted by all who, like myself, have had the pleasure of being associated, in any capacity, with you during past years.

" Your career has been an honor to the Church and highly creditable to yourself. You have faithfully discharged the duties of every position in which you have been placed. You have never shirked hard work or failed in the hour of trial. The Church has trusted you and has never been disappointed. I am thankful that it is your privilege to pass the evening of life free from anxiety and care in the scene of some of your important labors—a place where you are known and loved. May God be very gracious to you, and crown you at last in his glorious kingdom ! "

The following telegram was sent to him from Milwaukee, Wis. :

"The Sunday School Union and Tract Society, in joint anniversary assembled, send to the first Corresponding Secretary of the Union hearty greetings, and the expression of their desire that God may grant him in his retirement from active life a continuance of divine favor and of spiritual strength."

The New Jersey Conference, through a committee, addressed to him a letter containing these among other loving words :

"We recall with great pleasure the years when you were with us in full strength. And we count it no small honor to have had you associated with us in Conference relations.

"We are persuaded that your dilligent hand set in motion waves of influence, which have already contributed greatly to the upbuilding of the Church of our mutual choice and fellowship."

The students in alumni meetings, and in personal letters, addressed to him words of affection and expressive of their lasting appreciation.

The following item appeared in the New York *Advocate :*

"The Rev. Dr. D. P. Kidder will be seventy-five years old on Saturday, October 18, 1890. His vast number of friends and former pupils will be glad to know that his mind is clear and active, that he attends religious meetings, visits friends, enjoys his letters, and is looking serenely forward to the final 'welcome home.'"

This brief passage stirred up tender messages by telegram and letter from far and near.

Comforting, however, and helpful as these communications were, his greatest and his unfailing consolations were, as might be supposed, in spiritual sources. Anything concerning religion and his Church roused and interested him. The weekly visit of the *Advocate* was eagerly looked for. Until his last illness he never missed his attendance at the church and prayer meeting.

He was attentive, as heretofore, to his religious growth, and was careful not to decline in spiritual strength. His inner life and ruling thought appear in this covenant and prayer, written at this time and found among his papers after his death :

" O, infinitely great and glorious Lord God, my Maker, Preserver, and almighty Friend, condescend for the sake of my great Advocate and Mediator, the Lord Jesus Christ, to accept a renewed consecration of my soul and body to thee and thy service.

" In new circumstances of great trial and affliction, I feel more than ever my need of mercy and spiritual manifestation from thee, and also a pressure of obligation to be more watchful, prayerful, and believing. I specially feel the need of all those gifts of the divine favor by which my heart may be wholly purified and sanctified. I therefore pray for the baptism of the Holy Ghost in accordance with the provisions of thy grace and the high privilege of thy people. To this end I pledge increased supplication, earnest pleading, and corresponding efforts of faith, to take thee at thy word and rely calmly and confidently on thy promises. In this I plead for help that I may pray aright and be fully prepared by divine influence and grace to rise above all temptation and sinful proclivity, and thus to be placed in the position of a truly penitent seeker of the highest gift designed by God for humanity, but which is only to be found at the Redeemer's feet. I therefore humble myself beneath thy mighty hand, that thou mayest raise me up. Let therefore thy blessing come to me speedily in that form which thou seest will be best. Let me more clearly perceive the supreme excellency of my Saviour's character and atoning merit, and let my love to him glow with a warmer and purer flame. Let my sense of contrition for past neglects in the religious life be more intense, and my purpose to be faithful and obedient be more unwavering. Also I pray that my faith may be clear and scriptural, bringing the merits of my Saviour home to my soul in continual appreciation and unswerving reliance. While, therefore, I renounce all trust in myself, or anything that I can do, I claim with all my heart the benefits of his saving grace and promised intercession. So may I live that he may be within me continually the hope of glory, and that the Holy Ghost may occupy my body and spirit as his living temple. To this end may every evil thought be excluded, and every right and pure affection be exalted, and may the hallowing influence of divine power be felt in every faculty of my soul! Inspire and then answer my fervent and believing prayers. Thus may I speedily attain to all the mind that was in Christ Jesus my Lord, and may my soul, body, and spirit be made and kept blameless until transferred to the home of the glorified in the heavenly world. Amen."

Nothing so interested him as the Bible. He never tired of reading it or of having it read. It was the book he wanted first and last. Often, when his wife was reading some other book, he would say, " Now let us have a little more of the Bible." Many portions of Scripture he repeated in the intervals of reading and in sleepless hours of the night.

23

He had made it a practice all his life to commit Scripture to memory, and it was always a feature of the evening family devotions in his house that each one present should say a passage from the Bible, so that now in this period when especially the word of the Lord was precious to him he was never without his portion of daily manna. Traveling, as he was, through the wilderness, it was his solace to live by every word that proceeded out of the mouth of God.

As his strength failed there were chapters that he could recall only in part, and he would ask that they be read over to him.

Thus passed away four uneventful but gently ripening years. He had very little acute suffering. Much of the time he was unable to read for himself, but listened to reading with the same pleasure as in his more vigorous days. This duty of reading to him fell in the main to Mrs. Kidder. Her tender, strong, patient, and tireless spirit was an unfailing support and an unfading cheer as weakness fell on him and dimness gathered about him. His decline was so gradual that the change could scarcely be recognized, and even in the last two weeks, when confined to his bed, he seemed like one quietly going to sleep, till finally there was no awakening after midnight, July 29, 1891.

The funeral services were held at the family residence, 418 University Place, on Friday afternoon, July 31.

Dr. W. S. Studley and Dr. Miner Raymond read appropriate passages of Scripture, after which Dr. Sylvester F. Jones delivered a few remarks relating to Dr. Kidder's later years. He said in part: "His was an old age crowned with glory and honor, and cannot fail to win the admiration of all. His character was the outcome of heroic toil and endeavor. He was always in his accustomed place in the sanctuary when his health permitted. The energetic persistence of his spirit continued to be the distinguishing feature of his life to the end. The most beautiful thing in this world is a serene, pure, godly, and saintly old age. God keeps old people here below to let their light shine. Shining is being, not doing; it is character, not reputation. They shine in the ripeness of their wisdom, in the light of past achievements, in glory and honor attained, and in good works done and registered among men. There is not a cry so glad, a shout so joyous, as the ecstatic heartbeat of a soul as it leaps across the threshold of heaven. Such was the peaceful and triumphant death of Dr. Kidder." At the close Rev. Dr. Boring offered prayer. The interment was in Rose Hill Cemetery, near Evanston.

The news of his departure called forth from the press of the Church and the country generous comments, with summaries of his life. The religious papers, particularly of his own denomination, discussed his character and work in appreciative editorials, and all the organizations of which he had been a part passed resolutions expressive of their estimate of the value of his services. The Board of Education put on record the following: "Dr. Kidder found the affairs of this Board in disorder, and he immediately reduced them to form and efficiency. It may be safely said that his wise, careful, and prompt administration of the secretaryship laid the foundation of the present increasing growth and usefulness of the Board. He was a man of God, a sincere philanthropist, an unfailing friend of children and youth."

Dr. H. B. Ridgaway, President of the Garrett Biblical Institute, wrote: " It has fallen to few men to have lived so usefully, to have been connected so long a time and in so many ways with great movements calculated to advance the kingdom of God. When a young man he helped to mold the minds of children and youth; then in his middle life he assisted in fashioning the young ministers of our Church, and later on he was called to give system and effectiveness to our Board of Education. He has gone, and his works do follow him. A wise and good man, full of faith and the Holy Ghost."

Bishop Vincent sent this tribute: " Dr. Kidder was an early and faithful friend of mine, giving me wise counsel in the very beginning of my ministry, and always taking an interest in my work and success. He was always kind and candid as a brother, and I had great confidence in his judgment. Dr. Kidder was a man of lofty ideals, of calmness and dignity, of sincerity and consistency. He was a success in every position to which the Church called him, and his contributions to the cause of ministerial education should never be forgotten by Methodists.

"In Sunday school work he had foresight and common sense. His organizing power was displayed in his early efforts in behalf of the Sunday School Union of our Church. He was a quiet and humble Christian, very wise in speech, cautious, and full of kindness."

The allusion in this letter to the Sunday school cause recalls an interesting and impressive incident, namely, that during the very month in which Dr. Kidder passed away the Sunday School Union received a donation of $25,000—the largest gift at one time in its history. A hint this was, nay more, an assurance, that the cause to which he had given so large a share of his best years, was not only to remain a permanent department of beneficence in the Church, but was to continue in a manner yet more marked in its career of expansion and power.

Some given to tracing such coincidences would pause to note that the very page of the New York *Advocate* which published with comments the first news of this phenomenal gift, contained in the same column an editorial upon Dr. Kidder. As this was the first periodical which gave encouragement to the doctor's fruitful pen, the fitness of quoting a part of this editorial as the final word will be readily apparent:

"Dr. Kidder was an indomitable worker. It may be said of him truthfully that he filled five distinct spheres with general efficiency—missionary, pastor, Sunday School Union secretary, theological professor, and educational secretary.

"No one ever heard of his doing or saying anything inconsistent with his moral character and religious profession.

"He belonged to the class of men always laying foundations, working by a plan, and as sailors say, sailing with an even keel. If nothing startling was to be expected from him, everything solid grew under his busy trowel. He deserved well of his age, and received high honor from it. The work of his hands has been established, and everything that he ever touched in this country is strong and still growing."

THE END.

www.ingramcontent.com/pod-product-compliance
Lightning Source LLC
Chambersburg PA
CBHW021727110726
47902CB00005B/1376